DECEPTION

Simone —
Enjoy the read!
Steve Winer

DECEPTION

STEVEN WINER

Library of Congress Control Number: 2018910628
ISBN: Hardcover   978-1-9845-5185-6
                     Softcover   978-1-9845-5184-9
                     eBook   978-1-9845-5200-6

Print information available on the last page.

Rev. date: 11/02/2018

To order additional copies of this book, contact:
Xlibris
1-888-795-4274
www.Xlibris.com
Orders@Xlibris.com
784756

This book is dedicated to my good friend Robert D. Hensley. May he rest in peace.

I also dedicate this book to my wife, Linda, who without her encouragement and patience, as well as her creative thoughts, this book would not have been written.

CHAPTER 1

THE DARK CLOUDS were just starting to build. The Easterly winds from the West Coast of Florida and the Westerly winds coming off the Gulf of Mexico were starting to intersect over Fort Myers, Florida. It was just after 1:00 PM, Tuesday afternoon on August 18, 2013 and more than one hundred seventy five persons were crammed in the Memorial Gardens chapel expecting rain in a few hours. This day was a typical summer day in Southwest Florida, but this day was also the funeral of Joseph D. Hyland. It was an open casket, a decision made by Joe's brother, Daniel, the only remaining member of the immediate Hyland family. Joe had passed suddenly eight days prior. At the age of 56, most successful middle aged hard working business men are anticipating an early and lucrative retirement. However, Joe Hyland was not an ordinary middle aged business man. An autopsy had just been performed three days before the funeral. The investigation of Joe Hyland, his business partners and his development companies had already been started by the Lee County Sheriff's office and the Federal Bureau of Investigation years before Joe's death. Millions of dollars had been missing, for many years. The investigation was continuing while Joe lay in his coffin. Joe's autopsy results were just tentatively completed with toxicology results still outstanding. The current preliminary opinion of the Lee County coroner was inconclusive, subject to further tests. A surprise to most of the attendees that day. It had to be a heart attack, liver failure, or just all of Joe's internal organs shut down. Due to the coroner's tentative results and the years of investigation into Hyland's businesses, both Federal FBI agent, Arthur Winslow out of the Tampa, Florida FBI office, and Lee County Sherriff's detective, Luke Blakely, were two of the attendees at the funeral that day. Both law enforcement detectives were quite curious about Joseph Hyland's death. When there is a death like Joe Hyland's, the guilty person, if there is one, usually attends the funeral. Both detectives were taking pictures, offending nearly every attendee.

Just 4 years earlier, Joe Hyland was, at least on paper, one of the wealthiest persons in Lee County with a net worth of over several hundred million dollars. Joe had always been the center of attention, especially when local politicians and swanky businessmen were around him. He was a handsome man, six foot two inches, two hundred pounds, stark black hair, and gentle green eyes with a charming personality and whose persuasion of influence was difficult to be outmatched. Joe was a 1980 Michigan Tech graduate with a Bachelor's Degree in finance and a three year starter on the University's hockey team. A first team all-Western Colligate Hockey Association goalie both his junior and senior year. A veteran athlete who played in the Frozen Four his junior year. Losing to Minnesota in the championship game by a score of 1-0, in overtime. He was chosen, that year, as a first team all American. During Joe's senior year he was drafted by the Detroit Red Wings. However, Joe's destiny was not the physicality of being on the ice every night. Nor was it becoming a businessman in a small to medium town somewhere in Michigan. His aspirations were much greater than any rookie salary that could be offered by the Red Wings, while mostly sitting on the bench. He had a knack for finance, but his real skill was the ability to sell anything to anyone.

Joe, and his brother, were born in Traverse City, Michigan to a lower middle class family. His father struggled with nicotine, alcohol and keeping a job. While his mother ignored her husband's drinking, she continued to portray herself and her family as more of an upper middle class family. She would join any woman's club that would have her. She tried to hobnob with the upper crust of the City. But, it never worked, except in his mother's mind. Both Joe and Daniel knew that if they wanted to make something of themselves they would have to do it on their own. Joe's athletic ability and magnetic personality got him noticed by his high school classmates and made him one of the most popular in his class. Homecoming King, honor roll, football and hockey. He was the total package and his full athletic scholarship to Michigan Tech to play goalie for the hockey team was, at least in his mind, his ticket to wealth and notoriety. Daniel was never Joe. Everywhere he went in town and all during high school, Daniel was always Joe's little brother. Modest athletic ability, barely able to get "C's" in his classes, Daniel never had the opportunity to go to college. After high school graduation, Daniel went to work for a state wide grocery chain and worked his way up to manager of one of their local stores where he still worked on the day his big brother was being buried. Joe's mother passed of lung cancer during Joe's sophomore year at college. It affected Joe more than Daniel and confirmed Joe's future was not in some small town in Michigan. His relationship with his father was always fragile at best, but after his mother's passing, it became nonexistent for some time. Joe wanted no impediments to his future, especially a drunk unemployed father. At least for now, Daniel would have to deal with him.

After graduation from college, Summa Cum Laude, Joe had several offers, other than the Red Wings. Most of which were medium sized local Michigan companies. Joe could not see himself behind a desk, working with hundreds of other finance graduates and competing with MBA's. Joe had no ambition to continue on with school for a graduate degree, but he still was not sure where he was going. The climb to the top would take a long time and Joe wanted something different and much sooner. However, Joe had this unusual job offer from a large real estate development company, privately owned, based out of the small sleepy, up and coming town, of Fort Myers, Florida. The CEO and majority shareholder of George Harvey Communities, Inc., or better known as GHCI, was George Harvey. He was a graduate of Michigan and had a large winter home near Sanibel Island located on the Caloosahatchee River, which ran through Fort Myers to the Gulf of Mexico. George started his company, GHCI, twelve years before Joe graduated college. George built the company to almost a multi-million dollar conglomerate that George was preparing to someday eventually go public. GHCI developed and built luxurious high rise condominiums and large expensive sprawling homes, mostly in golf course communities developed by GHCI, on both Florida coasts, South Carolina and Georgia. George was strongly involved in Republican politics and was one of the larger contributors to politicians both in Michigan and Florida. George's Northern home was located in Ann Arbor, Michigan. George spent most of his time in Florida and had become a Florida resident due to the tax situation in Florida, which was much more beneficial for him and the company.

George had met Joe several times at the Michigan – Michigan Tech hockey games and frequently invited Joe to his private box at the Joe Lewis arena after some of those games.

The rivalry between Tech and Michigan was not quite like Michigan State, but was still considered a rivalry. George took a liking to Joe and closely followed his academic and athletic progress for several years. During Joe's college years and even after graduation, George would invite him to his Ann Arbor home, a few times, just to get to know him better. George felt that Joe may be the type of person who he could mold, in his own image, eventually giving Joe a lucrative future with his fast growing company. Joe's senior year, George arranged for Joe to come to Fort Myers for five days. First class, of course. Joe was introduced, by George, to the Mayor of Fort Myers, Governor of Florida and every high roller in the area. George offered him a job with promises of possible future stock options, lucrative expense accounts and a decent salary with other perks. Joe was flattered by the job. If Joe decided to accept the offer, it may have been his way out of Michigan, with a prestigious job in a different type of corporate world, without being behind a desk. If it was the offer it sounded like, Joe knew he may had found his opportunity. But Joe was not sure that Florida was the right place for his future. He needed time to think about it and find out a little more about life. Therefore, the two years after graduation from college, Joe reluctantly dabbled part time in graduate business school and a non-lucrative job on campus with the hockey team as an assistant coach.

Being frustrated for several years, with no real interesting and lucrative job offers, Joe finally decided to accept GHCI's offer and move to Fort Myers. He hoped that sometime in the near future, to become an executive for a publicly held GHCI. This move for Joe occurred in 1982. Eventually GHCI did go public at the height of the real estate boom in 2004 and its stock traded high on the New York Stock Exchange.

George Harvey became very wealthy, and between 2006 and 2008 George was even named George W. Bush's ambassador to France. Joe, however, didn't stay with GHCI long enough to see the company go public. And George was not at the funeral.

Leigh Mowery, Joe's ex-wife was at the funeral. Leigh never used the name Hyland, even when she was married to Joe, and always went as Leigh Mowery. Maybe, because Joe and Leigh lived together for some time before they got married. Or, maybe Leigh never wanted a man to control her. Leigh, was a perky petite five foot four inch woman with short cropped blond hair and very good looking. She was born just outside of Louisville, Kentucky and when she spoke everyone knew, by her accent, exactly where she was born. She was smart, cunning, dressed 'to the nines' and loved the better things in life. Their marriage was a surprise marriage even though they lived together for some time. In 2002, Joe and Leigh decided to give the one hundred plus guests at Joe's future development company's Christmas party a big surprise. The party was at the clubhouse of the plush golf development, known as The Riverview Golf & Country Club situated in Fort Myers, Florida, located on the Caloosahatchee River. This development was one of George Harvey's largest developments. Joe just got up on a chair half way through the Holiday party and announced that he and Leigh were getting married on the balcony overlooking the clubhouse pool and anyone who would like to attend should come on out and join them. It was a surprise to most everyone at the party. But the person most surprised by that event was Joe's attorney, Brian Kopp.

"How can you get married without some type of pre-nuptial agreement?" Brian whispered to Joe. Brian was one of the persons who thought something like this was coming and begged Joe not to do it without protecting himself.

"Don't worry, we have an understanding." Replied the smiling star struck groom.

"What the Hell does that mean?" returned the lawyer. "Don't you know what may happen to your assets? Divorces happens too easily and too frequently these days."

"Don't worry, everything is covered." Whispered Joe.

"I have no idea what that means, and I hope you know what you're doing." The lawyer retorted.

No one ever argued very long with Joe, no matter the issue, since most of the time, it was fruitless. His lawyer knew that. So the issue was dropped. Joe preceded to walk to the balcony overlooking the River and married Leigh.

Now, the date of the funeral, Leigh lives in a five bedroom home in Louisville, Kentucky, which she owns outright, unencumbered by any lien or mortgage. She had been divorced from Joe for more than four years, but she came to the funeral. She needed to find out where the assets were that, she knew, Joe had hidden. How will she get paid in the future to keep her home, her Mercedes and her membership in her country club? When Leigh entered the Chapel, there was no seat for her in the front row. Leigh was infuriated! Those seats were occupied by Joe's brother, Daniel, his wife and two daughters, Joe's longtime assistant, Cathy Rutter, who made most or the arrangements for that somber day, and worse of all, Ivana Hollings. Ivana, or "the vamp" as she is known by several people including Leigh, worked for one of Joe's companies for several years before his death and also had lived with Joe for a time. Ivana moved to a rental apartment several years before Joe's death, at Joe's request. But, Joe and Ivana kept seeing each other. Leigh was at Joe's funeral with an agenda. Where were all of Joe's assets? Did he hide them offshore? How much of his many millions of dollars are left? Who has control of them? Were there life insurance policies on Joe's life? Did any of the insurance policies make Leigh the beneficiary? Leigh was not only certain Joe would take care of her for the rest of her life, but she was promised so by Joe, even after the divorce. Joe knew Leigh needed certain funds to cover her life style, for which, he set her up. Leigh truly believed she was entitled to that life style. Did "the Vamp" possess any of those assets? Did Ivana have any control of any assets? Leigh was adamant to find out the answers to those questions.

Leigh first approached Brian, Joe's personal lawyer, about Joe's estate. But to no avail. She felt Brian had an obligation to tell her where Joe's assets were located, or, if there were any insurance policies. After all Leigh and Brian and his wife, Linda, were very good friends with Joe and Leigh for years. He was not just Joe's attorney, he and his wife were their friends. They had season tickets to the local hockey team and spring training for the Minnesota Twins. However, Brian was not going to break confidentiality with his client, even after death. Leigh continued to pump Brian as Joe was lying in his open coffin. But, again to no avail.

She then interrogated Cathy, Joe's longtime friend and assistant, even raising her voice fairly loud enough for many of the attendees to hear, but Leigh never really got any answers from Cathy. Leigh was frustrated since Leigh was certain that Cathy knew everything about Joe and was more than just an assistant, she also handled the finances for all of Joe's development companies. After some further harsh words to Joe's brother, Leigh decided there was no further reason to stay to the end of the service. Leigh then left.

It was nearly 2:00 P.M. and nearly all who had viewed the open casket were taking their seats. Joe's good looking facial features were mostly gone, but the mortician attempted to bring back those younger good looks. It was shocking to many that Joe had lost so much weight before his death. No one seemed to want speak to any other person about Joe's looks, but the fact that an autopsy was performed confused most everyone in the chapel.

When all of the seats in the chapel were finally occupied, about thirty or so people stood along the back and side of the chapel since all of the chairs were filled. Minister Daniel Hilson, had earlier discussed with Daniel, Ivana and Cathy about Joe's religious beliefs as well as events in Joe's life. The minister approached the microphone on the podium and in lieu of a religious ceremony, began to eulogize Joe and to pay the ultimate homage to a life well lived. Minister Hilson began to paint a splendid picture of a complete life and the many elements that went to make Joseph Hyland a great business man, philanthropist, including his many anonymous contributions made to enhance special interests in the community. He weaved together the many aspects of Joe's life which included many memories with friends, employees, and the business community. The Minister fashioned together the story of a unique life. Minister Hilson include several humorous events to help the attendees move past the sadness of that day. By crisscrossing memories of the highlights and attributes of Joe's life, the Minister was able to craft a charming and personal eulogy that gave justice to the life of a special person. Yet there were a number of attendees who personally knew about Joe's ups and downs, his happy times and finally the difficult and sad times encounter over his last several years.

Daniel was then called to the podium to say a few words about his brother. His remarks focused on the ups rather than the downs through which Joe lived. He outlined Joe's accomplishments, the awards he received from various charities and public officials as well as how he contributed to his family by providing tuition for Daniel's children to private schools, for family vacations, offered him a job in Joe's business and eventually the fact that Joe took their elderly father under his wing and provided for him up to his death. Daniel's remarks made many attendee reflect on their own personal experiences with Joe, many good and some bad. Many tears fell through those eulogies.

After listening to the eulogies, many wondered why there was some type of investigation surrounding Joe's death. Why were law enforcement persons attending the service? Why were the police observing the sign in book? Why did they want to ask some attendees some questions about the last several days of Joe's life? It just didn't seem possible to the attendees that Joe was involved with any wrong doing. Most attendees knew that the housing recession, which started in 2008, was not good for Joe, but it still was not part of Joe's personality or his ethics to be involved in any wrong doing, at least to the extent to have someone kill him.

After Daniel finished speaking, Minister Hilson told the attendees that the casket would be moved to the burial plot. Those that wanted to congregate at the burial site should meet at the grave plot in fifteen minutes. Several of Joe's friends and workers help carry the casket to the limousine parked just outside the side of the chapel. A light drizzle was just beginning and everyone knew that the summer afternoon rains were about to begin. Those that went on to the grave site, opened their umbrellas and began to walk down the road. Many others headed for their cars to go to work, home or a bar. Detectives Blakely and Winslow were finishing their notes that they were taking during the service and began texting their superiors. Both detectives left the funeral home to meet downtown at the Lee County sheriff's office. But first a trip to the County coroner's office seemed appropriate to check on any update concerning the additional toxicology tests.

Both law men wondered if Joseph Hyland was really the victim of a bad deed. It had been several years since the last police incident involving Joe had occurred. Several of his business partners died suspiciously. However, supposedly those events were eventually closed.

But, to this day, there has been questions about millions of dollars that were part of Joe's development companies that had been the subject of some deceptions by persons unknown. The money was still the talk of the town and still had not been located. Even the person who those funds belong to was still a mystery. Joe and his development companies were in the middle of those controversies. Joe's death, at such a young age, has again brought to light all of those past events and have given the authorities a new reason to reopen several investigations. How did Joe really die? Did it have anything to do with the missing funds? Were there more people involved in the suspicious deaths of Joe's business associates? Throughout all of the past investigations of Joe and his businesses, and the manner in which his business operated, more questions continued to surface each time something new came to life. This time it surfaced due to the untimely death of Joe Hyland.

CHAPTER 2

JOE GRADUATED TECH in 1980, he stayed at Michigan Tech and became an assistant coach for the hockey team for a year and started graduate business school. They both bored him. He quit both and decided to take the job at GHCI in 1982. The allure became too great. He needed to change his life. George Harvey started GHIC and owned the majority interest in the business with several minority shareholders, but George was only somewhat involved in the day to day operations. He had trusted the day to day operations to his lifelong Michigan school mate and fraternity brother, Bradly Whalen. He and Bradly had a special relationship. Nether George nor Bradly desired to discuss their relationship. Too much was at stake. Bradly owned twenty percent of the GHCI stock and got paid a quarter of a million dollars to run the business plus his yearly percentage of the profit. Bradly was organized, diligent, a little OCD, and knew every employee on staff. There were even rumors, within the company, that Bradley and George were closer than just a normal business relationship. Bradly was a tough negotiator. Bradly was also tough on employees who did not timely complete each task that was required. Yet he was fair. He had the respect of nearly all four hundred fifty employees. But most of all he always had the loyalty of George Harvey.

Bradly was quite taken back that George not only did not confer with him about hiring Joe, but that George was showing Joe the operations of the company and introducing Joe around without him. Bradly could only remember one other time that George did not discuss any hires or firing of employees with him before any decision was made. That was when George hired Roger Spector. George decided that Roger was going to be Joe's mentor. This took Bradly by surprise. However, Bradly had spoken to George on several occasions concerning George's interest in someone in Michigan. Bradley was aware that George had met Joe several times at social and athletic events. However, this was very out of character for his longtime friend and confidant, in fact, it made him a little jealous. George spent over six hours with Joe at The Riverview Golf & Country Club, which including a two hour lavish lunch at the plush Veranda restaurant in downtown Fort Myers. Most of the local sales managers for each local project also attended that lunch. Again, Bradley was a little jealous that he was not invited.

During that six hours, George introduced Joe to the Fort Myers staff and supervisors. He meticulously went over each of the pending construction projects, including the golf courses, clubhouses and all other amenities for each community. Most of the residential units at GHCI's developments were high rises condominium of 10 stories or higher or low rise, three to four story condominium. George consistently insisted that the full density approved, by the local governmental authority, for each project, was completely utilized. George told Joe that he would be spending about ninety percent of his time in the Fort Myers office at Riverview and the rest of his time traveling between projects in Florida and other states. To Joe, the Fort Myers sales office looked like it just came off the pages of Office Illustrated magazine. It was extraordinarily modern, spacious and expensively furnished. The office was well situated on a beautiful parcel of property overlooking the Caloosahatchee River with the Gulf of Mexico just in eye's reach from the large picture window facing west over the river from the third floor of the massive clubhouse.

George was savvy enough to understand that the most expensive condos and homes couldn't be sold without a first class sales office. Any prospective customer was immediately greeted by their own personal sales person who was available to them 24 hours a day. Each potential client was familiarized with the food and beverage amenities available in the sales office. If a sales person heard that one of the clients liked a certain liquor that was not available, at least two bottles of that beverage was added to the overstocked bar by the next day. Sales, money and influence, that was GHCI. George always believed that a sale was never lost due to lack of accommodation for any client. He loved making money. That belief was known by every employee and each employee knew that it was their responsibility to make George's wishes come true.

George finally called Bradly into his office to introduce him to Joe. George went on about Joe's hockey career and the fact that he was drafted by the pros, but decided, after a stint as a college hockey coach and graduate student, that working for GHCI was a much better opportunity over the long run. George then explained to Joe that since he was still new in Florida, it would be several months before he could take the real estate school course. That was a prerequisite to taking the State real estate sales person test. Until he passed that test he could only be paid a salary. But, Joe was assured that once he passed the tests, his commissions plus a base salary based on sales would start immediately. After one year as a sales person, Joe would then be eligible to take his Florida brokers test. Once he passed that test, according to George, the sky was the limit. Joe was a little confused, but he could see out of the side of his eye, Bradly was motioning as to don't worry about that, he'll explain the logistics latter. Joe appreciated the introductions, lunch and personal attention, but he wasn't quite sure as to what exactly he would be doing for GHCI if he couldn't be a real estate sales person or manager. More important, what and how was he going to be paid? Joe took this job solely based on the puffing of George Harvey over the last several years about growth in Florida real estate, the ability to work independently and the money that could be made. Joe, began to feel that it was a terrible mistake not to finalize all aspects of the compensation package, and his true job description, before agreeing to the employment. This turned out to be true.

George then indicated he had an appointment with the Mayor and he would leave him in good hands with Bradly.

"Good luck Joe, but I know you won't need it." George said as his voice tailed off as he quickly left the room.

"Does he just run off like that all the time? He just spent nearly the whole day trying to convince me I was the new star at GHCI?" Joe said to Bradly.

"You'll get used to it" Bradly uttered. "George has his own way of doing things. You probably have seen more of George Harvey today than you will in the next month" Bradly confessed. "The only person that seems to get George's attention, more than me of course, is Roger Spector. My understanding is that Roger is going to be your mentor." Confidently stated Bradly.

"Come on, let's have some coffee and talk. I'll let you know a little about your mentor and what you may be doing until you get you licenses. Roger really is a good man and, more important, you'll probably get your real estate licenses a lot sooner than George mentioned." Joe looked even more confused.

The two men walked for what Joe thought was close to quarter of a mile to get to the kitchen area. Joe thought he had never seen a kitchen so well stocked, not to mention two ovens, the largest refrigerator he had ever seen, the largest private bar, and a table with at least 25 chairs. It was probably bigger than Joe's parent's house.

"Roger Spector, is your mentor until you're ready to solo." Said Bradly. "He is a good man and a loyal employee. He is the leading sales manager for this development and has worked for GHCI for over two years. He also seems to get a lot of attention from George. Don't know why. He is a good person but, in my mind, nothing outstanding." That concerned Joe.

"We have a sales manager for each of the neighborhoods in each development, but Roger is in charge of the entire Riverview development. The density for this development is 2,550 units. We have a long way to go to sell out this project." Bradly continued. "We have two low rise condominium projects complete and have sold out all 300 units. In the first residential home phase, we have 75 single family homes which are either complete or closed or very close to be completed. We have 5 single home models. All have been sold and GHCI has leased them all back as model homes for a year. There are still 205 single family lots, in the first phase of the Residential single family lots, but only a few are sold. Still plenty to do in this project. Roger has done a good job for George, so far, in this development." Bradly unenthusiastically stated.

"What do you mean by 'so far' Bradley?" Joe questioned.

"You'll get to know the real George and Roger soon enough." Joe indicated.

"I still don't understand and what you meant about the fact that I'll get my sales licenses sooner that George mentioned?" Continued Joe.

"I am not saying George isn't a little quirky, or that people don't necessarily get treated unfairly here, but George likes results, good results, fast results, which puts a lot of pressure on his employees. George has his priorities and he has ambitions. And he has certain people he trusts more than others. However, George does not like the minutia of work. It is somewhat beneath him. It doesn't fly well with his peers." Bradley continued.

Joe still didn't get his questioned answered, but let it go by.

"And who are his peers?" Joe again questioned.

"People like Bob Graham, the governor; Connie Mack, the next Republican senator for the State, and most important, Governor of Texas, George W. Bush, who, if George has anything to do with it, will be the next President of these United States." Proclaimed Bentley. "That is one of George's major project. George will probably be Bush's Florida campaign manager when he decides to run for President."

"You got to be kidding" proclaimed Joe. "He never seemed that way when I was with him in Michigan. Does he really have those kinds of connections? And about my licenses, you never really answered that question?" Joe continued confused.

"Yes, George is well connected. You will find that out soon. You will also find out about your licenses very soon. Now, let's just leave that issue and we can both forget we had this conversation. My real quarry is why does a good looking, smart, capable person with job offers from a professional hockey team, several other successful companies, decide to come to Fort Myers, Florida and work for George Harvey?" inquired Bentley.

"I wanted a job where I could be promoted quickly, make good money in a short period of time and in a company that is a first class operation with some real independence." Replied Joe. "GHCI seemed to fit that profile, at least I thought it did, and, more importantly, it was in a warm part of the Country. I have gotten tired of snow and cold. And most important, I wanted to be as far away from my family as possible. George seemed to offer me all of that. At least I thought he did? So I took the job under the impression, from our several years of friendship, that the pay would be sufficient for my talents. I know I took a leap, but you seem to confirm it may have been the right one." Replied Joe.

"Let's see if that is what happens. Don't misunderstand me, this is a great company to work for. Lots of benefits, fairly good compensation if you're willing to work hard and do exactly as George instructs you to do. George may ask you to do 'favors' for him or GHCI on occasions. Don't even hesitate, just say Ok." Bradly confessed.

"What kind of favors?" questioned Joe?

"Again, let's just ignore that issue for now, just do your job, and you'll do very well. Obviously, George thinks a lot of you." Confessed Bradly.

Joe was still confused, and the confusion would continue as the day went on.

As Bradly and Joe moved into one of the plush conference rooms, Joe saw this young, trim, athletic looking gentleman sitting at a conference table working on some large project. He had a pair of black rimmed glasses and he kept pushing them up on his nose constantly.

"Joe, I want you to meet Roger Spector. He is going to be your mentor for the next undetermined amount of time until you can 'solo' as George likes to say. I will still be your immediate supervisor, but Roger should be able to teach you the ways of GHCI." Bradly said as he began to leave the room.

Roger was so indulged in his project he barely heard Bradly.

"I'm sorry, what's your name?" questioned Roger. I was consumed in this project.

"Joe Hyland, the new guy George just hired. George told me you would be my mentor, at least for a while." Replied Joe.

"Oh yes, you're the big shot hockey player. George loves hockey. Actually, George was involved in bringing the Florida Everblades hockey team to Southwest Florida. They're the equivalent of the triple A minor league team for the North Carolina Hurricanes. Once he really thought he may want to play the sport but he was never the athletic kind, nor is he the kind of person that likes to be the guy that gets beat up. He is the kind of guy who needs complete control and playing hockey was not his 'cup of tea' If anyone was going to get hurt in a confrontation with George, it certainly was not going to be George." Openly claimed Roger.

'Boy am I getting an education today." Replied Joe.

"I'm not sure what you mean by that, but didn't you know what you were getting into by accepting a position with this company?" questioned Roger.

"Actually, now I'm not really sure, why don't you educate me?' Requested Joe.

"How about dinner tonight? We can have a long discussion about your job description. Oh, by the way I didn't even ask if you have a wife or significant other. If so she is welcome to come. I am single and plan to be that way for a while. No prospects and no time for prospects. Not that I am gay or anything like that, but relationships, other than George and Bradly's, come second to GHCI. I hope I am not scaring you." Confessed Roger.

"No, there is no wife or significant other. I moved here on my own. George set me up in a one bedroom apartment just off McGregor Avenue, fully furnished right down to two flat screen TVs, dishes, eating utensils and food for a week." Replied Joe. "What's this about George and Bradly? Am I supposed to know something?"

"Don't worry about that. Someday I'll tell you the story, but not for a while." Replied Roger. "I'm kind of surprised that a good looking, highly honored athlete like you, doesn't have a 'looker' with him?" questioned Roger.

"Never found the right one, but not that there weren't a few who I dated, but in a small school like Michigan Tech, the women that I dated never had the same values or goals as me. They all wanted to get married after graduation, have kids and move to Detroit, buy a big house and brag to their girlfriends that her husband was the goalie for the Red Wings. Just not my style." Confessed Joe. "I wanted more, much more, and that type of woman just never hit my radar."

"Well, we can talk more about that tonight over a good steak. Did George provide you with some wheels?" asked Roger.

"A leased SUV. Biggest and most luxurious car I ever road in." replied Joe

"Good, I'll meet you at the Prawn Broker on McGregor Blvd, just about 3 miles north of here, at 8:00 PM. I'll make the reservation. Dress casual. I'm sure you can find it. On the same road as this development. Best seafood in town. We can talk as long as you want. You will need to get with the GHCI program soon, for good or bad. See you then." Confessed Roger.

Joe's confusion continued to grow as the day went on, but maybe some of his questions would be answered at dinner, at least he hoped so. He really seemed to like Roger. He was the type of person he may be able to be good friends with. He and George even sort of looked alike in some ways.

****

Joe and Roger meet at the restaurant about 8:00 that evening. Joe wore a jacket, but no tie. Since he remembered Roger told him to dress casual. Joe was just not sure what that meant. Roger had a Tommy Bahama shirt, with shorts and sandals. He looked like he was an usher at a Key West wedding. Joe seemed to get the idea. They each ordered a drink and Roger opened the conversation by asking Joe how well he knew George Harvey. Joe told him the stories about how George would meet him after the Michigan, Michigan Tech hockey games and invite him to his private box or a private party where they would chat about many things, especially Joe's future. Before each game, Joe would receive a call from George's assistant indicating that George would be in town for the hockey game and invited him to his box after the game. And on several occasion, especially after he graduated with his Bachelor Degree, George would invite Joe to his Ann Arbor home for a night or two to wine and dine him. Again, nothing really personal was discussed, but they spoke mostly about his classes at school, coaching sports, graduate school and life after college. Joe always cleared this with his coach, who had heard of George, but never met him. The coach was always fine with it so long as Joe didn't miss the bus back to campus when he playing or miss any games when he was coaching. Joe never did. Prior to Joe's trip to Fort Myers his senior year, George never gave Joe the impression that he was a candidate for a job at GHCI, since they spoke mostly about pro hockey and other business companies that had given Joe an inkling that a job interview, if not a job offer was a future possibility. Joe had been informed by his college counselor that George had called and spoke to him several times, with Joe's permission, about Joe's progress in school and if any pro team may be interested in him. Again, the counselor never gave Joe the impression that George was in the market to hire Joe, but that he sort of wanted to take him under his wing and help him. Nothing confidential was ever discussed with the counselor, such as grades, girlfriends, people he associated with, or family information, but each time a phone call was received by the counselor, Joe was notified. Joe was quite flattered that such an important person was interested in his future and he believed that maybe George Harvey could help him find the type of job Joe was interested in, never believing it may be with GHCI. George had only done this with one other person, Roger Spector, who George specifically choose to mentor Joe.

Without Joe's knowledge, George had his own investigators and inside people find out anything George needed to about Joe. And Joe never knew about this and probably wouldn't have believed it anyway. George was just too friendly and kind towards Joe to believe he would do something like that. George seemed a little off when he wasn't in the work mode. Joe just couldn't put his finger on it.

Roger found this conversation intriguing. He knew it wasn't George doing the investigating, it was Bradly. Roger had never seen or heard of George taking such an interest in anyone to this extent, except, of course, Bradly. Bradly was the jealous type, but Roger wanted to stay away from that and other very personal matters. Roger was a Southern boy from the Fort Myers area and went to a private high school and on to Vanderbilt University where he studied business and finance. Roger also did not have an MBA when George hired him. George knew Roger's family and had always held out the possibility of hiring him after he graduated. GHCI was Roger's first and only interview since he was hired on the spot by Bradly Whalen. Roger knew this could never happen without George's approval. This made Roger somewhat unhappy. However, Bradly pleased George and made sure Roger was indoctrinated into the company in the same fashion Joe had been that day. But it wasn't more than a week after Roger was hired that things started to become very unusual.

Roger continued. "One week after I was hired, Bradly Whalen, George Harvey's COO, summoned me into his office to discuss my progress at the company. Bradly asked me how I and my mentor were getting along." Roger said.

"I answered Bradly by indicating that I thought I was starting to understand the company and how it was set up and where it is looking to go." Continued Roger.

"Roger said that's not what Bradly was trying to get at. He wanted to know if my mentor was teaching me about the real estate laws in Florida. He wanted to make sure I understood the legal procedures for the purchase and sale of real estate. What the requirements, both legal and ethically, were required by a Florida Real Estate Broker. What are the closing costs involved in a closing. Who is required to pay those costs? What are Transfer Taxes, and how do you calculate them? What are Intangible taxes and how are they calculated. What is title insurance? When is it used and how is the cost calculated and who is required to pay for it. Is title insurance even required to close real estate? He kept questioning me as to whether or not I knew if I could draft a closing statement for a residential sale. Things like that" said Roger.

"Why is that unusual?" questioned Joe. "Aren't those the type of issues that you're required to know for this job?"

"Yes. But, he also grilled me about many other real estate matters which, only working for the company for a week, would be difficult to know." Said Roger. "But the vast majority of his questions were concerning matters that I would have learned in real estate school. After I completed the real estate class, I would be required to take a real estate school test. If I pass that test, then I would be eligible to take the State Real Estate test to get my sales person license."

"What's the difference between a sales person license and a broker's license?" asked Joe.

"A lot" said Roger. "A sales person cannot collect a commission and cannot get paid by a buyer or seller of real property. They can only get paid by a broker or real estate developer. They cannot work for themselves selling someone else's property and get paid a commission. They must work for either a broker or a real estate developer. Then, and only then, can they get a portion of a sales commission. And most important, if a person who is not a licensed sales person works for a developer, such as GHCI, they can only get paid a reasonable salary and any bonus that they may get paid by GHCI during the year, or at the end of the year, cannot be calculated as if it were based on a portion of how much the employee sold of GHCI's inventory during the time they were an employee."

"So, what I think you are trying to tell me is that since I am not licensed by the State, I am entitled to be paid only a reasonable salary and no matter how hard I work, I cannot get a portion of any commission from the sale of a condo or single family home?" questioned Joe.

"You got it." Answered Roger.

"Is there some reason you are telling this to me?" said Joe.

"Because I am your mentor and you will not be taking the Real Estate test in the same manner as all other candidates in the State of Florida, or, even like all the other sales associates currently working for GHCI. In the next couple of days, Bradly will be calling you into his office and ask you similar questions he asked me. Be prepared. George has contacts all over the State of Florida and beyond. Some of his employees are not like employees of other real estate developers. George has tagged a few of us to be very different. Why he tagged you, I really don't know. You and I are the only two working for GHCI that have been chosen. George and the Commissioner of the Real Estate commission in Florida are best friends, and maybe even more. George believes that money and friends are interchangeable. For some time now George has had, as part of GHCI, a real estate school. Don't ask me how he did that, because I don't want to know. But within one week after I started with GHCI, Bradly gave me the school's real estate test and went through each of the questions with me. He even gave me the answers. He told me exactly what to write down as the answers for each of the questions, even if he told me to put down the wrong answer. One hour later he took the test and marked it up and indicated I got 88%. To this day, I don't know which ones were wrong. Bradly didn't want everyone from this school to get perfect scores. You only need 70% to pass, so no telling what your score will be. But it will be greater than 70 %." Roger reluctantly said.

"You're just kidding!" said Joe not really believing it.

"I haven't told you the rest of the professional story." Roger continued.

"When I looked at my graded test, the date on the test was listed as more than one year from the date I was given the test. I was in school in Tennessee on that date." Continued Roger.

"No you weren't' said Bradly. "I have a copy of your transcript and your diploma from Vanderbilt." He told me to look at it. After Roger examined those documents, Roger asked how in the world was he able to change those documents. This was impossible. Someone would know about this. All Roger's records indicate he was in Tennessee that year. All Roger's instructors, counselors, friends and parents know he was there.

"Bradley said he knew that." Said Roger. "The question Bradley had was how much do I want this job. I had been hired about a week earlier getting paid $28,000.00 a year. If I played ball, my salary would go to

$60,000 per year plus a percentage of every sales commission in the Riverview development. That was more money than I could calculate. Bradly was cool and calm and said 'you are now the new general sales person for Riverview, if I wanted it, it was up to me.' And it could even turn out better." Continued Roger as his confusion to Joe. "However, Bradly said I could quit right then and that the test and conversation we had never happen and all of the documents he had would be destroyed. Bradley would deny anything done or said in that room. I had never done anything illegal intentionally all my life. At least I didn't think so. He said the original school documents are in a safe place and the new originals have been replaced. GHCI have people in the Vanderbilt registrar's office. GHCI have people in several universities. How did I think I got accepted to Vanderbilt? Did I believe I had the grades and test scores to get in. George and my parents are good friends. George convinced my parents to have me apply to Vanderbilt, even though I thought that I couldn't get in. Don't worry, Bradly said, they don't know about this. George just said that he had great contacts at Vanderbilt. George just got my parents to give me a little nudge towards Vanderbilt. Bradly then required I sign a confidentiality agreement concerning the events of that day. I asked him if I could think about it. He said that I had 10 minutes to think about it. He said who would know. Only you and I are in this room and I am not talking. And if I knew what was good for me, I would not do any talking. The Real Estate Commission isn't going to do any checking. They take the documents they receive from their accredited schools, especially the one from GHCI, at face value. It will just get buried in a bureaucrat's file. The confidentiality agreement will have GHCI cover my ass." Roger naively said to Joe.

"Bradly told me there was one more matter to finalize the transaction." Again continued Roger. "I couldn't guess what that would be. Since the date on the Real Estate test was dated more than one year prior, I was now eligible to take my Broker test. I almost lost my lunch! He said if I agree to the deal, we can take care of that right then and there. Even the confidentiality agreement was ready for signature. Nowhere on any of the documents was George Harvey's of GHCI's name. It was just GHCI's Real Estate School." Roger again confessed.

"Why are you telling me this?" asked Joe. "You don't even know me."

"I do know you, and I know George Harvey." Answered Roger. "I knew you were coming, remember, I was to be your mentor. He didn't spend over two years grooming you without some end game. The last broker who got his license in this fashion had my job in this development and moved to California. I spoke with him, but he would say nothing, including if he even has a job." Continued Roger. "It's now my turn to be the broker for the development. George Harvey was once the broker for all the Florida developments. He got sued, big time, for matters that really don't matter now. However, George was furious!" Confessed Roger. "That was the first time, and only time George Harvey got sued personally. That will never happen again. The way things are run around here I am not sure I want the job. But, I know I have to. I have my personal reasons. There are things I know about George that he doesn't know I know." Continued Roger emotionally. "The one issue I am concerned with relates to liability. The broker who lists the property, is the one with the liability with all real estate transactions in the development. We have 55 sales people for this development and it will be my reputation and future at stake." Confessed Roger.

"I know George knows something about me. He doesn't know that I know. I want to keep it that way. I know George thinks he is helping me, but even if I don't believe this is helping me, I am just going to continue to work as if nothing has changed." Roger said sadly.

"Again, I am not sure how the relationship between GHCI and the last broker ended but I don't want to know. I do know that GHCI is thinking of carving out and selling a large condominium parcel from this development in the next year or so. It is currently up for approval and permitting with Lee County. The transfer, I believe, is for several reasons. GHCI is very unhappy with the General Contractor and the architect for the project. Sure, GHCI could fire them, but they don't want any legal fights over the contracts. As part of the separated property, there is a large parcel of mangroves behind it on the river. Even if that development can support 3 buildings, each 10 or more stories high, the view to the river will be mostly impaired by the mangroves. That will affect the purchase price and the income is not in the ball park GHCI is used to considering for that type of risk." Said Roger. "This worries me. That would mean another developer will be in Riverview. I believe George has something on his mind about this parcel and just wants to get rid of it. And I believe you have something to do with it."

"What's a mangrove? And how do I fit in?" Asked Joe.

"Mangroves are some of the most protected seagrass beds and coral reefs in Florida. The mangroves trap sediment and pollutants needed for the uplands that would otherwise flow out to the Gulf of Mexico. Mangrove beds provide a further barrier to silt and mud that could smother the reefs. In return, the reefs protect the seagrass beds from strong Gulf and ocean waves. Without mangroves, this incredible productive ecosystem would collapse. Buildings would fall into the water. Mangroves are like kindergarten, seagrasses are like secondary schools, and the coral reefs are the high schools and colleges for the local fish! And, once the fish graduate from the university, they return to spawn. Mangrove roots collect the silt and sediment that tides in the river carry out towards the sea. By holding the soil in place, the trees stabilize against erosion. Seedlings that take root on sandbars in the river help stabilize the sandbars over time and may even create small islands. Mangrove forests, like the one behind this parcel in the development provide many of the resources upon which coastal people depend for their survival and livelihood. At low tide, people can walk across the tidal flats to collect shellfish, claims and shrimp. At high tide, the fish move in to feed among the protection of mangrove roots, turning the marshy land into rich fishing grounds. They are fully protected by the State and to have those trimmed or even removed takes an act of many State agencies. GHCI does not want to spend the necessary time or money just to give some rich people a beautiful view." Expounded Roger.

"Wow! I never knew, but I never even saw them until last week. Didn't even know what they were." Exclaimed Joe.

"Since the parcel is located within Riverview, GHI can still make money, not only from selling the parcel for a pretty penny since the parcel has a density of 111 units which include 4 units per floor for 9 floors and 1 penthouse on the top floor with 3 buildings amounting to 111 units. It's located right over the Caloosahatchee River. GHCI will get paid on the sale of the parcel and a piece of each of the real estate commission since anyone who will purchase one of those units will need to come through the Riverview front gate and stop at the sales office. One of the GHCI sales persons will show the property and GHCI will get a commission on each sale. Plus a different broker, not one of GHCI's will be in charge of the development since it will be sold to a third party not related to GHCI. My guess is that person will be you Joe." Confessed Roger.

"Wait a minute, you are going too fast for me." Exclaimed Joe. "Are you telling me that Bradly will be calling me in his office soon to give me both the real estate license test and the brokers test in the same day so he can groom me for the brokers job on a parcel they plan to sell?" questioned Joe.

"I believe so. George Harvey is so very convincing that he can probably include you in the deal with the parcel to the next developer, in fact I am positive it can happen. They will train you here and prepare you for the sale." said Roger. "If they don't sell it to a third party, George will make you a deal you cannot refuse."

Joe just sat there for a minute. He still had not even finished over half his steak since this conversation was so difficult for him to comprehend, that it really scared him. The most frightening part of the entire conversation was the fact that George Harvey, his friend and confidant, may have deceived him to take this job so he could take control of his life without Joe having any say.

"Roger, I like you. I cannot believe you have only known me for a short period of time but yet you have confided in me about something that is so hard to believe, that I am still not sure you aren't just putting me on." Joe said with a bad feeling in his stomach.

"This is the truth, Joe. I do like you and from the little I know about you and heard about you I still feel comfortable, as well as some obligation to let you know what you are getting into." Again confessed Roger.

"Between you and me and the four walls here, I have been thinking about some way to get out from under this hold GHCI has on me and I have been looking for the right person to do it with. I really believe you may be that person. I don't want you to say anything to me yet. See what happens over the next few days. I may be wrong about you becoming a listing broker. But, let's plan to get together for a drink after you and Bradly have had your get together. Then we can talk again. I think you may feel much more different than you did just a few days ago. I have a suggestion that just may work for the both of us. It may be a little dangerous, but if we handle it properly, calmly and professionally, it may just work." Said Roger.

"No obligations, but is it a deal, at least to talk about it?" asked Roger.

What could Joe say after hearing a story that is not only hard to comprehend in such a short period of time, but could take him out of the control of his professional life and end up being used as a patsy due to some stupid mangrove problem? This is not what Joe had in mind when he came to Fort Myers.

"Deal, I guess." Said Joe. "First, I'll let you know if this unbelievable situation I seem to have gotten myself into really plays out.

****

The next day Joe went to work at 8:00 AM at the GHCI office. He was never informed what time, or where to report, but he just assumed GHCI's main office at that time seemed reasonable. He must have guessed right since Bradly was waiting for him and told him welcome to work. His first task, as told to him by Bradly was to go to the large closet in the in the kitchen area. There he would find a closet full of clothing. He was told to take a dozen GHCI polo shirts, with the GHCI logo on them, in his size, two each in a different color. Bradley said he would need both khaki and black pants with socks to match each color of the shirts. There were also blue sport coats in the closet, with and without the logo, in all sizes and he should take 3 of those with the logo and 3 without the logo to wear with the khaki pants. He should also retrieve 6 white, long sleeve, button down shirts, in his size, to go with the sports coat. After he retrieved those, Joe told him to go to the Cole Hahn store at the mall in Fort Myers and tell the manager that he works for GHCI. They will provide him with all of the Khaki pants and black pants and socks he needs

They would also fit him with 6 pairs of the proper shoes to wear for work and work events. Bradley said that all of those clothes and shoes were for work and work events only. The store will charge them to GHCI's account. Joe was never to wear them to any social occasion or to a bar unless it's with other employees for a work gathering.

After he had accomplished all that Joe was informed that there was a sales meeting at 1:30 in the main conference room and should be sure to be there in one of his new polo shirts, khaki pants and new shoes and socks. Bradly intended to introduce Joe to all of the sales staff.

Joe asked Bradly what his job description would be and who he is to report to.

"That will all be discussed in the afternoon meeting. Glad to see you are anxious to get started" Bradly touted. "See you there."

At 1:20 that afternoon, Joe walked into the main conference room at the GHCI main office wearing a bright green polo shirt with a GHCI logo on it, a pair of black pleated pants, black knee high socks with little green dots on them and a pair of tie up black shoes. Luckily, after all of the clothes shopping left Joe some time to get to his apartment and iron the clothes so he would look crisp and professional for his entrance. As Joe walked into the room he observed between 25 and 30 young men and women wearing all different color polo shirts with the GHCI logo. The men had on either black or khaki pants and all of the women were wearing khaki skirts. There were several plates of donuts and muffins in the center of the large conference table with rows of bottled water and crystal glasses. Cloth napkins were rolled up next to several dozen stainless forks and china plates. Each of the persons present made an effort to introduce themselves to Joe and several indicated that they were sales or assistant sales manager for a specific neighborhood at the Riverside development. Others were sales persons and a few were administrative assistants. Two of the men indicated they were the manager and assistant manager for the club house and restaurants and one man was the golf professional. There were 4 large slim televisions on the East wall of the main conference room, each one divided into 4 equal parts. Joe could see several people, all dresses similar to those at the main office in each of the 16 squares. Each was sitting at a different conference table. At exactly 1:35 Bradly Whalen walked into the main conference room and told everyone that the meeting was to begin.

"It seems that most everyone in this room has already met Joe Hyland, our new Broker." Bradley said to the surprise of Joe.

"He is starting today and I wanted everyone to meet him. Joe, each of those televisions on the wall is set up in the main conference rooms for each of our developments in Florida, Georgia, and South Carolina and our newest development in Knoxville, Tennessee. You will be able to meet each of those hard working members of the GHCI family when you start your tour of each of our developments." Continued Bradly.

"Joe has been on our CEO's radar for some time and we are honored that Joe decided to choose to work for GHCI over several highly touted companies. Even more astonishing, is that Joe picked GHCI over becoming the Detroit Red Wings newest goalie. Joe was an All American hockey player for Michigan Tech the year they went to the Frozen Four several years ago. Too bad they lost in the championship game to Minnesota, but it certainly was not Joe's fault, since the game went into overtime and Tech lost 1-0. I watched that game on ESPN and Joe made some incredible stops. And yet, here he sits, and not a hockey pad on him. I want you all to give Joe a GHCI welcome and treat him to the very best when he is on his tour. We hope to indoctrinate him into our system so he can tackle the task of GHCI's new position of supervising Broker for one of our new divisions." Continued Bradly all to the surprise of Joe and Roger and every other person in the GHCI Company. Is this really true or it just a diversion until the back parcel at the Riverside development is sold? "Over the next few months Roger Spector will be mentoring Joe on the ins and outs of our organization and preparing Joe for the next step on the ladder here at GHCI." Proudly announced Bradly.

"I thought this would be a good time to let all of you know that within the next several months, GHCI will be carving out Divisions and promoting people to Division supervisors. All of this will be explained to all of you in a memo that each of you will receive in the next several weeks. Do not worry, none of your jobs are at risk, in fact some of you will probably be promoted." Proudly announced Bradley.

"Now, I will let Joe take the floor and let him give you a little background on himself so you can get to know him a little better. When you each get a chance to speak with him personally, I am sure you will see why George Harvey is so high on him." Said Bradly, as he turned to Joe.

Joe had never been afraid of public speaking, in fact, he really enjoyed it, but he would have felt a little more comfortable if he had been given some notice that he would be the center of attention at this meeting. But Joe, got on his feet and proceeded to give about a 20 minute talk on his background and reasons for choosing GHCI. The one item that was left out was the fact that everyone in the room, except Bradley and Roger knew he wasn't a licensed broker or even a licensed sales person. Worse than that, he knew very little, if anything about the real estate business in Florida. A fact that no one else who intensively listened to his short speech even thought about.

After Joe's speech and about 10 minutes of small talk and a few questions from the television audience, Bradly adjourned the meeting and told everyone to go back to their appointed tasks.

Bradly turned to Joe and said, "Good job. I suppose you are curious about all of this? Come to my office in 10 minutes and I will explain everything to you."

That may have been the longest 10 minutes of Joe's career. But Joe went into Bradly's office 10 minutes later.

"Joe, as to the breakup into Divisions, you will learn about all of that when the internal memo comes out. It may be a little longer than the next several months. But when you get the memo, you and I will have a long talk about your duties in that job. But as to the fact that I called you our newest Broker, I need to talk to you about that." Bradley confessed.

For the next 3 hours, Joe and Bradly went through the exact same conversation and exercise Roger had explained to Joe the night before. It wasn't that Joe was surprised about what was occurring, but the surprise to Joe was the fact that Bradly did it so soon after he started. And what was this about a Division Broker? After Joe had just become a licensed broker, he knew the next person he had to speak with was Roger.

CHAPTER 3

T HE DAY AFTER Joe Hyland's funeral, Cathy and William Rutter were at their home, located in a fashionable development just east of Interstate 75 in Maribelle, Florida. All of the homes and condominium are valued at no lower than one million dollars. The development was so large that the developer incorporated it as a separate City with its own zip code.

The Rutter's were having dinner on their lanai, since William had just grilled two one inch thick filets, baked potatoes and grilled Brussel sprouts. They were drinking a slightly fruity cabernet, when they heard the doorbell ring.

"Shit!' said William. "This always happens when we're in the middle of eating."

"Who the hell can that be? Its 7:30" questioned Cathy. "Maybe we should just ignore them."

"It probably has to do with Joe. I just hope it's not Leigh or Ivana. I just don't want to speak with either of them right now." Said William.

"They still think Joe left millions of dollars hidden somewhere and both of them believe that they are entitled to those assets and money." Angrily said Cathy. "If they only knew the truth, for God's sake, I handled most of his bank accounts."

"We don't know if it is them. Let's just answer the door and get rid of whoever is there. It may just be someone soliciting and selling candy bars." Said William.

The doorbell rang again. "I guess they aren't going away by themselves. I'll get it." Angularly said William.

William open the door and there was Luke Blakely.

"Hello, I am detective Luke Blakely of the Lee County Sheriff's department, and you must be Mr. Rutter."

"Sheriff's Department?" said William, "What do you want at this time of the night? We are in the middle of dinner."

"I am sorry, I am with the homicide bureau of the Sheriff's office. I just have a few questions for your wife." Replied Luke.

"I assume this is about Joe Hyland. Can't this wait until tomorrow morning? After all his funeral was just yesterday. And what does the homicide division have to do with Joe's death?" Said William with a tone Luke really took offense too.

"Sir, I am really tired. Yesterday a Judge granted the Sheriff's Department a subpoena for you and your wife's financials. My partner and I have been reviewing your bank accounts, financial transactions and documents in the public records for all of the real estate you and your wife have purchased both here in Lee County and in Naples and Collier County and in the Caribbean over the last several years. It was exhausting." Luke replied. "Now can we sit and talk?"

William reluctantly showed Luke in and sat him in the den while William went to get his wife. He was not happy telling Cathy what Luke just told him, but Cathy said, except for the fact that he has interrupted a great dinner, for which she was really in the mood, she didn't have a problem speaking with him.

As Cathy and William walked into the den, Luke said to them "Nice house."

"How did you get through security, without a call to us?" Asked William. "And, by the way, you're sarcasm about our house is not a good way to get started interrogating my wife." Retorted William.

"There was no sarcasm, I just really like the house. A lot of big homes in this development. I usually don't see so many expensive homes like this. My job don't usually bring me to these types of neighborhoods." Luke stated apologetically. "And it's not my intent to interrogate anyone. No one is going to the precinct, I'm here just to ask your wife a few questions. She did work as Joe Hyland's main financial assistant for several years. And, by the way, I am a police officer. It's not hard to get through any security, no matter how much money is behind the gate."

The first thing that came to Cathy's mind was how in the world the police got a subpoena for their financials. When she confronted Blakely about that, he explained to her in a calm and straight forward manner that the reasons for obtaining subpoenas were the police and prosecutors business. Luke was there to do his job and nothing else. He also indicated that subpoenas were issued for several other people's information and the Rutter's were not the only ones singled out.

"Joe's death was not a crime, for God's sake, he was in my house when he died. He was sitting at my dining room table eating dinner when he said he had pains in his chest and I called 911." Claimed Cathy. "What in the world does our finances have to do with Joe's death? Is there something that you're not telling us? Has Joe's death been determined a homicide? And if not, what the hell are you doing here at this hour of the night?" Cathy's voice getting louder as she starts to realize maybe this is a mistake talking to the police.

Luke assured the Rutter's that Joe's death has not yet been determined a homicide, but it is still considered undetermined and the coroner and the police have an obligation to try to close the matter. He continued that the reason he was at their home was to do just that. Cathy did work very closely with Joe for several years and she was involved in many meetings with Joe, his major employees and his lawyers concerning decisions that affected everything dealing with the financials of all of Joe's properties.

"What does that have to do with anything? It was Joe's companies, I was just his assistant. I was just a glorified secretary." Cathy uttered harshly.

"We believe that your position with Joe's companies was much more than that. As I indicated to your husband, my partner and I just spent many hours reviewing your finances including your salaries, yes plural, and other benefits you received as Joe's assistant. So, why don't you start from the beginning and tell me when and the circumstance concerning how you met Joe Hyland and how your relationship matured up to the point when he died." Asked Luke.

"You got to be kidding! I say again, what does that have to do with anything concerning Joe's death?" Cathy exclaimed.

Luke's experience as a police officer for 20 years told him that this curtesy call on the Rutter's was not going to work.

"Mr. and Mrs. Rutter, I see that this is not going to work here and at this time. I will expect you in my office tomorrow at 9:30 AM and we can go over the questions I have for you and we can discuss your finances." Said Blakely.

"That is not acceptable. I will contact a lawyer and we will straighten this all out including this illegal subpoena your office obtained." Stated Cathy.

"I don't think that is necessary, Mrs. Rutter, but it is your right and it will just make things a little more complicated. But I will still wait for a call. Here is my card. But if I do not hear from you by end of day tomorrow, I can assure you that the subpoena will be extended to your presence before a grand jury." Warned the detective.

"Bull Shit. Don't try to scare me. You may think that I am just a naive woman. I'll have my lawyer call you when he can. Now get out of my house!" said Cathy.

"I am sorry to have interrupted you during your dinner. Maybe I should have just made arrangements to meet at my office in the first place. My apologies." Said Luke

Luke left the Rutter's home. William asked his wife what was that all about. She assured William that this is all a big mistake, almost to be a joke. Why this has gone this far was inconceivable to Cathy. Joe died of a heart attack due to his health condition. He was lucky to be alive for the last 12 months. Cathy knew Joe had been drinking heavily again the night of the dinner when he died. He was probably on drugs as well. Cathy had been trying for over a 15 month period to help him control his drug and alcohol problem. She even arranged with some of his old friends and business associates for him to go to an inpatient program for 30 days to dry out and then to join alcohol anonymous. Joe just never would say that he had a problem. Prior to his death, Joe never admitted he had any alcohol or drug problem. In Joe's mind, all of his ailments were medical. He visited every specialist in town to determine what was wrong with him. If he didn't like the diagnosis from any doctor, he just tried another. There was no way he was depressed or self-destructive. He was just going through a bad time in his life. It was not Joe's fault. It couldn't be. Joe always believed he had always did everything right. He prided himself about that. As he said over and over every time someone tried to reason with him for almost two years, "I did nothing wrong! This is not my fault." Joe expected everyone who worked for him including his cadre of lawyers to fix his business problems. The housing recession was not his fault. Why should he be punished for doing the right thing?

"I am calling Brian Kopp first thing tomorrow and he can do his magic to get the police off our backs. This whole thing is ridiculous!" Cathy stated. "Maybe there is some way we can salvage our dinner."

"Let's just open another bottle of wine, that will probably do the trick." Said William.

****

Alex Terian, the assistant County Attorney assigned to the Hyland case also successfully got a subpoena for the financials for Leigh Mowery. His office reviewed her financials. There were some unusual transactions that were discovered by his office. Denise Hudak, was the investigator for the County Attorney's office. She went to law school at Nova University for a year, but had to drop out due to the death of her father and other financial and family reasons. She had no siblings and had to work to help her and her mother make ends meet. She was assigned the task of interviewing Leigh. Denise, a long time hard working investigator, who worked as an investigator for the Pinellas County attorney while she was in law school, was a woman with good instincts, highly knowledgeable on the law and with a high closing rate on matters assigned to her. She was very skeptical about this entire case. This case was not even classified as a homicide matter yet. She really was not sure why she was working on it. She made inquiry with her supervising attorneys several times who seemed to avoid any direct answer and just told her to investigate Leigh Mowery as she may relate to Joe Hyland's death. Reluctantly, she studied the autopsy and sheriff's reports and the only unusual facts in the reports was that at the time of death of Joe Hyland, besides eating baked chicken and broccoli as his last dinner, he had an alcohol content of .14, almost twice the legal limit. He had other traces of drugs in his system including Singuliar, Chantix, Xanax, Amitriptyline, Oxazepan and Phenobarb. Most of those are anti-depressants and sleeping disorder medications which when used together was usually for the purpose of causing a suicide.

Those drugs would never have been prescribed to Joe by a competent physician, for one reason, due to the condition of his liver. He had yellowing of his skin due to the accumulation of bilirubin in his blood; various bruising by the decreased production of blood clotting. His medical history indicated chronic fatigue, weakness of his limbs, and loss of appetite. Another reason for a physician not to prescribe those medications was Joe's kidneys. They were in the late stages of chronic kidney disease. Again his medical history indicated foamy and bloody urine, swelling of his hands and feet, constant pain in his back, high blood pressure, episodes of vomiting or nausea and puffiness around his eyes usually when he woke up. Any competent doctor would have seen most of those symptoms even without a complete examination. Joe had been hospitalized twice in the weeks before his death. He was put on a strict high carb diet, with absolutely no alcohol. Denise could not see any way in the world that this is a homicide. Denise, through her research, was aware that Joe had traveled to Amsterdam many times each year for the last ten years and all of those medications would have been easy to access there. So it was her conclusion that Joe was drinking heavily and taking these medications in small doses over a period of time. Her conclusion was that no one killed Joe Hyland. But why the inquiry? Why the inconclusiveness on the death certificate. It should have read possible suicide. But she knew that it was not her conclusion to make. She needed to write up a report on the whole situation. In Denise's mind, the real investigation was the missing millions of dollars. No one wanted to raise that at this time since it had been temporarily closed 4 years earlier. So before she started to write her report, she put her notes in her brief case, including financial notes from years before, and went to the Ritz Carlton hotel in Naples to speak with Leigh Mowery.

The phone rang in Leigh Mowery's room at the Ritz about 11:00 AM two days after Joe's funeral. Leigh picked up the phone to hear the front desk indicating that she had a visitor from the Lee County attorney's office.

"Not now I am getting ready to go out." Said exhausted Leigh. "Tell him to leave his card and I will call him latter."

"It's not a him. It's Denise Hudak, an investigator and she has a subpoena." Said the desk clerk.

"What the hell you talking about? A subpoena for what? They probably think I killed Joe. I wish I did, but I am not talking with her. Tell her to go away. What kind of crazy people work in that shitty police department? I have no intention of speaking with them." Leigh exclaimed in disgust.

The desk clerk attempted to explain to Leigh that the woman has a subpoena and she indicates she will call the Sheriff's office to have two deputies here to restrain her while she speaks to you. He indicated that Denise had assured him that the subpoena is just for your financial, not for any testimony.

"Shit." Am I supposed to come down to the lobby or is she coming to my room?" asked Leigh.

The desk clerk handed the phone to Denise who indicated that the two of them can talk any place she feels comfortable. After a somewhat cordial discussion on the phone, with assurances by Denise that the County attorney's office has no intention of discussing the death of Joe or accusing her of any foul play, Leigh told Denise to come up to her room.

To Leigh's surprise, Denise was dressed in a nice pair of black slacks, black pumps and a white button down shirt under a camel blazer. Leigh was still in her robe and had no intention of going anywhere at that time.

"Where's your police outfit? I thought you were from the sheriff's office." asked Leigh.

"I am not an officer, I am just an investigator." Answered Denise.

"So what's with this subpoena for finances? I don't even know what that means. And what does that have to do with Joe's death? You must have got the subpoena from some Court and they wouldn't have granted it without some belief that someone killed Joe. Am I a suspect? Do I need to hire a damn lawyer? If I do, I am not talking to you." Leigh said with some emotion.

"No one is accusing you of killing anyone. If you want to hire a lawyer, that's your right, but you're not under arrest. I am here to confirm some financial matters I uncovered after I was given the subpoena by my boss. I do have to admit that it is a little unusual to have a subpoena granted for financials where there is no confirmation of any homicide, but I am just an investigator and I do what I am told. I have a job just like most people." Confessed Denise who actually felt a little empathy for Leigh.

"OK, so ask me your questions". Said Leigh.

Denise took out her notes from her brief case and started to summarize her finding about Leigh's financials including some other information. She started by telling Leigh that she was born in 1959 in St. Matthews, Kentucky, an upper-class suburb of Louisville. After graduation she went to Louisville University for 2 years when she dropped out and moved to Fort Myers, Florida and shared an apartment with several girlfriends with whom she attended high school. Fort Myers was an up a coming, fast growing city. She took a course at a local real estate school and received her real estate sales person license. In 1981 she went to work with Tisch & Tisch Real Estate Company. She never took the broker test and only listed and sold residential homes for several year.

"What does this have to do with my finances?" Questioned Leigh. I don't need a history lesson on my life. Get to the point."

"This is just background information I discovered in my investigation. If I have the facts wrong, please enlighten me." Said Denise

"Whatever!" exclaimed Leigh?

Denise continued with the information from her notes. During the time she was listing and selling residential homes, she listed several resales in The Riverview Development & Country Club. She actually never sold any of those homes. She got paid for the listing, but sales people from GHCI actually sold the homes. She shared the commission with them. Denise's information indicated she started dating Joe Hyland at that time. He was actually a broker at the development. One of her girlfriends also dated a Roger Spector who worked with Joe at the time. But that relationship never lasted more than one or two dates. Denise could not find any other times Roger dated anyone while he and Joe were friends and coworkers.

"Tick tock!" murmured Leigh." Are there finances someplace in this history lesson?"

Denise ignored Leigh's remarks and continued. In 1999 she and Joe purchased two condominium units on the 8th floor in building 1 of Lago Del Sol. A door was cut out between the two condominium and she lived on one side and Joe on the other. Each decorated their own sides. Joe had a decorating company decorate each side. But she picked out the decorations and furniture package she wanted and Joe picked his. Largo Del Sol was a condominium project being developed by a company formed by Joe, Roger and a Florida company with an owner of the company being some person from the Netherlands. As it is known, the public records in Florida do not require the owner of a company to be revealed. Joe was the manager of that company. Denise thought that Leigh could reveal the name of this unknown person. She gave Leigh a few seconds to come forward with the name, but Leigh just continued to listen.

The two condominium units were titled in the names of Joe Hyland and Leigh Mowery, as joint tenants with the right of survivorship. But yet the two of you were not married.

"How am I doing so far?" inquired Denise.

"Oh hum." Uttered Leigh.

Denise continued where she said that before the purchase of the two condo units, Joe and Roger seemed to break off their business relationship and their friendship. How it ended, Denise was not sure yet. But the annual report, required by the State of Florida each year for the Largo Del Sol Condominium Association, didn't have Roger's name as an officer or director as it did the year before. But Leigh's name was there as a director and Secretary of the Association. Denise indicated that about that time, Leigh and Joe were an item, and were in fact living together. Denise could not understand the two different condo units, but the only remodeling of the condominium was an 8 foot door between the units. Nothing else in the units were changed. So if, for any reason Joe or Leigh wanted to sell one of the units, all that had to be done was take out the door and drywall the area. No one would ever know they were connected. Also some time before that acquisition, she went to work for the company that was developing Largo Del Sol, but she worked in the office. She never used or even renewed her sales person license again. In 2002 Leigh and Joe got married at a Christmas party put on for their friend, business associates and employees of Joe's company.

"Do you want to take a break?" asked Denise.

"A break from what? I have not heard anything about my finances. I'm not a lawyer, but the subpoena is for my finances and so far I have not heard about dollar one." Stated Leigh. "If you don't have anything, maybe you should just leave."

Denise ignored that comment and gazed at her notes again and started to go on. She decided to keep the rest of the non-financial information private and moved on. In 2005, Leigh left Fort Myers and moved back to Louisville and purchased a $1,250,000 home with cash. She opened several bank accounts, including a money market account with $100,000.00; a regular checking account with $50,000.00 and a broker's account with Merrill Lynch with $2,850,000.00. If Denise's numbers were correct, that adds up to $3,000,000.00! Every three months thereafter, Leigh deposited an additional $50,000.00 in her money market account. That went on for 5 quarters. Then it suddenly stopped. All of that money came from one of Joe's companies that he formed over the last several years. No prenuptial agreement has been found. No Settlement Agreement is in the public records concerning the divorce that became final in 2008. Denise did find the Divorce Judgement in the public records. But, that was 3 years after she left Fort Myers. There are records of travel between 2005 and 2009 from Louisville to Fort Myers on several occasions. There is a record of Leigh having a Court hearing with just her lawyer and the judge in 2009. Joe did not attend the hearing when the divorce judgment was finalized. There was no contesting the divorce. All financial matters were settled before the divorce became final.

"Did you and Joe come to an agreement about the terms of the divorce when you moved back to Louisville in 2004? Why did it take over two and a half years to finalize your divorce since the divorce action was filed in 2006? But you received over $3,250,000.00 and a $1,250,000.00 home before the divorce action was actually filed. Can you explain that?" questioned Denise. "That is really strange. And to top it off one of the two condominium at Largo Del Sol was deeded to you by Joe in 2008 after the divorce judgment was filed in the public records. Very strange. Don't you think?"

"That's enough. You seem to know everything about me even though some of the facts I heard were not quite right." Said Leigh. "I think your time is up. As long as I am not under arrest and there are no financial documents in this hotel room, this interview is over." Claimed Leigh.

"I appreciate your time Mrs. Mowery." Said Denise in a calm and friendly way. "If I need something more, I'll be in touch."

"You do that." Said Leigh. I'm sure you can find your way out."

Denise left the hotel to go back to her office to start to write up her report for her boss. Leigh got her cell phone and called Cathy Rutter.

****

Some of the non-financial information that Denise left out of her talk with Leigh dealt with Ivana Hollings. Denise's boss never mentioned Ivana, but during her investigation, Ivana surfaced. Denise could not find out much about Ivana, it was like she just appeared on the scene in 2000. Ivana had a sales person license and applied for a sales job at one of the developments that Joe was developing. Denise knew that if Ivana has a Florida sales person license, she had to have a background. Denise's curiosity was one of her better traits and made her the great investigator she had become. So before she started to draft her report for the assistant County Attorney, Denise decided to do some digging.

Ivana was a cousin of Roger Spector. Roger and Ivana would meet once and while for a drink to just catch up. Ivana went to journalism school in Tallahassee at Florida State. She was good looking and a fairly good student. She finished in the middle of her class with her bachelor degree in journalism. Ivana was tall, thin, blond hair, highly confident, her personality and movements showed that. Her main desire was to be a reporter on television. She auditioned several times in Tallahassee, Orlando and Miami, each at several stations. She was hired by several different stations from, time to time, but never lived up to the quality of a reporter any of those stations expected. It just did not seem to be a good fit for her. She was never sure why she could not succeed at any of those stations, but her ego rationalized that those stations just couldn't recognize good talent that was right before their eyes. She became depressed. After she was let go from the fourth station she had worked at, she decided to come to Fort Myers and pour her heart out to her cousin Roger. They talked for hours one evening and Roger finally suggested that she may want to pursue another vocation. Since Roger was working for GHCI, he thought that he would have no problem getting her a job. He convinced Ivana to go to real estate school and get her sales person license, then he would do the rest. With her personality and good looks she would make a good sales person.

Roger and Ivana were meeting and having their drink at the Red Lion Business Club. That establishment was a high end private business club located on the Caloosahatchee River where local business people paid dues of only $500.00 a year to meet and greet other business people in a cozy bar overlooking the River; or have a gourmet dinner with their business associates or their families in the plush dining rooms. There was also dedicated rooms for business gatherings and events. Everyone, who was someone, in Fort Myers was a member of the Red Lion Business Club.

Just a few bar stools away from Roger, Joe Hyland was having a drink with Robert Coulson, a local builder/developer who was attempting to become a preferred builder of single family homes in The Riverview Golf & Country Club. Joe and Robert had met a few weeks before though a mutual real estate agent friend. Robert was building mostly smaller sized homes on real estate parcels his development company would acquire from larger developers. Robert would have the parcel platted and approved for 20 to 30 homes to build homes about 2500 square feet plus or minus. Robert was doing well, but he wanted to expand his company into much larger developments like Riverview and build upscale single family homes in the range of 3500 to 5000 square feet, or even larger. Robert was with his attorney at the bar, Brian Kopp. Brian had been representing Robert for several years and had become good friends with Robert as well as his business and personal lawyer. Robert introduced Brian to Joe and they all started a conversation about the real estate business in Fort Myers and the Naples area. They all got along together well and each of them even drank the same thing, Crown Royal on the rocks. Joe noticed Roger was having a drink with a good looking blond, but he kept his cool and stayed on point with Robert and Brian. She was now sitting alone and then came up to Roger and told him she would see him latter. But before Ivana left, Joe called Roger over to an open stool by Roger and Brian. Introductions were made all around. Ivana then left. Joe ordered Roger another drink, but Roger said he had had his limit when he was with his cousin. Joe made inquiry of Ivana and Roger told them all the sad story. Joe was intrigued. After some small talk between all of these entrepreneurs, Joe said to Roger, that sometime tomorrow he would like to meet him either back at the Red Lion or somewhere other than The Riverview Golf & Country Club. Joe had something he wanted to talk to Roger about. Roger agreed to meet Joe at 6:00 the next evening back at the Red Lion. Roger then moved on and Brian, Robert and Joe continued their conversation over another Crown Royal.

CHAPTER 4

IT WAS NOVEMBER 14, 1987, at 6:30 the next evening and Roger was sitting at the bar at the Red Lion Business Club having a vodka tonic and Joe still had not showed for their meeting. Roger finally decided to give Joe a call to see where he was, or if he may have indulged a little too much the night before and forgot about the meeting. There was no answer and the call went to voice mail. Roger did not want to leave a message. Maybe Joe was with a client, but he would have called Roger to let him know that he would be late. He thought he would finish his drink and meet up with Joe at a later time, but he really needed to talk to Joe about something very important.

About 10 minutes later, Joe arrived at the Red Lion Business Club bar. Roger could tell that he had been drinking. Joe sat next to Roger and asked Bob, the bartender, for a Crown on the rocks. Like most private clubs, Bob had seen Joe come in the bar and had started to prepare the drink before Joe even sat down.

"This my kind of club. Said Joe. "My drink is ready for me before I can even find my stool."

Roger asked Joe where he had been or did they miscommunicate on the time. Joe, who was a little tipsy, said that he had run into Roger's cousin, Ivana. She was at the reception area at The Riverview Golf &

Country Club development about 4:30 and was asking the receptionist for Roger. Joe had seen her and recognized her from the evening before. Joe went up to her and introduced himself and told her that he had seen her with Roger at the Red Lion Business Club bar the evening before. He told her that Roger had been his mentor when he started working for GHCI. Ivana told Joe that she was going to complete real estate school in several days and then study for the school's real estate sales person test. She also mentioned that Roger was going to get her a job at the Riverview development as a sales associate after she passed the State real estate test. She was at Riverview to see if Roger would give her a tour of the development so she knew what she was getting herself into. Since Roger was not there at the time, Joe volunteered to give her the tour. She very cordially accepted Joe's offer.

The tour started with the clubhouse and after showing Ivana around the locker rooms, card room, billiards room, conference and banquet rooms and the four restaurants, they went to the main bar on the third floor of the building. That bar had walls of windows giving one a 360 degree view of the entire development, including both golf courses. Joe told Ivana that there were other smaller restaurants around the development and they could grab a golf cart and view the condos and single family homes and lots as well as the other amenities. Ivana gave Joe one of those looks that made Joe want to say that maybe a drink would be a better option. Ivana confirmed Joe's thought and they sat at the main bar where Joe ordered a Crown on the rocks and Ivana a vodka on the rocks, two olives.

They started to talk about Roger and other small talk about real estate until after the second drink. The conversation then became a little more personal. Somehow, time went by and when Joe finally looked at his watch it was after 6:00. Joe confessed to Ivana that he had an appointment with her cousin and he was late, so maybe they could finish their discussion about each other's lives at another time. Ivana consented and said to say hello to Roger. Joe accompanied Ivana to her car and then was on his way to the Red Lion.

"That's the truth Roger." Said Joe. "Ivana is quite the woman!"

"She is off limits for now Joe. She has been going through a bad time and is just coming out of a depression." Confessed Roger. "She doesn't need you 'charms' at this time. Let her finish school, get her State license and I'll make sure she gets a sales associate position at

GHCI. You know we are several of the 'chosen ones' at the company. I know George and Bradley will hire her as a sales associate. Besides she is their type for the job." replied Roger.

"She is every man's type." Retorted Joe.

"Just drop it." Said Roger. "Anyway, I have something more important to discuss with you."

"OK, OK." Replied Joe. "I'll back off, but if she approaches me, it's not my fault."

"That's not good enough. Forget her, let her live her new life. She needs time to concentrate on getting her life and priorities together. Joe Hyland will just screw that up! Anyway, you're going out with Leigh. Isn't she good enough for you? So stay away!"

"No problem. You have my word. Now, what is that you wanted to talk about?" Questioned Joe.

Roger started to talk to Joe about his frustrations with GHCI and the time it has been taking for him to start making some real money. Roger reminded Joe about the speech Bradly gave when Joe started working at GHIC and the new organization with division mangers, etc. None of that has happen. Both Roger's and Joe's take home pay has not considerably increased over the last nearly five years since Joe came to work, especially considering the increase in business.

George is getting more involved in politics and working towards bringing the company public and less on the day to day business. Luckily the real estate market is starting to do much better so the company can sort of run itself. But that can't happen for long. To top it off, Bradley seems to be making more and more of the day to day corporate decisions, some of which George may not know about. That probably includes the proposed new structure of the company and executive pay. Roger and Joe are executives in the company and by now have expected considerably more authority in running, not only sales, but a chunk of the operations of the business including receiving considerably more compensation. Joe listened closely and indicated that the same thoughts had come across his mind also. He just wasn't sure how to handle it.

Roger then confided in Joe about a person who he knows through some real estate business that they have done together. He is from the Netherlands, has considerable funds available to him, has great connections and wants Roger to go into business with him since he needs an American citizen for his business. This Dutch citizen wants to start taking advantage of the real estate boom that he foresees over the next decade. Roger has spoken to him and Roger, was assured, he would not just be a straw man for him and his Dutch investors. Roger could be a part of the business and take, not only a substantial salary, but a large percentage of the profits. Roger has also told him about Joe and believes that Joe would be a great asset since he is a considerably better front man than Roger, a great sales man and could greatly enhance the business. He has asked for the three of us to meet to discuss the issue. He and his investors are really anxious to get started as soon as possible.

Joe then brought up the elephant in the room. The fact that their licenses were not properly obtained is sufficient for George and Bradly to keep them from leaving the company, and worse, competing with their company. Roger said, he had thought about that issue deeply. Roger has come to the conclusion that, at least in his mind, neither George nor Bradly will bring up the issue since it would be in their best interest to leave things as they are and let our licenses stand.

First, any illegal connections for receiving our licenses will reflect directly on Bradly which will fall over to George. Roger and Joe know that, even though George was not directly involved with how we received our licenses, he had to know. After all, it is his business and he is very aware how real estate licenses are obtained. Joe remembers George specifically telling him the procedure to receive a broker's license in Florida.

Second, George and Bradly want to take the company public. Any illegal activities involved with the business would stop that in its tracks. George would lose multi-millions of dollars and Bradly would lose his share also. In fact, it is probably in George's and Bradly's best interest that we are not around when the company goes public. Plus, everyone seems to know about George and Bradly's relationship. I am sure they want to keep that as quit as possible.

And third, George really wants to sell that 5 acre parcel in the southwest corner of Riverview. It is already approved for three high rise buildings with a density of 111 condominium. With my Dutch connection, and sufficient backing, our new development company could make that parcel its first undertaking. The units can start at about half a million each and go up to more than 2 million for each of the three penthouses. With sufficient funds, which my Dutch connection says is virtually unlimited, the mangrove issue probably can be favorably resolved. The better the outcome with the mangrove parcel, the more the purchase price for each unit. Then each unit will have a view of the Caloosahatchee River on one side and the manmade lake on the other. Plus, this will help George's financials look better with the Security and Exchange commission and his stock price. The project can begin right away. Permitting for that parcel can be completed as soon as the plans are completed and reviewed by the County. All made sense to both Roger and George. Anyway, what would Roger and Joe have to loose just to speak with the Dutch man?

"Set it up Roger. I'm in." Confidently replied Joe.

****

Denise had just returned to her office at the County Courthouse to her 12 by 12 investigators office the evening of August 20, 2013. She had completed her preliminary background on Joseph D. Hyland, for which she knew there was a lot more to investigate. She really only knew him by reputation and the articles she read in the Fort Myers News Press and local gossip magazines as well as studying the Assistant County Attorney's file on him, which was far from complete. A man who was worth hundreds of millions of dollars a few years ago had to have some type of auspicious background and maybe an enemy or two. She had not acquired much in the way of facts from Luke about Cathy Rutter. She wasn't even sure if Luke would receive a call back from her, or her attorney, about any more in depth discussions that could lead Denise to some kind of conclusion for her report. However, the subpoena for Cathy and William Rutter's finances showed a net worth of just under $10,000,000.00. Denise was aware of William's holdings in Montana, which were substantial, but Cathy who was a bank loan processor and a glorified secretary doesn't just acquire that kind of money going to work 9 to 5! She still needed to do some more in depth investigation as how she acquired that small fortune. There is more to Cathy Rutter than meets the eye. She jotted down some notes on Cathy for follow up on her and the money. But her intuition still told her that she didn't have anything to do with Joe Hyland's demise.

Her interview with Leigh Mowery, if you can call it that, was a one way interview with Denise doing all the talking. In other words she accomplished nothing that day.

Denise was still convinced this was not a homicide and did not get any feelings that either Cathy Rutter of Leigh Mowery would have had any connection with such a homicide. Leigh lived in Louisville and was there for more than year before Joe died. She was not the kind to hire someone to kill Joe since she still believed he was going to be her meal ticket for a long time. Cathy, even with all that money, had true platonic feelings for Joe. Joe hired her away from her bank job at Wells Fargo that she truly disliked. Joe had worked with her on loans for condos and single family homes at The Riverview Golf & Country development as often as possible when she was working retail for the bank. That is how Joe met Cathy. He was impressed from the first time he met her. She has a depth of knowledge on real estate and mortgages, charm and ambition.

Wells Fargo was more than cooperative when it came to The Riverview Golf & Country Club. The Chief Operating Officer for residential loans and George Harvey were very good friends. George had even intimated to him on several occasions that he may have some position for him in his development company. Cathy was aware of that fact, but knew George uses that technique to charm whoever he needs to at any given time. Cathy knew George about as well as anyone could, due to their backgrounds, which was better left confidential. Cathy was just passing her time as a loan processor and she felt that her true talents were not being utilized by the bank. She wanted something for which she could thrive in fulfilling results and would give her that feeling of accomplishment she really longed for. Joe was that person.

After Joe hired her away from the bank, she did everything for him as his personal assistant and financial advisor. She enhanced his business experience as a business person and financial officer of a hundred million dollar company in a way no other person could have. She loved the man as a boss and philanthropist. She was actually proud to work for him. Denise believed that was the reason she acted towards Luke the way she did during their interview. However, no one thought about mentioning, that as good as Cathy was, she never did became a director or officer of any of Joe's companies. Maybe that was her idea?

Denise's gut also knew that Joe's brother Daniel, his wife and two daughters had nothing to do with this. They lived in Michigan and lived completely separate lives. Joe just sent them money when they needed it and sometimes when they didn't. Joe put his two nieces through college. Not the types who would want Joe dead. But the real reason, for Denise's conclusion, was that Daniel wasn't smart enough to even think about pulling something off like that. In fact, Daniel didn't even want to have anything to do with Joe. Joe tried on several occasions to get Daniel to move he and his wife to Fort Myers, where Joe could put him to work somewhere in the company. But Joe never received any response from Daniel about those offers.

So Denise wrote a short memo to Alex Tarian, her boss, indicating that she needed more time to complete the investigation. So far, her instinct was still either an unintended death or suicide and she was leaning to the former. She wasn't sure what reaction she would receive from her boss concerning the matter, but she had been working for the County Attorney's office for a long time and was well respected in her job. She really didn't care about his response. Her next move was to interview Joe Hyland's business partners and employees and continue her quest on Cathy Rutter's and Leigh Mowery's fortune. Denise knew Joe's life was an open book to Cathy and Leigh and even his closest employees. The more ammunition she could uncover about her thoughts on the incident and the alleged missing funds, the better the conclusion when her report was completed.

There was still one other issue that confused Denise. She understood that not only was the Sheriff's homicide division investigating Joe's death, but a Federal agent was working with the Sheriff's department. Arthur Winslow, a Federal homicide investigator was also in the background, but still being brought up to speed on the investigation from time to time. Denise could not grasp as to the reason the Feds where involved, in any manner, in a local homicide or a four year old theft of money investigation. Where there other mysterious deaths somewhere in this maze she was trying to wind her way through? Just something more for her to think about.

****

In December, 1987, Roger had called Josef Rynsburger, his Dutch connection to set up a meeting with him and Joe. Rynsburger was only in Fort Myers a few times each year. He was going to be there before Christmas that year. Josef said he wanted to bring one of his employees, Bram Meulenbelt, with him to the meeting. Bram had been with Josef since he stated his investment business and Bram was also friends with the banker who would be funding the transactions. Josef wanted to make sure Bram knew all the facts from the beginning. Roger had no reason to say no. So a meeting was set up December 10, 1987 at 5:00 PM at a small Italian restaurant, Mastello's, an out of the way place off of College Avenue and Summerlin Boulevard, in Fort Myers whose bar usually had a sparse crowd at that hour.

That evening, Roger and Joe entered Mastello's just before 5:00 and was greeting by the owner, Carlo. Roger knew Carlo for some time since he frequented all of his restaurants for years. Carlo greeted them and Roger told them they wanted the corner table in the bar. Two others would be joining them in a few minutes. Carlo sat them at the requested table and Roger order his vodka tonic and Joe his Crown on the rocks. The bartender, Brian, brought them their drinks and asked if they wanted menus. Roger told him that they were there for just some drinks. About 20 minutes later a limo drove into the parking lot at Mastello's and stopped at the front door. Josef and Bram exited the limo. Josef put down his glass of wine, put out his cigarette and Josef told the limo driver to wait for him in the back of the parking lot. Josef would call him when the meeting was over. They both entered the establishment and Carlo welcomed them. Josef said they were meeting several men in the bar.

"Must be Roger's party." Said Carlo. "Follow me."

Carlo took Josef and Bram to the corner table and they all sat down. Brian came over to take drink orders. Josef said he wanted a bottle of 1985 Masseto Tenuta Dell' and bring 2 glasses. Brian had never heard of that wine but offered to bring him a wine list. Josef disgustingly ask for their best Italian wine. Brian said they had a good 1984 Chianti Reserve of which, Brian didn't even know the brand. Josef nodded to Brian as if that is all you have, then bring it. Josef than took out a pack of cigarettes and started to lite one. Roger indicated to Josef that smoking cigarettes was against Florida law in a bar where food is served. Josef actually knew that, but Josef always attempted to try to get away with whatever he could.

"Roger, why didn't you set this meeting in a bar where I could smoke?" angrily said Josef.

"Sorry about that, but it really never entered my mind." apologized Roger.

"Roger, Roger, Roger, why are you sometimes such a disappointment. I hope Joe is a little more gifted than you." Laughed Josef.

Brian was standing there watching all this in ah! He then offered the others another drink. Both Roger and Joe accepted Brian's offer.

"Let's get on with it." Said Josef. "Oh, by the way, this is my assistant Bram Meulenbelt. I hope you don't mind if he joins us. He has been with me for years and handles so much crap that I don't have time for.

"Roger, I know about you and your job with George Harvey, that obscene man." Said Josef. "So Joe, I know that you work for George also and the word on the street is that you are, how do you say it? An 'up and comer' in the business and real estate world. Tell me about you and your background." Inquired Josef. All of the time that Josef was talking, Bram was taking notes.

Joe started off with where he was born and went through his life story to the present in about 10 minutes. Joe did not want to bore Josef too much. Josef asked Joe about his ambitions and how far he would go to get what he wanted. Joe, at that time was honest, but ambitious, and indicated he would really like to make a lot of money and be a part of a large, if not the largest real estate developer in the area. He would like to, someday, use some of his wealth to help people in the community and hopefully, someday get married and have lots of kids and hope they all turn out to be doctors and businessmen. Joe felt bad his brother was not ambitious like him or he would have his brother and his brother's two daughters, eventually work for him get them away from Traverse City. Anything that Joe Hyland would design and build would be the biggest and best in the area. He wanted to become well known and have everyone frequent his businesses, whether, hotels, restaurants, housing developments, all with lots of amenities. Joe wanted it all.

"But how far would you go?" Josef asked again.

"As far as I could without going to jail." Replied Joe.

"I'm sure you didn't mean quite that." Said Roger.

"Well that's what I heard." Said Josef. "And I like it."

Josef than started talking, looking directly at Joe and not even glancing towards Roger. He said that he has been investing in real estate in the Netherlands, Italy and Austria for about 10 years now and has down very well. He never uses his own money. He intimated that he has a relationship with the current officer of a bank located in Amsterdam. This officer is up and coming and has a lot of say in every loan. He has made his bank a lot of money with Josef's help. They had been boyhood friends in Amsterdam and went to business school together. After school, Josef's friend, went to work for AFC Bank N.V. They are headquarters in Amsterdam. In just a few months at the bank, he was appointed to the commercial loan committee. The bank is very aggressive and not only wants to lend money for acquisitions or refinancing of real estate, but they want to expand into the United States. By the way, my friends name is Hagan Vinke. He is one of the most successful bankers in Europe. We have had several discussions about where and how to invest in the U.S. We have come to the conclusion that Florida, and Southwest Florida in particular, is going to grow economically much more quickly, with prices accelerating faster and higher than any other place in the State. Josef indicated that the bank and Josef are looking for partners to start this venture. Money is no object. The bank will loan all of the necessary funds to put together ventures that make sense in this area. Josef continued by saying he knew Roger and worked with him. He watched how George Harvey had taken a beautiful parcel of real estate on the Caloosahatchee River, when it was foreclosed by the Savings and Loan Company in 1979. George remodeled the golf courses and clubhouse to give the best value for every square foot of the property. He is turning it into the most valuable development in this area! He is making a fortune." Said Josef. "And you know how ethical he and his inner circle are." Smirked Josef, and even Bram chuckled. "But he had to use a lot of his own money to do this. We can do the same thing with AFC funding 100% of the funds. Maybe even more.

"Impossible." Said Joe in astonishment.

"Nothing is impossible if there is enough for everyone." Replied Josef. AFC is headquartered in Amsterdam. It is an old established Bank stated around 1822. It now has new blood, my friend Hagen leading that group. It is big. It has total assets of over 80 billion euros; over 3,500 employees; with a net income last year of over 116 million euros. Its parent company is NL Financial Investments, which is owned by the

Dutch State. As long as it keeps making money, the State stays out of its business. So for the last several years Hagen has been promoted to Executive Vice President of the bank, made chairman of the foreign loan committee, and it has been doing nothing but making money." Proudly stated Josef.

"What's the catch?" asked Joe.

"No catch, but are you aware of the limitations of Dutch banks when they loan money outside the Netherlands and also become investors in the project?" asked Josef.

"Invest in the project? The bank will be a partner? To what extent and again what is the catch?" inquired Joe.

Josef went on to explain to Joe, again not even glancing at Roger, about restrictions put on Non-US Banks by the Federal Reserve. There is this Federal Banking law called the Bank Holding Company Act of 1956. The "BHC". And another Federal law called the International Banking Act of 1978. The "IBA".

"Never heard of them." Said Joe.

Josef, as if he never heard Joe, went on to explain, that under the IBA and certain Regulation of the BHC, a foreign bank may engage in permissible US non-bank activity only if it is a "qualifying foreign banking organization", or "QFBO".

"I am confused." Said Joe.

Again, Josef, as if he never heard Joe, said that under certain circumstances, which Joe and Roger did not need to concern themselves with, a foreign bank may engage in investments in US businesses and real estate developments. If the bank forms a foreign subsidiary company and that company would then not be prohibited from directly investing, selling, distributing, owning or controlling some of the voting shares of an entity. So if the bank underwrites, sells, or distributes securities in the US, it is not against the Netherlands or US laws, so long as the bank or its subsidiaries does not own or control or vote more than 10% of the stock of the US entity.

"What the hell does that mean? "Said Joe.

"That is my job to take care of. You just run the development business." As he is looking directly at Joe.

"So, what I gather is that the Netherlands Bank is going to be a partner, at least to the tune of 10%." Replied Joe after some thought.

"Now you are starting to understand." Said Josef.

"I don't like it." Said Roger.

"You don't have to like it Roger, but that's the way it is." Angrily said Josef.

"Here is how it is going to work. We set up a Florida entity that will purchase a parcel of real estate and be the development company. Joe, you and Roger set up your own entity that will be the managing partner of the development company; you two can figure your own percentage between yourselves; I will set up my own US entity in the US as a non-managing partner; and the bank will set up a Netherlands entity to be a partner. The percentage is 10% for the bank; 40% for me; and 50% for you two." Explains Josef. If we do it that way none of us will have to put up any money for the acquisition or development of the property. It will all be covered by the bank.' Explained Josef.

Josef knew that before all this could happen, both Roger and Joe would have to resign from GHIC, take care of their Broker license problem, for which Roger had previously explained, and initiate a new entity as the development company. Josef was certain that Joe, not Roger, could figure all of that out and no one would be the wiser.

"Bartender, can you go fetch my driver out in the back?" yelled Josef to Brian.

"His name is Brian." Said Roger.

"Whatever! Let's get this matter going. Joe, would you do me a favor and come ride with me. I need to speak with you about something else. I'll have my driver drop you back here for your car when I go to meet my lady friend, Alyssa, for dinner." Said Josef.

"And I'm not invited, or you can't talk about it here?" asked Roger. "And you are married Josef. Who is this lady friend?" again asked Roger.

"No, you're not invited. This has nothing to do with you. And my wife and my lady friends are no one's business except mine." Angrily said Josef.

"Sir, your car is out front." said Brian.

"Thank you." Said Josef as he handed Brian a $50.00 tip.

Josef, Bram and Joe all got in the back of the limo and found a comfortable place to sit. Josef told his driver to go to the Veranda restaurant downtown Fort Myers. The Veranda is known as one of Fort Myers' oldest and most expensive and most charming places to dine. It is a great place for business men to entertain and also for romantic dinners. Joe was very curious about what Josef wanted to talk about, but he opened the conversation asking Josef whether he travels with his wife to the US when he comes. Josef was not upset, even after Roger's comment at the bar, but informed Joe that he had been married for 27 years, but his wife is ill and it is difficult for her to travel. Joe then dropped the subject.

Josef looked at Joe and told him that he was impressed with his background and how much George Harvey respected him and has taken Joe into his inner circle. Josef was even more impressed that George was able to convince him to come to Southwest Florida to work for him. Josef was not a big fan of George Harvey. The only thing George Harvey stood for was George Harvey and what people could do for him. But that fact was not going to let Josef stop him from working with George on his newest relationship's first project. Josef was aware of the corner 5 acre parcel at Riverview and he had his eyes on that parcel as the first project with Joe and Roger.

"Joe, I like you and I know we can make a lot of money working together. Much more money than you have ever thought about." Started Josef. "But before we get together to start our venture they are several matters that need to be addressed. First, you need to quit your job with GHIC and resign as a Florida licensed broker." Continued Josef. "I know about GHCI's connection with the Florida Real Estate Commission and how you and Roger received your licenses. I do not want that issue hanging over our new venture. And you need to convince Roger to do the same." Josef's voice started to get more intense. "I am going to make money on these deals whether the deals succeed or not and don't ask me how. That is between Hagen Vinke and myself." Said Josef as he looked out the window to see how close the limo was to downtown.

"Second, I will make sure that you make a very good living on these projects, but you need to assure me right now that you will put everything you have on the line to become rich. "Said Josef

"What does that mean?" Questioned Joe.

"That means that you can form your own real estate company, without Roger, whether he knows about it or not is your business. Hire a licensed broker of your choosing to qualify the company so the company can receive a profitable commission on all sales, and you keep the profits, after all commissions are paid. But you do not get a real estate license. I don't want you even working with the Florida Real Estate Commission while we are partners. As the only owner of the real estate company, you don't need to be licensed to take profits of your own company. I will not be involved with that company, It will be all your baby." Confessed Josef.

"Third, the bank needs to sell our deals to the bank's foreign loan committee, even though my friend Hagen controls that committee. In order to do that, all of the property and profits, of each project needs to be personally guaranteed by you and all your companies. My companies and I will not be personal guarantors. That may be a hard one to swallow, but money speaks and it is talking very loudly to you right now." Forcefully stated Josef.

"Lastly, and most important, I want Roger out. It doesn't have to be today or even next week or next month. You can form your development company together, but, before whatever project we are involved in first, Roger has to be out of the picture before the first loan is finalized and closed. He cannot sign anything to do with the loan, including guarantees. I will leave the timing and method and how it is accomplished up to you. I need to stay out of this matter. This is not only me talking, but it is the bank talking also. Can you live with those conditions?" Josef said as if a final ultimatum.

Joe was surprised at all of the conditions put on this matter. After all, Joe just met Josef that day and all of this is sprung on him in a few short hours. Joe could tell by Josef's mannerisms that he wanted an answer now or the deal would be off. But he had to ask.

"Josef, everything you said about the businesses sounds promising and I really think we can do business together and we can be a good fit. But the deals with Roger and GHIC I may need to think about at least as to timing." Cautiously uttered Joe.

"I understand loyalty and a need to digest everything that has been said today. But, I am a person of quick decisions since that has always been my way and it has always worked for me. I am also good at judging character. Look, I just met you today also, yet look at what I am offering you." Retorted Josef. 'I need an answer before I get out of this limo. Think quickly!"

Joe looked at Josef's face for what Joe thought was an eternity, his heart said to say that he needed time to think about it, but his mind said, "Deal."

"That's what I was looking for, now hire yourself a lawyer and start forming entities. And when you resign from GHIC, talk to the powers that be about that corner parcel at Riverside. Negotiate the best deal you can. Keep Roger in the deal until we start to negotiate a loan for acquisition of the real estate. Roger and George Harvey are very close, for some unknown reason. It will help and lessen the blow on GHCI if George knows Roger is in the deal. Remember, money is no object. It's an all cash deal. Best of all it will lessen the blow to GHIC when you and Roger resign. At least they know they'll make money on you and George will think that Roger will make money on his own." Josef said in a very nice tone.

Josef got out of the limo at the Veranda, told the driver to take Joe back to his car and Bram back to his hotel. Josef was meeting his friend Alyssa at the Veranda. She was about 25 years younger than Josef and he liked it that way. However, Joe's life would now change forever.

CHAPTER 5

O N AUGUST 21, 2013, three days after Hyland's funeral, Luke Blakely, Arthur Winslow and Alex Tarian were all in Alex's office, on the top floor of the Justice Center in downtown Fort Myers. Luke had attempted to speak with Cathy Rutter two days before, and Alex's investigator, Denise Hudak had spoken with Leigh Mowery, the ex-wife of Joe Hyland one day before.

Alex started the meeting. "Denise is sure that this whole investigation concerning Joe Hyland's death is a waste of time and she should be doing something more productive." Said Alex. "She has been with this office before I was hired by the States Attorney, and she is smart. She has only reviewed the autopsy report, my limited file and interviewed only Leigh Mowery." Alex went on. "I can keep her on the case and get her to bring Cathy Rutter in for questioning concerning her small fortune. Denise can talk to some of the employees of Hyland's companies, but she is going to probably come to the conclusion in her final report that Joe Hyland was not murdered. She will say it was either unintended or a suicide." Continued Alex. "I can keep that report confidential for just so long. But the press is starting to ask questions. Why an autopsy? What are the authorities doing by not releasing the results of the autopsy?" finished Alex.

"It still is possible Hyland was murdered." Said Luke. "We still have not located Roger Spector, Hyland's old business partner who seems to have fallen off the face of the earth. Maybe he is dead? Or maybe he is involved somehow? All of Hyland's other business partners that we know about, and the President of the Dutch Bank, who loaned Hyland all the money, are dead. And they all died somewhat suspiciously." Luke continued. "Something is missing here. I know that all of Hyland's developments that had unsold units, or developments that were partially finished, or real estate businesses that were actually operating with a negative cash flow, were foreclosed by the Dutch Bank. Hyland was smart. How did that foreclosure occur if the Bank had loans outstanding with more than a sufficient amount of money to complete all of the developments? Where did all the money go? And even more strange, there was no foreclosure judgment recorded in the public records. Deeds from each of Hyland's companies for all of his company's unsold condos, unsold lots, unbuilt parcels of real estate and also the mine were deeded to the Dutch Bank. The only document in the public records is a dismissal of the foreclosure action. So there must have been some kind of settlement between Hyland and the Bank. Hyland died with an estate of a small fortune of money of which we have no idea, but it was a lot, at least to us. Maybe in the range of over $2.5-$5 million. That may have not been very much to the Bank in the scheme of all the developments. But, why did the Bank let Hyland keep that money? Only his condo was exempt from a judgment. That was worth only $400,000.00. It would have been easy for the Bank to just finish the foreclosure and take everything. Hyland's lawyers must have had some damn good defenses for the Bank to settle. Hyland probably kept more than $5 million in the settlement. After all, this was an enterprise worth over a billion dollars." Luke laughed. "You would think it was important for the Bank to show its shareholders that they were serious about this foreclosure.

"I knew there was a lot of money involved, but we are in a league we have never seen around in this County. I knew that the press wrote about the foreclosure and said it was the largest in the County's history, but we are talking about a market value of the properties in the foreclosure worth more money than I can comprehend. Enough money to murder someone?" asked Alex. "We need to follow the money. There is a lot more to this than meets the eye. Maybe I will get Denise to investigate each of the projects Hyland and his partners were involved. Let's have her follow the money. Who knows what that will indicate? How many Dutch partners did Hyland have Arthur?" asked Alex.

"Only one that I can find. His name was Josef Rynsburger. He was a real estate investor in Europe for several years before he hooked up with Hyland. He did use the same Dutch Bank for all of his transactions in Europe, but that doesn't seem unreasonable. And his banking friend who was his funding connection was not the President of the bank at that time." Said Arthur. "He only became President when Rynsburger and Hyland and Spector started they're companies here in Florida." Continued Arthur.

"This Rynsburger must have been very well healed or had some great connections with the Dutch Bank or additional investors or the Bank wouldn't have loaned him or Hyland that kind of money." Said Alex. "And we know Hyland and Spector didn't have a pot to piss in when they started these development companies." Alex continued. "What happen to this Roger Spector? Maybe we should talk to his old employer, George Harvey, and also get Denise on the trail of Spector." Alex said. "Mean time, Hyland's death is still suspicious, or maybe we should set up a little diversion and set up the press with a probability that the corner is leaning towards a homicide. It may help us in the investigation. That will also get the press to do some more investigation. Who knows where that will lead us? OK everyone?" Questioned Alex.

"I am not sure we should deceive the public before we know more about all of the partners in these developments. We also need to know what else has gone on in these developments. We need to know where all the money came from and where it went and if there really is money missing before we start some unfounded conspiracy?" Questioned Luke.

"Any other suggestions?" said Alex

"First I think I need to go to Amsterdam to do some investigation on our friendly banker and Rynsburger to find out their full backgrounds, their business associates and the full relationship with the Dutch Bank." Suggested Arthur. "Making a statement to the press at this stage of the investigation may backfire on us. Let's do some more in depth investigation both here in Lee County and Amsterdam and meet back here in a week or two. Mean time we should keep in touch so we all know where we are during that time." Said Arthur.

Alex knew that Arthur was right and a deception concerning Hyland's death would be premature. So Alex asked Luke to talk to Hyland's ex-wife and Cathy Rutter again. Denise will follow the money and set it all out on paper so we can review and analyze the trail. Alex also thought it may be helpful to speak with the Dutch Bank's local counsel who actually filed the foreclosure matter and try to find out how and why there was a settlement and what those terms were. Even Hyland's attorneys may be a good source on those questions. Alex knew that client confidentiality would be an issue, and more than likely there was even a confidentiality agreement as part of the Settlement, but good investigators can usually get something from the lawyers, at least to start a trail to follow. The plan to make a determination about Hyland's death and his partner's deaths was now being put in action.

****

Luke called Cathy Rutter the next day to set up a meeting to discuss her relationship with Joe Hyland and his companies. Cathy indicated to Luke that she had called Brian Kopp, Hyland's corporate and personal lawyer, concerning having him represent her in any discussions concerning her finances and her relationship with Joe. Once that has been finalized, she would call Luke to set up a meeting.

Brian Koop, Joe's attorney, said to Cathy during their conversation, that even though Joe has died, he still represented Hyland's companies and possibly Joe's estate, if and when he is retained. Representing her personally may be a conflict of interest. But Brian suggested that since the foreclosure of all of the developments and properties owned by Joe's companies is complete and a final Settlement Agreement was made between the Bank and Joe personally on his personal guarantees as well as all of Hyland's companies, that Brian should advise the surviving Board members of all of the companies to meet and voluntarily dissolve all of them. There is no reason to keep them active. There are no creditors for any of the companies. All of the law suits, by contract purchasers of the condos, lots and development parcels, as well as the company's contractors and their sub-contractors have been resolved. Once all of the development company's dissolution are complete, Brian believed he would be able to represent Cathy.

Brian also indicated that he would not accept any retainer to represent Joe's estate. The personal representatives of the estate, Daniel Hyland, Joe's brother, and Southern Trust Bank, can handle the estate matters. They can hire their own attorney. Cathy knows all of the Board members so she can contact all the Board members and request a Board meeting so that a resolution can be passed to have the documentation be drafted for the dissolution of all the companies. Brian, relayed to Cathy that he is not a criminal attorney. If the discussions turns towards a criminal matter, Brian would recommend to Cathy a good criminal attorney. But for the immediate discussions, he told Cathy that he can be at the meeting so long as he sets the ground rules for him to be there. Cathy is very bright and a good business person and could probably handle the meeting herself. But if she feels more comfortable with Brian there, this matter may be able to come to a conclusion in a better structured and timelier manner. Brian also, in the back of his mind, knew that he needed to know what was going on in the County Attorney's office concerning this investigation. Brian has been involved with all of the legal, and most of the personal matters, with Joe and his companies prior to his death. If there are large sums of money missing from all, or some, of the loans, it would be a good idea for him to be involved in those discussions. After all, Brian closed every loan Joe made with AFC Bank. Brian was also the title agent for the Title Companies that insured title to the properties. Brian wasn't worried so much about that, since the properties have been sold to the Dutch Bank, and Brian was sure some attorney checked the title to all of those properties before the Bank would have taken title. But Brian still had some bad feelings about law suits if there really was money missing.

Cathy called Luke and set up a meeting with him and she told Luke that Brian Kopp would attend. Luke wanted to know if Brian was to be there as her counsel. She explained the situation as Brian told her and Luke agreed.

Luke then called Leigh Mowery at the Ritz Carlton Hotel to try to set up a meeting with her before she left the area to go back to Louisville. Leigh said that she meet with his investigator a day ago and his investigator was trying to intimate that Leigh was somehow involved in Joe's death or stole or laundered money. Luke assured her that that was not his intent, however, if she wanted to be represented and have her counsel present at the meeting that would not be a problem. Leigh said that she felt it was the County Attorney's responsibility to find where any of the missing assets were. She was certain she was entitled to those assets under her Divorce Settlement Agreement. Luke assured her that he would consider that after a full discussion with her and retrieval of any missing assets. Leigh was not really comfortable with that statement, but she knew she did not have the resources or the patients herself to find the missing money, so agreed to a meeting. She would decide about counsel before the meeting and Luke would know her decision at the meeting. It was set at the Ritz in one of their small conference rooms the day after the meeting with Cathy Rutter. Leigh was unaware that Cathy had agreed to meet with the County, but it was Leigh's intention to call Cathy after she hung up with Luke, where she would find out about it. From Leigh's last phone conversation with Cathy a couple of days ago, she got the feeling that Leigh was on her own. Cathy was not going into this investigation with Leigh as an allies. Even though, at one time when they worked together at Joe's office they were best friends. They went out together with their husbands socially and many times just by themselves. They loved the Half Time Bar & Grill just around the corner from Joe's office. The bartender was on a first name basis with both of them. They ate breakfast and lunch together almost every day. One of them would drive to Juicy Lucy's fast food restaurant down the street. Breakfast sandwiches, hamburgers and fries and lots of gossip. But those days seemed to be over. Leigh had to get herself together and decide on a lawyer, or not.

Denise was giving her marching orders from Alex. Luke would take care of the interview with Leigh. He wanted Denise to investigate each and every company of every development that Joe Hyland was involved. What was the name of every company; who were the Board members; officers; managing managers; silent partners; everything else including most important who were the owners; their percentage of ownership and their contributions, whether money or other consideration.

"Thank you for having Luke interview that Bitch!" said Denise. "But ownership and contributions? How do you expect me to do that? You know we have tried to find that information before in other high profile matters. We had to go to Court to get that information. Remember this is Florida." Denise confessed.

Alex explained to Denise that she is the best investigator the County has ever had and that is one of the reasons she has been there so long. Alex knew Denise has her ways. He explained that no matter what she does, or how she does it, he would have her back. Alex made sure Denise understood that she was to do whatever was necessary to find out the information.

"Get me an organizational chart with all of the goodies, and be discrete." Requested Alex with authority.

"Shit, you get me out of having to interview the Bitch, but then ask for the impossible." Exclaimed Denise.

"I have confidence in you Denise. This is the largest foreclose in the history of this whole area, by far, and a then a suspicious death soon thereafter. Things novels are made of." Said Alex. "The press is on are back to finalize this case."

"I'll do it, but you better have my back. And this death is not suspicious. It was a natural death and you know it." Confessed Denise.

'Well, Miss Smarty! We don't know that. You may be the one to find that out." Said Alex.

"Well, there should be something in this for me if I can solve your made up puzzle."

'It may not be such a made up puzzle. One other task. Find out where Roger Spector is and how he is involved in this mess." Again requested Alex.

"Who is Roger Spector?" asked Denise.

"He was Joe Hyland's partner when the first company was formed. He worked with Hyland at GHCI and was his mentor. He has seemed to have disappeared. So do your job. Keep me informed. You have two weeks." Ordered Alex.

Denise was not happy, but she has done investigations like this before, just not as big or with as much publicity, but she knows where her bread is buttered. But Roger Spector? She wondered if there was more to this than she thought? But after some contemplation and deep thought, she still had her same thoughts on Joe Hyland's death.

Arthur called KLM airlines and booked the next flight to Amsterdam. His instructions were clear. His thoughts included the fact that the murders may not have been in Fort Myers, but there may have been several in Europe. All over a whole lot of money stolen in the US. This was Arthur's instructions. Find the killer or killers of Josef Rynsburger, Hagen Vinke and maybe even others. He found that much more intriguing than a fake murder of a big shot in a small town in the US.

CHAPTER 6

FOUR DAYS AFTER Joe's funeral in Late August, 2013, Luke Blakely, Cathy Rutter and Brian Kopp meet at Luke's office at the County Sheriff's office at 10:00 AM. It was hot that day, a typical summer day in Southwest Florida. Luke looked like he had not taken a shower in two days. He was wearing the same suit and shirt when he meet with Cathy several days before. He had not shaved in several days and he looked like sleep was a thing of the past for him. Cathy was wearing a new Chico's outfit and Prada shoes with just the amount of jewelry as to not be "dripping in it". Brian was well groomed, wearing a pair of expensive pleated black pants and a Tommy Bahama polo shirt. Brian always dressed business casual since he did not frequent the Courtroom often. He was much more comfortable dressing the way his clients dressed than trying to show off in $1,500.00 suits.

"You called this meeting." Brian said to Luke.

"What's your status for this meeting Brian?" replied Luke. "May I call you Brian?" Questioned Luke.

"Of course." Replied Brian. "Cathy has asked me to join her in this meeting to help her with any legal matters that may come up. I have represented Cathy for several years on her personal business matters. We are here pursuant to a subpoena for financial information. The subpoena asks for her last 3 years tax returns which I emailed you before this meeting. I also included a current financial statement and her last 12 months of bank statements as requested in the subpoena. Cathy is aware that I am not a criminal lawyer and if it turns out a criminal lawyer should be here representing her, this meeting will end. So to sum it up, I am her representing her financial interests only." Outlined Brian.

"That's a typical lawyer answer. I have no idea what you just said." Brian said looking confused. But I have no problem with you attending the meeting." Said Luke.

The meeting started with Luke asking Cathy about her background up to the time she meet Joe Hyland. Cathy replied by starting when she graduated The University of Montana with a B.S. in business and finance. During her junior year, she met her husband William Rutter at an alumni event for the University. William had graduated the same University several years before and Cathy was there at the request of her college counselor for networking purposes. Cathy began dating William Rutter after that meeting and married about 6 months after she graduated. William came from a wealthy family that owned several thousand acres of land in Montana where they raised mostly cattle, but they dabbled in the thoroughbred horse business. They never raced any of the horses, they just used the facility for breeding the horses. They're main income source was cattle.

Cathy lived in one of the houses on the ranch with William after they married and William wanted her to go into his family business. She tried that for a year, but Cathy really didn't find any challenge and really didn't like the cattle business. She wanted to move to a larger metropolitan area where she could utilize her business and finance degree for something more interesting with more job satisfaction.

That caused a small crisis with their marriage, but after some time, a compromise was reached for the two of them to stay together. William would work the ranch for 8 months a year and then spend 3 to 4 months with Cathy where ever she ended up working. It wasn't the best compromise but they were both willing to try it and it has worked so far with no complaints from either party.

Money was not a problem. William was not rich, but his portion of the ownership of the ranch, after his parents died, was one third who he shared with his two sisters. The sisters did not live on the ranch and just took their portion of the profits quarterly and were happy living their lives in Bozeman, Montana. William received a reasonable salary for operating the business and his potion of the profits quarterly. His net worth was in the neighborhood of four to five million dollars. His yearly income including the salary and profits was about $250,000.00 plus or minus. That information was confirmed in the tax returns and financial statement provided to Luke.

After some investigations and numerous interviews for her new vocation, Cathy was hired in the commercial loan department as a loan reviewer for Wells Fargo Bank in Boise, Idaho. She wasn't happy with the location, but she worked there for the experience and got very good reviews. However, Cathy wanted to move to a more up and coming city where she could be promoted more quickly to a commercial loan producer, where the money was. Her employer was amenable to her request. She was a very good employee and Wells Fargo was a large and fast growing company and was buying banks all over the Country. The most up and coming area where Well Fargo had purchased banks was the west coast of Florida. There were openings were she could transfer, at her choice, to either Tampa, Sarasota or Fort Myers/Naples area. William was not happy about the location which was not only far from where the ranch was located, but hard to get to. But Cathy wanted to move to a location she could utilize her skills and not start from the bottom and be able to move up. This could happen in one of those areas. This was a new area for her employer and they were putting substantial resources into those areas. Cathy finally, after little thought, decided to move to Fort Myers. This area was the fastest growing areas of the three locations. Cathy started in Fort Myers as a loan possessor. The major plus for Fort Myers was that she had her sister, Martha Edwards Spector and nephew, Roger Spector who lived there. Roger was in the real estate development business, for which Cathy thought would certainly help grow her business.

In the course of her employment, in her new job, she went to Riverview Golf & Country Club to meet the sales staff and to try to grow her business. The homes and condominiums were some of the most expensive in the County. There she meet Joe Hyland. Roger, her nephew worked with Joe at that development. She would on occasion take them out to dinner for business development. Originally, Roger and she were not that close, but by seeing him more often they did grow much closer and had a good family and business relationship. During the course of one of the dinners with Joe and Roger, George Harvey's name came up. Cathy had heard that name from her boss who was friendly with him. However, she remembered hearing that name from her sister some time ago. Cathy just could not connect why she and her sister knew George.

Both Roger and Joe quickly turned the conversation away from George and told Cathy that George was the visionary for the company and wasn't directly involved in the day to day operation of the developments. Prior to the purchase by Wells Fargo, the old bank didn't have the personnel resources or necessary capital to give many loans in that development. However, with Wells Fargo backing, it was now possible to obtain as many loans as possible. At first, Cathy worked on construction loans for new product at the development. Cathy did such a good job, she then started working on final loans to the third party purchases for the condos and homes. It was a good relationship for the Bank and Cathy was starting to receive a good reputation around town.

In 1988, at Roger's request, Joe and Roger asked Cathy to go to dinner with them. They all had a long conversation, in confidence. Joe and Roger were contemplating leaving GHIC to start their own development company. They were not sure how quickly that may occur, but told Cathy they had considerable backers with sufficient funds to build large developments. They believed the first development would be a 111 unit high rise in the Riverview development. That was not set in stone, since they had not yet spoken to George Harvey about them leaving the company nor about purchasing the parcel. However, Joe and Roger's financial backer's indicated that whatever it takes, in terms of purchase price, or other conditions, to but that parcel, would be met by the backers.

After that transaction would be complete, Joe and Roger were instructed, by their backers, to start looking for other large parcel to development. Their backers wanted to move fast and keep the construction of large developments moving since this area was beginning to boom and real property prices were increasing as fast as any place else in the nation. Joe and Roger offered Cathy the position as the Chief Financial person and personal assistant to Joe and Roger for their new, to be formed, Development Company. Salary and benefits were discussed and Cathy knew she couldn't turn it down, since money didn't matter to the backers, and it would be a new challenge, if it really happened.

They agreed to keep the move quite until all of the parties come to an agreement with their own powers that be. They estimated the creation of the new company and all conditions with all parties would take four to nine months, but in reality, it took less than that. Cathy continued to get calls, from time to time, over the next few weeks from Joe, just to make sure that she was still on board and to keep her up to date on the purchase of the corner parcel in Riverview and creation of their development company. It was strange that Cathy never heard from Roger, concerning any business matter, after that first dinner. She saw him around town, but he would just say hello, never really spoke to her. They were friendly at Cathy sister's home, but out in public, Roger was like a different person. Cathy thought that he just didn't want anyone to know about their future plans. But it was still very unusual.

"That's my background up to meeting Joe." Said Cathy. "Did I miss anything you want to know? Brian emailed you my last three years tax returns so you know what my husband makes. Any questions so far? Said Cathy.

"I appreciate your candor on your background. And thank you for the documents. Now I would like you to tell me about working for Joe Hyland's companies." Asked Luke. "Also, I would like you to cover how your net worth is near 10 million dollars. I see you husband counts for nearly half of that, but there is still a big difference." Questioned Luke.

"You saw her financial statements and tax returns. However, the vast majority of her net worth was accumulated between 1201 and 2007. The tax returns for those years are not available since they have already been destroyed since the statute of limitations on those years have passed, but Cathy can explain how the wealth was accumulated." Said Brian, "Since the relevant tax returns are not available, what else do you need? And I am really trying to understand how all of this relates to Joe Hyland's death?" directly stated Brian. "Are you working with the IRS or something? Please enlighten me." Questioned Brian.

"That issue does not concern either of you at this point of the investigation." Said Luke with a tone in his voice.

"That's not good enough!" angularly said Brian.

"Listen, just have your client answer a few more questions and we can all go home. Otherwise, I will have no alternative except to have one of the County Attorneys call the Judge to make your client answer the questions" retorted Luke with a slight smile.

"Brian, I have nothing to hide. He has already seen my recent tax returns. I can probably explain the rest. I have nothing to hide. I did nothing wrong." Interrupted Cathy.

"OK, but let's get this done and I will still need some information about Joe's death." Brian reluctantly said.

"Joe's death is not at point here. Just finish the questions." Said Luke. And yes, I read her tax returns." Stated Luke. "They do not explain how she accumulated such wealth." Admitted Luke.

Cathy started to explain the procedure she used to make her money while she was working for Joe. Being in the real estate business she could see that real estate was appreciating almost on a daily basis. The area was booming. Cathy wanted to get in on the boom. She spoke to her husband and explained to him her plan on taking advantage of the real estate boom. She indicated that they would need about $60,000.00 to $70,000.00 to start and if her plan worked, they could recoup those funds and then work on the profits and not put any more of their money at risk. William, after some thought and a lot more discussion with Cathy, agreed to have Cathy use those fund that were in savings so long as that was all she would put at risk. Joe said to Cathy that real estate is selling before the shovel is in the dirt. He finally believed that Cathy should take advantage of the situation, especially at the start of the alleged boom. Cathy had substantial funds to start the investment process and that is why Joe had agreed to let her start her investments in real estate even while she was working for Joe.

If Cathy purchased an unbuilt condo unit for $650,000.00 and she puts down 10%, she signs a pre prepared purchase agreement that has been approved by the State of Florida and she just fills in the blanks. So no lawyer or closing was necessary. It's just a normal purchase agreement to purchase a condo. Cathy then puts the condo on the market for $900,000.00 because, in her mind, prices are escalating so fast the condo would be worth that much within the two years, or most of the time even led time, it would take to build the building in which the condo is located. Cathy would then have up to the time the condominium is completed, before she would have to close on the condo, and to sell and assign the purchase agreement to a third party. During that time all that was at risk was the $65,000.00. Within the time it took to complete the condominium, she was always able to find a buyer. She would assign the purchase agreement to the new buyer by signing a simple assignment document which included an assignment fee of the difference between what the new buyers purchased the condo for in the amount of $900,000.00 and what Cathy originally paid for the condo or $650,000.00. That left Cathy with an assignment fee of $250,000.00. The new buyer closes on the condo when it is completed and pays the $650,000.00 purchase price. Cathy makes $250,000.00 clear. She never closes with the seller. Most of those transactions happen in one of Joe's developments. But she did the same type of transaction in other developments, including Riverview. Cathy always knew that if she could not find a buyer she would be obligated to close on the condo for the original purchase price, if she couldn't assign the purchase agreement before the condo was completed. But due to the inflationary real estate market in this area of the Country, Cathy never had to close on any of those transactions. And she would always find a buyer substantially before the condo was completed. She made nearly $4 million dollars over a 6 year period with this method of investing.

"Why did you stop in 2007?" asked Luke.

"I saw that market inflation was starting to decline and it was taking longer and longer to find buyers and I also could not get the purchase prices I wanted. So I decided I had made enough and did not want to risk having to close on a condominium or home." Replied Cathy.

"Did you pay taxes on the money you made in this scheme?" questioned Luke.

"Don't answer that question." Piped in Brian. "The statue has run on those gains and that has nothing to do with how she earned her money."

"I did pay my taxes, just for the record." Said Cathy. "Even though the tax returns are not available, I do have a file on every transaction I was involved with during that time."

"I don't need to see those files, since they will not involve paying taxes." Said Luke. "Let's move on."

"Let's talk about your work with Joe. You were his CFO when he started his companies, can you tell me about your job description?" Asked Luke.

"Don't answer that question Cathy that is not part of the required information in the subpoena. And for the record, Cathy was never an officer or director of any of Joe's development companies." Stated Brian.

"I won't answer any more questions, I believe you have the information you requested." Interrupted Cathy.

"Maybe, but are you willing to volunteer some information about your job, your responsibilities, and how money came into the company for payroll and expenses while construction of the projects were in progress." Asked Luke.

"She is not willing." Said Brian with an attitude. "If you want any more information get a Court Order."

"You will be hearing from us again, Mrs. Rutter. I would not plan on leaving town for a while" Said Luke.

"Get real detective. Is this some type of witch hunt? And we still do not know how this has anything to do with Joe's death." Stated Brian. "Until we understand that issue, or if you have some evidence of Mrs. Rutter stealing any of Joe's money, please enlighten us. Otherwise, Cathy is done with your questions. Let's go Cathy." Said Brian.

Cathy and Brian left Luke's office and went out to talk about the matter over a cup of coffee.

Luke realized he really didn't get much out of that interview and he would have to take a different approach with Leigh Mowery.

****

Arthur had just boarded his Delta flight from Fort Myers to Atlanta where he would have an hour and a half wait to board the KLM flight to Amsterdam. Prior to leaving, Arthur contacted the Amsterdam police and spoke with Senior Amsterdam police officer Visse Jansen. Arthur gave him some background on the current investigation on Joe Hyland's death, his connection with AFC Bank, and the deceased President of the Bank, Hagen Vinke. Arthur told the officer he would be in Amsterdam the next day and if could obtain the investigation files on the deaths of Hagen Vinke, and if there is a file on the death of his wife, Sofie; and Josef Rynsburger and if there is a file on his wife, Lena, he would really appreciate it. The officer wanted to know the approximate date of those deaths and Arthur really didn't have exact dates but just told him it was around 2008 for Lena Rynsburger; 2009 for Sofie Vinke; 2010 or 2011 for Josef and for Hagen. The officer was a little confused since this is the first time anyone had asked him about these incidents in the last 4 to 5 years. But since the U.S. FBI was interested he would look into the matter, or at least see if there are files on the deaths. Jansen remembered something about Vinke's death, but would need the file to refresh his memory. Arthur said he would contact him when he arrived and settled into his hotel. He would be staying at the Conscious Hotel Vandelpark since it was somewhat close to the main Police station in the OUD-WEST area of the city. He had stayed there before. It was reasonable priced. The air didn't work very well and there were no controls for the air in the rooms but worst of all there was no mini bar. But otherwise it suited him fine. Officer Jansen seemed very cooperative, probably because he was a little curious about why the FBI wanted information on these matters.

****

It was getting close to September, 2013. Denise had to really get herself up to complete the investigation tasks that Alex Tarian had assigned to her. She really believed there must be something going on that she was not aware of to have her spend her time investigating Joe Hyland's companies and to find this Roger Spector. Who the hell was Roger Spector and how does he fit into this whole mess? But everyone has to make a living. So she said to herself, "Let's just do this crazy ass investigation so I can move on to better things!"

Denise went on the internet and it wasn't very hard to find Roger Spector. A married man, 58 years old, with two children, a boy and a girl. Roger was born in Fort Myers to Martha and Eugene Spector. He went to Bishop Verot High School on an academic scholarship. One of the most prestigious private Catholic high schools in Lee County. His parents were not Catholic, but they must have had some connection with someone with some influence to get Roger into that school. After graduation, he went to Vanderbilt University. Denise knew that Roger's parents couldn't afford to send their only son to Vanderbilt at a tuition and fees of $37,392.00; room and board of $6,584.00; and other living expenses of a couple thousand dollars. And that was per year for 4 years. After he graduated with a B.A. in business and finance, he went to work two weeks after he returned to Fort Myers for GHIC. That means George Harvey must have known him or his family or he got great grades in college. Nothing on the internet mentioned any awards or graduation rank. Denise knew she had to use all of her investigation skills to find out about how good old boy Roger Spector got into and graduated from Bishop Verot and Vanderbilt. He must have been the smartest person in Fort Myers or have some kind of sugar daddy. The only connection she has now dealing with money or influence is George Harvey. Roger left GHIC ten years of seniority after he started and went to work with Joe Hyland as partners in constructing Largo Del Sol in The Riverview Golf &Country Club. A development owned mostly by George Harvey until he eventually took it public. But Largo Del Sol was completed and sold out before GHIC went public. Why would George Harvey let Roger and Joe Hyland develop a valuable parcel of Riverview on their own? Why would Roger Spector leave GHCI with 10 years into the company?

Joe Hyland's companies went on to develop several other very large developments, in Fort Myers and Cape Coral, an adjacent town to Fort Myers just across the Caloosahatchee River. Cape Coral was considered a bedroom community since most people lived there and worked in Fort Myers. The population of Cape Coral was near 120,000 which was more than twice the population of Fort Myers. The acreage size of the city made it the largest City between Tampa and Miami and only second in acreage size in the State of Florida to Jacksonville.

Denise then went on SunBiz.org which is the Secretary of State's web site for public information. She Typed in Joe Hyland's name and up came a dozen or so sites. Roger is not currently mentioned in any of the corporate reports on the web site for any of Hyland's companies. Roger was mentioned as an officer and director of the development company for Largo Del Sol in 1989, but his name was never mentioned thereafter. He is not mentioned in any more of Joe Hyland's other developments thereafter. What happen to Roger?

Denise had found all this out in about 15 minutes on the internet. Now it was time to really do her investigating thing. What she found so quickly was the big picture, but what is the real story? Where to start? How about checking out her police connections and see if their boy Roger has a record or has a clean slate. But first, since she is a senior investigator in the County Attorney's office, Denise decided to check court records that only she could have access to.

The first documents Denise looked at were Roger's birth certificate and Eugene and Martha's wedding license. At first glance it seemed perfectly normal, but a closer look showed a slight discrepancy. The marriage took place in June, 1955. Roger was born September, 1955. The wedding took place 3 months before Roger was born. A little unusual for those days. Denise then went to other Court records which reviled a sealed civil proceeding entitled Martha Edwards, which was Roger's mother's maiden name, vs. George Harvey. Unusual for a civil proceedings to be sealed. Except it dealt with George Harvey. What in the world could that reveal? Denise had been working the Corridors of the Courthouse for many years and had accumulated many friends and people who owed her favors. Would she be able to get one of her friends who owes her that favor to let her take a peek in the file? She spoke with several of the clerks she had talked to before who had always been very cooperative, but getting a sealed file open seemed to scare each of those clerks. She hadn't collected much information on Roger Spector yet, but she thought it may be important to unseal the file and see what it was. The one person she knew who may be able to have the file unsealed was Alex Tarian. The Assistant County Attorney has a lot of influence around the Courthouse. She decided to call his cell since there was no answer at his office. There was no answer on his cell, but she left a voice message about the sealed file and asked if he could attempt to get it unsealed so she could review it. She gave him the Court file number and hung up.

Denise then went to the passport department at the Courthouse and flashed her County Attorney's badge and asked for a copy of Roger Spector's passport. The clerk went into her computer, no questions asked, and found a copy of the passport. She printed it out for Denise. It was obtained on December 12, 1987 and was renewed on December 8, 1997 and renewed again on November 30, 2007. So, Roger has a valid passport, for whatever purpose that may be in her investigation?

Denise then went to find the last known address of Roger. The public records indicated that during the time Roger worked for GHCI and was partners with Hyland he rented a condominium in one of the neighborhoods in The Riverview Golf & Country Club. She checked the ownership of the condo and the records revealed the owner was, no one else but, George Harvey. He purchased it preconstruction and closed on it in 1985 and sold it in September, 2001. Roger vacated the condo in June 2001 with no forwarding address and no record of any local address after he vacated the condo.

For the last 12 years, Roger has not had a local, Fort Myers, address, at least not under that name. If he wanted to kill Hyland, why wait 12 or 13 years to do it? Denise was still sure Hyland was not murdered, so why was she still searching for this guy? Since it was getting late that day, Denise decide to call it a day and get some rest. She would start fresh in the morning putting together the companies involved with Joe Hyland's developments. She will see where that goes to determine her next move on attempting to follow Roger Spector's trail.

Just as Denise had removed her makeup, gone through her nightly routine and caught a little of the Tonight Show with Jay Leno, her phone rang. The caller ID said Alex Terian.

"What are you doing calling me at this time of night Alex? Did your wife kick you out and you need a place to crash?" Queried Denise.

"Sorry to call you so late, but your voice message got me thinking." Said Alex. "The sealed file you mentioned, are you sure it is a civil matter?" questioned Alex. "It is rare for civil matters to be sealed. It has to be something big or someone with some big clout to have a civil case sealed."

"You called me at 11:30 at night to tell me that? Angularly said Denise. "This couldn't wait until tomorrow?"

"I just want to make sure you said civil matter. The only way I know of a civil matter being sealed would be if the matter started out criminal and it was adjudicated back to the civil courts by a Judge or by agreement of the parties." Said Alex.

"This is interesting. I'll get one of our clerks tomorrow morning to go back to the dusty files of 50 years ago to see if there is any record of a criminal matter with the caption you indicated in your voice message." Said Alex.

"You are really after this Spector guy, Alex. I still don't understand. What does this have to do with Joe Hyland and a death that I am 99% sure was natural?" Again angularly said Denise. "Now let me go to sleep. I'll be in late tomorrow and don't call me again tonight."

Alex had a gut feeling that there may have been many County Attorneys who would seal matters, if pressured by the right person or persons. After Denise's voice message that gut feeling came to him quickly.

****

The next day, August 30, 2013, Luke Blakely got up early, took a long hot shower, put on a crisp starched white shirt, the only black and white stripped Versace tie he had and a clean black suit. He needed a new start on this Hyland thing. He was getting nowhere and was starting to believe that maybe Hyland's death was not a homicide. The County Attorney's office looked for missing money over 4 years ago coming up with Nada! Maybe he is spinning his wheels just for the press and the publicity Alex and the County Attorney's office may get if they actually solve this puzzle.

Just because Hyland use to be so rich, the County is spending a lot of money on what may turn out to be a wild goose chase. But after some thought, Luke decided he was going to go to Perkins restaurant and have the largest steak and egg breakfast they have and give this matter one more push. He would call Leigh Mowery for a one on one meeting. If he can meet with her alone and without a lawyer around, maybe he can really do some interrogating. Then, maybe he can finally make a decision about this case so he can realistically tell the County Attorney's office his thoughts.

Luke called Leigh and reminded her who he was. She remembered and said that she is not sure why he wants to speak with her again. She lives in Louisville and just came down to Fort Myers for Joe's funeral. She hasn't been in Fort Myers for more than a year before Joe died. So she couldn't have killed Joe.

"Killed Joe! What a laugh! Who would want to kill Joe Hyland?" Blurted out Leigh. When the real estate boom was going on he gave more money to charities than the average person made in a year." As she went on. "He paid his help well, built a great product and sold every condo before he even started construction on it. People camped out for days just to get in a lottery to see if they had a chance to buy one of the condos. The money just rolled in" Again going on. "Then the crash came. That damn bank in Amsterdam. They forced him to build that hotel condo in Cape Coral. Everyone, even his own lawyer, Brian Kopp, begged him not to start the hotel. But for whatever reason he built it." And she went on and on. "He was promised by that damn Bank that they would take care of everything. I don't know what happen, you need to talk to Brian Kopp. He knows the story." Leigh seem to just want to get this off her chest. "Joe asked me for a divorce. I didn't want the divorce. I know it was because he was seeing Ivana that 'Vamp'. It was so stupid. You don't kill someone because they cheat on you. You divorce them." Leigh knew she was just rambling. She really believed in her heart, Joe was savvy enough to hide money in case of a crash or his partners wanted out or the Bank would break their promise to take care of him. But she needed to stop talking.

"I never said you killed Joe, in fact, I never even intimated you killed him." Luke interrupted Leigh's tirade. "Something happen to Joe and the County Attorney's office is being pressured by the press to find out what happen. The press is, also, still on the issue of some illusive millions of dollars that may be missing years ago. Don't know why they can't just leave it be. I just want to ask you some background questions about his business and your life after the real estate crash." Said Luke. "It shouldn't take very long. I'll meet you at the hotel and then you can be on your way. Is that simple enough. Just some background." Lied Luke.

"What about my life?" Questioned Leigh.

"Simple things like when your divorce was final and when did you move back to Louisville. Things like that. Simple." Luke lied again.

"Ok, I'll talk to the reception desk and get us a small conference room. Just ask where it is. Meet me at 3:00 this afternoon." Agreed Leigh.

"How about if we meet in a public place. It may be more comfortable for you. The bar should be fairly empty at 3:00. How about a booth in that beautiful Ritz bar. I'll even buy you a glass of wine or a drink or whatever you want. OK?" Asked Luke.

"OK. I'll be there." Reluctantly answered Leigh.

At 3:00 that afternoon Luke showed up and went directly to Bites, the lobby bar, a wonderful bar overlooking the courtyard. Luke order an ice tea. About 10 minutes later, Leigh joined Luke at his table. Leigh was dressed in a Talbot's afternoon wear of white slacks and a navy blue top. With her short blond hair cropped just behind her ears, a diamond tennis bracelet, two diamond rings on each of her middle fingers and a large diamond in each ear. Luke was impressed. He remembered her from the funeral, but this time she was dressed as if she was going to a fancy afternoon party. Leigh ordered a Robert Mondavi Reserve chardonnay. Luke mentioned that he remembers her form the funeral, but she looked much different and less coiffured. Luke thought she was really beautiful, but he didn't say that. Leigh told him this wasn't a date and she wasn't in the mood to be picked up by anyone. She just wanted to get on with it.

Luke wanted Leigh to give him some background on where she's from, how she choose Fort Myers, where she worked and when and how she meet Joe Hyland.

Leigh started by saying she attended St. Francis private high school which cost her parents what seemed a fortune for them and her mother worked two jobs for a couple of years, bless their hearts, they both passed some time ago. She graduated in 1977. She then attended Sullivan University for two years working at an accounting office and administration associate's degree. She hated the accounting part so she never really graduated. Several of her girlfriends and her would come to Fort Myers Beach for Spring break and stay at the Lani Kai on Fort Myers Beach. Leigh always liked to have a good time and she found the perfect place on the beach, with a rock & roll band until 2:00 AM, to enjoy her week stay each year. She loved the area and the weather and thought about maybe moving there after she graduated to look for a job and meet some interesting people in the area, especially Naples. That's where the rich people live. She wanted the good life. Louisville was such a bore to Leigh when she was young. Since her parents passed, when she was in college, she really didn't have any ties in Louisville except for a couple of girlfriends she spoke with from time to time. She hated accounting so she left school right before graduation and a girlfriend and her drove Leigh's, 1985 Ford Taurus to Fort Myers to try to find a life. Leigh had about $10,000.00 with her after her mother's estate was probated and the house she lived in for 18 years was sold. Her mother was the last of her parents to pass. Her girlfriend, left the Fort Myers area about two months after they arrived since she ran out of money and didn't have much luck with finding something, making enough money to survive. She really didn't know what she wanted to do, but she did enjoy sitting by the pool. Leigh hasn't spoken to her since.

When Leigh arrived in Fort Myers, Leigh took some temp jobs as a receptionist and went to real estate school at night to get her sales person license. The class was only a month long and $500.00 and it would at least give Leigh a respectable profession and the ability to meet people. She knew they were plenty of realtors in the area, but Leigh was always confident in anything she really wanted to accomplish. She graduated from Real Estate school on time, passed the school test and two months later passed the State test to get her real estate license. During the time between graduation and taking the State test, Leigh went to a real estate job conference and spoke with several local firms who were looking for additional sales associates. She had several offers, but only one said they would let her work as the receptionist immediately until she passed the State Test. That was the firm of Tisch and Tisch Real Estate Company. They had 12 associates with a good reputation and wanted to grow. Leigh was very personable, dressed well and had that slight southern accent that made the broker at the firm think that Leigh could charm many a skeptic into buying a home.

During this background dissertation by Leigh, Luke was just fascinated with her good looks the way she was so animated with that great Kentucky drawl. He could see why any real estate firm would want her on their staff.

Leigh went on and confirmed she had been working at Tish and Tish for about 3 years and struggled to have ends meet. Once she started as a sales associate, she only got paid when she sold a home, or, someone else sold one of her listings. She found the hardest part of the real estate business was getting a listing. But her looks and charming Southern drawl helped her get quite a few. She saw from the other associates that the salespeople that listed the most made the most money. Getting a listing was just a little too hard for Leigh. So she started to think that maybe she needed to get a real job with a regular paycheck. Her money was running out. Maybe a husband, or at least someone to live in would solve the problem. She had meet some interesting people, but none that interested her enough to go out with more than a couple of times. Leigh wanted more. She wanted a better life than when she grew up. She wanted to meet that special guy. She had meet several woman she became friends with and they would go out on the town several times a week. But meeting a man in a bar was not Leigh's cup of tea. However, those nights, so far, were the best part of her life.

"So what about Joe Hyland? Does he fit in here somewhere?" Asked Luke.

Leigh who loved to talk, especially about herself answered, "I was just getting there." She now seemed to start to enjoy just to be able to talk to someone about her life, even if it was a detective. She didn't do anything wrong.

Leigh then told Luke about showing some potential clients some condominiums in The Riverview Golf & Country Club. While at the development, she actually got her clients to sign a purchase agreement for a newly built $450,000.00 condominium. There were lots of contingencies in the agreement, but she felt they really liked it and would eventually purchase it. Leigh needed someone from Riverview to sign the purchase agreement for the developer. She took her clients to the sales office to present the offer to the developer. Joe Hyland was the only one there, and he had the authority to sign the agreement. Joe looked at the agreement and then at Leigh and asked her if he could have a word with her in private. So they went into a small conference room. Joe asked her name and shook Leigh's hand. He said he had not seen her at the development before. She said I haven't had any clients that could afford to buy here. This was her first. He said that the prices on the units for sale were not negotiable and no contingencies would be allowed in the purchase agreements, including for financing. Also, the contract she used was not the authorized purchase agreement approved by the State for new condominium in this development. He knew she must be aware of the procedure for the sale of new condominiums in Florida, after all she was a licensed realtor.

She was aware of the proper procedure, but Leigh's hopes for a sale and a commission were based on the terms in the contract her client's wanted to sign.

She was somewhat embarrassed. She told Joe that she knew about the condominium law in Florida. But all realtors try to do what is necessary to get the sale. Joe laughed and said 'good try' to Leigh. Leigh was quite enamored with Joe. He was really good looking and really trying to be nice about the whole matter. He was really a good guy. Joe, trying to keep the conversation going, asked where she was from, since he just couldn't put her accent to a location. She told him she was from Louisville, Kentucky. He complimented her on her accent, and said that he would sit down with her and her clients and go over the approved purchase agreement and see if they could work together to convince them to buy the unit.

The two of them, both Joe and Leigh worked great as a team talking to Leigh's client and finally convinced them to sign the approved Purchase agreement. There is a 15 day recession period on the purchase of new condominium in Florida and the clients believed they could have an answer about their financing for the unit within that time. So Leigh got a sale.

"That's how we met. Sort of a long way around it, but I finally got to what you wanted." Said Leigh.

"Then what happen. "Said Luke.

"Joe asked me out to dinner that night. And the rest is history" laughed Leigh.

"Well, I am really here for the rest of the story Ms. Mowery" confessed Luke.

"I know that, but once you get me started talking, I just can't stop. And call me Leigh." said Leigh. "Do you think I could order another chardonnay?" questioned Leigh.

Luke called the waitress over and ordered another round.

Leigh then told Luke about her and Joe and the fact that they started to date, off and on for a while, and then about a year later, fairly regularly. Several months later they were at dinner one night when Joe told Leigh that he and a friend of his, Roger Spector were going to leave GHIC and start their own development company. Leigh said he must have really liked her because this bit of information was, according to Joe, very confidential. Neither he nor Roger had told their employer and they still had not put together documents with their investors for the project. Leigh swore herself to secrecy. She was flattered that Joe would trust her with such important confidential information. But Joe had other ideas. How about you joining the company as a sales person. Joe was going to start a real estate company for the sales of the units in the project and Leigh could be a sales associate. Joe knew she could make a lot more money selling developer products than looking for obscure listings or try to sell other people's listings.

Leigh wanted to know where the project would be, but Joe wasn't at liberty to divulge that information yet. Lots of hurdles to cross before they could talk about that. Meantime, Leigh still had her job with her current company and as soon as the deal was all set, they could work out their terms. If they could work something out, Joe knew she would be a great asset to the sales force.

Eventually, Joe and Roger worked out everything with their investors and she went to work for Joe. She never did work for the real estate company. He was not impressed with my selling ability. She didn't blame him. When all was ready to go, Joe asked if Leigh would work in the office and help Cathy Rutter who was the financial person for the development. Both of them knew sales was not really Leigh's thing. She was happy to take the office job and Leigh and Cathy eventually became good friends. Cathy even told Leigh that Roger was her nephew. Leigh thought that must have been the way Cathy got her job. Little did she know?

"When did Joe and Roger finally get their ducks in a row and actually tell their employers they were leaving to start their own development company and what project did they start? More important who provided funding for the project?" asked Luke.

"Detective, I have been very cooperative with you so far and have told you my life story. You know Joe and I lived together for several years and I know you know we got married and I know you know we got divorced." Leigh stated as she was finishing her second chardonnay. "But I was just an administrative assistant for the owners of the company and Cathy. I just did what I was told." Said Leigh. "I am not getting into Joe's financial business except to say the real estate market took off when he started his first project and he made lots of money."

Leigh was getting nervous about what she would say and how that would play out in this investigation. She was willing to just say a few more things and she wanted to go back to Louisville the next day. She had a dinner date with Cathy and William Rutter that evening and she needed to get ready. All she would tell Luke was that a company was started, Joe had several partners, one of whom was Josef Rynsburger from Amsterdam. She and Joe became very good friends and also with Josef and his wife Lena. They did a lot socially together. Life was enjoyable since whenever the Rynsbuger's were around, money became no object.

The first project was Largo Del Sol in the Riverview development. She said to Luke that was a surprise to her since George Harvey, who was the developer of Riverview was also Joe's and Roger's employer. Leigh also told Luke that it was strange that there was no hesitation by George Harvey to sell the Largo Del Sol parcel to Joe's development company. But a strange thing happen just before they broke ground on the first phase of the project. That phase consisted of the first 10 story building with 37 units and all of the amenities for the entire project. Then Roger left. Leigh didn't know what happen. Joe never mentioned it to her. Leigh even asked Joe about Roger and he told her Roger wanted out, so he let him out. Strange.

"Who was Joe's and Josef's other partners?" asked Luke.

"I really didn't know for a long time, but during the divorce I found out that their partner was a bank in Amsterdam that loaned them the money for all their projects." Confessed Leigh. "Can I have one more glass of wine, I think I am going to need it."

Luke called the waitress over again and ordered another Chardonnay.

"Since you worked for the financial person and Joe, you must know where the initial funds came from to purchase the real estate to start the Large Del Sol project. It had to take a few years to draft the plans, permit the project and build a 10 story building and all the amenities. Payroll had to be met and bills had to be paid and the land had to be paid for?" Luke asked without trying to upset her. He could see she was getting into a conversation she was uncomfortable with.

"All I know is the bank paid everything. Every month Cathy put in a requisition for expenses for everything including the future profits on all the units, on each building, that the partners were supposedly going to make. She sent it to the bank and the bank wire transferred the funds the next day. I think Cathy called it a draw." Said Leigh with some trepidation.

"How about the land? Who paid for it?" asked Luke.

"I told you." As Leigh was finishing her third glass of chardonnay. "The Bank. They paid it all. Joe and Josef didn't have to pay anything."

Luke was very confused. Leigh is either lying, or something strange is going on. Banks, whether U.S. banks or foreign banks, do not work that way. Luke also found it strange that a foreign bank was a partner. He didn't think that was legal. Most interesting was the statement that the Bank was paying profits, in advance, to partners even before unit one was even built, sold or closed. But he didn't want to push her too far, as he saw she was somewhat upset. So he changed the subject.

"Tell me about your divorce." Said Luke. "We'll change the subject."

Leigh was confused. This detective wants to know about my divorce? He doesn't want to know about my marriage or the two of us living together before we got married or how we lived in separate condos while we were married? Or about any affairs either of us had. Leigh thought about it. Ok, she thought she would accommodate him since the rest really wasn't any of his business. He probably knew about it anyway. Everyone else did.

"One day, out of the blue, Joe and I were having dinner in my side of the condo and he said to me that he wanted to get divorced." Calmly uttered Leigh. "I said it's Ivana, isn't it? Do you love her?" as Leigh started to tear up.

"Who is Ivana?" asked Luke.

"She was a sales associate that worked in Joe's Real Estate Company. She was also Joe's broker's daughter." I know that they were seeing each other on the side. I heard it from several people." Said Leigh now a little more composed. "He said we would always be good friends but it was the right time to cut the marriage ties. He promised he would take good care of me monetarily so I would never have to worry again about money. Like I said, during those days, money was no object." As Leigh was starting to tear up again.

Leigh went on with the conversation indicating that Joe had had a long talk with Brian Kopp, his attorney, and Brian was going to write up an Agreement where she would get $3,000,000.00 cash up front; a large home of her chose, up to $1,250,000.00 in Louisville; and a stipend of $50,000.00 every 3 months for 10 years. Leigh said Joe wanted her to move back to Louisville! She thought it was a joke, But it wasn't. He said that we will not need lawyers involved for this divorce. They could work this out just between themselves. Leigh went on to tell Luke that, even though Leigh didn't want to get divorced, the offer was more than fair. Brian could document the terms for them. She said she was very sure that this was all because of Ivana and Joe was just trying to buy her off. Joe never really answered that question.

Leigh called Brian the next day and asked him if it was true. Brian said that he and Joe did have that conversation, but Brian knew that both Leigh and Joe were too good of friends so he would not be involved with any domestic problems between Joe and Leigh. However, Brian was having one of the other lawyers in his firm, who does divorce work, write up the agreement Joe spoke to him about and it was generally what Leigh outlined in her phone conversation with Brian. Brian was sympathetic and felt horrible about it. He was not really surprised that Leigh knew nothing about this divorce and the terms until after Brian spoke with Joe since that would have been the way Joe handles social matters. Brian was confused, but that wasn't unusual when it came to working with Joe. He really thought Leigh should contact her own lawyer and discuss the matter, but he didn't say that. Joe was furious with Brian when she told him about the call to Brian and Brain's response. Leigh knew she was getting screwed somehow, since she had heard rumors that Joe had hundreds of millions of dollars. Leigh was really in a state of shock and didn't quite know where to turn. Most of all she didn't know what to do about Ivana. As it turned out, the Agreement that was drawn up was never signed by Joe. There was no divorce. Brian was furious with Joe. Brian tried to tell him that this would come back and bite him in the ass! Joe didn't want to hear that. He told Joe that he and Leigh had an oral agreement. Brian knew oral agreements for divorces didn't work. But there was no arguing with Joe.

Leigh moved to Louisville and purchased a large home. Joe gave her $3,000,000.00 cash. He started giving her $50,000.00 every 3 months, but that stopped after about a year and a half later. Sometime after that, Leigh hired the best divorce lawyer in Fort Myers and sued Joe for divorce and wanted a full accounting concerning where he had all his money and what his net worth was. Leigh never found out the answer to those questions. Joe pleaded poverty and if money was to be had, it couldn't be found. His wealth was in bricks and mortar and raw land. Leigh didn't want those assets to be sold. She had been paid in advance. However, she tried desperately to restart the $50,000.00 per quarter again. After all, he promised her. They did get divorced and Leigh was deeded her side of the Largo Del Sol Condominium and Leigh deeded Joe his side. The door was removed, and the wall was boarded up. Leigh got to keep the Louisville home and all the money Joe gave her. Leigh was still sure there was more money and somebody was trying to get rid of her. Not even the lawyer hired by Leigh thought the deal Leigh got was a bad result. Her own Lawyer never found any more substantial money. Only real estate assets that Joe said not to touch. She felt he would take care of her once those were sold and Joe got his profits. Leigh was very naïve.

Leigh never took another step into her condo at Largo Del Sol. She put it on the market and sold it for $450,000.00. Leigh and Joe never saw each other in the same room again. The next time Leigh put her eyes on Joe, he was lying in a casket.

Luke didn't know what to say. Leigh got up, said thanks for the wine and she hoped she never saw Luke or anyone else in law enforcement again. Leigh then walked away.

Luke ordered a drink. He felt he really needed one. Again, it seemed that he just couldn't get the necessary facts to prove any wrong doing in Joe Hyland's matter. But he did find out some things that were really unusual about Joe's business practice. He will be curious about what Denise finds out about Roger and all of Joe's companies and their transactions and hopefully Denise will determine the money trail.

CHAPTER 7

R OGER SPECTOR CALLED Bram Meulenbelt several days after the conversation with Joe Hyland and Josef Rynsburger at the Mostello bar concerning investing together in projects in Southwest Florida. Roger wanted Bram to speak with Josef and confirm that this "deal" they discussed was really going to happen before he set up a meeting with George Harvey and quit his job. Roger was not even going to entertain quitting until the deal, as discussed, was set in stone to set up a development company to purchase the corner parcel at Riverview. Most important, Roger was not sure how much money George wanted for the parcel, or if he would even consider selling it to Roger and Joe. This was a mandate if Roger and Joe were just going to quit their job on the spot with GHIC.

Roger also wanted authority to make an offer and what was the most they could ask for? Bram asked Roger what he thought the parcel would be worth if they can build the permitted 111 units and all of the amenities. Also, the permitting for the cutting and trimming of the mangroves would have to be included in the price, since that was not part of the original permitting for the Riverview project. Without the trimming of the mangroves, the prices would have to be adjusted.

Roger said he and Joe had been discussing the project. They believed it would cost about $600,000,000 to build and market the 111 units and to build the amenities. They know the loan would be substantially less since the profits from the sale of units in the first building can be used to help build the next building and so on. It also may take at least half a million dollars to permit and trim the mangroves, if they could do that at all. They would ask an average of $650,000.00 per unit depending on the floor and the view. The asking price would start at $450,000.00 for the lowest floor inside unit, there would be 3 units per floor, to $850,000.00 for the corner units on the floor below the penthouse. The first 2 floors would be parking garages, each fully wall boarded with an automatic garage door. All of the garages would be for 2 cars. The penthouse garages would be for 3 cars. The 3 penthouse units would sell for at least $1,000,000.00 each, probably more, depending on the mangrove situation. Bram said he would speak with Josef and get back with him as soon as possible since Josef wanted to tie up that parcel as soon as possible.

Bram told Roger that Josef doesn't do developments with just one loan. There would be one loan for the acquisition of the land. Next, the second loan would be for the first building plus the amenities. The third loan would be for the second building. The fourth loan for the third building and the last loan for the mangrove matter. Roger was somewhat surprised, but many developers do it that way as well as many banks require the developer to do it that way. So Roger believed it was his responsibility to just see how much George wanted for the land.

The next day, Roger received a call from Bram indicating that Josef had spoken with the Dutch Bank. The offer was to be no more than $30 million dollars for the land. Roger said that is crazy. That's $5 to $10 million too much. Bram said than be a good negotiator. But you have the authority for up to that amount. Make the purchaser on the Purchase Agreement, "a company to be formed". We can take care of structuring the company after we tie up the land.

"How much will the loan be for? And who will put up the remaining funds to close and construct the project?" Asked Roger.

"The Bank will loan the development company about 120% of all land and construction costs for each building plus additional amounts for the mangrove parcel, payroll for employees, rent and maintenance for a very nice corporate office, and the salaries for you and Joe." Said Bram very calmly.

"What? Are you telling me that no one, except the bank, who is one of the partners, has to put up any funds for this project? Also a separate loan for each building? Shouldn't we use the profits from the first building to build the second building and so on? Roger said with a questionable voice.

"The Dutch Bank who is loaning the money, and the Dutch partner, will be two different entities. There are some other amounts that the Dutch Bank will fund in addition to the amounts I just quoted you. But we will go over those once we get the land under contract. You and Joe can sign the purchase agreement for the development company. You must put a 150 day 'free look' provision in the purchase agreement to make you and Joe feel comfortable that you are not personally on the hook for the purchase price while the development company negotiates the loan with the bank. You will also need to get someone to do an environmental assessment on the land, soil samples, and start the permitting process for trimming mangroves. Contract for anything else that you believe needs to be evaluated, so the Purchase Agreement can be finalized within those 150 days. And get a good lawyer to represent yourself and Joe. Josef has his lawyer and the Bank will have its own lawyer" Said Bram sort of questionably.

"You sound a little pessimistic Bram. What's wrong? And why so many lawyers. They cost a lot of money you know?" asked Roger. "But the most important question is how does the loan get paid back with all of that borrowed money part of the loan package?

"Nothing I can talk to you about. That's between Josef, the Bank and the Banks investment company. It's their problem. You will make lots of money. The units most likely will sell for more than you estimate since the market value of real estate in Southwest Florida is booming and it will take a couple of years to fully build out all 111 units. The price on the units in the first building will sell for substantially less than the units in the last building. We need to act soon. Trust Josef, he knows what he is doing." Assured Bram.

Roger said that he would talk to Joe and set up a meeting with George Harvey to start the process they spoke about. Then they both hung up the phone.

Bram was nervous and a little unhappy he was not able to tell Roger the complete story of the loan, but Josef told him to keep it quiet for now. Roger was enthusiastic, but nervous about paying the loan back. But he was more nervous about speaking to George Harvey about his job. He was perplexed at the amount Josef and the Bank were willing to pay for the land and the amount of the loan or loans, and what the final terms of those loans may be. Roger called Joe and they decided that Roger would initiate the meeting with Harvey since he knew him much better. Roger said they needed to meet in a secluded place. Roger indicated that he was friends with Bill and Janet Nelson who owned, the Grind, a small coffee establishment on Cleveland Avenue and Andre Lane in South Fort Myers. A perfect secluded place to meet. There was a small conference room in the back of the establishment. Roger would reserve it once the date and time was set up for the meeting.

When Roger hung up with Joe, Roger wondered why Joe was not surprised at the amount that Josef would pay for the land and the amount of the loan and its terms. Roger did not know that Joe had already had that conversation with Josef in the limo a few days ago. Joe's concern was how he was going to tell Roger that he will not be involved in this or any other project. He was still trying to think about a logical way to approach that issue. Both were thinking about George Harvey. That was also going to be hard. But the wheels had started to spin and the fate of this partnership had now begun. Joe was excited but understandably nervous. Roger was just scared.

****

On August 31, 2013, Denise was in her office very early, on her computer checking the Florida Secretary of State's web site on all of the companies with which Joe Hyland or Roger Spector were associated. There were many. She was in the process of putting together, what she thought, was a loosely knit organizational chart. She had no clue how complicated the matter would become.

She was starting to do her research when her phone rang. The caller ID said Alex Tarian.

"Hello Alex. What are you doing up so early? Slumming it?" joked Denise.

"Denise are you sitting down? Asked Alex.

"I have been sitting for over an hour researching Hyland's companies at your command. If my back starts to hurt, I will file a workman's comp case." Again joked Denise.

"This is serious." Said Alex.

Alex then relayed the story that Alex got his friend, Judge Blatton to have the Clerk unseal the 50 year old file on George Harvey and Roger Spector's mother. I told the Judge that I was working on the Hyland matter to determine the cause of death and if there was any criminal activity involved. I also told the Judge that I had a reliable confidential source that puts George Harvey and Joe Hyland together in Michigan for many meeting some years ago, and Hyland was now an employee of GHIC, a company that Harvey has a majority ownership interest. It must have been enough to get his old friend to get an Oder to have the file unsealed.

The complaint in the file was a paternity action brought by Martha Edwards, Roger's mother, against George Harvey. The matter was filed when Martha was pregnant with Roger. There are no depositions, interrogatories or any evidence in the file. That was not unusual 50 plus years ago. Lawyers just filed a case and then settled it or went to Court. All negotiations were usually oral, over the phone, or in meetings. If meetings took place in a Judge's chambers, there were usually no records kept of it. The only documents in the file, other than the Complaint and Harvey's Answer was a Settlement Agreement between the two parties. George Harvey did not admit that he was Roger's father, and the Agreement does not indicate whether or not he took any type of paternity test. However what ever happen Harvey agreed to pay for all of the child's schooling including a private high school of the mother's choice; a private college of the child's choice; and Harvey guaranteed employment for the child for at least 10 years after he graduated from college. He also gave Martha Edwards $10,000.00 cash.

"Can I get a copy of that Agreement?" said Denise.

"No, it stays sealed." Said Alex.

"Alex, it's a great feat that you got the file unsealed, but could you please tell me how Roger Spector fits into Joe Hyland's death?" questioned Denise. "I know they worked together for GHIC for some years. Then they quit their jobs and went into business together as developers. They purchased a parcel of land in one of GHIC's developments to build a large condominium project. Where they got the money, I am still working on. How they got George Harvey to sell them the parcel after they both quit, is strange, but this paternity Settlement Agreement may have something to do with that. Maybe Roger knows about George being his father? But the birth certificate has Eugen Spector as the father. I'll check adoption files to see if Eugene ever adopted Roger. But, most likely, Eugene claimed Roger as his child from the date of Roger's birth. Maybe that was to make sure Roger would be employed and maybe George gave him a sweet heart deal? However, Roger and Joe Hyland split and Roger left the partnership sometime during its first year of development, or at least Roger was no longer a decision maker in the company. And now he is nowhere to be found." Said Denise. "Do you think he had something to do with Hyland's death, or maybe George was involved?" questioned Denise again. "Do you think, Roger or George poured liquor and forced drugs down Hyland's throat before he went to dinner at Cathy Rutter's home 10 years later?" laughed Denise.

"Why not?" Said Alex.

"What's the motive on Roger or George's part?" Again questioned the bright investigator.

"Find out!" said Alex. "There has to be something there somewhere. Maybe Joe found out about George being Roger's father and that may have had something to do with it. This is all too much of a coincidence between Spector, Hyland and Harvey. And I don't believe in coincidences! Call me when you have an answer." And Alex hung up.

Denise just stared out the window. She thought, what is going on here?

Denise than made a call to one of her connections at the Court House and asked her to do her a favor. She asked, in confidence, for an adoption search with the names, Eugene Spector, Roger Spector, Martha Edwards and George Harvey and to go back to the year of Roger's birth, 1956. Denise's friend was close with Denise and Denise knew that this search would remain confidential. Her friend told Denise that since the time frame was so old it may take some time. Denise acknowledged that, and told her to give her a call when the search was complete. Denise said to her, "I owe you."

Denise went back to her corporate search on Joe Hyland. She found over 30 entities in the public records, most of them being limited liability companies. A few were corporations.

Denise looked at each recorded entity. Each of the entities, had Traverse City Development Company, Inc., a Florida Corporation as the managing partner of all the LLC's. Joseph D. Hyland was the Registered Agent for each entity. The addressed used by Hyland was Traverse City Development Company Inc.'s corporate office on Summerlin Boulevard. Of all of these 30 plus entities, Roger Spector was named a Vice President in only one company, Traverse City Development Company, Inc. and only during the year 1988. Thereafter, Roger's name never appeared again. There were a couple of different types of recorded entities. There were two entities that were incorporated by Hyland as Real Estate Companies. Both of them had two unknown individual, whose name Denise had never heard of as the managing partner. Denise surmised that the reason for these unknown persons named as managing partners was for the purpose of having those persons qualify the companies as a Florida Real Estate Company. A Florida broker must be a managing partner of a real estate company. Florida Real Estate Rules require that. The broker did not need to have an ownership interest in the company, but was responsible to manage it. The question, Denise had, was why did Joe Hyland not use his broker's license to qualify the company as a real estate company? Since Hyland was indicated as the Registered Agent of both companies, Denise came to the conclusion that Hyland may have also been the only owner of those companies. Strange? Denise thought that she would have to check further on that issue. A call to the Real Estate Commission on the status of Hyland's broker license would be necessary. She put that on her list along with the adoption issue.

There was one other unusual recording in her search of the Secretary of State's website. An entity came up titled, Rynsburger/Traverse City/SLS Investments, LLC. That entity perplexed Denise. Again the managing partner was Traverse City Development Company, Inc., Hyland's development company. The Registered Agent was Hyland. The principal place of business was Hyland's corporate office. No other names were in the public records. In Denise's mind, this may have been the company that was the overall development company for all of the projects, and somehow shared in the profits, but, due to being an incorporated entity, no liabilities. Again, not only strange, but it seemed all parties have been very meticulous to leave no trail to follow.

Denise, in her numerous years on this job, was certain there must have been personal guaranties for each of the loans. Hyland, and his development companies, would be the logical persons to give their guaranty. Roger Spector was no longer involved. At least that is what it seemed to Denise. That would explain why Hyland lost nearly all of his assets when the market crashed. Why would Joe Hyland agree to take on over a billion dollars of liabilities for these developments, but not have other individuals take on the liabilities with him? Yet, were all these other entities and individuals entitled to profits? Just more questions. Denise then checked the public records on Rynsburger and SLS Investments, but nothing appeared. Again, very strange. She added that item onto her check list to further investigate. However, Denise knew Arthur was on his way to Amsterdam to do some investigating. So Denise texted Alex to let him know she found two names which may, or may not be, Danish, but told him about Rynsburger and SLS Investments and asked him to relay those names to the Dutch authorities to see if they could find anything in the Netherlands connecting those names to the investigation.

Denise then resumed her investigation in the public records. For the most part, Denise determined that all of these multiple entities that were incorporated were mainly for 6 large developments. Each development was much different than the next. The developments dealt with the following projects:

(1) Largo Del Sol, a 111 unit, 3 building high rise condominium plus amenities in The Riverview Golf & Country Club. This project had been completed and built out and turned over by the developer to the unit owners;

(2) Coconut Cove Park, a 486 condominium development project consisting of 95 condominium duplexes and 37 condominium eight plexus plus amenities located on a large parcel of property on one of the main Highways, U.S. 41, named Cleveland Avenue, and nicknamed Tamiami Trail in South Fort Myers. This development was completely built out and all but 48 condominium were sold by Hyland's development company. The 48 remaining units were purchased by the Dutch Bank, ANB Amro N.V., who was not the lender, but an assignee of the Mortgage and all Mortgage documents for the project. AFC Bank was the original lender. By an Agreement in Lieu of Foreclosure, which Denise could not find, The Dutch Bank, ABN Amro then sold those unsold units to individual end users;

(3) Snook Point Development, a mixed use development located in the City of Cape Coral on the Caloosahatchee River at the mouth of the Gulf of Mexico. This development consisted of 6 neighborhoods. The first neighborhood was a 124 unit four plex condominium consisting of 31 buildings, plus amenities. All 124 units were completed and sold out by Hyland's development company and the neighborhood was turned over by the developer to the unit owners. The second neighborhood was a 210 unit, 3 building high rise condominium plus 60 pool cabanas around a large pool with additional amenities. All 210 units and all 60 pool cabanas were completed and sold out by Hyland's development company. That neighborhood was turned over by the developer company to the unit owners. The third neighborhood was a 60 lot subdivision, which was a Home Owner's Association for 60 residential homes, to be built by preferred builders who were selected by Hyland's development company. All 60 lots were sold by Hyland's development company to individuals or preferred builders to build model homes. Only several homes were actually built when the neighborhood was turned over by the developer company to the lot owners. Since all lots were sold and none were owned by the developer company, the developer had to turn over the neighborhood to the lot owners. The fourth neighborhood was a large development tract which was permitted for 345 low rise condominium with the buildings to be no more than 3 stories tall. Nothing was ever built on this parcel of land by Hyland's development company. The Dutch Bank, ABN Amro who was assignee of the Mortgage and all related documents by AFC Bank, who was the original lender for the project, ended up purchasing the parcel of land through some unfound Agreement in Lieu of Foreclosure. The fifth neighborhood was a parcel of land permitted for 240 units in 3 high rise condominium buildings located on the Caloosahatchee River. None of the units or buildings were ever built by Hyland's development company. The parcel of land was purchased by the Dutch Bank, ABN Amro by assignment of the Mortgage and related documents by AFC Bank through the unfound Agreement in Lieu of Foreclosure. The sixth neighborhood was a mixed use neighborhood consisting of a 250 unit hotel condominium in a 20 story "L" shaped building. The proposed condominium documents, which Denise found during her investigation, were never recorded in the public records. It was required that each owner use their unit as a hotel room by either putting it in the

Hyland Development Company's Management Company or the owner could rent them themselves, with approval of Hyland's development company either themselves or through an independent rental company. Other elements in this neighborhood were a conference center, several large upscale restaurant, 12 commercial units and a 210 slip marina. The condominium hotel building was completed by Hyland's development company, but no units were ever sold. The commercial units were completed by the Hyland's development company but none of the commercial units were ever occupied. In fact, the condominium documents were never filed with the State of Florida so a condominium hotel was never created. The entire Hotel, commercial units and the 210 slip marina were sold to the Dutch Bank, ABN Amro by an Assignment of the Mortgage and all related documents by AFC Bank, through the unfound Agreement in Lieu of Foreclosure.

(4) A parcel of undeveloped property called, International Capital Park, encompassing 60,000 acres in Orlando, Florida, adjacent to the University of Central Florida. The intent was to develop a mixed unit development, to include an unknown amount of residential units, an unknown square feet of commercial space, an 8 story hospital associated with the University of Central Florida which would be a teaching hospital for medical students, and a 6 lane major highway which would intersect the property as a second entrance to the Orlando airport. A small amount of infrastructure was started by the Hyland development company on this parcel, however, all of that real property was sold to a third party prior to the foreclosure action being commenced. The purchase price, according to the transfer fees on the deed, to the third party, was considerable less than the amount owed on the mortgage.

(5) A 185 acre undeveloped parcel of land which was fully platted for 2,050 single family homes and amenities called Hidden Woods, just outside Of Orlando, about 4 miles from Disney World. Hyland Development Company contracted with preferred builders to purchase lots and build models and homes for third party purchasers. 75 lots were sold by Hyland's development company and homes were built on most of those lots. The remaining 1,892 lots were purchase by several developers prior to the foreclosure matter being commenced. Again, the purchase prices, according to the transfer tax on the deeds, to a third party purchaser, was considerable less than the outstanding amount on the mortgage.

(6) Alico Aggregates Mine, a 4,200 acre parcel pf property with several mines located there on. There was a mining permit in place to mine 1,875 acres of the property at the time Hyland's development company purchased the property. They were 1,100 acres of environmentally sensitive wetlands. The mines were close to several residential developments and there were several lawsuits filled against the mining company concerning blasting. The mine was purchased by Hyland due to the fact that the Federal Government was in the process of taking bids for sand and gravel for the construction of a third lane for interstate 75 which was just several miles from the mine. Hyland's company was not awarded the contract. Still, the mine grossed $25 million dollars a year. However, the business was still losing money. The mine was sold to the Dutch Bank, who financed the purchase, ABN Amro by Assignment of Mortgage and all related documents by AFC Bank, through the unfound Agreement in Lieu of Foreclosure. A deed was recorded from the Developer to the Bank for this property and all of the personal property used in the business.

Denise then determined that all of the other entities that were formed by Joe Hyland were ancillary companies for those 6 developments. The companies were involved with management purposes, cable television for the residential parcels, utilities for the parcels, mortgage brokerage companies for purchasers of the residential units, etc. Hyland and his unknown partners tried to cover as many bases as they could to maximize their income and profits on the projects.

Denise then went into the Lee County public records to look up the mortgages from AFC Bank N.V. to each of the entities to determine the amounts of the mortgages and the terms and conditions for each of the developments. However, only the Mortgages, Assignment of Rents and Profits and UCC Financing documents were recorded in the public records. Also, all of the Mortgages and other recorded documents to ABN Amro were also recorded in the public records. Those documents did reveal the amount of the mortgages, which in Denise's mind seemed extremely high. Those transactions had to be further investigated. All of the recorded documents incorporated the normal and usual terms for those types of documents. The real "nuts and bolts" for each of the development loans would be in documents that were not recorded in the public records such as the Not, Loan Agreements as well as any personal guarantees that existed.

Ultimately, in Denise's investigative mind, the real estate bust that occurred in 2008 caused all of these developments to be over extended due to the inflated mortgage amounts, and all of the development that were not completed by 2008 were "under water". Denise was sure that the value of the unsold properties was far less than the outstanding amounts remaining on the mortgages. The total amount financed for all the developments were well in excess of $1.6 billion dollars! The public records revealed a foreclosure amount of just under a billion dollars. That was the largest foreclosure in the history of Lee County. All of the developments, except Largo Del Sol and a few other neighborhoods in the developments were not involved in the foreclosure. Denise determined there were a lot of condominium and lots sold by Hyland's development company. All of the net proceeds of the sale of each unit or parcel would go to the lender as a pay down on the principal amount owing. The lender would then release the mortgage lien on that unit or parcel sold, so the ultimate end purchaser would get good title, free and clear of all liens. Denise added all the sales of the residential units and parcels and there was nearly a billion dollars that was paid down on the mortgages. After all the principal on the mortgages were paid off, the rest should have been profit for the developers. That does not seem to have been the case here. Denise was confused and wondered why. This is not how these types of transactions are supposed to work?

During the day, Denise took a few minutes off from looking at the Secretary of State's web site. She needed a diversion. She went on line to see if there were any articles in any of the local papers about the developments or Joe Hyland. Denise found an article with an interview with Hyland about the Snook Point Development. This article confirmed her beliefs about something strange going on. The article was from the Business Observer, a local Cape Coral neighborhood paper. It indicated that one of the staff reporters for the paper interviewed Hyland about the Snook Point development, specifically the hotel condominium. The article read as follows:

"When the Business Observer interviewed developer Joe Hyland about building the $250 million dollar condo hotel in Cape Coral in 2007, the headline read 'The Bravest Developer.'

Indeed the Lee County developer was one of the boldest entrepreneurs in the region. Hyland died on August 8, 2013, at the age of 56.

Hyland, who had moved to Southwest Florida from Michigan in the early 1980s, acquired Snook Point Marina and the 175 surrounding acres at the mouth of the Caloosahatchee River in June, 2001, from Fairfield Properties. He paid $35million in cash and 3 months later he sold 44 of the waterfront residential lots, mostly to one Michigan entity for $29.5 million, nearly recouping his investment.

Hyland, through his company Traverse City Development, Inc. continued to develop Snook Point through the real estate boom. Investors were so anxious to buy townhouses and condos there that they camped out for two days for the opportunity. In February, 2002, Hyland sold more than 100 townhouses in 5 hours and grossed $50 million dollars.

The market continued to surge through the mid-2000s and in 2004 Hyland's company sold 219 condos at Snook Point for an average price of $1 Million a unit. One building sold out in just two hours.

But Hyland's spectacular run ended just as dramatically when the market collapsed. The Dutch lenders backing Hyland's Snook Point and several other developments in Lee County filed one of the region's largest foreclosure totaling just under $1 billion dollars. It seems to this reporter that there must have been more to it than meets the eye since there is no way Hyland could have owed that much after all those sales.

In 2007, Hyland knew he was taking a gamble with the condo hotel at Snook Point, telling this reporter 'if the market doesn't come back in three years we're all in trouble.'

He indeed was the bravest developer!"

This article confirmed Denise's thoughts about some strange maneuvering with all of this money. A billion dollars will make anyone kill someone. She began to try to put all of this together. She knew she had to sit down with the Alex, and Luke Blakely, review her and their findings and try to figure out just what happen. More investigation would be necessary. Maybe Luke had found out some information or maybe even the FBI agent had some additional facts. The fact that the FBI was involved seemed more logical to Denise now that she found out that the money for the developments all came from the Netherlands. Plus there was a strange entity formed with the Dutch investors concerning some sort of arrangement.

Denise then got a call from her friend from the Clerk's office concerning Roger's adoption. It seems that no adoption ever occurred whereby Roger Spector was adopted by anyone. Denise wondered whether or not George Harvey was still his legal father. What would that mean? Does Roger know about any of this? Questions, questions. What a web, thought Denise.

One more call for Denise before she would call it a day. She knew after sitting in front of a computer all day, she would need a drink. The next call would confirm that. The call was to the Florida Real Estate Commission to determine the status of Joe Hyland's real estate license. She was shocked to hear that Hyland let his broker license lapse in 1999 and then officially withdrew it that year. He was no longer licensed at all. A person who was going to borrow over a billion dollars for the purchase and sale of real estate would never withdraw their real estate license. There would be too much money to make. Denise did not think about asking about the dates when he received his licenses. It had been a long day and she was tired. She was just shocked that Hyland no longer had a broker's license. But stranger than anything else, the person on the phone indicated that in looking up the withdrawal of Hyland's broker's license, there was a letter from the same real estate company indicating that a Roger Spector also withdrew his broker's license at the same time. The person on the phone from the Commission told Denise that Broker's, especially from the same real estate company don't usually withdraw their licenses. They usually move them to a different real estate company to continue selling real estate. Denise asked the person on the phone the name of the real estate company Hyland and Spector were working for. The person said The GHCI Real Estate Company. Denise asked who the qualifying broker for that company was. Denise was told a Mr. George Harvey. Denise was speechless. What could all this mean? She thanked the person on the phone, hung up and poured herself a double scotch.

****

Roger was very nervous about making this call that he dreaded, but knew it had to be done. Roger had found out about the fact that he was, in fact, George Harvey's son. He found that out when he was 18 and doing some research for one of his college classes on his background for a paper He noticed the date discrepancies between his birth and the marriage of his parents. He spoke with several people who knew his family well and figured it out. He never mentioned that fact to George or his mother or his father. He believed that if anyone of them wanted Roger to know about it one of them would have told him. Roger grew up with a great father who treated him just as a good father should. Let sleeping dogs lie, thought Roger. However, his investigation answered a lot of questions for Roger as to his schooling and job.

Roger knew George's cell phone and called him to set up a time to meet, at The Grind coffee shop, in the small conference room to have a discussion. George wondered what the big mystery was. George wanted to meet at the sales office at GHIC, but Roger was adamant about an offsite meeting. Did you get engage, or did you get her pregnant? George was just pulling Roger's leg with those comments. He knew Roger well. What's this all about? George had a very busy schedule with a calendar filled with matters dealing with complex issues concerning lenders and contractors for his developments, personnel problems, and politicians with favors needed for the politicians, meaning money, and favors for George by the politicians. Maybe Roger found out who his real father was? But How?

George had just several increments of time around all of his other meetings for this strange meeting at The Grind with Roger. Roger did not tell George that Joe would be attending. He thought that would spark too many questions. Over the last several years George and Roger had many short meetings in and away from the sales office at Riverview. They finally agreed on a 30 minute meeting that Friday at 3:30 at the Grind. George mentioned that it had been too long since he spoke with Bill and Janet Nelson and tasted one of their wonderful cappuccinos. So George decided not to think twice about the subject of the meeting. George thought the meeting probably would be about some changes concerning the sales people at Riverview, or maybe Roger's salary or commission. Sales had started to slow down. It was the summer time in 1998 and that is usually the slow time of the year. The real estate boom was just on the cusp of beginning.

Roger and Joe were in the back conference room at 3:30 that Friday. Joe and Roger were drinking ice coffee. The Grind usually closes at 3:30, but for George Harvey, the Nelson's would stay around for an extra hour or so. There was always something that had to be cleaned or fixed in a coffee shop. George showed up about 3:40 and yelled to Janet to get him one those great cappuccinos. He went to the back conference room and Joe was there with Roger.

"What is this an ambush?" declared George.

"No George, I just didn't want to mention that Joe would be joining us. It would have sparked too many questions. Said Roger. "We needed to speak to you about several important matters that concern the both of us."

"What in the hell can be that important?" Queried George.

Joe actually started the conversation. He had been with GHIC for a shorter amount of time and Joe knew George had always favored Roger. So Joe thought that this message should come from him. Roger didn't complain since he was nervous enough about this talk.

"George, I am going to be blunt and honest with you. You have always treated me well since the first time I met you in Michigan." Started Joe on this nerve racking discussion. "Roger and I have been approached by Josef Rynsburger, who you know, since he has done business with you in the past." Continued Joe.

"He is the guy that purchased one of my personal small homes on that large parcel in Buckingham that had an 8 car garage. Is that the guy?" interrupted George.

"Yes." Said Roger, I sold him that parcel."

"Glad to get rid of it, never saw any need for it." Again interrupted George. "I know that fellow is a foreigner and he had 6 or 7 expensive cars, including a big limo, and he needed a place to store those expensive wheels. What crazy thing does he want this time?" asked George thinking it's got to be something strange for this meeting to be held at The Grind.

Joe tried to start the conversation over again and bring it to the point. He told George that Josef wanted Roger and him to go into the development business with Josef in Southwest Florida. Josef has obtained a very large commitment for funds from a Dutch bank and would like Roger and Joe to form a development company with Rynsburger for several development projects. Josef has offered them 50% of the business for just their real estate development knowledge and for them to take charge of running the developments. Josef and the Dutch bank would be minority owners since a foreign bank can only own 10% of any real estate development in the States.

"Wait. Said George. "So this Josef will own 40% and his friendly bank will own 10%? The way I count the beans, that doesn't make anyone a minority partner. You both will own 50%. That is a recipe for a deadlock and most deadlocks end up with the person with the money winning." As if George was teaching them a lesson.

Roger then decided to intervene since he was the one who did all the business with Rynsburger over the years.

"I know Josef and we have all sat down and came to an understanding that Joe and I will make all of the development decisions. The bank will make the money decisions, and Josef just wants his portion of the profits." Said Roger.

"So let me get this straight." Said George. "You two have already made up your minds that you are starting your own development company and will be leaving GHIC?" continued George. "And when is this parting happening?" questioned George.

Joe, then again took over the conversation. Joe told George that neither Roger nor Joe wanted this parting to be on bad terms. In fact, Joe indicated that the new development company wanted to do business with GHIC. Joe brought up the idea of purchasing that 5 acre Southwest parcel at Riverview and building the permitted 111 units. Joe reminded George that GHIC was reluctant to start that development due to the mangrove problem. Joe assured George that they would pay GHIC a fair price for the parcel and their development company had budgeted sufficient funds to permit the trimming and cutting down of part of the mangrove parcel. GHIC would not have to pay anything for those permits or do any of the cutting and trimming and most importantly have any liability from any purchasers concerning the mangrove parcel.

"Josef and his bank sure have put some thought into this as well as budgeting a lot of money. That project will be very expensive. It's not just a couple thousand dollars to develop that parcel. You all know that." declared George.

"We know that and we have covered that with both Josef and the lender." Said Joe. "And GHIC will benefit on real estate commissions since any potential purchaser will have to come through your sales office." Smiled Joe.

"I don't like it. Both of you are Real Estate Brokers and I am sure that between the two of you, you'll find a way to cut GHIC out of the commissions." Said George with that business man attitude. "And you haven't even talked price or terms and conditions!" again George said with that same attitude.

"George, Roger and I have agreed to withdraw our Broker's licenses immediately. We will contact the Florida Real Estate Commission and formally withdraw all of our licenses. Neither of us want GHIC to even make an issue about the new development company playing games with your commissions." Confessed Joe.

George and the Commissioner of the Real Estate Commission were very good friends and had worked on many a deal together. George was not afraid to call his friend to find out whether or not Roger and Joe actually do withdrew their licenses. In the back of George's mind, it would be ridiculous for them to do that, but yet George was aware of how they received their licenses. Actually, it was a smart move on the part of both Joe and Roger.

George went on. "What's the catch? And why a GHIC parcel for your first development? Questioned George. "Was this Josef's idea or his Dutch Bank?

Joe then put on his charm and tried to convince George this was best for all concerned. The money and promotions that were supposed to come through for them had really never occurred. Whatever the reason, is not Roger's or Joe's concern and Joe was sure George had a reasonable reason for all of that. The idea to purchase the Riverview parcel was Joe's and Roger's idea. Again, they wanted to leave on good terms and be able to work with George and his companies in the future. Joe indicated that they had thought about this intensely and had agreed to take the risks involved with these types of developments. But how many times do people get an opportunity to go into business, as a full partner, and have nearly unlimited funds to start several large developments at once. Joe tried to convince George that Southwest Florida was just about ready to have a real estate boom, and both Joe and Roger wanted their piece of the action. George had already got his, and replacing Joe and Roger would not be that hard. After all they were just glorified sales persons. Most important, they all wanted to part on good terms and remain friends and maybe even continue to do business together.

Roger continued the conversation saying, ironically, that George has always been like a father to him and treated him very well. But even kids needed to leave the nest to try to make it on their own. George started to soften after he heard Roger say that.

"I reluctantly agree to this joint agreement to end your employment with GHIC effective as of the first thing tomorrow." Said George with a nostalgic feeling. "Go see HR tomorrow and make all the arrangements." Said George. "And I truly wish you the best, but you guys have chosen one of the hardest professions to make money, but, again, I wish you luck."

"I want to make one more request before you guys leave, but before I do that, I assume you will have a draft of the proposed purchase agreement on the Riverview parcel on my desk in the next few days or so. I want to handle the negotiations personally." Said George now with a better attitude. "Joe, do not take offense, but we have come to an agreement on your employment and the withdrawal of your broker's licenses, but after you leave, I would like to speak with Roger alone for a few minutes. After all he has been with me for some time." Said George.

"I understand." Said Joe. "Roger, I'll catch up with you tomorrow morning at about 10:00 at HR."

"Thanks Joe, and good luck. You'll need it." Replied George.

After Joe left, Roger and George stayed in the conference room to talk. George was very concerned about this whole idea about this big development company and this Josef Rynsburger, a foreigner and some Dutch Bank he had never heard of. When asked by George, Roger admitted that he and Joe had not spoken about their 50% interest and what portion each would get. What if there was a dispute between Roger and Joe? How would it be resolved? What if there was a dispute between Roger and Joe and the foreigners? How would it be resolved? The last thing anyone would want to do in the midst of a large development would be to dissolve the partnership in the middle of construction and sales for that development. I'm sure any lender, no matter how friendly would want personal guaranties and every lender George knew had to answer to their shareholders. Anyone who signs a Reservation or Purchase Agreement to purchase in that development may have a good reason to cancel their agreement. George conveyed to Roger that these things must be worked out.

George admitted he had a soft spot for Roger. George liked Joe, but not in the same way. Roger was flattered. George told him that if there was ever any dispute or problem that comes up in this new venture, George wanted Roger to come see him immediately and he would make sure Roger was taken care of. Again Roger was flattered, but Roger said he was a big boy and could handle whatever problems that may come up. George insisted, since he did not trust these foreigners and made Roger promise to George that he would come to him the minute it looked like he was not being treated fairly. Then George said to Roger not to worry about the parcel in Riverview. George, Roger and Joe will be able to work out the price and terms all in a reasonable manner and George even admitted that he would be proud to be working with Roger on the project. Roger was somewhat taken back. That was one of the nicest things anyone had ever said to Roger. Roger knew why he had said that. Then they both went on their separate way.

Joe, as he was driving home, thought that he would now have to find somewhere else to live since he was living in George's apartment. But if the terms were fair maybe he could even stay there for a while. Joe also knew he had to earn sufficient money in which to live his new life. The car he was driving was also leased by George. Another issue to deal with. Joe needed to negotiate with Josef a salary to pay for his living expenses. Joe was now on his own. However, he felt that Josef knew about these types of issues and they could all be resolved.

But in the back of Joe's mind was the fact that sometime in the next few months he would have to find a way to tell Roger that he was no longer going to be a part of this new venture. For some reason, it just didn't seem fair, but Joe knew if he wanted to really make money and get along with his new partners, he would have to find a way to take Roger out of the new venture. Sometimes life is difficult, but business is a Bitch!

CHAPTER 8

A RTHUR WINSLOW WAS a seasoned FBI Detective. He had worked his way up the agency to the Detective in charge of white collar crime in the Tampa office. Lee County is under the jurisdiction of the Tampa office. Only the elected County Attorney of Lee County and Alex Tarian, the assistant County Attorney on the Hyland case, knew Arthur was with the white collar crime division. From the beginning of this investigation, the County Attorney's office believed that there was some type of fraud or deception consisting of millions of dollars between, one or more persons and AFC Bank, involved with the Hyland developments. The motivation behind these possible frauds or deception claims is purely financial, to secure a personal or business advantage over other persons. These are not victimless crimes. A single scam can destroy a company, devastate families by wiping out all or a large part of the family's wealth or life savings or cost investors billions of dollars, or even all of these.

The FBI's white collar crime work integrates the analysis of intelligence with its investigations of criminal activities such as corporate fraud, mortgage fraud, bank fraud and embezzlement and works with local law enforcement when other criminal activities are interwoven with the white collar crimes, such as a possible homicide.

One of the elements white collar detectives work on is investment crimes. These schemes, sometimes referred to as "high yield investment fraud" involve the illegal use of fraudulent financial instruments. These types of fraud occur when bankers or investors, along with their partners, set up illegal fraud schemes as no risk investments, guaranteed returns, usually in advance, and involve complex strategies. These schemes are usually set up to victimize their own investors or partners in a transaction involving loans. This is completed and utilized since partners usually trust the perpetrators. When perpetrators find out about these schemes, violence can occur even, homicide. Hence the FBI and local law enforcement work together to accomplish the goal of each agency.

This is what Arthur Winslow and Alex Terian believe may have happen with Hyland, his close friends or partners and the Dutch lender, or someone who works for the lender. The foreclosure of all the Hyland real estate and loss of the personal wealth of Joe Hyland may be only one deception that may have occurred. Other incidents causing death to certain individuals could have also been a deception to protect the underlying scheme. Arthur's mission is to determine if these deceptions occurred.

It was just over two weeks after Joe Hyland's death, at the end of August, 2013, that Arthur Winslow landed at Schipol, the main passenger airport for Holland. It is located 11 miles from the main Amsterdam police station. Arthur took a taxi to his hotel, the Conscious Hotel Vondelpark. It took Arthur about an hour to get to the hotel due to some heavy traffic. Once settled in his hotel, he contacted senior Amsterdam police officer Visse Jansen. The officer told Arthur he had searched the records and computer concerning the deaths of the four persons he had requested. Arthur was told that no investigations were ever initiated on those deaths and no criminal files existed on those deaths. Jansen was curious as to who these persons were. However, the officer did say he retrieved the death certificates on all four person. He did an internet search and a police search in the Amsterdam records on the names. The search didn't reveal any criminal record on any of the four persons, but Officer Jansen was sure he had heard the names of the two men before. He said he would think about them overnight and maybe something will click.

Arthur asked what time the next morning he could come in to the station to discuss the reason he was in Amsterdam and discuss these individuals. Officer Jansen told him any time after 8:00 AM would be fine. Arthur agreed that he would be there at 8:00 sharp. Meantime, Arthur asked if the officer could fax copies of the death certificates to him at his hotel. Officer Jansen was very accommodating and did so immediately. He had the fax number for most hotels in his computer.

Arthur asked for one more favor. Where would be a good place to get a drink and have dinner close to the hotel? The hotel didn't have a restaurant. Officer Jansen asked Arthur if he liked sea food. Arthur answered in the affirmative and Jansen suggested the Mossel and Gin Restaurant. It was close to the hotel. It is known for its steamed mussels, shrimp, bitterballen and grilled octopus. The gin and tonics were the best in the city. Jansen suggested he eat outside. Sidewalk cafés are the city's specialties. Great people watching. Arthur thanked him and took him on the suggestion. Arthur had 3 gin and tonics and plenty of seafood. That dinner was just the trick for Arthur to finally have a good night's sleep. The flight over to Amsterdam was tiring, so Arthur didn't even look at the death certificates that night. He thought they would be there in the morning.

The next morning. Arthur got up early and found a hard roll, butter, and a small bottle of orange juice hanging in a small cellophane bag on his door knob. He thought, what a unique way to serve breakfast when there is no restaurant. Not much, but unique. He ate it all while he was getting ready. He also noticed a red light flashing on his phone. He picked it up and the clerk, at the desk, answered and told Arthur he had a message he could pick up when he came down from his room. A message? Who could that be from? Officer Jansen? Alex? His office in Tampa? Or was it just the four death certificates that were faxed to the hotel the evening before. It would have to wait.

Once Arthur had taken his European shower, brushed his teeth and dressed, it was 7:30. He wasn't quite sure how far the main police station was from the hotel, so he went down to the check in desk and asked the clerk for his message. Arthur read the message form Alex about the two names Denise found in the Florida public records. He also received the four death certificates. He was glad that maybe he may have some sort of leads.

Arthur asked the desk clerk how far the police station was from the hotel. The clerk, who couldn't understand why one of the guests needed to go the police station, told Arthur it was about 10 minutes by taxi. To get a taxi in Amsterdam is not like New York. They are very hard to hail down. Usually you could only get them at a designated taxi stand. Those stands were in the major squares or at large hotels. Arthur's hotel certainly was not one of those hotels where taxi's hung out. Arthur asked the clerk where he could find a taxi and he was told to walk west for about a block he would find a taxi stand.

Arthur got to the police station just after 8:00 that morning and Officer Jansen was there to meet him. After they exchanged some pleasantries, the two of them sat down in Jansen's office to chat about why Arthur was in Amsterdam. Arthur explained to the senior law enforcement officer that he was an FBI agent from the Tampa, Florida office. He was with the white collar crime division and he was investigating possible fraud dealing with certain loans that the AFC Bank N.V. had made for several real estate developments in Southwest Florida. The amount of the loans were very large, somewhere over $1 billion American. The exact facts were not determined and Arthur was in Amsterdam to see what he could find out. Officer Jansen, than blurted out, that he just remembered where he had heard one of the names on one of the death certificates.

"What are you talking about?" Said Arthur.

"The name, Hagen Vinke. I remember that name. He was, I believe, either the President or on the Board of Directors, or someone with an important job at AFC Bank. The time frame was somewhere about 2000 until he committed suicide in 2009." Declared Jansen.

"How do you know he committed suicide?' said Arthur.

"It's right here on the death certificate." Said Jansen confused that Arthur didn't read that.

"Holy crap! Your right. He did commit suicide. Or at least that's what it says on the certificate." Said Arthur a little embarrassed. "The doctor who signed the death certificate of Hagen Vinke is Dr. Nicolaus Timmerman. In fact, he signed the death certificates on all four!"

"Quite a coincidence." Said Jansen.

"I don't believe in coincidences." Said Arthur.

"Well, here is another coincidence." Started Jansen. "AFC Bank was purchased or merged, or something like that, with the Netherlands largest bank, ABN Amro Bank in about 2010!"

"And the coincidences keep coming." Said Arthur. "I just got a lead on a Dutch man named Rynsburger today. He was involved somehow, with Hyland in the same real estate developments in many Southwest Florida real estate developments."

The two law enforcement officers started to discuss the facts they learned in just a several minutes.

An Amsterdam bank loans Joe Hyland's development companies over $1 billion American between 1999 and 2008 or 2009. That same bank was in the process of being purchased by the largest bank in the Netherlands somewhere about 2010. The borrowers cannot pay back the loans from the Amsterdam Bank. Then, the largest foreclosure in the history of Southwest Florida is initiated by the new purchasing Netherlands bank. That new Netherlands bank does not finish the foreclosure, but instead settles with their borrowers. The President, or whatever he was at the bank that was sold, supposedly commits suicide before the two banks merge. The same doctor signs all four death certificates for two related business men and their wives. The two banks merge in about 2010. Joe Hyland dies suspiciously in 2013. Hyland's original partner in his development company in the States disappears just before the first loan from the original Netherland's bank. The first development then starts construction in 1999.

"Visse, listen to us, and we have only been investigating for about 20 minutes." Declared Arthur. I think we may be on to something."

"How do you want to do this?' said Jansen. "Who should look into what or whom?"

The two detectives decide that Jansen would try to find out more about Rynsburger and how he may fit into this scheme, if at all; check out the doctor and his relationships with the four deceased; and find out the position of Hagen Vinke at the bank, when the banks merged and anything that can be determine about the loans to Hyland and if Vinke was involved. Arthur would be in touch with his law enforcement connections back in the States and continue to try to find out anything he can about the loans or relationships including Hyland's first partner who disappeared. They would meet again the next morning at Jansen's office about 9:00 to compare notes.

****

Denise Hudak and Alex Terian agreed to a meeting in Alex's office at 10:00 AM on August 27, 2013, just over 3 weeks after Joe Hyland's death, to go over Denise's investigation into the Hyland's developments. Who were his partners, from where the money came and went, and lastly, what happen to Roger Spector?

Denise went over each of the 30 plus limited liability companies and corporations formed by Joe Hyland between 1999 and 2008. Denise explained the complexities of each of the developments. She explained what was sold in each development by Hyland's real estate companies. Denise further explained to Alex that AFC Bank, the original lender for all of Hyland's loans, was sold to ABN Amro about 2010. The new bank assumed all of the assets of AFC Bank including all loans connected with Hyland's development companies. The new bank was the bank that initiated the large foreclosure action. She then went over which properties were foreclosed.

After that explanation, which barely kept Alex awake, Denise said she had three observations she would like to be considered in the final determination of this investigation. Alex, had no problem with that. He highly respected Denise's intuition since she has solved many investigations over the years.

"However, before I go into those matters," requested Denise, "Have you heard from Arthur Winslow from Amsterdam?"

"I have and he does have some leads." Said Alex." The President of the bank that loaned Hyland's development companies all the funds, committed suicide in 2009." Replied Alex. "That was just when the Netherland's largest bank, ABN Amro, was in the process of doing their due diligence and auditing the largest customers accounts at AFC Bank, which is normal procedure when a bank is in the process of acquiring a bank."

"You got to be kidding?" replied Denise.

"The investigation is still going on so don't jump to any of your quick conclusions, Denise." Quickly replied Alex. "The doctor that signed the death certificate for the Bank President also signed the death certificate for Josef Rynsburger." Alex went on. "Again do not jump to conclusions yet." Requested Alex.

Denise listed to those facts and was not sure how they all fit together, but she had a gut feeling something from Amsterdam very likely connects with Joe Hyland's death. She may becoming a believer that some criminal wrong doing had been done to Hyland.

Alex, feeling an urge of full disclosure with Denise, since she was now heavily involved in the case, told Denise that Arthur Winslow was actually in charge of the Tampa FBI office, white collar crime division and is really investigating fraud dealing with the loans to Hyland's development companies. Our office is the one working on any possible homicide or homicides.

Denise was a little pissed off, but has been around long enough to know that there usually is a reason for holding back information from investigators in certain cases. The County Attorney's office does not want their investigators to go off on tangents that may not have anything to do with the case. But she felt she should have been told from the beginning of the investigation. She is far from a rookie.

"Tell me about your observations." Asked Alex.

"First, as to the money loaned to Hyland for the developments financed by AFC Bank, the amount was more than $1.5 Billion. The mortgages in the public records specifically state only the amounts loaned for each development. No Notes, Loan Agreements or personal guarantees are in the public records. There are no indication of how draws were allocated or how often they were utilized." Stated Denise. "Everything in the public records points to Joe Hyland, and maybe all of his entities, being the only persons to sign personal guaranties for all of the developments in the total amount of about $1.5 Billion. Josef Rynsburger and any of his entities or the Bank's entities would not have been personally liable. The reason for that is due to the fact that none of those persons, or their entities, were named defendant in the foreclosure action. Only Joe Hyland and all of his development companies were the only defendants in the foreclosure court action." Continued Denise.

"The company Rynsburger/Traverse City/SNL Investments, LLC makes me believe that AFC Bank formed an entity so as to become a partner in all of the developments. I believe there are some restrictions on the percentage a foreign bank holding company may possess in a U.S. development if the Bank's parent company is loaning the money. However, I am certain the Bank is a partner. The amount of the foreclosure is just under $1 Billion. After painfully going through all of the hundreds of units and lots and parcels sold by Hyland's development companies in all those developments, there is no possible way that the amount of the foreclosure can be the correct amount unless someone, or multiple persons, were skimming off the top of each draw, or skimming somewhere else. There is a possibility that the default interest rate and penalties and other costs could have been so high as to cause the high foreclosure amount, but very unlikely. I added over $1 billion dollars in sales. I realize there are costs for sales like realtor's fees, transfer tax, property taxes, etc., but I really believe someone was stealing money. The default interest which may have been outrageously high, was not in the foreclosure file in the public records. That information would be in the Note or Loan Agreement which is not usually put in the public records. Interest was only 2.5 points over the then Liber rate or about 4.75% average on all loans. That interest rate would not cause the amount of the foreclosure to be so high." Continues Denise.

"Alex, someone or multiple persons were stealing money on each draw and designating that money as to some other expense." Stated Denise confidentially. "The first development, Largo Del Sol, seems to be on the up and up. All units were sold at market value, except for two units. Joe Hyland purchased those units, for no cash, yet the deeds transferring the units to him indicated a market value transfer through the transfer taxes paid on the deeds. That alone may be a violation of State laws." Denise continued. "The loan was paid back in full with no problems. It may have been that Hyland's profits on that development may have been in kind, by receiving the two units. But that does not mean money could not have been skimmed from that loan. However, that is not true with any of the other developments. I need to speak with Brian Koop, Hyland's attorney, about that and several other minor hiccups with that development." Said Denise. "Otherwise the only way to find out about skimming on the draws or skimming somewhere else is to fully review the draws. Maybe Cathy Rutter will cooperate and show and explain to me the brake down on those draws. Otherwise we will need to get a subpoena for those records." Finished Denise.

"Good observations, Denise." Alex complementing her. "What else?"

"As I said, there was over $1billion in sales before the foreclosure. When I called the Real Estate Commission, both Joe Hyland and Roger Spector withdrew their brokers and salespersons licenses. Can you imagine the amount of commissions that could have been made on over $1Billion in sales? No rational person would give that to other sales people in any real estate company. I believe that Joe Hyland, was the only owner of the real estate company, and I have no reason not to believe that. He could have made a lot of profits on those sales. However, nowhere in the neighborhood as much as if he where the broker. That one is very hard to understand. Again, I need to speak with Hyland's attorney about that issue." Said Denise,

"Another good observation and a little perplexing also." Said Alex. "What else?"

"I found, on line, an interview with a reporter from the Cape Coral Business Observer with Joe Hyland when Hyland was in the process of permitting the condo hotel at Snook Point. It was the middle of the decline in the real estate market and Hyland was going to build a 250 unit condo hotel. The average price for each unit was set at $1million dollars. The loan was for $250 million. It's in the public records and part of the foreclosure. The interview did not seem like Hyland really wanted to get a loan for that project. He laughed it off, but I have a feeling someone was making Hyland build that Hotel. Even Hyland said he would be in financial ruin if the real estate market didn't turn around in three years. Hyland had to know it wouldn't. He was in the middle of the downfall and he knew what was coming." Said Denise. "I believe that hotel was being built for whomever was skimming money from the loan draws to take their last big score!" admitted Denise." I also believe that the majority of the outstanding bank funds that were not paid and became a part of the foreclosure action, came from the hotel, the convention center and the commercial units, all located in Snook Point which was the last loan with AFC Bank."

"Good work!" Admitted Alex.

Denise and Alex discussed everything that Denise had brought up that morning including the loose facts of Arthur's investigation. Including the fact that the same doctor was involved with the bank's President and Josef Rysnburger's death cannot all be coincidences.

"Let's wait to hear from Arthur and reconvene to determine where this thing goes from here. Meantime, Denise, will you speak with Catty Rutter about those draws and see if she may be cooperative. Also Hyland's attorney can give us a lot of insight. Try to bypass that client confidentiality crap. Everything we spoke about is in the public records. Maybe he can just enlighten us." Suggested Alex.

"One more item." Said Denise. "I believe that through my investigation and my connections that I have determined that George Harvey is Roger Spector's father. I have come to the conclusion that

Roger may not know about it, but his father Eugene Spector must. As part of the settlement, Roger's mother got $10,000.00 cash and all of Roger's schooling was fully paid for. Roger also received a job commitment for 10 years from George Harvey. What that means, I have no idea, as it relates to this investigation." Said Denise. "But I'll bet a month's pay it does have something to do with it."

"You're probably right, but work on the other matters first. If there is some connection it will surface." Instructed Alex.

****

In January, 1998, Joe Hyland and Roger Spector had successfully negotiated a purchase agreement for the 5 acre Southwest parcel of property at The Riverview Golf & Country Club with Bradly Whalen. Joe thought it was so much easier than he thought it would be. It was almost as Bradly and George were like the same person, or at least had some connection. The purchase price was $20 million cash after a 150 day 'free look' period. Hyland and Spector's Development Company, Largo Del Sol Development Company, LLC would be responsible for finalizing the permitting and trimming of the mangrove parcel thereafter. Josef was pleased. The purchase price was substantially less than what was authorized to purchase the parcel. GHIC agreed that Joe and Roger, and their partners would be financially responsible for the mangrove issue, however, that GHIC would cooperate fully with Joe and Roger to accommodate the permitting and trimming of the mangrove parcel.

Everything was now being put in action. The parcel was already permitted for 111 units. The rest was designing a site plan, having the lawyers draft the necessary documents including, condominium documents, purchase agreements, reservation agreement, etc. Both Roger and Joe agreed to hire Brian Kopp, as their attorney. Quit a few real estate people had told both of them that Kopp's firm is the best real estate and business litigation firm in the area. They have office all over Florida and several offices in other States. Perfect for their new venture. Brian could work on the real estate matters and one of his law partners could work on the land use matters for the permits to trim the mangroves.

Josef's task was the money and the lender. Josef had already starting the application for the loan even before the parcel's purchase agreement was executed. Almost like Josef new something no one else did. Before GHIC had to close on the land, the new development company had 150 days to get soil samplings, check all the necessary permits, and all other miscellaneous matters that are involved in putting together a large real estate development.

However, there was one more issue to be resolved. It was one week before Joe and Roger were going to sign their names to the loan application for Largo Del Sol. Joe remembered what Josef said to him in the limo the night of their first meeting. Roger must be taken care of. Roger must not become a partner in any of these developments. It must happen before the application for the loan with AFC Bank is submitted. This fact has been haunting Joe for months. How does he do that? Roger had been working as hard as Joe on the site plan, the condominium documents and the permitting for trimming the mangroves. Both Joe and Roger had withdrawn their real estate licenses together from the Real Estate Commission. Roger could never get a real estate license again. Its Josef's fault thought Hyland. Joe questioned whether he should try to get Josef to reconsider, but he knew Josef, from the first time he met him, would never change his mind. He had some reason and it must be important. Joe also did not want to jeopardize his future. It had to be done. The loan application had to be submitted without Roger's name.

Joe could lie and tell Roger that after several months working together, Joe determined that the partnership would not work with the two of them working together, so one of them had to go. Roger would never believe it and he would question why the one to go would have to be Roger. They both gave up an awful lot to form this alliance. Oh, what to do and how to do it? And it must be done quickly. Joe even thought for a short moment of faking an accident so Roger would get hurt permanently and have to leave the partnership. They took out life insurance and disability insurance on each other in case one of them died or was injured. But that is not the way Hyland did things. Kill or maim Roger? No way. Be a man, Joe thought. Tell him as much of the truth as possible. But is there any other way? Roger has arranged his whole life around this alliance. He gave up his company car and leased a new one. Gave up his condo that GHIC rented him at a reasonable price and rented a more expensive condo. Agreed to take less salary until the loan for Largo Del Sol was approved and the first draw was received. And on and on and on.

After much thought, Hyland decided to talk with George Harvey. George had always treated Joe well. The negotiations for the land parcel at Riverview went well and Harvey seemed to have taken some kind of shine to Roger. Hyland would tell Harvey the entire scheme. If he needed to, he would blame the invalid real estate licenses GHIC required Joe and Roger to accept. This way, Joe got Roger out of any possible legal trouble in the future. Harvey's connection with the Real Estate Commission could only last so long. Clearing that issue up was a good thing. Both Joe and Roger where ill advised to even think of such a scheme. Yes, Hyland thought that Harvey would be furious, but the deed is done and maybe Harvey would take back Roger in some capacity, or at least help him get a good job. He was not going to tell Roger up front, he believed he should speak with George Harvey first and then talk to Roger.

So that is what Hyland did. He made an appointment to see Harvey privately and tell him the truth and let the chips fall where they may. To say that the meeting went well is one of the biggest overstatements Joe Hyland had ever imagined. George was furious. He threatened to pull out of the Purchase Agreement for the Riverview parcel. He threatened to call the police. He threatened to black ball Joe from ever being able to work in the real estate industry again. The threats went on and on. After Hyland was able to calm Harvey down after 20 minutes of ranting, Hyland decided to bring up the real estate licensing scheme. It didn't seem to slow Harvey down, after all who would the State believe, George Harvey of Joe Hyland?

After a full 30 minutes of ranting on the part of Harvey, he finally calmed down and asked Hyland why in the world he would have done such a thing. Hyland, in his most ashamed voice said that he never would have partnered with Rynsburger if he had known that this was going to happen. Hyland was not lying, but he was not completely forthcoming with Harvey. But Hyland was capable of selling almost any argument to Harvey.

"George, it was either him or me and I always knew you had a soft spot for Roger from the first day I came to this company. Why, I am not sure, but I know some how it's personal." Declared Joe. "This incident has shown me that I will always have to watch my back with my new partners." admitted Hyland. "But this has been what I have always wanted. It is my chance to be someone in this County and beyond." Pleaded Hyland. "Don't take this away from me. If I can do anything for Roger, short of bring him back in the new venture, I would do it. I would owe you both." Again pleaded Hyland. "I feel awful."

"You will owe Roger for sure, and I will make sure you owe me." Exclaimed George. "This is one of the lowest acts that anyone has done to a decent person who I know and have admired." Said George now a little calmer. "Now get out of here and I don't want to see you, even at the closing of the 5 acre parcel." Said George. "I will take care of Roger. Tell him to come and see me this afternoon. Don't tell him anything. I will tell him. I don't want you to spin this in some Rynsburger fashion." Claimed George.

Joe left with the harshest sour feeling in his stomach as he has ever had. What did he just do? What will this cost him over his whole career? But Joe made the call to Roger. Hyland didn't tell Roger about anything just that George wanted to see him that afternoon. Roger pressed him, but Joe, as meekly as he ever has been, just told him to go see George.

****

Joe left the meeting with two completely different feelings. First, he was glad he didn't have to have a confrontation with Roger. George was bad enough, but that confrontation for Joe was over and Joe was sure George would, in some form or another, take care of Roger. Joe just didn't want to have any further confrontations, especially with Roger and was very hopeful that would not happen. Joe was not sure what he would say or do if Roger confronted him. However, would it be George or Roger who contacts him about some sort of severance compensation? Roger had been there for some time. George would make sure Joe paid good money for this. Joe was not really sure whether he could make a better deal with George or Roger. But after some thought, it was Josef who wanted this done. Josef held the money strings. Joe was basically broke, except what Josef was giving him weekly to barely live. Joe knew the salary would highly increase over time, but right now Joe was just making ends meet. Maybe, Joe should refer the issue to Josef. But he would need to speak with Josef first. Last thing Joe wanted was to have

Harvey or Spector call Josef out of the blue about that issue. He would have to contact Josef about this issue soon.

Second, Joe had to get moving to finalize the paper work to have Roger removed as an officer and director and owner of the development company including an Agreement with all the terms of the severance and full releases. Joe would have to call Brian Koop, that day, to get the paper work started. It could all be finalized by mail so Joe didn't have to confront Roger again.

Joe also had other things on his mind. Joe wanted to make sure that real estate sales persons were hired by Traverse City Real Estate Company, LLC. This was Joe's company and any profits were all his. The sales person's agreements had been drafted by Brian Kopp a few days before. He had already hired a broker some time ago, Laura Wills, a 50ish year old seasoned sales person who had been in the Fort Myers area all her life. She knew everyone. Laura had located a nearby office for the real estate company. Josef had advanced Joe sufficient funds to get the office under lease and furnished. Josef would be reimbursed sometime in the future once the project was selling. Once several furnished model condominium were completed, the real estate company could then use those models as a sales center. Laura had already qualified Joe's real estate company as a qualified real estate broker some time ago. Luckily in Florida, ownership of real estate companies was not of record. Now that Roger was out, Joe was the lone owner of the company. He wanted to make sure that the Real Estate Commission did not know of his ownership of the company. Josef assured him that the Dutch connection in these developments would not interfere with the real estate commissions earned on any of the Developments. Also, Ivana was Laura's daughter and Roger was Laura's cousin. Fort Myers was still a small world. Joe was oblivious!

Laura had been busy hiring real estate people. She had 10 outstanding offers from reputable licensed sales people, with incentives that Joe Hyland was going to move quickly and get hundreds of units on the market. Presales would be able to be started soon. The word got around town and real estate agents came out of the wood works to look for employment with Joe's real estate company. One of those agents was Ivana Hollings, Roger's cousin. Joe was not aware of that. Joe had been too busy with the purchase of the land and all of the professionals to be able to get the first shovel into the dirt for Largo Del Sol. Laura had been constantly contacting Joe as to when they would be able to offer at least non-binding Reservations Agreements for condominiums at Largo Del Sol. Joe's answer was always the same. As soon as Brian Koop notified him that the State of Florida, Department of Condominium had approved the Reservation Program.

"Well tell him to hurry up." Exclaimed Laura." My sales people are salivating on getting buyers."

"I should hear today," said Joe. "Brian tells me that a Reservation Agreement does not take very long to be approved. Hope to call you today. Remember, all deposits should be made payable to Kopp's law firm. His firm is going to keep all deposits in their trust account." The firm's trust account for all deposits for all developments will be opened at Southern Trust Bank, as per the relationship between that bank and Joe in the past. Brian had no problem with that. Brian's firm would also close all development units.

"Also, the condominium documents are not complete and will take several months before they are approved by the State. We cannot turn the non-binding Reservation Agreements into binding Purchase Agreements until those documents are complete and temporally approved by the State." Continued Joe to Laura. "So make sure all the agents keep in touch with their clients regularly. We don't want them to cancel their reservations and buy another product!" exclaimed Joe. "We will have all amenities and the first high rise building finished in 18 months or less, according to the contractor."

"Don't worry, Joe. I am on it. I have hired the best around." Confidently said Laura.

Ivana, when she was hired by Laura, knew Joe was the boss for this project and in fact he was her real boss even though Laura was her broker. Ivana had plans for herself and Joe sometime in the future. He will be very rich one of these days and her goal is to be there to share it with him. Ivana also knew that Leigh Mowery and Joe were presently dating. Leigh was hired by Joe the day he opened his main Company office on Summerlin Boulevard. Cathy Rutter was also hired as the company's financial person and Joe's personal assistant. Leigh Mowery was hired as Cathy's assistant and Joe's backup assistant. Things were moving ahead. However, in the back of Joe's mind was what was going to happen to Roger. It was strange that he had very few comments about Roger's absence, other than Laura. She didn't believe Joe for a minute. She had met Josef Rynsburger and was sure it was his doing. But there was too much money at stake, so Laura quieted down. Joe just said that Roger determined that the stress of this amount of money was not for him and wanted to get out as soon as possible. Joe then called Brian Koop and got his assistant. He told her to get the paper work started to remove Roger from the real estate company and the development companies. Then he made the tough call to Josef. Joe told him about the confrontation with George Harvey and the fact that George would meet with Roger and talk to him and hopefully take care of him. But Joe knew that some type of severance compensation would need be given to Roger. George Harvey will make sure that happens. Without even a pause, Josef said give him $50,000.00 for a full, final and complete release on all matters. Have your lawyer draft the Agreement and get it signed soon. Josef then hung up. Joe called Brian's assistant back and told her to get Brian to add the $50,000.00 consideration to the agreement and to the necessary documents. Joe was amazed. Not even a discussion. This adventure with Josef is going to be a either a whirlwind or a big bust!

****

Roger showed up at George's office about an hour after Joe called him.

"What's going on George?" opened Roger. "I received this unusual phone call from Joe to come and see you. He wouldn't tell me anything about it." Said Roger.

"Sit down Roger. I have something to discuss with you." Started George. "It's like this. Joe and his asshole Dutch partners have decided to fire you! I really believe it had something to do with that Rynsburger. He has always been a pain in the ass to work with." Admitted George.

"What do you mean fired me? How can he do that, I am an owner?" questioned Roger." What the hell am I supposed to do?" finished Roger.

"To tell you the truth, Roger, after much thought after my meeting with Joe, I really believe you are better off without them. They are all greedy sons of bithchs! Joe will probably be going broke in a few years. He has no idea who he is getting involved with. I believe that Joe thinks this real estate boom will last forever. He is naïve. I have never seen a boom continue for years." Calmly said George. "The key is to know when the turn is coming. Joe is too greedy!" said George. "His partners and that Dutch Bank will toss him aside when they want to. He'll end up broke, or worse." Said George. "And I really like the guy. Too bad for him."

"However, this is still unbelievable. Joe didn't even have the guts to tell me myself. What the hell am I going to do? "Asked Roger again.

"Roger, look at this as a blessing in a disguise. I have some plans for you and if it all goes the way I believe it will, you will be well off in a few years!" said George. "Do you trust me?" asked George.

"I don't know who I trust." Said Roger, then after thinking about what he just said, "I am sorry George, and I do trust you. You have always been fair with me and looked out for me."

George and Roger then sat down for some time, and discussed different alternatives. George gave Roger several lucrative alternatives, all good opportunities. But George kept saying, do you just want to move on, or do you want to move on and cover yourself when this real estate boom dies. Roger didn't know what exactly that meant. It may take a little time and a lot of patience, but Rynsburger and even Joe, the turncoat I never thought he would be, may just get theirs.

"I don't understand George. What does that mean?"

Roger was then offered opportunities in Georgia, on the east coast of Florida, Tennessee, and then something different, Aruba! George admitted to Roger, in confidence that he had down some underhanded things to be able to have the opportunity to build the largest condominium hotel in Aruba. It's located right next to the Marriott Hotel on Palm Beach, right on the water in the high rise area where the big spender's go on the Island. The hotel will have 790 rooms, 60 of them suites and every amenity possible including the largest casino on the Island. First class all the way. After all of those bribes, and all the other things George had to give, which he wouldn't even mention to his priest, he purchased the land to put up this hotel. The land is in an Aruba land company. This will have nothing to do with GHIC. It was George's hedge against the real estate boom going flat.

The Wyndham Hotel Group has agreed to manage it. They had a hotel in Aruba some years ago, but it was bought out and turned into an all-inclusive resort. Wyndham has been looking for an opportunity to get back to Aruba. It will be a gold mine.

Best of all, Roger, Aruba use to be a territory of the Netherlands and even though the Aruba people have received their independence from the Netherlands, the Netherlands still has a lot of influence there. Many Dutch people still take their annual vacation in Aruba. Also, and most important, the bank that is funding Joe and Rynsburger has a branch there. And that may be the key to some type of scheme for Roger to get back his dignity that Hyland took from him. George implied that a plan may be brewing. But there may be other ways to get back against Rynsburger. Time will tell.

Roger still had no clue what George was intimating. Roger pleaded with George to explain it to him. George told him again not to worry about it that he would handle it. George really wanted Roger to take the Aruba job and George knew Roger would never regret it. George also assured Roger that Roger didn't have to be concerned about Wyndham being bought out again. George told Roger that lots of George's resources were being put into this project. Wyndham hotel Group has 7,645 luxurious properties all over the world. A 50 year Agreement is in the works for this hotel. Wyndham has properties in 66 countries and was originally founded by Trammel Crow in 1981. George indicated that in 1981, he was one of the original partners of that hotel chain. A few years later, George was bought out at his suggestion when he wanted to start developments in Florida. But he left the company on good terms and Wyndham is happy to see George come back. Especially now with his political connections.

"Take some time to think it over. Your single and free right now. A stint in Aruba may be the cure to some of your current woos! I want you to learn the casino business and, and if you still like Aruba when the hotel is finished, you can run the casino. You'll make a fortune." Said George. "And maybe, that one day will come where you may just out smart Hyland. At least I hope so!" Declared George.

"This has all come too fast. I need some time." Admitted Roger.

Before you start taking that time, George and Roger had one more issue to discuss. George was furious that Roger was thrown out and there was no discussion of severance compensation.

"Go back to Joe and confront him and get at least $25,000.00 cash before you sign any of the documents they may be in the course of drafting to take you off the development and real estate companies."

Said George. "Don't call me back unless you get at least that much."
Cautioned George. "Sometimes you have to be a man or even a jerk!"

Starting the next day, Roger would be put on GHIC's payroll again.
George told Roger to speak with HR and tell them you will be working
for GHIC and to reinstate your salary with full back pay. Then let me
know in a few days if you will take the offer in Aruba. I will set you up
in one of the Aruba Company's rented condos in Aruba. It's paradise.
There will be plenty for you do there while you are learning the casino
business

"Have you ever been to Aruba?" asked George.

I was there with several guys some time ago on a gambling
weekend." Said Roger.

You won't believe what they have done with that Island in the last
few years. And it is only going to get bigger!" said George.

After the meeting with George, Roger got up the courage to call
Joe and give him a piece of his mind. But once Roger stopped talking,
Joe was very conciliatory and blamed the Dutch people. Joe offered
Roger $50,000.00 to sign the necessary releases and apologized to him
in every way he could. Roger was surprised he didn't even get a chance
to ask for the severance compensation. But he was happy he didn't. Still
Roger said that he would never accept any apology. Roger intimated
that George felt that Joe was getting into something that he will never
get out of and only bad things would happen to him over the next few
year with these Dutch people. George knew of these people and the
reputation of the lender and Joe should watch his back, so to speak.
Roger just couldn't wish him good luck, but Joe did wish Roger good
luck and a good life. Roger did not tell Joe about all the different offers
he received from George. Roger specifically said nothing about Aruba,
and Joe had no idea what was coming in the next few years. Roger also
was in complete limbo when he hung up the phone. What was next
for Roger?

CHAPTER 9

A FTER THEIR RESPECTIVE investigations, Arthur Winslow and Senior Officer Jansen meet at the main police station in Amsterdam at 10:00 AM several days after their first meeting in late August, 2013 to compare notes on all of the coincidences that came up during their first meeting. Officer Jansen said he would start first.

Officer Jansen determined that Hagen Vinke started working for AFC Bank right out of college in 1989. He worked at low level jobs for several years, but caught the eye of the influential employees of the bank. He was ambitious and always willing to take on tasks others refused. He was the first one at the bank each morning and the last one to leave in the evening. His ambitions paid off. In 1992, he was promoted to a junior loan officer for the Bank from which he handled well through 1995. One year later the word 'Junior' was taken off his title. He was considered an up and comer, worked very hard and landed some of the largest loans and most successful loans year after year. In 1996 he was voted on the Board of Directors of the Bank and was promoted to Executive Vice President in charge of foreign loans. That included any loans outside the Netherlands including the United States. Vinke had many connections in every country where AFC made loans. His main connection in the United States was Josef Rynsburger, his very good friend from his high school and university days. Hagen Vinke and Josef Rynsburger were from the same City and went to the same schools together. Both men were born in Utrect which is a City and a Municipality in the Netherlands Capital and the most populist city of the Province of Utrect. It is located in the Eastern corner of the Randstad Conurbation and not far from the center of Amsterdam. It is the fourth largest city in the Netherlands with a population of near 320,000 people.

Vinke came from an upper middle class family who were moderately wealthy. Vinke's family owned several commercial and residential rental real estate properties. Rynsburger was somewhat jealous and always wanted to work for the Vinke family. Rynsburger was infatuated with the real property business, but he came from a more middle class family and his father was a just a laborer. They were, however good friends and Rynsburger and Vinke ended up going to the same high school and university. Rynsburger was intelligent with a great mind for numbers and economics. Both went to the Utrect University which was one of the largest and most prestigious Public Universities in The Netherlands. The year they started Utrect, on the academic rankings of world Public Universities, it was ranked 56th in the world and the highest in The Netherlands. Both men entered the Departments of Economics and Banking. Rynsburger received a scholarship for the amount of tuition and costs that the Netherlands didn't pay. The Netherlands payed that portion of University tuition and costs for anyone who cannot afford the school, but qualifies for the school. Both did very well.

Upon graduation, Vinke went to work for AFC Bank and moved his way up. After several years on the Board of Directors, Vinke was appointed by the Board as President of the Bank in 2000. As President, he also held a position on the foreign loan committee. Since he had much experience with foreign loans, especially the United States, most of Vinke's contemporaries looked to him for his thoughts and insights for approval of most foreign loans, especially the United States. The bank had flourished under Vinke and his loans were some of the Bank's most profitable. Officer Jansen's source tells Jansen that Vinke always seemed to need to prove himself. His family was fairly wealthy and he needed to prove to his parents that he could also be successful. Making money was in his blood. He was always looking for the next big deal. Personally, that is why Jansen believes that he and Rynsburger were such good friends and business partners. Rynsburger was always coming up with schemes to get richer. Vinke thrived on that.

Also, Vinke and his two sons were not on the best of terms. Both sons were gay and Vinke was embarrassed and hoped that that issue wouldn't affect his position at the Bank. In the Netherlands, being gay was not a shame that a family usually hides, but Vinke felt differently. They all became estranged early in Vinke's career. This also affected Vinke's relationship with his wife. However, it was just never mentioned between them. Sofie, his wife, was very hurt down deep since she hardly ever got to see her sons. But the family survived, all in their own manner.

After graduation in the 1980's Rynsburger worked for a real estate company obtaining listings and selling real estate. He studied and worked the residential and commercial real estate business for several years. In 1992, after Vinke was appointed a junior loan officer, Rynsburger obtained a loan from the AFC Bank through the efforts of his friend Vinke. For some unknown reason to Rynsburger, he was not required to put down any funds for the loan. He obtained a 100% loan, including costs. Very unusual. He was, however, required to get several guaranties due to his financial situation. Not only his parents had to sign a guarantee, for which they were not that enthusiastic, but he also obtained a guarantee from a longtime family friend, Dr. Nicolaus Timmerman. This was the doctor that signed the death certificates of the four individuals being investigated.

Rynsburger purchased his first property in the Netherlands, rented it for a few years and sold it for a nice profit. Josef believed he was on his way to great wealth in the real estate business. With his friend Vinke at AFC Bank, and his family friend, Dr. Timmerman, he believed he could virtually write his own check. Vinke's source believed that Rynsburger would give advice to Vinke on different methods for the Bank to make money. Most of that advice then had Rynsburger involved in some manner. Rynsburger always made money. Vinke knew that and relied heavily on his friend's advice. Because of advice from Rynsburger, Vinke's opinions were being more and more followed by, not only his peers, but also some of the more seasoned lenders. Josef and his family's friendship with their family doctor, Dr. Timmerman matured month by month, especially after the doctor was guaranteeing Josef's loans. The doctor would always get some type of gratuity from Rynsburger for his guarantees. Since the Doctor had trusted Josef enough to guarantee his loans, Josef later convinced the Doctor to go into the real estate business with him.

Dr. Timmerman was not sure at first, but Josef seemed to do so well he thought it would be interesting, and maybe even a little profitable. The Doctor was also fond of having wealth and believed that wealth was the way to impress his patients and other people in the community. In the world in Amsterdam, real estate ownership was a big part of being, or, at least looking wealthy. Their real estate company purchased several properties in the Netherlands, all with AFC loans, and all through Josef's friend Hagen Vinke. Their real estate company did very well with Josef running the business and the doctor funding all of necessary funds over and above the loan amounts Josef could obtain from the Bank. Dr. Timmerman was extremely impressive with Josef's knowledge on real estate and especially finance. Josef was still obtaining 100% loans for all his acquisitions. However, Dr. Timmerman was under the impression, from his partner, that their partnership loans were 70% loans to value. Dr. Timmerman's investment in the partnership was the illusive 30% down. Josef never really said anything about the particulars of each investment since all of the financials that Dr. Timmerman reviewed looked proper. Rynsburger started deceiving friends and family at a young age.

After 15 months, Dr. Timmerman got the feeling that something was just not right. His returns were getting smaller and the property values were going up. Rents were going up and sales were increasing. But the doctor's return was diminishing. Dr. Timmerman did not want to confront Josef due to their friendship and social circles. The doctor was not hurting for money so he just decided to leave the partnership without any dispute. He decided to tell Josef that the reasons for dissolution of the partnership was for two reasons. First, he didn't seem to receive the return on his investment that Josef had originally forecasted he would receive. The doctor was not happy about that, but he just left it as that. Second, he told Joseph that he just wanted to concentrate more on his physicians business. However, the doctor really was a little leery as to what was actually occurring in the partnership and felt Josef may be a little too aggressive for the doctor and maybe something was going on that the doctor didn't want to know about. The doctor was certain Josef could handle the business himself without any more of his guarantees. The partnership and the properties were liquidated so the doctor's guarantees were cancelled and Joseph and the doctor made a fair profit. Josef's profit was much more handsome than the doctor's due to the deceptive manner Josef communicated the loan situations. The doctor was still a bit confused on the handling of the real estate investment partnership and, in his gut, had some misgivings. However, Josef and Dr. Timmerman still remained friends for some time, until much later when the facts about Josef and Hagen's loan deceptions were revealed

Josef also introduced Dr. Timmerman and his spouse, Elise, to Hagen Vinke and his spouse, Sofie. It was Dr. Timmerman who then became Sofie Vinke's internist when she was diagnosed with colon cancer in 2006. Dr. Timmerman was also Josef's spouse's doctor when she was diagnosed with lung cancer in 2007. The six of them, which included the Doctor's spouse, Elise, became close and went on many trips together and socialized often. Even though Dr. Timmerman was not an oncologist, just an internist, he was still Sofie's and Lena's main physician. They both trusted him absolutely. However, Dr. Timmerman never fully trusted Josef completely thereafter.

In 1999, Josef decided to take his ill gained profits from the Timmerman partnership and start purchasing real property in Amsterdam and eventually developing property in The United States, specifically, Southwest Florida. Josef, had an innate impression for picking the correct real properties that would increase in value quickly. He felt that Southwest Florida was going to boom over the next 10 years or so. Josef was very greedy, as well as perceptive, and wanted to have "his piece of the American pie". All he needed was the right people to front for him who would trust him implicitly as Dr. Timmerman did at first. And with Josef's bank connections, there were many ways for Josef and Hagen to make their fortune.

"So far, this is all fascinating." Said Arthur. "Please continue, I can't believe you learned all of this in such a short period of time."

Officer Jansen, continued. Josef took numerous trips to Fort Myers, Florida and purchased a large condominium there as his office for his real estate business in Florida. The condominium was big enough so his assistant, Bram Muelenbelt, could also stay there. Bram would help Josef with issues that came up, from time to time, dealing with the U.S. properties and the Dutch loans. Bram would, on occasions, go to Florida without Josef to work on issues that would come up with Joe Hyland or Hyland's attorney. Josef was not always available to go to Florida every time an issue occurred. Josef had business in many parts of Europe also. Bram also was instructed to retain a separate law firm to represent only Josef's interests and Brian Koop, Hyland's attorney worked with those attorneys, from time to time, on common issues dealing with the Hyland developments. The lawyer was from the Feldman & White law firm out of Miami, Florida. Albert White was Josef's lead attorney.

Joseph, as part of his U.S. portfolio, purchased several condominium in The Riverview Golf & Country Club as rental properties. There, his salesman was Roger Spector, who worked with him on his purchases. Spector, during one of Josef's and Bram's visit, introduced both of them to the majority owner of the development, George Harvey, and also Bradly Whalen, George's partner who actually did most of the real estate management. For whatever reason, Bram did not get the feeling that Harvey and Rynsburger hit it off well. Bram was also perceptive enough to know that the relationship between George Harvey and Bradly Whalen was more than just business. George Harvey had heard about this Dutch man who was in Southwest Florida to make a name for himself. Each found the other very arrogant and difficult to deal with.

"These coincidences seem to be coming one after another and are very fascinating. You will remember, Roger Spector is our missing partner of Joe Hyland." Said Arthur.

"I understand that." Said Officer Jansen. "But I have yet to find out what happen to Spector after he and Hyland broke up."

"I'll see what my colleagues in the Lee County Attorney office may have found out about that." Said Arthur. "Please go on."

Officer Jansen went on to confirm that Josef Rynsburger was involved in at least 6 very large developments, each with multiple loans with Florida development companies. All of the development companies had different names, but the principals were all the same, including Joseph D. Hyland and his development company, The Traverse City Investment Company, Inc.

"I am sure your people at your County Attorney's office can find out more about those development companies." Said Officer Jansen. "I have no way here to do that."

"We can, go on." Said Arthur. "This is still very interesting."

Jansen went on. After the first loan was closed with AFC, the other loans started to came very quickly thereafter and each loan was larger each time. Officer Jansen's connections at AFC Bank had indicated that the amounts of the loans were probably much larger than they should have been under normal banking practices in the Netherlands. His source could not give any opinion as to loans for U.S. real estate. All of the draws for each of the loans were on a monthly basis and always were requested by Joe Hyland's financial person, Cathy Rutter, an employee of the development companies. Again, my source said that influential people at the bank were starting to take notice. However, Vinke was the expert on U.S. loans, and he assured the committee that this was normal for these types of loans. So few questions were asked. However, after the third loan, Board Members and loan committee members started to question Vinke about the loans and some unusual payments from the requested loan draws. At first, Vinke could appease them by saying that, by the time these large developments are fully constructed, with most of them taking several years to complete, the value of the units would probably double, or at least increase drastically in value, which would always keep the Bank's collateral out of jeopardy. The loan to value between the mortgaged real property value and the outstanding principal loan amount was always, at least in the reports from Vinke to the committee, within the parameters set out in the original loan documents. Those numbers would come from the inflated values of the real estate in any particular loan. That gave the loan committee some feeling of security, but most of the members of the committee were still concerned. However, nothing more was done by the bank to review the loans. The Bank was receiving its percentage of ownership in each of the developments, as well as all of the interest due, on a monthly basis. All of this looked very good on financial reports.

The final loan by AFC to Hyland's development companies was for a hotel condominium in Cape Coral, Florida. That loan was brought up in the loan committee for approval, just about the time the Florida real estate boom was starting to whither. That loan was the largest loan yet requested by Hyland. Also, about the same time ABN Amro, the largest bank in the Netherlands, had just made a preliminary offer to purchase AFC Bank. ABN believed, at least on paper, that AFC Bank was very profitable. Banking consolidation was also becoming the norm about that time in the Netherlands. A sale of the Bank would mean an audit and a complete review of AFC's largest loans as well as other random loans. Vinke was still pushing hard for this hotel condominium loan to be approved. No one on the committee was sure whether or not interest in the purchase of the Bank was actually going to happen, so the committee's work went on as normal. From Jansen's source, until about 3 months before the condominium hotel loan was submitted for approval, all of Hyland's development company's loans had been performing satisfactorily, but not as well as Vinke had predicted. At that time, the interest payments due on the then outstanding loans were becoming more difficult to cover out of each monthly draw. This was due to necessary required payments for the development company salaries, construction cost to ensure no liens by subcontractors would be filed against the properties and other necessary payments. It was those other necessary payments that concerned the Bank. All of the loan documents had a cap on the amount of funds that could be requested. There was never a problem with collecting the Bank's interest when the draws were distributed in the past. But the last three draws were somewhat more difficult for the interest to be distributed. However, Vinke would always due his magic to make sure the Bank received its interest. Also, the Bank was aware that sales were slowing in Florida, but Vinke, again, convinced the committee that the slowdown was only temporary, and the City of Cape Coral seemed to be immune from any slowdown.

On one hand, this large loan for such a first class hotel in the United States was a great loan for the Bank to have on its portfolio. This was a condominium hotel with 250 units. The loan for the hotel was for $60 million and once completed, the purchasers of the condominium units in the hotel would pay the purchase price, at an average of $1.5 million per unit. That would come to be a large part towards paying off that loan. Plus the operating revenue from the hotel, which would still be a part of the developer revenue stream would be substantial. The Bank had a lien on those funds, so the bank would receive a large portion of that revenue towards the pay down of the loan. In addition, a franchise fee from the ultimate hotel chain that would operate the hotel, and operate all the amenities and restaurants, would be paid to the bank since the Bank also had a lien on those funds. Lastly, since the Bank's subsidiary was a partner in the venture, profits for the bank's ownership interest in the hotel would also be collected. There were several major hotel chains negotiating for management of the hotel and to have its name attached to the hotel. The loan for the conference center and additional commercial space was an additional $25 million, but that loan was not on the table for approval at that time.

On the other hand, committee members were concerned about the guaranty that all of the units would be sold and closed by the time the hotel construction was completed. It would take about 2 ½ years to build the hotel and all amenities. With the real estate market starting to loss its luster, how much of a risk was the committee ready to take? If the hotel failed to happen it would be a disaster for the Bank. But Vinke and Rynsburger were adamant that this hotel was the essential fragment of the Snook Point development, in order to protect the Bank's interest. There were other parcel of property at Snook Point, for which the bank held as security for this loan. Those parcels were for the purpose of building additional residential units to make Snook Point a destination site in Cape Coral. The hotel convention center was essential to that development. It was something that that City had never seen before in its history. Without the hotel/convention center, the money invested in that development would be much harder to recoup by the Bank.

Vinke had been a real money maker for the Bank and Rynsburger developments were a chunk of that. It was a close call on the vote by the committee but Vinke's arguments produced a positive vote by the committee. After much debate, the loan was granted.

"Had they only read the local papers in Southwest Florida at the time, the Bank would never have allowed the loan in the first place. The Board and loan committee should have had access to Florida real estate information with all those loans outstanding." Continued Jansen. However, Jansen had a feeling that Vinke and Rynsburger had other ideas, other than profits for the bank. Jansen's informant says that even Hyland's attorney and Rynsburger's attorney pleaded with Rynsburger and Hyland not to build the hotel at that time. Getting $1.5 million a unit several years after the hotel was commenced would have been very difficult. These facts were not communicated to AFC. At least Jansen's informant believed that. Whether Vinke or Hyland had anything to do with that is unknown.

Jansen's source said that the audit by ABN Amro of the Rynsburger loans showed something that was somewhat out of the ordinary. It must have been quite substantial since, ABN Amro were thinking about withdrawing their offer to purchase the Bank unless AFC

Bank contributed some substantial deficiencies that were found in the Rynsburger loan audit and several other Vinke loans. In addition, ABN Amro required an immediate change in some of the officers of the Bank, with all of the specific changes and deficiencies specifically laid out in writing for the audit committee of ABN Amro to review.

****

The day of the internal announcement about the audit and change of officers was made public to the Board of AFC, Vinke blew his brains out! He was on the Berenstr Wolvenste Bridge over the Keizersgracht Canal. Why he was there no one knew. One of the most famous monuments facing that canal is the Homomonument a memorial that commemorates gays and lesbians. Some people thought that Vinke's sons were in his mind when he shot himself. That was just a rumor.

When the police arrived at the scene where Vinke died, Dr. Timmerman was already there. The doctor had indicated that Vinke called him from the Bank and wanted to meet him at the bridge to talk about something very confidential. Vinke said it had to do with Josef Rynsburger. The doctor told the police that he witnessed Vinke shoot himself in the head. The doctor was kneeling over the body when the police arrived. Timmerman was trying to revive Vinke by giving CPR. The police checked Vinke's right hand to determine if there was gun residue on his hand. There was. There was no gun residue on Dr. Timmerman's hands. The doctor said he tried to revive Vinke, but he was killed instantly. The police knew Dr. Timmerman, who had practiced medicine in the area for years. The police had no reason to believe that the doctor was not telling the truth. Also, the doctor had no idea what it was that Vinke was going to tell the doctor. It all seemed very strange.

"Don't know if that had anything to do with any of this, but it is an interesting fact that Vinke's wife passed just a few months earlier." Said the officer. Doctor Timmerman was Mrs. Vinke's doctor. He signed both death certificates, for Hagen and Sofie Vinke since he observed both deaths. Also, no autopsy was performed on either of them since the death occurred in the presence of a doctor. Both bodies were cremated several days after their deaths. Neither of their two sons ever married and were not that upset when they heard the news of their father's fate. They were both in their forty's.

Both sons went to work soon after their father's and mother's death for a newly organized company called Ikea. Even though that company had been around for 40 years, new management was ready to change the company's image and expand outside of the Netherlands. One of the first places for that expansion was Florida. Vinke and Rynsburger had much invested in Florida Real estate. Again, Jansen was not sure what any of that may mean as to this investigation, but it is something that should be looked into. Both of his sons went to Florida and they are still there working for Ikea. A suicide should always be investigated, but the doctor must have been very convincing. He had all the right answers to the questions.

"What a story!" said Arthur, "How did you find this all out so quickly?"

"My brother in law worked for the bank as a commercial loan officer until the sale of the Bank to ABN Amro. However, there is another important fact that Arthur needed to know about Vinke's death. No gun was found anywhere near the body, nor was there any suicide note.

"Wait a minute!" Exclaimed Arthur. "Are you saying Vinke was murdered?"

"Everything I just told you is third party information. It's probably about 60-70% true. It will have to be further investigated." Claimed Officer Jansen. "I will continue my investigation and see if I can confirm any of what I just told you." Promised Officer Jansen. "But remember, that is only the first two death certificate signed by Dr. Timmerman. There are still 2 others."

"What about the gun?" said Arthur? What happen to it?"

"Dr. Timmerman said it fell into the canal after Vinke shot himself. However, a 9 millimeter shell casing was found next to the body. It had Vinke's fingerprint on it. Vinke was next to the edge of the bridge when he shot himself in the head and the gun may have fallen into the canal." Said the officer.

"But the police must have found it, right?" asked Arthur.

"No, it was never found. The police believed it was washed out by the tide since the tide was moving out quickly at the time Vinke shot himself" said Officer Jansen.

"I don't believe it." Said Arthur. "We are missing something here. We need to see if the doctor has the gun."

"Why would Dr. Timmerman kill Vinke? Asked Jansen. "The police had no motive at all. They were friends."

"I am really losing my touch. "Said Arthur. "I didn't even see the cause of death as suicide. Although the death certificates are all in Dutch, but you would think I could have figured it out."

"That's the query." Posing the question to Arthur. "The death certificate says suicide!"

"I don't understand?" questioned Arthur. "If there was no gun or note, why a determination of suicide? Just on the word of a friend, the doctor? Did the gun actually fall into the canal? Could the tide have be that formidable?"

"The Police dragged the canal. They found no gun." said Jansen. "However, it's been 4 years since that happen. It's too late now. There is nothing there to look for now."

"I don't know what Dr. Timmerman saw or what he was told, but according to my sources, no gun was ever found." Explained Officer Jansen. "But I will find out. As I told you from the beginning, no investigation file on the suicide of Vinke was ever open. At least I can't find one and there is nothing in the computer, not even a police report that they showed up at the scene." Confessed Officer Jansen. "Under these circumstances a report and investigation should have been done. This all happen about September, 2009. Dr. Timmerman must have had some influence. It is just hard to believe."

"Will you see about some type of investigation on this Vinke matter?" You have the tools and as senior officer, you should be able to get a computer expert to determine if something was deleted from your computer system?" questioned Arthur. "If nothing else, at least an interview with Dr. Timmerman may be appropriate. When you speak with him, maybe you can find out some information about the other two death certificates?"

"Did you find out anything about Roger Spector or about the Hyland's developments or the loan amounts and what the issues were with the draws?" Asked Jansen.

"I have been in touch with Alex Terian, who is handling the matter in Lee County, Florida. His investigator has under covered a lot of facts dealing with the Hyland developments and the loan amounts, however, they are still working on the draws and use of funds." Said Arthur. "The investigator is still going to speak with Hyland's financial assistant and his attorney and see what else they can determine. I will have them send you their current report to bring you up to date and I will let Alex and his investigator know what you have preliminarily determined."

"See if you can finalize all of the facts you have found from your source. However, I am not sure the County Attorney will believe me about Vinke's death" Continued Arthur. "Some of those committee and Board members must still be around somewhere. See if you can speak with a couple of those people. I am going to go back to Fort Myers to meet with the rest of the investigation team. I will communicate with them about your findings in this investigation. Great job! I will be in touch with you in few days and we can discuss our findings further."

****

It was just 4 weeks after Joe Hyland's funeral. Labor Day weekend, 2013 had come and gone. Denise had just spent many hours of investigation to find out about Hyland's development companies and their loans from AFC Bank. She also addressed other unusual matters such as the real estate licenses of Hyland and Spector and especially the relationship between George Harvey and Roger Spector. What happen to Roger Spector? Denise likes to keep her list, so they were on her 'to do' list. She didn't treasure speaking with George Harvey about Spector. She thought that he probably wouldn't give her the time of day anyway. But she had to move on.

Now it was time to talk to Cathy Rutter. Denise had already spoke with Leigh Mowery which didn't go very well. Denise really didn't find out much more than she knew when she walked into the hotel to speak with Mowery. Maybe Cathy will be more cooperative. Denise, thought it would be more courteous to call Rutter and set a time verses just showing up. Cathy answered the phone and Denise indicated that she was the County Attorney's investigator and she had some questions about Joe Hyland and his development companies. Cathy indicated she had already spoken with a detective Luke Blakely. Denise acknowledged that fact but indicated that additional substantial investigation had been done since then and there were some more information that they needed concerning attempting to wrap up the investigation.

"What investigation? Said Cathy. "Are you investigating the death of Joe Hyland or something about missing money from 10 years ago?" Again questioned Cathy.

"Both." Said Denise truthfully. "The investigation concerns the manner of Hyland's death as well as the draw procedures for the loans that the development companies and AFC Bank were operating under."

"Why is it the County Attorney's business as to how Joe Hyland operated his business?" questioned Denise. "I can sort of understand an investigation into Joe's death by your office, but the operations of the development companies is not your office's business." Claimed Cathy.

"You are correct about my office's interest in Hyland's death, but there is currently an investigation ongoing by the Tampa office of the FBI concerning possible white collar crimes dealing with the operation of Hyland's development companies and the Dutch Bank." Confessed Denise. "So, I would like to speak with you about both."

"As you probably already know, I was the financial assistant for all of Joe's development companies, so if there is a criminal investigation concerning those companies, and as a person involved with the finances for those companies, I will not speak to anyone until I can get legal counsel." Said Cathy very astutely.

"You said the magic word." Admitted Denise. "When can I expect a call from your attorney to set up a meeting?"

"You will receive a call soon." Said Cathy.

Then Cathy hung up.

****

It was now early in March, 1998, and several days since Roger Spector had his discussion with George Harvey and Joe Hyland. Roger was just devastated about what had just happen to him. His whole life changed in just the matter of a couple of hours. Roger still was not sure why George Harvey still even wanted him to work for GHIC. He was happy to have a job, but Aruba? Roger was happy George was expanding into the hotel business, it was a logical progression for someone like George. But why couldn't it be Miami or West Palm Beach or somewhere nearby? The opportunity for George and the Wyndham investors, whoever they may be, must be quite overwhelming or George would never choose a project so far away. A casino business. Big time money. That's probably part of it. And George asked Roger to manage that part of the business. Probably the biggest profit maker of the whole investment. Roger kept going over and over in his mind if he really wanted to do this. The offer George gave him was better than he could find anywhere in the states, but so far away.

Roger had seen the HR people at GHIC the day before and he had already received a check for his back pay for the last several months. Roger knew why George was being so good to him. Roger, after much thought, decided that maybe a change in scenery was a good idea. He was just ready to call George to accept the Aruba offer when his phone rang. It was his mother and she was crying.

"What's wrong mother?" Asked Roger. "Your father just had a massive heart attack. He was just taken to Lee County Health Park. He is in the emergency room. I'll meet you there." Cried his mother.

Roger didn't know what to say. He knew his father was a little overweight. He had too much fatty food in his diet, never exercised, and had high blood pressure. Roger realized he was just too busy with his life to try to convince his father to change his life style. Roger made it to the emergency room just in time to tell his father he loved him before he passed.

"What happen?" Roger said to the nurse caring for her father.

"This was a massive heart attack." Said the nurse. "Your father came in to the hospital with profuse sweating, cold and clammy skin, labored breathing, his face pale and other parts of his body cyanotic, blue lips and tongue, practically no blood pressure and unable to stay conscious." The nurse continues. "We did everything we could to try to restore a normal heartbeat with an automatic external defibrillator. He was too out of it to give him the necessary drugs to try to restore normal functioning of his heart." The nurse still continued. "The doctor was going to try surgical intervention, but in the doctor's opinion, your father's overall condition was not conducive for it." She finished. "I am so sorry for your loss."

Eugene Spector was a good father to Roger. He did his best to provide everything Roger needed to the best of his physical and financial means. How his father paid for all of his schooling was not a mystery to Roger, but there was not a father Roger knew who did as much for Roger as any other father did for him.

"I am so sorry Mom." Said Roger as he took his mother in his arms and held her.

"What am I going to do now?" cried his mother. "He took care of everything. I would not even know where to start."

"Don't worry, Mom. I'll handle everything." Said the hurting Roger. "Let me talk to the doctor and see where we go from her."

Roger and the resident doctor went into a small office and spoke for a while. Then Martha Spector saw Roger pick up the phone and call someone. He spoke for a while to some unknown person and then hung up. He then resumed talking to the doctor. Roger had called Memorial Gardens Cemetery where both of his parents had purchased cemetery plots years ago. Roger stuck his head out the door and told his mother that arrangements had been made for the cemetery to pick up his father tomorrow morning. They would both go over to the cemetery office to make all the arrangements. Roger was going to go home with his mother and stay with her that night. Then Roger said he had to make another call.

Martha Spector knew she would have to call her sisters, one of whom lived in Portland Oregon, and Cathy Rutter. Martha also knew that her sister in Portland wouldn't come to the service since that sister and Eugene really never got along and they only saw each other once every four or five years. Martha had to be strong. But she knew she had Cathy. However, she and Cathy lived in two different worlds. She had to show Roger she could survive on her own. Other than Cathy, she had no other family and her husband had no siblings and Roger was their only child. But Martha had a large circle of friends. She was involved in a book club, a crafting group who met every Wednesday for crafting classes at The Owl and Pussycat, then they all went out to lunch. They even went to dinner every two or three months. Her friends would help her through this tragedy. After all, several of her many friends had gone through the same thing or even worse. Several had even lost children. Thinking about that helped her keep going that night.

Roger then came out of the office and asked his mother if she had the email address of her crafting friends and book club members. He was going to email them about this tragedy. Roger knew the comfort they all could bring her. But the next day all arrangements had to be made for his father's funeral. He had really never thought about something like this before. He thought about calling his Aunt Cathy, he knew she would help out his mother financially, but they weren't that close otherwise. However, Roger knew Cathy would be there for her over the next few weeks.

It's not like Roger didn't know that something like this would happen someday, but how do you prepare for it. His father was just 76 years old. He was just going to make a call letting George Harvey know he was going to Aruba. Then this happens. But Roger was somewhat confused. His second call was to George Harvey to let him know that he would not be able to leave for Aruba until after his father's funeral and until his mother was ready for him to leave the Country. George said something very unusual to Roger during that call. George told Roger that he wanted to come with him to the funeral home and help him and his mother out with the funeral arrangements. Roger knew why he would say that, but Roger knew that it wouldn't be the best thing for George to do. Roger refused the offer and thanked him for his kindness, but he believed it would better with just Roger and his mother. George understood.

Several minutes later, a nurse came out in the corridor and asked if a Martha Spector was there. The nurse told her there was a call for her and she could take it in the office. Roger was stunned. Who even knew they were there? Martha went into the office and picked up the phone. The door was closed so Roger could not hear the conversation, but he saw his mother crying. They spoke for some time and when his mother came out of the office, Roger asked who that was. Martha said a very good friend. Roger knew who it was, but he let it go.

"Please let's go home so we can get to the funeral home early in the morning. Be sure to email all my girlfriends when we get home, but tell them not to call until tomorrow. I will be all right now." Calmly said Martha.

Roger had no idea what just happened, but they both went home after a good bye kiss to their husband and father. Cathy came to Martha's home that evening, but just stayed for a short time. It was up to Roger to handle matters.

****

Joe Hyland had been working 15 hours a day for the last 18 months and it was almost the end of 2000. The first tower of Largo Del Sol with two floors of garages, 36 residential units between 2500 square feet to 3500 square feet and a penthouse with 6000 square feet was completed. All of the roads and parking areas for all three towers, the required manmade lake for drainage, and all amenities including a huge kidney shaped swimming pool with a large island in the middle, complete with several windmill palms and several spindle palm trees on it, two hot tubs, a 7500 square foot clubhouse with full kitchen, conference room, game room and card room. All complete and all sold out. Joe was happy and the Dutch bank wanted to know when the first closing would occur so they could get paid back.

The loan for the second tower had been closed nearly 6 months ago and that tower was half way complete. Josef and Hagen were having AFC Bank's attorneys draw up the loan documents for the third tower so it could be closed as soon as the second tower was finished. Joe and Leigh had become a couple and the first thing Joe did when the County approved closings for the condominium units in the first tower was to bring Leigh up to the floor just beneath the penthouse unit and told her that Joe and her were moving into the two 3500 square foot units as soon as they furnished them. Joe said it's time for them to really become a couple and move in together. They had been a couple since the day Cathy Rutter hired her as Joe's assistant. Joe had known Leigh for a few years before when he worked for GHIC and Leigh was selling real estate. They went out a few times but never exclusively. Joe had several young ladies he would take out, from time to time, or on occasion, a weekend vacation to the East coast of Florida. Joe's favorite place in South Beach was Lowes Resort right on Ocean Drive in South Beach. He loved to frequent Prime 112 and China Grill since they had the best food and wonderful people watching. He loved to hob nob with the famous and wealthy. Joe did not like to spare any expense. Joe's expense account was quite large. Josef made sure of that. Bram, Josef's assistant, did not appreciate that since he had to account for the funds to the bank each month, but Josef controlled the money strings and Bram went along. Leigh was just one of those lucky ladies, but so was Ivana. Leigh never appreciated the fact that Ivana and Joe went out from time to time. But once she came to work for Joe at his real estate company, everything changed.

"Why are we going to live in two units? Asked Leigh.

"These two units are part of my profits and I won't even claim them to the IRS. Also, I want to have you decorate yours any way you want, so you can enjoy your side. I'll have mine decorated as a man cave. I need a pool table, several big TV's, several refrigerators, one for beer only and a huge bar!" gleamed Joe. "We will only cut a door between the two. I don't want to make them one big condo. In a few years, we will sell them and build a huge house on the River." Said Joe. "So get your decorator and send me the bills. I will get Cathy to put them in one of the draws to the Bank for the next tower."

"Sounds good to me." Gleamed Leigh. "Well, we'll just let the games begin."

"Your right." Said Joe. "We are going to start rolling in money. Josef knows how to play this system for all of us."

Ivana was furious!

On the way back to the corporate office from the happy couples new love den, they met Bram as they were walking in the office.

Bram was in Florida to check on the Largo Del Sol project for Josef. He needed to make sure that Joe was on the timetable that had been set for the project. No problem with the construction time table, but the mangrove issue was stuck with a hearing officer for the Lee County Board of Commissioners.

There has been excessive opposition to the trimming of the mangroves. There are two contradicting reports on the effects of the trimming. One is written by Hyland's development company's environmentalist and the other by an environmental group who oppose everything dealing with the echo system of the Caloosahatchee River. A hearing is being set in a couple of months. Each side will have its chance to testify as to their positions. The purchasers of tower two units and the new owners in tower one units are furious that this issue has not been resolved yet. They were all told by the sales staff, both for Riverview and Largo Del Sol, that the mangroves will be trimmed to give them the maximum view of the River. Luckily, so far, it has not stopped sales. All of Tower two is sold out. There are non-binding reservations for all units in tower three waiting for binding purchase contracts. Bram knew that Josef would not be happy about the mangrove issue.

But Bram was in town for two other very important matters.

First, Josef had heard about the last non-platted parcel of property located in Cape Coral, just across the Caloosahatchee River from Fort

Myers and at the mouth of the Gulf of Mexico. It consisted of 175 acres. The original owner of the property was one of the original developers of Cape Coral in 1957.

Cape Coral began when two brothers, the Rosen brothers, flew over the peninsula of Florida known, at that time, as Redfish Point. The brothers spent two weeks flying around Southwest Florida looking for land to develop. Flying over what would become Cape Coral, Leonard, one of the brothers, tossed some coins out of the window of the plane. They later found the coins, and that was the place where both brothers decided to start their venture to fix up Redfish Point. The development started so fast that the area didn't know what hit it. They changed the wilderness into a waterfront paradise, a place for selling and buying dreams. The brothers formed the Gulf American Corporation which developed Cape Coral. It became the largest master-planned community in the United States. The Rosen's platted most all of the land, put canals everywhere so most everyone who built a home on a lot would be on water so that the buyers could take their boats out to the Gulf of Mexico. The Rosen's sold lots so fast, they couldn't keep up with the amenities needed to keep the city, with the most acreage in Florida, active. Gulf American Company owned some land on the River that was not platted. That company provided a boat and gasoline every Sunday so Cape Coral residents could go water skiing. Another way the Rosen's drew crowds to Cape Coral was with the famous "Rose Gardens", which open in 1964. The Waltzing Waters, Porpoise Pool, Rose Gardens, Aloha Lagoon and Pavilion of Patriots entertained prospects and residents for six years until it just got too expensive to maintain. So the Rosen's sold that entertainment land, of about 175 acres, to General Acceptance Corporation, a finance firm from Pennsylvania. At the time of the sale, the brothers had been accused of dirty sales practices, for which a history of Cape Coral may show that the accusations were really politically motivated. Be that as it may, that same year, the community incorporated and became the City of Cape Coral. General Acceptance Corporation did not have the vision that the Rosen's had and the rising costs, declining land sales, and other problems caused General Acceptance Corporation to go into bankruptcy. The company that purchased the "Rose Garden" property out of bankruptcy, Fairfield Properties, Inc. was now, 30 plus years later, selling the most expensive parcel of real estate left in the City of Cape Coral for $35 million.

Josef was fascinated. Cape Coral was a bedroom community in 2001. By purchasing this parcel, a development of a mixed use project could be built with high end high rise condominium, a large first class hotel with a convention center and substantial commercial retail space with several fancy restaurants. With a proposed density of at least 2200 residential units, a very large profit could be made. As a bonus, there was already a 275 slip marina, fuel tanks for boats, and a small restaurant that was part of the property. That meant whoever purchased the property would already have some income while they were developing the property. Bram was in Florida to meet with representatives of the owners of the parcel to try to put a Letter of Intent together so that Joe Hyland's development company could incorporate another entity to develop the "Rose Garden" property. A perfect parcel of property for Joe Hyland's development company to start their next project. Also a perfect development for another loan from AFC Bank. And the larger the loan, the more excess money could be added to the loan for "pre-paid profits" for Hagen and Josef. With money not a problem, it didn't take long for Bram to have a short two page non-binding Letter of Intent completed by "a company to be formed" as the buyer and Fairfield Properties, Inc. as the seller for $35 million.

Bram had completed his first task he came to Florida to accomplish. He gave the Letter of Intent to Joe Hyland and asked Joe to give it to his lawyer, Brian Koop, to draw up a complete purchase agreement with a 150 day 'free look period' so the property could be tied up and Joe could hire the necessary professionals to evaluate all the necessary elements for developing the mixed use development as Josef had anticipated.

The second task Bram was requested to do was to deliver a document to Joe Hyland to give to his lawyer, Brian Kopp. This document was to be put it in Koop's firms safe. The document was drawn up by Hagen Vinke and Josef Rynsburger.

"What is this document, Bram?" Asked Joe.

"I really don't know." Answered Bram. "Josef just gave it to me with strict instructions to have your lawyer put it in his firm's safe."

"The manila folder isn't even sealed. You must have looked at it and read it?" Said Joe.

"I learned a long time ago, not to do things like that. I like my job with Josef. When I am told to do something, I do it. Sometimes I am not really sure I want to do everything Josef requests, but, that's the job" Answered Bram.

"Why my lawyers safe?" asked Joe again. "Why not his law firm's safe?

Joe just got a shrug from Bram. So Joe, the curious person he was, opened the manila folder, took out the document and looked at it. It was written in Dutch. Joe wouldn't be able to read it even if he wanted to. So Joe agreed. How could it hurt? But in the back of Joe's mind, he had the feeling that this was the agreement between Hagen and Josef as to how certain excess funds from each of the loans for all of the developments would be divide up between the two of them. That would be how Josef's longtime friend, Hagan Vinke, got his kick back on each loan. Joe couldn't know this for sure, but Joe was not naïve, he saw how Josef, who came from a meager background, and Hagen lived. They were making money somewhere in addition to what was coming out of the development loans. Joe was a 50% owner and he was making a good salary, but not the type of money to purchase the types of automobiles and homes and entertain like Josef and Hagen. In fact, Hagen was not even supposed to be making any money off these loans. He just approved them as chairman of the foreign loan committee and President of the bank. Joe didn't believe that he was doing anything wrong, so Joe just honored Josef's request.

The next day, Joe dropped in on Brian Koop at Koop's office. Joe was always welcome there without appointment. He brought in so much work for the firm, he knew half the lawyers in the Fort Myers office. Joe told Brian about the Letter of Intent for the Cape Coral property and asked him to draft a Purchase Agreement for the property.

"You got to be kidding, you haven't even finished the Largo Del Sol project, and you still have to close the loan on the third tower?" Questioned Brian. "And you're buying the most expensive parcel of property in Cape Coral, at the asking price of $35 million?"

"Yes and expect a rough draft of the loan documents from the Banks attorney in about 3 weeks. The loan will be for $45 million." Said Joe. "I spoke with Josef and he believes they need the extra money for environmental investigation, soil tests, your lawyer's fees, fees for the land use attorney to discuss the density and mixed use, zoning for the property with the Cape Coral City attorney, for the engineer to plat the property, etc., etc."

"But $10 million extra?" said Brian surprisingly.

"Yes." Said Joe. "And by the way, when you draw up the purchase agreement, Josef wants the new company you're going to form, to purchase the corporate stock from the entity that owns the property, Fairfield Properties, Inc. We are not buying the real property. We are purchasing the corporation stock."

"Are you all nuts?' said Brian. "That corporation has been around for over 30 years. You have no idea what problems exist with the company. They may have IRS problems, employee problems, and unknown liabilities for a million different matters. No one buys a 30 year old corporation. They just buy the assets of the company." Said Brian further and with force.

"This will save us almost a half a million dollars in transfer tax." Said Joe. "And by the way, the name of the company that is buying the corporation is Snook Point Development Company, LLC."

"At some point, Joe, you are going to have to transfer the real property into Snook Point Development Company, LLC, and then you will have to pay the transfer tax at that time." Advised Brian. "And, oh by the way, do you want me to charge you by the hour or by the pound for this purchase agreement?" jokingly said Brian.

"Funny man. You know our arrangement, and as for the transfer tax, let Josef take care of that. His attorney says he has a way to avoid the transfer tax completely." Retorted Joe.

Brian had been practicing Florida real estate law for over 20 years and had no idea how the transfer tax was going to be avoided. He was also very leery about purchasing the corporation instead of the property. But Joe was the client. Brian thought to himself that he will just write a letter to Joe confirming everything about this conversation and copy Josef's attorney at the same time. Maybe that may bring them around to reality. It would also cover Brian and his firm's butt!

In Brian's mind, he wasn't quite sure how Joe and Josef were getting all of this credit for these loans and especially with no capital being put up by the borrowers for any of the projects. But in all of Brian's years of practice, he has seen almost everything. And this client is adding to his 'first time seen that' list.

Just before Joe was to leave he turned to Brian and said, "Oh, by the way, here is a manila folder with some documents in it. Please put this in your safe under my general file."

"What is it?" asked Brian.

"I have no idea, it's in Dutch." Said Joe. "Just keep it there until Josef or I ask you for it. OK?"

This was not a problem for Brian. He kept documents for a lot of his clients in the firm safe. So with no further discussion, the original of some agreement between Josef and Hagen was hidden in the safe of a third party lawyer. No one except Josef Rynsburger and Hagen Vinke knew what the agreement was about or what the terms were.

And no one would.

CHAPTER 10

DENISE WAITED A week, until September 12, 2013, for Catty Rutter's attorney to call her to arrange a meeting to discuss Hyland's death and his development companies. So Denise, a little upset with Cathy Rutter's lack of cooperation, reluctantly called Cathy Rutter at her home and asked when her attorney would be calling for the meeting. Cathy, also distraught about all these interviews, also reluctantly said she would have him call her that day. Just after noon, Brian Koop called Denise and said that, his client Cathy Rutter, had asked him to call Denise.

"You know what this is about" angrily said Denise. "When the hell are we getting together to discuss Joe Hyland?"

"Do you mean discuss Cathy Rutter?" retorted Brian.

"We need to discuss both and possibly other unknown people." Said Denise.

"This may be a short meeting." Said Brian.

"Whatever, however, we need to do this. We need to try and wrap this matter up." Said Denise.

"OK. How about tomorrow morning at 9:30 in my office. It's just several blocks from your office." Said Brian.

"I'll be there." Huffed Denise.

Then she hung up.

Over 4 weeks after Joe Hyland's funeral, Denise Hudak, Brian Koop and Cathy Rutter met at Koop's office. When they all went into the large conference room, Koop's assistant brought in coffee, water and some sweets. Denise started to talk and Brian interrupted her.

"Denise, before you start this interview, I just want to make sure that everyone in the room understands my presence here." Started Brian. "I have been Joe Hyland's lawyer for about 14 years. I represented him personally and I represented all of his corporate interests. I am not a criminal attorney. I have represented Cathy individually on several occasions for specific real estate transactions and some civil legal advice. Since she was the financial assistant to Hyland for all of Hyland's companies, I would be representing those companies and Cathy, as her or their interests appear. If it turns out, which I don't believe will happen, Cathy needs criminal advice, then this interview will be over. Does everyone understand that?" Asked Brian.

Both Denise and Cathy acknowledged that fact to Brian.

Denise started the conversation by summing up what had happen in relation to Cathy since Joe Hyland's death. Denise indicated that it was her understanding that the day after the funeral, Luke Blakely, a Lee County detective, came to her house and spoke with her and her husband, William. Luke had a subpoena for your financials, but the conversation only lasted a short time and no real substance came out of that meeting.

"Is that correct so far Ms. Rutter?" asked Denise.

"Yes." Replied Cathy.

Denise then went on and indicated that several days later, Cathy and her lawyer, Mr. Koop, met with Detective Blakely at the County Sheriff's office. There Cathy gave the detective a timeline of how she moved to Fort Myers to work for Wells Fargo Bank as a loan officer. Denise also indicated that Cathy's husband only lives full time in Southwest Florida for about three to four months a year. The rest of the time he resides on his family ranch in Montana. While Cathy is a full time resident in Southwest Florida she does travel to Montana from time to time. That while working for Wells Fargo, Cathy had the occasion to handle some loans for individuals who were purchasing residential homes and condominium in The Riverview Golf & Country Club. In the course of working on those loans, Cathy meet Joe Hyland and Roger Spector, two of the sales managers for the development. Cathy worked with both Joe and Roger multiple times on various loans."

"Wait, Cathy Rutter did not initially meet Roger Spector at Riverview." Interrupted Brian. "Cathy is Roger's Aunt. He had known her for a long time."

"Oh. I didn't know that." Said Denise. "But that is good to know."

Denise then went on. "Mrs. Rutter even had an occasion to meet the owner of GHIC, the developer of the project, George Harvey."

Denise thought these meetings happened somewhere in the neighborhood of 1997 or 1998. Sometime after those encounters Cathy and Roger Spector and Joe Hyland meet privately to discuss the fact that Roger and Joe were in the process of possibly starting a new development company. They would be going out on their own and develop a condominium project. Mrs. Rutter was also under the impression that when the new development company was finalized and Roger and Joe separated from GHIC and all of the 'I's had been dotted and all of the 'T's were crossed, that Roger and Joe wanted Cathy to quit her job with the Bank and go to work with them in some financial capacity such as a COO or CFO. In fact, less than a year later, that is what happen.

"So far so good?" asked Denise.

"Kind of. First, this all happen 10 to 12 years ago. I cannot remember the exact dates. Second, I was never an officer of director of any of the companies except some of the condominium associations. I was a financial assistant to Joe Hyland for all of the development companies only. Not his real estate company nor did I do any financial matters with any of the condominium associations." Answered Cathy.

"I understand." Replied Denise.

Denise continued to summarize the last meeting with Luke Blakely. After that point in the conversation, Luke started to ask Cathy some questions about her finances and how her net worth was in the neighborhood of $10 million. Denise's recollection of the notes on the conversation was that Cathy gave information as to quite a few real estate transactions that she had completed over a several year period beginning after she started to work for Roger and Joe's development companies. Denise's recollection was that William Rutter, Cathy's husband, put up the original funds for Cathy's first real estate purchase and after that no more money was transferred from her husband to

Cathy for future investments. Cathy and her husband made several millions of dollars flipping homes during the real estate boom. Between the value of the funds that Cathy and her husband earned on their flipping business and including Cathy's husbands assets, the net worth of Cathy and William Rutter grew to just under $10 million. After that conversation, then Luke began some questions about Cathy's work at Joe and Roger's development company. At that point the interview stopped since Cathy's attorney indicated that was not part of the subpoena that was served on her.

"Did I summarize it as you remember it Ms. Rutter?" asked Denise.

"Yes, with the exceptions I mentioned." Answered Cathy.

"Good. Let's continue from there." Said Denise. There is no subpoena involved in this interview. You have complied with the subpoena that was served on you concerning your finances. We have reviewed your information and find it all to be credible." Continued Denise. What I would like to discuss first is you relationship with Roger Spector." Asked Denise.

"He is my Nephew. He decided that he no longer wanted to be a partner or employee of the new development company very early on." Said Cathy. "He was there one day and the next day he was gone. I was asked by Joe to contact Brian Koop to draft the paper work to take Roger off as an officer and director of The Traverse City Development Company, Inc. and Traverse City Real Estate, LLC; cancel the Operating agreement for both those companies; and draw up an Agreement for separation of the relationship between Joe Hyland and Roger Spector for all matters dealing with those companies."

"Do you know who the original officers and directors of those two companies were?"

"Yes." Said Cathy.

"Who were they? Asked Denise.

"All that information is in the public records in the Florida Secretary of State's office." Said Cathy.

"I know that, but would you please tell me anyway? Asked Denise.

"Joe Hyland and Roger Spector were directors. Joe Hyland was the President and Treasure. Roger Spector was the Vice President and Secretary." Said Cathy.

"After Roger Spector left the companies, who became the officers and directors? Asked Denise.

"All in the public records." Said Cathy.

"But would you please tell me anyway? Asked Denise.

"Joe Hyland became the only officer and only director. Of both companies." Said Cathy.

"Did you ever become an officer or director of any of those companies? Asked Denise.

"No. I helped with the financial information for the companies." Answered Cathy.

"Where is this going?" asked Brian Koop.

"Just some preliminaries before we get into some of the real meat of the interview." Said Denise.

Let's get to what you are really looking for. This is not a formal deposition, Ms. Rutter is here as a curtesy." Said Brian.

"OK." Said Denise.

"Ms. Rutter, do you know where Roger Spector is today?" Asked Denise.

"Yes." Said Cathy.

"Where is that? "Asked Denise.

"None of your business." Answered Cathy.

"Do you know how much money, if any was paid to Roger Spector to leave the Development and Real Estate Company?" Asked Denise.

"No, as far as I know there was a confidentiality clause in the Agreement signed by Hyland and Roger. Also that was over 12 years ago." Answered Cathy.

"Cathy, just answer the questions, don't offer up any other information." Advised Brian.

"After Roger left the companies, who were the owners of those two companies?" asked Denise.

"Joe Hyland." Answered Denise.

"Who was the broker who qualified the real estate company?" Asked Denise.

"Public Records! But it was Laura Wills." Answered Cathy.

"Was Joe Hyland a broker in the real estate company, or was he even a sales person?" Asked Denise.

"No." said Cathy.

"Again, where are you going with this line of questions? So far this is all a waste of time. Everything you asked could have been found in the public records. And I am sure you have already done that." Said Brian a little annoyed. "Either ask what you have come here to ask or let's all go on with our lives."

"OK Brian, let's do that." Angrily said Denise.

"Ms. Rutter, how many developments was Traverse City Development, Inc. involved with? And what were the names of those developments? Asked Denise

"I don't remember, there were too many companies to remember them all." Answered Cathy.

"I don't understand your answer. I am not asking you to name every company that was formed by Joe Hyland for purpose of cable TV services, utility installation services, management services, consultation services, etc. and etc." Said Denise. I am only asking you, as financial advisor for Traverse City Development Company, Inc., how many real estate developments was Travers City Development Company, Inc. involved in where residential homes or condominium, or commercial lots were platted and sold, or condominium, whether residential or commercial were constructed and sold or residential homes were constructed and sold or commercial buildings or hotels were constructed and sold or rented, etc.?" explained Denise.

"I believe there were 5 real estate developments that Traverse City was involved with." Answered Cathy.

"Can you name them for me and tell me where they were located? Aske Denise.

"The first one was Largo Del Sol. It was a high rise residential condominium project located in The Riverview Golf & Country Club.

The second was Snook Point Development. That was a large mixed use project located in Cape Coral.

The third was Coconut Cove Park. That was a large low rise and duplex condominium project located in South Fort Myers.

The forth was International Capital Park. It was a large mixed use project located in Orlando.

The fifth was Hidden Woods. A large platted development for residential homes. It was located just outside Orlando." Answered Cathy.

"Was there not a sixth real estate project?" asked Denise.

"It was not a real estate project, it was Alico Grand Mine which was a mining business. It is located in South Fort Myers." Answered Cathy.

"How were each of these six projects structured?" asked Denise.

"Don't know. Answered Cathy.

"Yes you do, please explain the structure to me. Asked Denise.

"She said she didn't know. Move on." Said Brian.

"She knows, Brian. Ms. Rutter, do you know how many loans were obtained for all of these six projects?" Asked Denise.

"I can't remember." Answered Cathy.

"Where there 6, or where there 20, where there 100? Any ballpark number?" Asked Denise.

"A lot." Said Cathy.

"From which banks were the loans for each of the 6 developments obtained? You can go through the developments one at a time. "Asked Denise.

"There was only one bank involved in all six of the developments." Answered Cathy. It was AFC Bank from The Netherlands. They were located in Amsterdam."

"How many loan officers did you or anyone else from the development companies deal with on each of the developments, or were there more than one loan officer for each of the developments?" Asked Denise.

"Just one for every loan for every development. His name was Hagen Vinke. He was the Senior Loan Officer for foreign loans. He was also the President of the Bank" Answered Cathy.

"Where you and or anyone else involved in putting together the monthly draw requests for the loans for these projects?" asked Denise.

"Yes." Answered Cathy.

"You and who else?" asked Denise.

"I finalized the draw requests. Lots of people were involved in determining what funds were needed each month for each loan. "Answered Cathy.

"What did the draws consist of? And I mean by that, when you put together these requests, what were the purposes of the funds you were requesting to be used in each development? And who did you send the request to? "Asked Denise.

"Each request was different and had different uses for the funds. Each request went to one person, Hagen Vinke. No exceptions" Answered Cathy.

"Where there any specific purposes for the use of the requested funds which were always in every one of the requests?" asked Denise.

"What are you trying to find out here? Asked Brian Koop.

"The question is straight forward, no tricks." Said Denise.

"Here is where we stop." Said Brian. "If you want any more answers about the loans and or preparation of draws or uses of the funds from each of the draws, Ms. Rutter will require full immunity for any criminal matters, including criminal conspiracies involved in preparing the draw requests, and the distribution of the funds received by the Bank for such requests and any other matters dealing with these 6 projects. This is not to say that Ms. Rutter did any criminal acts or was a conspirator in any criminal acts, but this is a requirement for her to discuss any further, the draws and funds received concerning the 6 projects." Requested Brian. "Talk to your boss and to the FBI and get the immunity in written form so I can have a criminal lawyer review them. You can send the immunity forms to me here at my office."

"Wow where did that come from?" Denise uttered confused.

"From Ms. Rutter's attorney." Said Brian.

"OK, I'll speak with my boss and get back with you on that issue. Ms. Rutter. Do you know a Josef Rynsburger?" Asked Denise.

"Same request. Include Mr. Rynsburger in the immunity agreement." Requested Koop.

"Have you heard of the companies, Rynsburger, LLC? Or Rynsburger/Traverse City/SLS investments, LLC." Asked Denise.

"Again the same request. This interview is over. The more you ask, the more I will require to be in the immunity agreement. Cathy don't say another word."

Denise did not argue, but now Denise was convinced something had been happening with the money from the loans for Joe Hyland's developments. What it was, she wasn't quite sure. She had a theory, but was not quite sure she would discuss it with anyone without further investigation. Denise had heard about the suspicious deaths of Hagen Vinke in 2009 just as AFC Bank was being purchased by a larger bank. She also knew about the suspicious death of Josef Rynsburger in 2011. Both of their death certificates were signed by Dr. Nicolaus Timmerman. So were the death certificates of each of their wives. As Alex Terian always says, 'I don't believe in coincidences'. Who is this Doctor? More to investigate. This all started as a no where to go investigation of a drunk named Joe Hyland, and now Denise is not sure what in the world really happen to Hyland and all of the others who died in this twisted probe dealing with well over $1 billion.

Denise was cordial when she left Brian Kopp's office and thanked Cathy Rutter her for her cooperation.

As soon as she left, she called Alex and told him what had just happen. Alex said that Arthur was on his way back to Fort Myers and will be in the office the next day. Alex suggested that they all get together after lunch tomorrow to discuss what has been uncovered and what still needs to be investigated. This matter has too many roads to follow without any real end game here. It's time to ratchet it up and see what falls out.

After Denise hung up with Alex, the name Roger Spector came to her mind. Where does he fit into this? Why did he leave the development company? Why won't Rutter tell her where her nephew is? Why doesn't anyone else know where he is? Does George Harvey have anything to do with this? After some thought, Denise dismissed her thoughts on George Harvey. How could he be involved? However, given what has surfaced so far, maybe he is involved?

****

About 5 weeks after the death of Eugene Spector, Roger Spector went to the main office of GHIC to speak with George Harvey. Roger had been receiving weekly paychecks from GHIC in the mail at his mother's house. He had given up his last apartment where he was living while he working with Joe Hyland. It was on a month to month lease. He had left no forwarding address and did not change his mailing address at the local post office. Roger moved in with his mother until she was ready to live on her own. Roger was amazed at how quickly his mother was adjusting to her new life. But he thought that maybe it was because he was there and he was handling all of the necessary details for the survivor of the death of a spouse. Also, his Aunt Cathy Rutter would come by several times a week to spend time with his mother. The time Roger spent with his mother also gave Roger time to think about what he wanted to do with his life. Aruba sounded more fascinating as the days went by. A whole new start. A whole new vocation and one that is quite intriguing. Since George has been so good to him, he also thought that someday he may be able to come and work for George at one of his real estate developments. He knew he couldn't get a sales license in Florida, and probably any other states since he didn't want anyone looking into his past records for his sales and broker licenses. So Roger thought he would speak with George and make some kind of final determination.

George was in a meeting when Roger arrived and George's assistant told him it would be just a while. During the time he was waiting for George, Roger was thinking about his father's funeral. It was just a grave side service. His father requested that type of funeral, as well as a pine box. His father was practical and didn't want his family to spend a fortune on a funeral. What a waste of money. There were about 40 or so people attending the funeral. His parent's minister said some nice words about his father, but they all came from him and his mother. The minister really didn't know Eugene well. They attended church only on major holidays. But one thing that stood out was when Roger looked behind him from the front row at the graveside, he saw George Harvey. He didn't think much of it at the time, but it was a nice gesture for a busy man to come to the funeral of the father of someone who quit his job with the man's company. But yet, George has been more than accommodating since Roger quit. It did make him think about George in a whole new light. Most people do nice things to advance things for themselves. What is it that George Harvey may want now that Roger's father has died? Was he going to tell Roger that he was Roger's biological father? Or was he really just being a nice man?

Then George came out of his office and asked Roger to come into his office.

"How are you and your mother doing, Roger?" Asked George. "I am really glad you decided to come and see me today."

"Actually, my mother is getting along very well under the circumstances. She has a large circle of woman friends, many of them widows also." Answered Roger. "My father had seemed to take good care of my mother financially which was really a surprise to me. I had no idea how much insurance he had. My mother told me he purchased it when he retired from work. Five hundred thousand dollars as well as his pension. And with my father's social security, my mother can live better than me."

"I am glad to hear that.' Replied George. "Have you thought about what you may want to do in the future and whether you may be interested in my offer in Aruba?"

"In the last couple of weeks, that is all I have been thinking about." Replied Roger.

George then started to go over all of the terms of the Aruba employment including where he would stay, his expense account, his schooling for the casino job, his salary, which shocked Roger, his on the job training, at another casino owned by one of the partners in the Wyndham project. Most important the fact that he would be given a stipend for a flight home every 120 days for Roger to see his mother for 3 days. George really wanted him to take this position.

Roger was overwhelmed by the information and also thanked George for the money while he was staying with his mother. Roger really felt obligated. Then Roger thanked George for coming to his father's funeral. Roger knew he and his parents were acquaintances, and Roger knew why. But, still, that was really going out of his way.

Roger said he would take the job. George asked when he thought he would be able to travel to Aruba, with the caveat that he shouldn't go until he was sure his mother was going to be alright. George would have arrangements made for his two bedroom condominium to be ready for him and he would have use of a company car. George told him that in Aruba, there weren't many fancy cars so the car was a few years old with a few dings, but the way people drive there, there will be more dings before he gets another one.

Roger was just overwhelmed and told George he would start in a couple of weeks and he would call George's assistant when he was ready to leave. George brought up one unpleasant subject. George asked Roger if he had seen or spoken to Joe Hyland since his father's death. Roger told him no and he wasn't interested in seeing him again. George indicated that Joe was at the funeral, but he never got out of his car. He was with Josef Rynsburger and his assistant Bram. George wanted to make sure that Roger had signed all of the necessary papers so Roger and Joe were legally completely finished. Also, George wanted to make sure that Roger had received his $50,000.00 consideration. Roger said all of the legal matters were complete and he had received his money. Roger had also heard that the development at Largo Del Sol was doing very well, but there may still be problems with the mangrove situation. George confirmed Roger's facts. George said that Joe will be having a hard time with that mangrove situation and he wouldn't be surprised to see his development company and sales people get sued by some of the buyers. George said he had his pulse on the situation. Roger knew what that meant.

One last strange matter came up during Roger's meeting. George asked Roger if he had ever heard of a Dr. Nicolaus Timmerman. Roger found that quite unusual.

"No, never heard of the man. Who is he?" Asked Roger.

"I received a call about a week ago from the doctor. He was in town for a reunion of his medical school. He is from the same town as Josef in the Netherlands. He went to undergraduate school at University of Virginia and then Medical school at University of Miami. The reunion was at the Sanibel Hilton Resort. He said only about 30 showed up. Tough getting older. You lose them quickly. He said that he had heard that Josef Rynsburger had done business with me at several of my developments." George continued. "The doctor asked if I had ever had any problems with him in my dealings. The doctor said he and Josef's family were close and that he and Josef went into the real estate business together some years ago. Josef said he needed some capital and he could make a lot of money for them both. The doctor could continue his medical practice and Josef would take care of the business and keep the doctor fully appraised of what was going on. Josef assured the doctor he would get all of his investment back many times over."

What is this all about? I remember Josef Rynsburger. I worked with him when he purchased some units in Riverview." Said Roger. "Actually, I was the one who introduced Joe to Rynsburger when we started the development company for Largo Del Sol. I thought Rynsburger was more of a friend to me than Joe, but I was very mistaken."

"The doctor was suspicious about what Josef was doing with the money that the doctor gave him for down payments and other funds for various matters with the properties in their partnership. So the doctor finally asked Josef to dissolve the partnership. He told Josef that he was getting older and wanted to just concentrate on his medical business. They sold the properties and went their own way. However, they have stayed somewhat friendly since that time." Said George. "The doctor had his accountant hire a forensic accountant to see why his portion of the final distribution of funds were not anywhere in the neighborhood he should have received considering the way the properties were flourishing."

What happen? "Asked Roger.

"There was some deception going on. Josef has a best friend who is the President of a Bank in Amsterdam and also on the loan committee at the bank." George looked somewhat somber. "Josef told the doctor that they were getting 70% loans on the rental properties and the doctor was funding the 30% difference. In fact, the Bank was giving Josef a 100% loan and the President and Josef were splitting the difference. Josef used the rent to pay the inflated loan payments. Sometimes Josef was short and would ask the doctor for additional funds to be used to fix something on the properties, but he really needed the money to pay the inflated loan payments."

'You got to be kidding. And Joe is this man's partner?" said Roger. "And I worked with him on purchasing real estate here in Fort Myers?"

"The doctor just wanted to warn me about Josef and that I should be careful since he is always looking for investors for some sort of deal."

George assured Roger that he was going to keep an eye on Josef and Joe's investments and see what happens to these developments. George always really liked Joe, but George was certain that Josef found a real sucker. Joe likes money and if Josef keeps Joe just flush enough to keep his eyes off the ball, Josef and his banker friend will rob Joe blind. Josef was lucky that the doctor didn't want to pursue the matter. The doctor didn't want any publicity and really didn't' need the money. George really liked Joe, but was just upset as to the manner Joe dismissed Roger from their new development. As it turns out, Roger is lucky not to be involved.

This is the reason, George wanted Roger to move to Aruba. George knew it was a good idea to keep Roger's location as quite as possible. George did not want Josef coming around Roger, and moving Roger to Aruba, at least for some time, would solve that problem. George believed that Josef was scary! George felt bad for Joe, he knew it was Rynsburger's idea to toss Roger out of the developments. George was happy Roger agreed to take the Aruba job so as to keep Roger away from Josef and Hyland, at least for now.

George wished Roger luck over the next several weeks in getting his mother use to Roger's new vocation. But George would always make sure Mabel was never without what she needed.

****

Since the beginning of 2001, after Leigh had her condo completely decorated by Robb & Stucky, the best known and most expensive designer group in the area, things had been good for Leigh. Joe's condo furnishings, other than a bedroom, was going a little slower. Joe arranged for the contractor finishing tower 2 at Largo Del Sol to cut the doorway through the two condos. A beautiful 8 foot door was installed. It never closed. Joe and Leigh were going out to dinner almost every night to the best restaurants and clubs in the area so Joe could keep a high profile in both Fort Myers and Cape Coral. The couple never missed their Saturday night at the Red Lion Business Club. Bob, the bartender took very good care of them and their guests.

At the main office, Leigh and Cathy were eating breakfast almost every morning together as well as lunch every day. They must have kept the Juicy Lucy's on San Carlos Drive profitable every month. When Joe had business meetings or dinners at night, Cathy and Leigh went to their favorite bar and restaurant, The Half Time Lounge, just around the corner from the office. Joe was very busy finishing tower 2 and starting tower 3 for Largo Del Sol; working with his attorneys at Brian Kopp's firm on arguments for the hearing with the Lee County hearing officials on the mangrove issue; listening to Brian Koop's issues with the loan documents for the purchase of Fairfield Properties, Inc., the owner of the Snook Point property in Cape Coral; and working with architects and engineers on the platting and design for Snook Point. The Letter of Intent given to Brian Kopp to draft the Purchase Agreement was completed and executed by all parties. Snook Point Development Company, LLC was formed and the usual ownership interests were prepared by Koop's law firm.

Josef was coming to Fort Myers almost every six to eight weeks to check on the progress of the developments and Bram usually came with him. Sometimes Bram came by himself to represent Josef's interest. The entire Southwest Florida business community was talking about how this new developer, Traverse City Development Company, LLC was in the process of finishing a 111 condominium unit project in The Riverview Golf & Country Club and now they were purchasing the last large parcel of developable commercial and mixed use property in Cape Coral for $35 million. Where did these people come from? The community was fascinated.

Joe finally delegated to Cathy the task of finishing the decorations for Joe's condo. Not that she didn't have enough, but since Leigh and Joe became so close, Cathy was taking on more responsibility to take care of Joe's calendar including business dinner arrangements. Leigh was doing more shopping than working, but Cathy really didn't mind. Most of the time her husband was in Montana and she loved to work. Cathy knew exactly what Joe wanted in his condo and between Cathy and Leigh, the unit was finished in 4 weeks. Joe loved it. Pool table, foosball table, large U shaped bar and lots of large televisions. Even Leigh didn't mind eating there, sometimes. But most of the time it was full of contractors and construction supervisors, drinking beer, playing pool and just hanging out. Leigh understood why Joe wanted separate condos.

Joe did make time for at least two trips a week to the sales office for Traverse Realty to check on his realty company. Sales were good for tower 3 at Largo Del Sol and Reservation Agreements were being finalized for the first condominium project at Snook Point for 31 four plexus amounting to 124 condominium units along with the platting of 45 single family residential home sites. Preferred builder contracts were being drafted for potential builders to bid on the right to be able to build homes in Snook Point. The sales people were very busy promoting both projects with the thought of commissions dancing in their heads. Laura Wells, the broker was completely in charge and Joe was very happy with her performance and the people she hired. Every time Joe showed up at the sales office, Ivana Hollings was always there. It was if she knew when he was going to be coming. Everyone could see a little flirtation between the two of them, but Leigh was Joe's girl. That is what everyone at the office knew, except for maybe Ivana.

Once the $45 million loan was closed on the purchase of the corporate stock for the Snook Point property, Joe put on a grand opening event to end all events. Cape Coral had never seen such a party. On the location where the hotel would be built someday, 6 large tents were erected and at 6:30 PM one evening a group of nearly 650 people, mostly real estate sales people, contractors, builders and attorneys showed up. But many curious individuals who lived in Cape Coral were there just out of fascination. There was an open bar, appetizers overflowing and a 6 piece band. The Mayor of Cape Coral made his entrance by helicopter about 7:30. Speeches were made by Joe and the Mayor. Snook point was now the new cornerstone for Cape Coral. Everything about the party went perfect. Cathy Rutter made all the arrangements. She was getting better and better running Joe's business every day. Leigh was the star of the evening in her new Versace dress she purchase in South Beach. Joe was in heaven. Ivana hated it! Joe Rynsburger and Hagen Vinke attended the gala and looked around the property and thought, besides the acquisition loan for the property that just closed, there would be at least 8 more substantial loans for sub-developments on the Snook Point property. Life was going to be good!

About three months after the gala, Josef and Bram were in Fort Myers together when they came upon an 85 acre of unimproved property in the middle of South Fort Myers, just 2 miles south of The Bell Tower Shopping Center on the main road through Fort Myers on U.S. 41. Josef asked Albert White, his attorney, to look into the uses for the property. It was determined that it was zoned residential and had a density for just under 500 multiunit residential units. Josef asked Bram to stay on in Fort Myers, after he went back to consult with Hagen. Bram was to negotiate a Letter of Intent to purchase the property at whatever the asking price was. The usual 150 day free look period would be part of the agreement to tie up the property while Brian Koop, the architects and engineers could do what was needed to make sure the property was feasible for building 500 condominium units. Josef did contact Hyland before he left Fort Myers to tell him another project was coming soon. Largo Del Sol was about six months from completion, Snook Point was at least a ten year build out and now another 500 unit project. Joe thought this was crazy, but, as he was always told by Josef, 'money was not a problem'. All Joe had to do was take the responsibility to manage the construction and day to day operations for the developments and sell the units. He would become wealthy. And he was. Josef and Hagen would be very, very wealthy, with just a little deception!

After Hyland signed the Letter of Intent that Bram had negotiated, Coconut Cove Park was conceived. Brian Koop was given the order to draw up the purchase agreement and begin a three phase condominium project. The architect and engineer were given their orders for the planning and drawing of the phasing and construction for 95 condominium duplexes and 37 condominium eight plexus for a total of 486 condominium units. Loan documents would be on Brian Koop's desk for review in 6 weeks.

****

Josef and Hagen knew that the Southwest Florida real estate boom was now beginning in full force. It was just turning 2003. They both knew that there would be more developments and dozens of loans coming at a very fast pace. The foreign loan committee was watching the appreciation of Florida real estate and more than happy to keep giving Joe Hyland's Development Company more loans. It was good business for the Bank. But Josef and Hagen had to make sure that any skimming of loan funds off the top of the loans was done in a fashion that would not raise any eyebrows at the Bank, and look legitimate both from the Bank's prospective and from Joe Hyland's perspective.

The amount of money in each loan that exceeded 100% of the necessary funds to complete each project, part of which, includes the pre-payment of profits, were included in each monthly draw request and then had to be wire transferred to a location within the AFC Banking system, which, at Vinke's request, was done out of a branch of the AFC Bank in Aruba. Then it was transferred to a location in Florida so it looked as if the money was for the project. The Bank's 10% ownership in each development was given to the Bank immediately from the Aruba account. The rest of the money, was part of Rynsburger, LLC's 40% ownership in each development and the rest was some additional skimmed money. Just enough not to get it noticed by anyone.

Hyland was fine with this since he was getting paid a very high salary each month, plus he was making 100% of the profits, after commissions were paid, out of the sale of the units through his real estate company. His 50% of the profits from the developments were to be paid to Hyland after each loan was paid off. Joe was pricing the units extremely high, since they were not only being constructed extremely well, which was expensive, but they then adding the real estate boom, inflationary prices of real estate, on to the prices for all residential and commercial units. This allowed Hyland to charge prices much higher than they were worth. It also keep the professional flippers away. The reason for that was that by the time the unit's construction was completed, the appraised value for the unit would be at least the original price Hyland priced the unit, or, sometimes even more. Most purchasers, during this period of time believed the price of real estate in Southwest Florida was just not going to stop going up. Demand was much higher than supply during this boom which also caused the prices to be inflated. Every butcher, baker and candlestick maker were borrowing money on their homes, 401(k)'s, IRA's and close and distant relatives to get in on the action. They were all going to become rich!

So on each draw for every loan, 10% of the pre-paid profits attributable to the Bank were given to the Bank and 40% of the pre-paid profits for Rynsburger LLC, plus some extra added to the draws for 'nonexistent costs', but explained as a footnote on each draw, were wired from Aruba into an account in the name of Rynsburger, LLC at the Flagler Community Bank in Fort Lauderdale, Florida. The signor on that account was Hagan Vinke, in case Vinke ever had to justify the funds to the Bank's Board of Directors. It was pre-paid profits approved by the Bank's Board. Unbeknownst to the Bank, a small portion of those funds were then divided equally between Vinke and Rynsburger. Both needed that extra money for their good times and their 'man toys'. The rest remained in the account, to be distributed at some time in the future. The monthly draws also included the 50% pre-paid profit for Hyland, without Hyland's knowledge. Cathy was told that Vinke was holding that money for Hyland. Any extra amounts from each draw on every loan, over the pre-paid profits, for which Joe Hyland had no idea was happening, were wired into the AFC Bank's account where all the release fee amounts were wired each time a unit in any development was closed to a purchaser. In developments where hundreds of millions of dollars or more were involved, a few million dollars extra was a small amount to 'red flag' any draws over a long period of construction.

Then Vinke would wire transfer any extra amount into another bank account set up in the Aruba branch of AFC Bank. The signor for that Aruba account was Cathy Cutter, the person who crafted each monthly draw. She would then wire those amounts to two other bank accounts in Florida to remain for Hyland, or at least Cathy thought it was for him. But they really were for Hagen and Josef to take after the projects were complete. This was sort of an insurance policy if anything went bad during the construction and/or sale of the developments. Cathy relayed all of this to George Harvey since she was sure that Rynsburger and Vinke were going to cut out Hyland form his promised profit windfall. George had Cathy executed a Power of Attorney that George had drawn up by one of his Aruba attorneys, giving Roger a Power of Attorney over that Aruba account if, for any reason, Cathy's perceptions turned out to be true. A little deception against the Dutch bandits may be needed in the future. What a grand turn of events. Roger may be actually helping Joe Hyland take his revenge in the future. Who would have thought?

Once the 50% pre-paid profit of Hyland's funds were wire transferred to the AFC Bank account in Aruba, Cathy Rutter would wire transfer those funds to two different Community Banks, one in Fort Myers, the McGregor Community Bank, and one in Naples, Florida, the Tamiami Community Bank. Unbeknownst to Cathy, this way the funds would be on AFC Bank's balance sheet and be considered pre-paid profits for one of the partners, for which the loan committee had approved. The amounts that were wired to the Fort Myers and Naples community bank accounts were left in the account to accumulate until someday, in the future, it was believed that they would be distributed to Hagen and Josef. Cathy Cutter got a cash monthly payment personally from Vinke and Rynsburger for arranging for those wire transfers. Cathy believed that those payments were a separate part of her salary, although Catty was not that naïve. Cathy believed that the funds she wired monthly were actually to deceive both the AFC Bank and Hyland. Hence the Power of attorney, if needed.

This practice of skimming money from the loans had worked well for the first 4 acquisition and development loans for the Largo Del Sol development, and the acquisition loan and 3 loans for the first condominium project for the Snook Point development. AFC Bank's balance sheet always balanced on the loans since AFC Bank knew they were loaning over 100% of the proceeds of the necessary funds for both acquisition of land and construction thereon. The loan committee was under the impression that the additional funds were exclusively for the Bank's, pre-paid profits, the partner's pre-paid profits and for professionals such as attorney's fees, engineer's fees, surveyor fees, architect fees, etc.

AFC Bank had indicated in the loan documents that the principal due for each loan would be repaid when each unit, lot or parcel of land was closed and title transferred to the ultimate purchaser. That would pay down the principal on the loan. Interest was being collected on the full amount of the loan on a monthly basis as part of the draws on the loans. In addition, Joe Hyland, personally, and all of his development companies were executing personal guarantees on all funds, for whatever purpose, under the terms and conditions of each AFC Bank loan. No other guarantees were required. AFC Bank also secured all loans by cross collateralizing all developments for each project loan.

The Bank and the Bank's auditors were content with the arrangement. This was true since the Bank controlled each draw request. This deceptive scheme was working well, so long as prices continued to increase on the real estate that was subject to these loans. There were some skeptics on the foreign loan committee, but since the Bank was receiving its interest on all outstanding principal on a timely basis each month, principal was being reduced each time there was a sale, and the Bank was receiving its 10% pre-paid profit each month with a full guarantee on the outstanding principal balance of every loan, a majority of the loan committee members were satisfied. The full net amount of each purchase of individual lot or condominium sold by the Developer was always used to pay down the principal of the loan associated with the sale. No one but AFC Bank received any of those net sale proceeds. The Bank was happy.

Josef with the encouragement of Vinke, as the President of the Bank, continued to try to find large developments in Southwest Florida so as many loans as possible could be approved, and the circle of funds would continue to flow, under the same scenario, for which the Bank believed was also a great investment for the Bank's shareholders.

Just to confirm the agreement between Hagen and Josef as to how this deception was to continue and how the funds appropriated by Josef and Hagen under this scenario would be distributed, the two of them drafted a 1 page agreement, written in Dutch, memorializing the full Agreement. They both agreed, that the best place to keep the original Agreement would be in a third party's safe. After a discussion between them, it was determined that Josef would give the Agreement to Bram to bring to Florida and give it to Joe Hyland, who couldn't read Dutch, and have Joe give it to his attorney, Brian Koop. Koop would place it in Koop's Fort Myers Office safe with instructions that only Josef Rynsburger or Hagen Vinke or Joe Hyland could have it removed from the safe. If Joe Hyland asks Koop to do that then Koop could indicate that it was being held for his client. That would protect each of them from any third party knowing what was actually happening. Both Hagen and Josef understood, without even saying it to each other, that if the real estate boom did crash someday, they would still have the money they had appropriated from each loan in community banks in Florida and the persons who would be financially responsible to pay back all of any outstanding principal and other costs, such as interest, for all loans would be the guarantors, Joe Hyland and Hyland's development companies. The bank was fully secured since the Bank has every parcel of real estate and all personal property associated with every development mortgaged and cross collateralized. No one would come and look to Hagen or Josef for any deficiency. The Bank's loan committee had all facts for every loan when it was approved.

There were several misconceptions on the part of Hagen and Josef. No one had any idea that AFC Bank would ever become a candidate for acquisition by any other Bank. Also, Josef and Hagen were aware that Dr. Timmerman had hard proof that Josef and Hagen had done this similar type of deception to the doctor when Josef and the doctor were partners in their real estate company. However, they believed that the doctor had agreed not to go to the authorities, so there would be no publicity, and the doctor didn't want his wife or anyone else to know that he had been taken. But whether or not the doctor would keep quiet about this was an unknown. That's how George Harvey became aware of this scheme. Josef and Hagen could not have conceived of the deep down bitterness of Dr. Timmerman and the bitterness of George Harvey concerning what Josef and Hagen did to Roger Spector and to Joe Hyland. And last and most important, no one knew that the real estate boom would make such a huge crash in 2008-2009. Otherwise everything was just blissful and everyone, and their relatives, were making a fortune.

CHAPTER 11

I T WAS 6 weeks since Joe Hyland's funeral. In October of 2013, the weather in Fort Myers was a little cooler than the average. It was always enjoyable to have a touch of fall in Southwest Florida. Usually, the weather stays quite warm through the beginning of November. Seasons go from summer to winter. But this year there was a touch of fall. Always enjoyable. Alex Tarian, Luke Bradley, Denise Hudak and Arthur Winslow were all meeting in Alex's office in the Lee County office building to get updates on their investigations. All of the participants knew there were several investigations going on that needed to be solved. Some of the participant believed all of those investigations may be, in some way or another, all connected. But how?

This whole investigation started with Joe Hyland's death. Luke was not convinced that Hyland's death was even a homicide. However, if by chance it was, Catty Rutter may have had something to do with the death. She was there when it happen and her, and her husband, William were the last ones to see Hyland alive. Denise believed the same thing. However, the facts weren't there. Hyland and Rutter were very good friends personally and in Hyland's real estate developments. They both helped each other and each benefited from the other's help. Neither Denise nor Luke could find any motive for Rutter to be involved with Joe's death. Rutter helped Joe when he was very sick and was into drinking a lot. She was the one that got him help with his drinking. He was still an alcoholic when he died. However, up until his death, they remained good friends. At the time of Hyland's death, Rutter actually had more money than Joe. But money was still a motive. It always is. Rutter controlled the loan draws for Hyland's companies. She paid the employees, paid Hyland, paid the bills and paid the bank. Any excess from the draws, went to AFC Bank and probably Rynsburger, maybe as additional pre-paid profits or maybe as something else. But Cathy probably knew or suspected something. Neither Luke nor Denise could ever get anything out of Rutter about that issue. Was she a suspect? Maybe. Denise then relayed to the others in the room that her interview with Denise and her attorney, Brian Kopp, ended when Denise attempted to get Cathy to answer questions about the ownership interests in all of the development companies. Denise also attempted to get Cathy to explain the procedure in determining how much money was requested in a draw and for what uses. Lastly, Denise attempted to get Cathy to explain where and how funds were distributed after receipt of the draw request. Denise believed that the answers to those questions may very well have some real affect in leading the investigations to a conclusion. However, Brian Koop insisted that Denise receive full immunity for all matters that may result in those answers.

"Does that immunity extend to murder?" asked Alex.

"The word murder never came up in the immunity discussions." Replied Denise. "I have no reason to believe that Cathy was any way involved with Hagen Vinke's or Josef Rynsburger's death. The only death that she may be involved would be Hyland's. I believe it was never requested because Rutter and Koop believe that Hyland's death was not a homicide."

"Let's hold off on that issues until we have finished our discussion today to deal with this request of immunity for Rutter" Said Alex. "There may be other ways to get Rutter to answer those questions without immunity."

Who else would really benefit from his death? The next person considered was Leigh Mowery, Joe's ex-wife. Ex-wives are always suspects. The only motive Mowery seemed to care about was whether or not Joe was hiding some money from her during their divorce. Revenge was definitely not a motive for Mowery. There was no evidence to substantiate that. Even when Hyland cheated on her with Ivana Hollings, it wasn't enough for a revenge murder. It was, however, the strangest divorce any of the four in that room had ever seen before. Hyland gave Leigh well over $3 million, sent her to Louisville, Kentucky to live and paid her $50,000.00 every 3 months for over a year. Hyland was cheating on Mowery and decided he wanted Ivana Hollings more. So Hyland just told Mowery that he wanted a divorce. Hyland must have believed that Mowery wanted the same since she was well aware of Hollings. They both agreed to remain friends and with what Hyland offered Mowery she seemed to be fine with it. For all they knew, Mowery may had been seeing someone else. Rutter would not confirm or deny that. They were best friends.

Hyland promised to take care of Leigh, even after the divorce. Hyland told Mowery that Koop's law firm would have the divorce completed in a month, so long as she didn't contest it. No need to contest the divorce. All the money was given to her upfront and before a divorce was actually initiated. However, no divorce agreement was even ever drawn up. Once the quarterly money stopped, Leigh waited some time for Hyland to start paying again. She had no idea that sales at that time where starting to slow and Hyland was not earning as much as he did at the height of the boom. After close to a year with no more quarterly payments, Mowery finally initiated a divorce proceedings. Her lawyer and her lawyer's investigator spent months looking for funds that Hyland may have hidden somewhere. But, after several months the lawyer and investigator didn't find any more than he had when he died. Against Brian Kopp's advice, Hyland never even hired a lawyer for the divorce. Koop wrote Hyland another one of his cover the firm's butt letters about representation during a divorce proceedings, however, Hyland just let it go through. The only thing Mowery got in the divorce was one of the two condominium that Hyland and Mowery both owned jointly at Largo Del Sol. She then immediately sold hers for cash. No one in the room believed she was a suspect for anything.

Next there was Ivana Hollins, the woman who caused Hyland to break up with his wife and get Leigh out of town. They were a thing for several years. She was a bad influence on him, especially during the down time of the real estate boom. She was also a heavy drinker. It was mostly her drinking that caused Hyland to start drinking heavily. They also loved to party. But the turn down of sales and the complaints that the prices for his units were much too high, didn't help. Hyland needed his products to sell high to fulfill the outrageous obligations under the mortgages with the Bank. When Hyland moved out of his condominium at Largo Del Sol, he purchased a $1.5 million dollar home in the development just north of The Riverview Golf & Country Club. Hollings moved in and lived with Hyland until the foreclosure action by the Bank. Hyland had given Hollings $200,000.00 to decorate the home. Hyland finally ran out of money, went into rehab and Hollings left him. Hyland's real estate company closed and Ivana went to work for another broker. Hollings is now going out with some other rich guy now. No one in the room saw any motive there.

Next there was Josef Rynsburger, his business partner. He was already dead years before Hyland died, and so was the banker, Hagen Vinke, who loaned the development company all of that money. However, the issue of excess funds and illegal payments from draws, hidden money, theft, and deception was still on the minds of the law enforcement people in the room. How to find what happen to those funds was not going to be easy. That is probably the only crime that law enforcement may be able to prove. But how?

"Maybe you already tried this." Started Luke, as he looked to Alex. "Can't you get a Judge to give you a subpoena for all of Hyland's financial records, checking accounts, wire transfers, etc.?"

"Luke, I got subpoenas for Mowery and Cutter which came up with nothing. And it was not easy getting those subpoenas." Answered Luke. "There just is no probable cause for a subpoena for Hyland or his company records. No one is complaining about missing money. If someone really did steal some money, it would have started 13 years ago. The statute of limitations is probably run on the vast majority, if not all, of the funds. If someone really did misappropriate funds from draws on loans, neither AFC Bank nor ABN Amro are complaining. If it did happen to them it would have been discovered by the Banks during their due diligence period. If they did find something, it was worked out between the parties, since the Banks merged about 5 years ago. It just isn't going to happen. No Judge will let me go on a fishing expedition." Continued Alex as he was lecturing everyone else in the room.

"Further," said Arthur. "The IRS came after Hyland for past due income taxes due on the theory of 'forgiveness of debt' under his personal guarantees. That is a shit load of taxes. He owed taxes on just under a billion dollars! All of the records for his companies were destroyed well over a year ago when the IRS withdrew their investigation against Hyland and his companies. They knew that he didn't have the money to pay anything. So, more than likely, there aren't even any records to look at."

Hyland and all of his companies, both development companies, and all of the other 30 plus companies never filed for bankruptcy so no one really knows what was where. But also, no one really lost any money except Hyland. His employees lost their jobs and maybe a paycheck or two, but that isn't a motive for homicide. If anything, Hyland tried to help most of his employees to get other jobs or even gave them some money he couldn't afford. The Bank did file a foreclosure action, but never finished the law suit. The Bank got title to all of the Hyland's development company's unsold real estate, the Alico Mine and all equipment associated with it, under some Settlement Agreement through the foreclosure process. The foreclosure law suit was dismissed, title to all of the properties were transferred to the Bank and a Settlement Agreement was drafted and executed by all parties setting forth the Agreement between all parties. The Agreement must have had a confidentiality clause and was not filed in the public records. Only the deeds and the foreclosure dismissal was filed in the public records.

One thing everyone in the room knew, was that Hyland moved back into his Largo Del Sol condominium and the $1.5 million home and most of the furnishings, except for some things taken by Hyland, were transferred to the Bank. That must have been one of the provisions under the Settlement Agreement. Hyland kept his cars and some cash, don't know how much, and everything that was in his safe in his condominium. What was in the safe was unknown to everyone, including the Bank. Everyone in the room was sure that the Bank was not even aware the safe existed. What that all adds up to is an unknown to the people investigating the matter. Cathy Rutter is keeping quiet and Leigh Mowery probably didn't know what was in the safe since she never asked for any of it in the divorce proceedings.

Hyland worked for George Harvey and Bradly Whalen for some years until he left to start his own development company. No motive there, and Hyland even purchase one of Harvey's parcels of real estate for his first development! The separation must not have been completely cordial, but also didn't seem that there was much in hard feelings either.

After much thought and discussion, the only possible suspect was Roger Spector. That was probably a long shot. And no one knew where he was. They knew his father had passed some time ago, but after the funeral and a few weeks staying at his mother's home, he fell off the earth. Hyland and he split up just months after they both left GHIC to start their own development company. Hyland stayed on, Spector left. There could be some bad blood there. But that was 14 years ago! Still, it probably had to be investigated.

Otherwise, Hyland, during the real estate boom, helped anyone who needed help, gave lots of money to charity and was well liked by everyone. He put Cape Coral on the map and changed the development attitude of that City. When he was down after the bust, he was still well liked, he just became a drunk and unable to pay all his bills. There were hundreds of developers and ordinary people that hit rock bottom or worse during the real estate crash. Many had their properties and even their homes 'under water'. But no enemies came to mind.

Their conclusion, for purposes of this meeting, was that Denise would investigate the disappearance of Roger Spector and find out what happened to him and if he may even be a possible suspect. Also Denise would look into whether or not the death of Hyland was positively a homicide. She needs to speak with the County coroner and go over the autopsy. Maybe it was just a death from natural causes?

Next was Arthur's turn. His investigation was to determine if there was any fraud or theft involved with any of the dozen of loans AFC Bank gave Hyland's development companies for all of its developments. Trace the funds collected on sales of land, homes, condominium, sales from the products of the mine? There was over $1.5 billion in total loans. Just about a billion dollars in sales. No one has really been able to determine that. However, that is a lot of money. What kind of Settlement Agreement was made between ABN Amro, the bank that purchased AFC Bank's assets, including Hyland's mortgages, during the foreclosure? Was there some kind of scheme, and if so, who was involved and how did it work and where did the money go? The statute of limitations is still running on that. But is that a Florida matter or Netherlands matter? Everything about this case gets more complicated.

Arthur then gave the other three participants at the meeting a complete portrait of Senior Officer Jansen's investigation through his source, his brother in law, who was a senior commercial loan officer at AFC Bank during all of the Hyland loans. The entire account is unusual, to say the least, if not in violation of dozens of U.S. and Netherlands statutes. Arthur reminded everyone about several important points to keep in the back of their minds while completing their investigation. The lender was a 10% owner in all of the Hyland developments for which those developments received loans from the Bank. All the loans went to the developments in Florida. Arthur needed to determine if there was even jurisdiction in Florida for any possible indictments against ABN Amro, if there were really any violations of statutes at all. Second, Josef Rynsburger and Hagen Vinke were best friends and both died suspiciously. Complicating the matter, AFC Bank has been purchased by the largest lending institution in the Netherlands. How would that fit into the picture? Did ABN Amro Bank have knowledge of any fraud, theft, or deception by Hagen Vinke and Josef Rynsburger at the time ABN Amro purchased the Bank? Was it covered up by the purchasing bank? Vinke was dead before the bank was sold. However, Rynsburger was not.

Denise then conveyed her experiences speaking with Cathy Rutter, the person who probably knew as much as anyone, about how the loans were obtained and how the draws were distributed. Denise was sure, Cathy was not involved with any fraud, theft of deception of any funds. She was just a worker bee who did what Hyland, Rynsburger and the Bank asked her to do. However, were their funds illegally dispersed? Could the remaining funds still be in a bank account somewhere other than ABN Amro? Hyland, Vinke and Rynsburger are all dead. Maybe some or all of the money is still somewhere. It would be ironic if the money is still in some bank account under one or both of the dead men's name. Even their wives are dead. More complicated!

"This may be a good time to discuss immunity for Rutter, at least on any fraud, theft of deception by Hyland's companies. Also under her duties involved with all of the money that came through the development companies." Said Alex.

"If Rutter requested all the funds, for whatever the reasons, on each project, and then received and dispersed those funds, she seems to be the best place to start." Said Luke.

"I agree." Said Alex. "Let's not concern ourselves with the death of Hyland and Rutter's involvement in his death. Let's give her immunity. I'll get my office to draw up the immunity agreement and email it to Brian Koop for his firm to review. Once it is signed, than we can take a real shot at what Cathy Rutter really knows about all of these funds. I hope we're not spinning our wheels."

Arthur then conveyed the episode of the real estate partnership between Dr. Nicolaus Timmerman and Josef Rynsburger. That partnership was dissolved at the start of the real estate boom. Why? The reason for the dissolution was never revealed. Could there have been some deception by Rynsburger and the doctor concerning their loans? The doctor did not have any management responsibility for any of the real estate or partnership matters. The doctor was the only person who ever put his own money in the partnership? Rynsburger never used any of his money on any commercial matter he was involved in, including the partnership with the doctor. Vinke always made sure each loan was the full 100% that was needed or, on many occasions, more than 100%. Timmerman also guaranteed several of Rynsburger's loans at the Bank and all of the loans for their partnership. All of the loans were for 100% of the amount needed to fund projects. Yet the doctor put up money. Where did that money go? A coincidence? Another large coincidence was that Dr. Timmerman was the only person present at Hagen Vinke's suicide and Josef Rynsburger's death. The doctor signed both of the death certificates and certified and determined the cause of death for both. Arthur related the apparent suicide of Vinke and all the circumstances. Everyone in the room believed that there was much more to the story than Arthur uncovered. Whether or not this somehow fits into the Lee County investigation needs to be determined. Maybe Dr. Timmerman is another suspect. Could Dr. Timmerman and Hyland been connected in some way? Arthur was assigned that task.

When the four law enforcement persons were completed with their discussion, there was more confusion than certainty about anything. Someone or multiple people were very smart. Too many coincidences and too much alleged deceptions. However, each of the people in that room knew what they needed to do.

****

Brian Koop had just received another set of loan documents for review. It was the height of the real estate boom in 2005. All 111 condominium units for Largo Del Sol was completed, sold out and all units closed. However, that nasty issue of the mangroves was still pending. The first hearing initiated by Largo Del Sol Development Company, LLC was still pending for a final determination by the Lee County Hearing Examiner.

The purchase of Fairfield Properties, Inc., the corporation that owned the Snook Point property had closed including the loan for acquisition of all the land and its infrastructure. The attorney for Rynsburger formed a Delaware Trust through a Delaware Trust Company and transferred the entire Snook Point Property from Fairfield Properties, Inc. to the Trustee of the trust, an individual who worked for the Delaware Bank in their Trust Department. The Trustee of the Delaware Trust then transferred the entire Snook Point property to Snook Point Development Company, LLC, who had the usual ownership as all other developments. No transfer tax was due on the transfer under both Florida and Delaware law. At least that is what the Delaware lawyer handling the transaction with Rynsburger's attorney, Albert White indicated. A savings of almost half a million dollars in transfer tax, for a total attorney fee of a measly $25,000.00. Brian was amazed and said he learns something new about the law every day. He hoped this one was legitimate. At least he didn't have anything to do with it. The platting for the Snook Point property had been completed. The infrastructure was completed sufficiently for the first neighborhood to be completed and the loan to build the 124 low rise four plex condominium units and all amenities was closed. All 124 units were pre-sold and about half were completed and closed with people now living at Snook Point. 60 residential home lots were platted and 44 of the lots had been sold for $29 million paying off more than half of the $45 million loan for the acquisition of the $35 million Snook Point land.

The loan for acquisition and infrastructure for Coconut Cove was closed and the infrastructure was sufficiently completed for the first phase of 200 duplex and eight plex condominium units. The loan for the 200 condominium units was closed and construction was started on the 200 condominium. All 200 units were pre-sold.

The new loan Brian just received from the Bank, for his review, was for a 4,200 acre parcel of property with several mines on it. It was being mined for sand, gravel and aggregate for roads and the building of structures and other various uses. The 3 mines occupied 1,875 acres and the remainder of the property were wetlands. Bram and Josef located the mine in the southwestern part of Lee County off Alico Road about 6 miles east of Interstate 75, the major interstate North and South on the East Coast of the United States and ties from New York to Miami, Florida and it goes right through Fort Myers. The Letter of Intent was the same as usual with the 150 day 'free look' period. Brian Koop drafted the Purchase Agreement for the asking price of $37.5 million. There were a dozen contingencies which the owners were working on satisfying within 90 days. Not all of the contingencies were satisfied the day Brian Koop received the loan documents, but that didn't stop Joe Hyland from asking Brian to review all the loan documents.

The loan documents, except for the numbers, were essentially the same as all of the other loan documents Brian had reviewed and discussed with Joe Hyland previously, except for several items. First the loan was for more than the purchase price. The loan was for $45 million. Josef said that the mine needed operating capital. Second, Joe Hyland, personally, and all of his development companies for Coconut Cove Park and all of the development companies for Snook Point were personal guaranties. Brian had reviewed the financials for the operation of the mine and it was his personal opinion that the current operation could not support a loan as large as the one AFC Bank is offering. Brian wanted Joe, who would be ultimately responsible for operating the mine, even if he were to hire most of the current employees and an overall manager, to explain to Brian how the operations could pay all of its bills and still cover the loan payments. So Brian made an appointment to meet Joe at Joe's main business office.

When they met, Brian asked Joe about the guarantees and why only he and his companies were the only guarantors. Where was Josef's guarantee? Joe said that the deal concerning guarantees was struck when AFC Bank agreed to loan all of the funds for projects Josef felt where highly profitable in Southwest Florida. But Brian argued this was not a development, this was a going business and Joe knew nothing about mining. Joe said he had the personnel who did know about the business and there would be a greater demand for the products of the mine due to the continued real estate boom over the next coming years. Josef felt the mine could be ultimately sold in a few years for over $50 million. After all the mines had been mined to a depth of 90 feet, the property could be rezoned to a real estate development. All of the mines would be filled with fresh water and then connected to each other so each home built on the lake could have a dock and the home owner could have their own boat. A beach club would be built, so homeowners could take their boats to the club to eat, at one of several restaurants, play tennis, basketball, swim in the large community pool, or just lie on the beach under permanent cabanas. Other mid-rise condominium could be built so that an addition number of units could be utilized to optimize the profit for infrastructure for the real estate development.

Brian was shocked, but Joe is the client and Joe has asked Brian and his firm to take care of the transaction. Brian's firm would make a lot of money on this closing so Brian agreed to continue as before. However, Brian had one more important observation. The company that was purchasing the mine was Alico Grand Mining, LLC. The ownership of this company had changed from the past projects. Joe's development company had only a 40% ownership interest and Josef's company had increased its ownership interest to 50%. Yet Joe was still the only guarantor. Joe knew about this and said that he and Joe had a conversation about this, and for reasons, not important to Brian, the ownership on this project would change.

"At least tell me why the change." Asked Brian. "I am your lawyer and I should know everything going on to properly represent you."

"I will tell you that it is a confidential matter between Josef and the Bank and the Bank is requiring this change to finalize the loan at this level." Said Joe.

"So the Bank wants a bigger ownership portion of the project and since U.S. law requires the Bank ownership to be only a maximum of 10%, the Bank is doing it this way to deceive the Netherlands and the U.S." Said Brian.

"You don't want to know." Said Joe. "And that is all you need to know to close the deal."

"Joe, this is like the day you told me to prepare divorce papers between you and Leigh and you were giving her millions of dollars and you said it was an amicable divorce without any contesting. You two would remain friends and you would continue to take care of her." Said Brian with a little attitude. "Look how that is turning out, it's bleeding you. Trust me no divorce is amicable. Your time will come. You aren't even divorced yet and no divorce action has been filed! What the Hell is going on?"

"Don't look into the past. Things are going great, Leigh and I are still friends and everyone, including you are making a fortune!" exclaimed Joe. "So let it be!"

"Ok." Said Brian. "So let's talk about something fun for once. How about you, Ivana, me and Linda, Robert and Sandy Coulson all meet for dinner at the Red Lion next week. We haven't really got together socially since you and Leigh split." Said Brian.

"Finally a good idea." Said Joe. "Make a reservation. I have a business deal Josef and I want to approach Robert on anyway. Say next Tuesday. I know you and Linda meet Robert and Sandy at the Red Lion every Tuesday night for dinner. Add two more."

Brian agreed to dinner and let the other issues go. Brian just wrote Joe another cover the firm's butt letter about the ownership and guarantee issues. Nothing more was said. The matter closed several months later and Joe Hyland was then the operator of a large mine. It's not like he didn't have enough to do.

****

It was a cool night in November of 2005. However, the Southwest Florida real estate boom was as hot as a gas grill with T-bone steaks sizzling! Everyone in Southwest Florida was buying real estate and then listing it hoping to sell it in a month or two to other people for a large gain who then wanted to do the same. No one wanted to live in those homes, just sell and watch the money come in! People were invading their IRA's and 401(k)'s, paying penalties plus the income tax. No one cared, the money they could make on selling real estate will take care of their full retirement. They were taking their other retirement funds, selling stock, selling jewelry. They were taking out Equity Loan Mortgages on their homes, both second and third mortgages. And they're banks approved those mortgages since even the banks thought that they would be paid back soon after the real estate sold. The secretaries, the restaurant servers, the factory worker and the cleaning women. Get in now and don't miss the boat. The local newspapers had editorials on how the rising prices in real estate was increasing at 2-3%

per month. Never since the end of World War II were housing prices rising as fast as they were that year. It was bedlam.

Everyone was sitting around Robert Coulson's pool. He had a $4 million home on the Caloosahatchee River. There was Joe Hyland, Josef Rynsburger, and Brian Koop, who set up the gathering, Bram Meulenbelt, and Larry Morgan, Robert Coulson's son-in-law. Robert Coulson, and his wife Sandy, were the majority owners of Riverside Custom Homes, Inc. His son-in-law and his daughter, Carrie, were minority owners. The high end custom home building business was growing as fast as prices of homes were rising. Last year this family based custom home builder built 95 homes averaging $1.2 million each. This year they were on pace to build 120 homes averaging $1.5 million each. Profits were in the $12 million per year range to be shared by the family. Riverside Custom Homes, Inc. also had their own real estate company, with their other daughter Kendra as the broker, so they could also make additional money for the family on commissions for every sale of their homes. Josef and Hagen Vinke's mouths were salivating. Loans to build each of those homes. But Josef and Vinke had more in mind that evening. Robert and Sandy and Joe and Leigh had become good friends since they were introduced a few years ago at the bar at the Red Lion Business Club bar. The two couples, and occasionally Brian and his wife, Linda would all socialize. However, since Leigh left Fort Myers and Ivana came into the picture, the socializing became less and less. But tonight was not social, it was all business.

Josef and Bram had just come back from Orlando. It was time to expand to other hot markets around Florida. Just outside of Orlando, off Interstate 4, about 10 miles from the entrance of Disney World was a 185 acre parcel of real estate already platted for both residential homes and multiunit condominium, with a density of 2,050 homes and multiple amenities. The current owner was much overextended with his bank and needed to sell this parcel fast. The asking price was $18.5 million. Bram had a letter of Intent drawn up and Brian Koop was working on the purchase agreement when they were meeting at the Coulson's home. Josef has already spoken with the current project manager and several of the building supervisors who would be enthralled to be able to keep their jobs when the parcel is sold to a new owner. Brian knew that Josef and Hagen wanted Hyland's development company to build its own homes, instead of parceling them out to preferred builders. An endless streak of loans for each home and condominium. AFC was making money and skimming a little off of Josef's additional ownership so it still looked like they were a 10% owner, so that extra money gave the Bank more incentive to listen to Vinke and continue funding their projects. No one who audited the bank would even know the extra money was really for an additional percentage of ownership. It would just look like additional fees, for which the Bank booked the extra money on their ledger. The profits of the Bank increased and all shareholders, loan officers and Vinke, the President were happy working for a very profitable bank.

Brian started the conversation.

"Gentleman, some of you know why this gathering was called." Started Brian. "It wasn't just for the Crown Royal on the rocks, but I would have come just for that and Sandy Coulson's wonderful hors d'oeuvre's. Joe, why don't you tell Robert why we are here."

"Robert, our developments are selling like we never believed could happen. Josef and I and the Amsterdam Bank have decide to expand to other locations in Florida where the real estate market is almost as hot as here. We want to get into the home building and condominium building business. We want our companies to be able to do everything in each development from soup to nut." Happily said Joe. "Josef and I and the Bank in Amsterdam are willing to make you and Larry wealthy." We would like to offer to purchase the assets of Riverside Custom Homes, Inc. from you and Larry for $18 million cash."

"Are you kidding?" said Robert."

"That's not all." Continued Joe. "We are willing to give you, Robert, a one year employment agreement with a salary of $1 million to operate the business for us. Then you will be able to retire with plenty of money and do things you haven't been able to do since you are currently working 15 hour days, 7 days a week."

"Larry, you will get a 5 year employment agreement with a salary of $400,000.00 per year with all of the benefits you currently have but more." Continued Joe. "You will become the main development manager after Robert's employment agreement expires." Said Joe.

"This is a win – win situation for all of us." Said Josef. "Robert, you are 56 and you can retire early and do what you want."

"As a bonus, Robert, there will be no non-compete agreement in this deal." Said Joe. "If you want to start another home building company, and as long as you don't build within 5 miles of any of our developments, you can do that."

"Robert, you can have the rest of the year to finish the homes you have started and take those profits." Said Josef. "Any new homes would be under our new building company."

Brian then intervened on this conversation. "As you know, I represent everyone here except Josef. I cannot represent anyone here, if you were to go forward with this transaction since I have a conflict of interest." Said Brian. "I brought you all together tonight to discuss Joe and Josef's offer and if you all agree, I can document the transaction as long as you all make all of the decisions on the terms and conditions of the transaction and agree to execute conflict waivers for documentation and insert a provision in the Purchase Agreement confirming the fact that neither I nor my firm represents anyone in this transaction and all I will be doing is documenting the terms and conditions you all agree to." Continued Brian. "This is a complicated transaction, so if you all want to get your own attorneys, I will take no offense. I just want all of you to do what's best for each of you."

At that point Joe told Robert and Larry that Brian was working on a purchase agreement for a large parcel of real estate in Orlando with a density for 2,050 residential units. Joe indicated he would not be able to start selling and building for several months, so Joe told Robert and Larry that they should take some time and think about it. However, they would like an answer within a week so that they could prepare for where the Orlando project would be going from here. Robert and Larry were flattered and taken back at the amount of money offered, in cash up front for their business. They agreed to talk about it and get back with Joe in a couple of days.

Thereafter, Brian, who was always comfortable in his friend's home, went over and pored fresh drinks all around. While enjoying the drinks and food, both Robert and Joe exchanged compliments about the other and each agreed that if the answer on this offer is a "no" that there would be no hard feelings and things would always go on as before. It was quite an evening for everyone. Josef and Bram, then told everyone that they had to leave early since they were going back to Orlando early the next day. They said that they enjoyed the evening and complimented Robert on his beautiful house. And with one last try, indicated that Robert and Larry should seriously consider the offer. Josef really felt it was a better offer than it was worth, but Josef knew that Hagen would be able to sell a $20 million loan to the Bank's loan committee for the purchase of Riverside Custom Homes.

Robert Coulson and Brian Koop were very good friends and each respected the other's opinion. After Joe left for the evening, Robert, Larry and Brian sat down, poured another Crown on the rocks and discussed the offer that was just made.

"I would never work for Joe Hyland and especially Josef Rynsburger for all the money in the world." Exclaimed Larry. 'I say no to this offer, no matter how much money they are offering. After all, Carrie and I only own 10% of the business. $1.8 million, and then giving the IRS their share, won't let us make it to 50 years old. After working for them for 5 years, they'll never renew my contract, and we'll have to start all over again. My 10% vote is no!"

"I am impressed with everything Joe has offered for the business. It's probably a great deal for me." Said Robert. "But I don't want to work for them either. We are making really good money with no end in sight. No amount of money will change my mind. I like to work and things are good. Brian, tell Joe my answer is also no!"

"I think you need to think a little longer about this. They have offered both of you a lot of money" Said Brian. "This boom is not going to last forever. Maybe you should take your money, forget the 1 year employment contract and go out and start a new home building business." Continued Brian. "This is money in the bank."

"Brian, you know that the company has loans on all of the lots we have purchased and on the models and spec homes we have." Explained Robert. "Once those are paid off, the $18 million is down to about $9 or $10 million. Then taxes! I like it the way it is. I'm flattered, but the answer is no!"

The next day, Brian called Joe and told him that both Robert and Larry were very flattered with Joe's offer, but they are really not interested and want to just stay where they are and keep their course. Joe said, thanks to Brian for setting up the meeting, but we'll all just go out and make money our own ways. Joe then called Josef and told him the news about Coulson's decision.

"Shit." Said Josef.

Then he hung up.

Brian called back Joe to tell Joe he had the purchase agreement ready to send to him for the Orlando parcel. Joe told Brian that he should expect loan documents on his desk from the Bank's attorney for review in about 4 weeks. Brian thought about what Joe was getting into. The loans and amounts of money just keep adding up. How in the world is Joe going to pay all this back and to continue to manage this quickly increasing work load. How much longer is this real estate boom going to go on? At some time, the cost of real estate has to level off or start to fall. The ordinary 'Guy' out in the working world is just not going to be able to afford any place to live. Joe, and all of his assets, are all on the hook.

Brian knew that Joe was getting paid a very high salary and making some profits off the sales of the residential units and some profits from his real estate company, but what is he doing with all that money. His life style is over the top. If the shit hits the fan in this real estate boom and the crash comes, whether easy or hard, Josef and Vinke will walk away extremely rich and Joe will be devastated and looking for his next meal. Brian could see by all of the loan documents that a substantial amount of money is being paid to the Bank and Rynsburger up front out of each draw. Also, Joe's ownership, and profits, have been recently reduced with Joe's blessing. If they have reduced Joe's interest once, why not again. Where is all of this extra money going that Rynsburger and the Bank are receiving? Brian believes a large portion of the extra Bank's funds are probably finding its way to Vinke. Why can't Joe see this?

Joe is really enjoying being the front man on all of these developments and having local businessman and politicians call him for advice and being invited to all of the important functions around town. Someone has to get to Joe about this. Brian has seen Joe start drinking more and earlier in the day as the stress of this job is getting more and more difficult. Brian has even heard from several of his employees that he may even be taking some prescription drugs. He has been losing some weight lately. Every meeting at Joe's office, no matter the time, starts with Joe bringing out the Crown Royal bottle and ice and pouring a drink for everyone in the room. And Brian knows that when Joe offers you a drink, no one turns it down.

Brian has been trying to have a sit down with Joe on retirement funds and some plan for the future when all of this is over. Brian has attempted to get Joe to set up broker accounts and invest in annuities and to purchase a much bigger and more expensive home other than the condominium at Largo Del Sol since under Florida law, all homesteads and retirement accounts and annuities are exempt from creditors. Brian has even spoken to Cathy Rutter who has tried the same thing, but Joe really believes someday, if this does all end, he'll have so much money that he could do anything he wants. Life is going to turn out great for Joe. His one very large personality flaw, is that no one is able to tell him what to do personally with his life. He knows best and it is his job to take care of his people and not the other way around. Everyone, but Joe, makes personal mistakes, but this one will turn out to be a bad one.

****

Several days after Joe Hyland had received Robert Coulson's answer on the non-purchase of Riverside Custom Homes, Cathy Rutter opened a letter from the Lee County hearing officer's office. The determination by the examiner dealt with Largo Del Sol. This is 5 years after the initial petition. The determination was good news and bad news. The officer had ruled for the developer. The mangroves may be trimmed, on a periodic basis, as needed, down to the top of the first floor of the residential units. The mangroves, however, could not be trimmed below the parking levels. That was the good news. The bad news was that the mangroves could only be trimmed directly in front of the balconies of all the residential units. The spaces in-between the three towers could not be trimmed. What kind of ruling was that? If someone is on their balcony overlooking the river, The could see the river directly in front of them, but that person had a small view of the river if they were to look either North or South towards the river. The non-trimmed mangroves would impair a Northerly or Southerly view of the river from each unit's balcony. What this meant was that if someone was riding in a boat on the river and looked at Largo Del Sol, the mangroves in front of the buildings would look like a big 'H'. Who has ever heard of such a ruling? Reading on, the examiner found that the environmentalist's report funded by the County has merit where a full trimming of the mangroves would endanger nurseries for many fish species in the river; hinder the protection of the riverbank from strong winds and waves from natural wind and boat waves; hinder soil stabilization, and stimulation of nutrient retention and water quality through hindered filtration of sediments and pollutants. Despite the mangroves ecological and economic importance, mangroves are under threat. Therefore, a compromise of this trimming for this development was necessary. The examiner's findings and decision had to be approved by the full County Commissioner's before it was final.

Once Cathy showed Joe the decision, Joe was outraged! He first took out a bottle of Crown Royal and poured about three fingers of the liquor into the glass and drank it down in one swoop. He then called Brian and told him about the decision. Brian asked Joe to have Cathy email a copy to him since he had not received his copy from the County yet. Once Brian read the whole decision, he showed it to his partner, a land use attorney, who had been working on this matter since the beginning and argued the developer's case before the County examiner. Both attorneys then called Joe. They could both tell that Joe had something to drink and was a little out of it. But the land use attorney proceeded to discuss the decision with Joe. She said that the decision was a good decision for the developer. The developer had represented to the unit owners at Largo Del Sol that the developer would pay for and obtain permits for trimming the mangroves so all balconies would be able to see the river. That has been accomplished. Then the developer would pay for the first trimming. Thereafter, the unit owners would be responsible for any further maintenance or trimming. The owners may not like the full result, but the developer had done exactly what the developer had represented to the owners that he would do.

Next, after approval by the County Commissioners, the developer would hire a company to trim the mangroves exactly as set out in the decision. As an exhibit to the decision a drawing of how the mangroves should look after they are trimmed was attached. If the owner's do not like the decision, let their condominium association appeal the decision. The developer would then be out of it. It would now be between the condominium association and the County to try to resolve any of the owner's complaints. Joe liked what he heard, although he was still upset at the decision.

A few days later, as Brian thought would happen, the attorney for the condominium association called Brian to complain about the County's decision on the manner in which the mangroves would be trimmed. The Association attorney argued that the developer did not do what he represented he would do. Brian just echoes what he and the land use attorney had told Joe and told the attorney that if his clients didn't like the decision, he could represent the Association before the County Commissioners meeting when this matter came up for final approval.

The matter came before the County Commissioners at their next meeting. The attorney for the condominium association was there as was Brian. The association attorney argued his client's case and said that the decision was foolish and the trimming as set forth in the decision would look ridiculous. Brian told the Commissioners that the developer was fine with the decision. The County Commissioners voted 4-3 to accept the County examiner's decision. The matter was over. Finally, or was it.

Joe now could tell Josef and the Bank that the mangrove issue was finally over and Largo Del Sol was finally finished. This has been a thorn in the side of Josef and Hagen. Both of them believed that the project should be built, sold and the developer should move on. This issue has been going on for just under 5 years. Joe sent Josef and Hagen a copy of the County examiner's decision and a copy of the County Commissioner's final Order. Along with that, Joe sent the attorney fees bill for in the amount of $47,500.00 plus cost of $8,550.00. In addition to these fees and costs, the trimming of the mangroves would cost $187,000.00.

Joe asked Hagen to send the funds to his development account so the bills could be paid. Josef and Hagen talked about this and were furious with Hyland since he was the person that represented to the owners that the developer would pay for the first trimming of the mangroves. Joe never consulted Josef or Hagen about that issue. All Joe wanted were sales and he made that representation to potential owners. It was Joe's first development and was desperate to sell out the project. This started before the real estate boom actually began. Josef and Hagen decided to take the position that Hyland made the representation, so the costs should come out of his pockets. After all Joe had agreed to manage all the developments so long as he did not have to put up any of his own money. That would be provided by the bank. And Josef would find all of the property necessary to be developed. Now it was time to have him pay for his mistakes.

This information was given to Joe by Bram, the week after they received the news and the bills. Bram was sent to Florida for another parcel of property that Josef heard of in Orlando. Bram first stopped in Fort Myers and communicated the decision Josef and the Bank had come to about the bills for the mangroves. Joe was furious. There was no logic, in Joe's mind, that the Bank would not pay for the mangrove costs. That was all part of the development and both Josef and the Bank were aware of the mangrove issue form the beginning. It was Roger Spector that communicated the issue to Josef. Roger was the one who knew Josef first and the best and Roger felt comfortable telling Josef about the issue. Josef was aware that the mangroves was an impediment to selling the units at the prices that all of the owners wanted for the units. A representation about the mangroves had to be made. Everyone knew that.

Joe was even more furious that Josef had Bram tell him this news and Josef didn't even call or discuss the issue with Joe. Finally, Joe called Josef direct and after a heated discussion about the issue, Josef told Joe that their partnership should be dissolved. That Josef could find another developer to finish the projects. Joe learned a lot about Josef and Hagen over this issue. In the scheme of the full amount of money involved with all the projects, this was small change. But Josef would not back down. Joe finally agreed to pay the costs involved, but the relationship between Joe and Josef and Hagen would never be the same. The first problem was Joe had to determine where he would find the money. Joe was going to make Josef pay one way or another. Joe told Cathy on the next draw to increase certain specific costs by 10% and put those funds into Joe's personal account when she received the draw from the Bank. Cathy was curious why Joe was making that request, but considering what she has seen over the last 8 years, nothing surprised her anymore. This was a big mistake on the part of Joe. He would not hear the end of this decision.

CHAPTER 12

IT WAS NOW February, 2006 and the Florida Real estate boom, in most people's minds, was still sizzling! Josef and Hagen were skimming substantial funds from dozens of loans as the real estate mania continued. Josef was with Bram in Orlando Florida looking for additional projects when Hagen Vinke had just received the news that his wife, Sofia, was diagnosed with metastatic colorectal cancer, stage IV. Hagen took the news hard. His wife had been his rock through all of this time he and Josef have been committing their multiple deceptions. His wife, after having to go through radiation treatments and chemo therapy, would only have only about a 12% chance of surviving for 5 years. Going through these treatments, Sofie endured Alopecia, which is substantial hair loss; fatigue and lose of energy; substantial pain in the areas of the radiation treatments; constant vomiting and nausea; and neutropenia, or a loss of white blood cells which would usually help fight infection. She was miserable. Hagen had a very hard time with this. Hagen was so distraught, that Josef, from time, had to remind Hagen to keep his eye on the accounts at the Bank. And most important to make sure the wire transfers of the overages that went to Josef and Hagen were timely initiated. Josef was never the sympathetic type. But in Josef's defense, the last thing either one wanted was someone snooping into their scheme that had been working so well and nearly, if not, impossible to find with normal audits. Hagen had his wife check into The Netherlands Cancer Institute, which is a small specialized hospital, in Amsterdam, for patients like Sofie. The prognosis for Sofie was not bright. Hagen didn't know any of the physicians at the Institute, but had good reports on the facility. Sofie's internist had been Dr. Nicolaus Timmerman since they had become friends when Josef and the doctor were partners in various real estate ventures.

Hagen called Dr. Timmerman after Sofie was diagnosed and asked him if he would see her and be Hagen's go between with the physicians at the Institute. The doctor had only spoken to Hagen only when necessary for appearances since he found out about the deception that Hagen and Josef had committed against him while Josef was his partner. Timmerman did see Hagen socially on occasion since Sofie and the doctor's wife, Elsie, got along well and the families had always been friends. Dr. Timmerman was now a man of fairly substantial means and the amount of money that was deprived from him by Josef and Hagen was, in the doctor's mind, not enough to get the authorities involved. The doctor was the type of man that did not want a police investigation and publicity. The doctor was very adamant that if he were to find out about any other partnerships that Josef were to get involved, or any other real estate matters Josef and Hagen were to be involved, with other people, through the AFC Bank, the doctor felt it his obligation to warn those people. Josef and Hagen knew about this and were grateful to Timmerman about his discretion. However, their gratefulness was not great enough to refund the money that was held back from the doctor. That decision was really Josef's. Hagen was more sympathetic. Timmerman was a good man. However, a little bad feelings between them was livable. Returning the funds was not only not going to happen but they knew the doctor didn't want people to know he was swindled. Bad publicity for the doctor and his practice. The warning that would be given by the doctor to any future persons who could be deceived by the two thieves would be very subtle and not so overwhelming as to accuse Hagen and Josef as people who would intentionally steal or commit fraud. It was just a warning that Josef and Hagen were not very careful in how they handled other people's money. This all had to be in confidence. This is what the doctor did with George Harvey when the doctor was at his reunion in Southwest Florida.

Hagen contacted his two sons in Florida where they had been working for quite some time. It was the first time in many years Hagen spoke with them. Sofie and Hagen were extremely hurt, years ago, when they found out that their sons were gay. Since Sofie found out about her sons, Hagen forbid her to associate with them. But Sofie would speak to her sons whenever she could without Hagen knowing. Their sons 'condition' was embarrassing and really hurt Hagen. He thought that Sofie's illness may be the catalyst to bring his wife and sons together, so they could become a family again. It was something Hagen has missed terribly. His sons were so hurt when their own parents turned on them for something they had no control over, that they decided not to see their parents. Sofie, however, had been contacting them, from time to time, for years. They did give their best to their father, and sympathized with him, and indicated that they hoped they would be able to see him some day if he came to Florida. It was not a great phone call for Hagen.

Dr. Timmerman, a more companionate man, agreed to visit Sofie. He knew her, and liked her, from their social outings some time before the Rynsburger partnership dissolved. The doctor was not the type of person to hold the sins of the husband against the husband's wife. So Dr. Timmerman visited Sofie Vinke, from time to time, for several months, when she went to the Institute for treatments, The doctor discussed the medical progression of her disease with her doctors and then with Sofie. Sofie took comfort in her talks with Dr. Timmerman. Timmerman very seldom spoke with Hagen unless it was absolutely necessary and then only briefly. Hagen did get a feeling that Dr. Timmerman really didn't enjoy speaking with him, but was doing it for Sofie. However, Hagen, a man with great prestige at a highly respected bank, felt that when he asked someone to do something, that person would always follow his orders. He just didn't get that feeling with Timmerman.

****

Back in Orlando, Josef had spoken with Hagen who related the news about Sofie. Josef felt somewhat upset. He immediately called his wife, Lena, who decided to visit with Sofie almost daily and became Sofie's "go to person" while Sofie was going through the side effects of her treatment. Hagen was grateful for the friendship of Nicolaus and Lena. It helped him tremendously to be able to continue his very stressful work at the Bank and his more stressful schemes and meetings with Josef.

After a week in Orlando, Bram searched out a parcel of property in the heart of Orlando that was undeveloped where much of the infrastructure for the property had been completed. It was called International Capital Park. The owner of the parcel had financial trouble and the bank, who was holding the mortgage, was ready to foreclose. The owner was looking for a sale to put off the foreclosure, keep their credit, and make some kind of arrangement with their bank to accept the proceeds of a sale. Josef meet with the owner of the property and determined it was a 135,000 acre parcel that was zoned for multi uses. The density still had not been determined for the number of residential units nor the amount of commercial square footage. However Bram found out that since the property was near the University of Central Florida, the University had been in negotiation with the current owner to purchase a large parcel of the property for purposes of building a teaching hospital and a medical school for the University. The negotiations were still on going as Josef was contemplating the purchase. Bram had also determined that the State of Florida was contemplating purchasing a portion of the property for the purpose of constructing a 6 lane highway as a second entrance to the Orlando airport, which was desperately needed. If the negotiations with the State could not be finalized, the State was ready to file an eminent domain action to obtain the property. All of this was music to Josef's ears. The asking purchase price for the property was the outstanding principal amount of the owner's mortgage plus all accumulated interest and all costs to close, all in the neighborhood of $65 million. But, for Josef, money was no object. Josef told Bram to draft the usual Letter of Intent and when fully executed, send it to Brian Koop to draft the purchase agreement.

Brian was shocked when he saw the Letter of Intent along with the survey of the property that took 18 pages of survey's paper at 36 inches by 48 inches! The purchase agreement would be huge and complicated. Bram told Brian to draft the agreement at the asking price. Loan documents would be on Brian's desk from the bank's lawyers in 6 weeks. This was a huge closing. This transaction made the Alico Mine closing look simple. 14 families were involved in the ownership of the property. Kopp's fees would be huge!

Due to dozens of title problems with the property, which all had to be fixed, and several internal conflicts with the families involved in the ownership of the property, as well as the urgency on the part of the bank holding the mortgage, it turned into a three day closing while all the problems were solved. The loan documents were again similar to all the of the other acquisition loan documents. However, Joe Hyland's development company's ownership in this parcel was diluted again to 35%. Joe and all of his companies were the only personal guarantees for the loan of $72.5 million. Brian again had a long conversation with Joe about the guarantee and the dilution of his ownership interest. The amount of personal guarantees outstanding for Joe Hyland was now over a billion dollars. Joe's response to Brian's rant was a usual Joe Hyland response, 'what's the difference between a billion dollars outstanding in guarantees or five million dollars of guarantees'. If things go bad, it doesn't make any difference. Joe was convinced that the real estate boom was still alive and well. This boom would still be around until all of Joe's developments were completed and paid off. Then everyone will all be rich! What a fool, Brian thought.

However, the dilution of Joe's ownership was a very big thorn in Joe's side. After he saw the dilution of interest, Joe immediately called Josef to discuss this issue prior to executing any loan documents. Joe was under the impression that the dilution to 40% on the mine was for the mine only and his 50% would be kept for all future acquisitions. Josef was not as cordial about this call as normal. Josef reminded Joe about the screw up on the mangrove parcel at Largo Del Sol and the inability of Joe to convince Robert Coulson to sell Riverside Custom Homes. The first issue, Joe reminded Josef that Joe paid all the fees incurred with the mangrove parcel out of his pocket. The second issue, dealing with Robert Coulson was something that could never have happen. Coulson wouldn't have taken any amount of money for the company. There was no way that deal could have been made. Joe arranged the meeting because Joseph asked him to. Josef was not in the mood to discuss either issue. The ownership interest is what it is and that was it. Then Josef indicated to Hyland that he was aware of some of the draws that have been requested by Joe's office over the last year. Josef indicated that those draws were fully complied with by the Bank, without complaint. Over that period some extra funds had been put in those request. Josef said that he was aware that Joe was probably recouping his mangrove fees from the Bank. Nothing was said by either Joe or Hagan, but that is why there was a dilution of Joe's ownership in this acquisition. What goes around comes around. Josef made it quite clear that Joe needs to do his part in this partnership and not try to screw his partners. But Josef told Joe straight up not to try to deceive a deceiver. Joe knew he had made many millions of dollars over the last few years, so to continue with this conversation would have been fruitless, if not dangerous. The International Capital Park property closed in March, 2007, and Joe Hyland, with his reduced equity interest, executed all documents as drafted.

Sofie Hagen passed two weeks later. Dr. Timmerman, his wife Elisa, Hagen, Josef and his wife, Lena were at her side when she passed. Dr. Timmerman signed the death certificate. Nicolaus wanted to leave as soon as the death certificate was signed. Elisa just didn't understand why he wanted to leave Hagen so soon. But they both left. Hagen and Joe knew the reason and admired the way he had treated Sofie during her illness. Nicolaus went beyond the call of his personal and professional duty for Sofie. Hagen would not forget that.

Hyland flew to Amsterdam for the funeral. The night after the funeral, Josef, Hagen, Bram and Joe had dinner. They went to Restaurant Vermeer, a very expensive dining experience located in the Red Light District, with one of the best, but most expensive wine lists. Josef ordered two 250 Euro bottles of cabernet. All of the meals on the menu changed daily depending on what fresh seasonal foods and ingredients were available. Each meal was at least 125 Euros each. During diner, they discussed each project and their status. Hagen, due to his circumstances with his wife's death, was extremely quit and still depressed, so Josef did all the talking.

Largo Del Sol was completed. There were no law suits by the Condominium Association for construction defects or the mangrove parcel.

"Good job on Largo Del Sol, Joe" said Josef. Nothing was said about Joe's recoupment of the mangrove fees.

"I understand that two of the three phases in Coconut Cove Park are completed and sold out with just a few units left to close. All the amenities are complete including the roads for phase three." Said Josef. "However, I understand that all of phase three is sold out, but some of the purchasers are asking for their deposits back."

"There are a few who are claiming defaults by the Developer under their purchase agreements. I believe it is due to the fact that those purchasers believe the price is now too high and either want the price reduced or their money back." Said Joe gingerly. "They are all claiming different reasons for developer violations under the purchase agreements."

"Like what?" asked Josef?

"Some of the claims include the fact that we are in violation of some Federal law, I think Koop calls it the Federal Interstate Land Sales Act or ILSA." Said Joe. "Others are claiming the square footage of the units are not the same as set forth in the prospectus. Others claim the amenities are not the quality or the size that were represented to them. Things like that."

"What does Koop say?" asked Josef.

"He says they have no case." Replied Joe. "But I do believe the real estate boom has slowed slightly for a short period of time. Prices all over Lee County, not just our developments, are now at a price that some people are finding it hard to finance their units. The appraisals on some of the properties, initiated by the purchaser's lenders, are coming in lower than the purchase price. Lenders are demanding their customers put more money down to comply with their loan commitments. However, I still believe it is just a slight slowdown and prices will start to move up again. Prices, over the past several years, have been going up so fast, in such a short time, a short slowdown may be needed"

"What's our response?" again asked Josef.

"Koop says once the units are completed, send the purchasers their 20 day notice to close, and if they refuse, take their 20% deposit, cancel their purchase agreement, and resell the unit. We have no contingencies in our purchase agreement for financing, so appraisals should not matter with closing the units. " Replied Joe. "And I believe I can probably sell the defaulted units for more money than the original purchase price!"

"I don't want their deposit, I want the current purchase price in full. Make them close." Demanded Josef.

"Can't do that. The State of Florida, Department of Condominium, will not allow a developer to have the remedy of specific performance to require a purchaser to buy a residential unit." Replied Joe. "The developer's only recourse is to take their deposit and resell the unit."

"What a crock of shit." Harshly replied Josef. "How many of these assholes do we have.

"Right now about 8," replied Joe. "However, there are so many asshole attorneys out there, that they need to find ways to make fees to survive. Therefore, if an attorney comes across a purchaser who wants out of their purchase agreement, those slimy attorneys are advising their clients that they can find some way to declare a default with their purchase agreement and demand their deposits back. Then the attorney ask his client if they know any others in the same position. The attorneys are killing us." Said Joe.

"Do something about this Joe. Get Koop on it and stop this. We need to close units." Angrily stated Josef.

Hagen finally replied after listing to all of this banter, "The loans will not work if the bank only gets the deposits. It is a red flag on the loan and the loan will be audited based on this problem. The bank needs the entire purchase price or the shit may hit the fan." Meekly said Hagen. "I can hold off the Board of Directors for only a short period of time."

"Gentleman, Even if we settle with some of the purchaser by giving 10% of their deposit back and keeping the other 10%, I know my sales people can sell the unit quickly." Remarked Joe. "There are still thousands of anxious people to get in on this real estate boom. We may even be able to make more money when a buyer defaults, especially if we take the entire 20% deposit."

"I don't want this problem." Insisted Josef. "Joe this is just another mess up you will need to clean up. You are managing these projects. Fix the problems."

Joe was not in the mood to argue and just wanted the conversation to end. He knew if it continued, the same issue with the Snook Point Hotel commercial project would come up. Even though construction on the hotel had not started, Reservation Agreements for units are being cancelled daily. They are all non-binding Agreements and this will really hurt the Snook Point development if the hotel cannot be built. So Joe changed the subject towards Hagen and his wife's death. Joe tried to console Hagen, but it was difficult. Meantime, Josef was furious about what may be happening back in Florida. He and Hagen had a lot of money on the line as well as draws that neither one of them wanted to be forensically audited. Jail is not a place Josef would be able to tolerate.

Even though Hagen may not have been thinking the same thoughts as Josef, jail would also not be a place he would be able to tolerate. Death is a better remedy. Hagen would have his time, in the next few weeks, to think about that issue.

Meantime, Hyland skipped the rest of his wine and started ordering Crown Royal neat. Josef was seeing something happing to Joe, but just wasn't sure what it was. Josef thought Joe was tough and could live through these types of issues they were currently facing. Josef still hoped he was right.

The 3 partners and Bram finished their meal in record time. Usually, Josef liked to dine for at least 3 or more hours. It was a time of pleasure and true relaxation for him. But tonight, the meal was over in one and a half hours.

"You know what to do Joe, now make sure you and Koop get this done. We have contracts and the purchasers have to honor them. Don' let some greedy fucking attorneys do anything that would upset the plan Hagen and you and I have with the Bank. Hagen has just lost his wife. Don't let him loose his freedom!" exclaimed Josef as he and Hagen left the restaurant with Joe sitting there with the bill in his hand. What did Josef mean by the fact that Joe was somehow involved with "this plan" with the Bank? Joe knew that Hagen was collecting pre-paid profits for the Bank on their interest in the projects and Josef was collecting his pre-paid profits on the projects for his interest. The loan committee must have approved that or the loans would never have gone through. But what was the scheme Josef was alluding to. Hyland knew Josef was not happy with a few disgruntled buyers in Coconut Cove Park, but that was just a drop in the bucket compared to all of the money involved in all the Florida projects. What was going on? It was something Joe was trying to figure out on the plane from Amsterdam back to his Largo Del Sol condo in Fort Myers. The answer would come to him soon enough. But not after several more Crown Royals.

****

It was June, 2001, Roger Spector had just lost his father four months earlier. He was out of a job since Joe Hyland and Josef Rynsburger has just told him he would no longer be involved in their new development company. It was devastating. Roger had quit his job, given up his real estate broker's license and readied himself for a new adventure as an entrepreneur. Luckily, George Harvey liked Roger, for obvious reasons. George always made sure Roger fell on his feet. While Roger lived with his mother helping her through the grieving period after the death of a spouse, George Harvey had his company, GHIC put Roger back on the payroll. Roger felt bad just getting paid so he would come over to The Riverview Golf & Country Club and do odd jobs. He was the starter for the golf course several days a week; helped in the restaurant and other odd jobs just to justify in his own mind he was not just taking charity. Once his mother started to do things again with her circle of friends and her sister, Cathy, came around a little more, Martha seemed to be able to coop with life much better. Roger was now ready to try the Aruba job.

Roger Spector then told his mother about his offer from George Harvey to be the casino manager for the new Wyndham Hotel & Casino being built on Palm Beach in Aruba. He told her all about the salary and benefits and the ability to come and visit here periodically, all as part of his benefits of the job. Roger didn't really want to go to Aruba, but the offer was just too good to pass up. While the hotel was being built Roger would be working at La Cabana Beach Resort & Casino learning the casino business. One of George's partner in the new Wyndham casino is also a partner in the La Cabana casino. Roger would be staying at one of the La Cabana condominium for no cost until the Wyndham is completed. George is also providing Roger with a used automobile. Roger's mother didn't seem as surprised or sad as Roger thought she would. It was if she already knew about it. But how could that be?

"It's a great opportunity and George Harvey is a generous man." said Martha. "You need to live your life. I appreciate the time you spent with me during those first few months after your father died. But it's time for you to move on."

Roger was ready and even exited to start a new job in a new place. He packed everything he could carry on the plane and shipped the rest to the La Cabana Resort. No more Joe Hyland or Josef Rynsburger. A new life. Roger hadn't spent any of the $50,000.00 he received as consideration to transfer his interest in the development company to Hyland. So he got himself a cashier's check for that amount and it would be his first deposit in his new checking account in Aruba. Roger had few friends except for the people he worked with at the Country

Club, so there were really no good byes except for George Harvey and his mother. Off he went to the great unknown with much enthusiasm.
****

It was December, 2007. Josef and Hagen were meeting for dinner at the Bridges restaurant in the Red Light District in Amsterdam. Josef enjoyed eating and socializing in that part of Amsterdam. That classy restaurant is located inside the Hotel Sofitel. This restaurant was the perfect destination for a seafood diner. It was known for its fresh fish, wine pairings for each course and outdoor dining. It had been almost a year since Sofie died. Hagen had not gone out much. This dinner was both a social gathering and business meeting for Hagen and Josef. Both of them had heard that the real estate boom was stating to slow and more and more buyers were abandoning their purchase agreements and leaving their deposits on the table. It was cheaper for a purchaser to lose their deposit, than to purchase a property whose price was falling on a monthly basis. Especially if they were purchasing it for investment. Investors do not want to start off with an investment 'under water' where the mortgage is higher than the value of the property. As they were eating their appetizers, Josef started the business part of the evening.

"Have you got your update on our projects in Florida? Asked Josef. "It is starting to be a little worrisome."

"I have heard and so has the Bank's Board of Directors. They want to meet with me next week." Replied Hagen.

"Right now Phase 3 of Coconut Cove Park seems to be the biggest problem with purchasers. Luckily, it's our lowest priced properties." Said Josef. "At least most of Phases 1 and 2 are closed. Although there is some big shot Fort Myers condominium attorney who is claiming that at least 67 of the units in Phase 2 have Chinese dry wall problems. I don't even know what that is." Admitted Josef.

"It's a mold problem with dry wall that came from China out of contaminated mines The Chinese just dumped the bad batch on the United States market at a reduced price and developers purchased them quickly." Said Hagen. "We didn't buy them, our general contractor purchased them. I understand the problem is rapid all over the Southern states, where the real estate boom was the highest, not just our development."

"We'll get Joe and Koop to handle that problem, even if we have to sue our general contractor." Replied Josef. "I am more worried about the closings in Phase 3 of the project. As I understand it, Coconut Point Park has closed way over half of the units and only a few of them have Chinese dry wall problems. However, the rest of the unclosed units, either the purchasers have walked and Koop has sent the Bank the deposits, and the rest of the units, are either in litigation or are threatening litigation if the purchaser does not get their deposit back." Angrily stated Josef.

"My real concern is Snook Point." Said Hagen. "We have approval for the loan for the hotel but if it cannot be built, that development will not be a success. The hotel is the main attraction for the whole project. If it's not constructed, everything in that community goes down the shit hole!"

"We have no pre-sales on the hotel. It will take a little less than 3 years to complete. We can sell the units during the time the hotel is being constructed, even if we lower the purchase prices a bit." Said Josef. "We must get Hyland to get the permits and start construction of the hotel soon! That is absolute."

"We won't have a problem with Joe, the problem will be Koop and that damn Cathy Cutter. She is too smart for the job. She needs to listen more and keep her mouth shut. And that bitch that Joe is living with, Ivana. She loves money, but she does know her real estate. Joe is being pounded on all sides to not build the hotel." Declared Hagen.

"I don't care who pounds Joe and for what reason." Said Josef. "We tell him what to do and he needs to do it or he doesn't get paid. No matter what, it has to be done, Joe will do it if we tell him to. He has no money tied up in the project. He'll still get paid monthly. We'll make him build it! End of story."

"I'll send Bram there to talk to Joe and tell him that the first draw will be coming on the hotel and he needs to start to get purchase agreements. Koop has confirmed that since the hotel is considered a commercial condominium, the State does not have to approve the documents or purchase agreements. Get Joe's sales staff to start writing purchase agreements and get the 20% deposits. Promise them anything! Get Rutter to prepare the first draw as usual and send it to you for disbursement." Demanded Josef. "And make sure our money is in every draw request."

"I will, but I need to hear what the Board of Directors have to say about the project." Replied Hagen. "The loan has been approved for well over 100% of the construction costs, and I hope the Board understands the importance of this hotel being built."

The two went on to their entrees and talked a little more socially for the rest of the evening. It was getting harder for Josef to be social with Hagen. Too much money was at stake!

They did confirm with each other that, other than the Hotel, everything built so far was sold and closed at Snook Point. However, only the 124 low rise condominium, and the 210 unit high rise condominium and 60 cabanas have been built and all sold. There is still over 1400 units left to be built at Snook Point not including the hotel. Only two homes have been built on the 60 waterfront lots, but all of the lots have been sold. That's all they cared about at Snook Point. No one mentioned the acquisition loan. Even though the sale of the residential lots paid down a great deal of that loan, the loan was for more than 100% of the acquisition. There were still several million dollars outstanding. And interest was accruing. They were both thinking about that at that time.

The mine was in full operation and producing a small cash flow. Not enough to fund the large loan by AFC Bank, but all bills and employees were being paid. However several employees have been laid off to save some money. Most important, Hagen and Josef were being paid.

The amenities at Hidden Woods in Orland were almost complete and 6 model homes had been completed and furnished. No other homes had been sold yet, but 35 lots have been purchased by preferred builders. In the back of both Hagen and Josef's minds was the fact that they are now glad that they didn't buy Riverside Custom Homes. Each knew what the other was thinking, but nothing was said.

The International Capital Park in Orlando is still in front of the city council for final approval for a determination of residential density and commercial density. Negotiations are still in progress with the State on purchase of land for the airport road and the University is still negotiating for a parcel for the hospital.

Hagen reported that their bank account in Fort Lauderdale now has $4.550 million dollars in it. It is a nice cushion, but it has been depleting since both Josef and Hagen like to live well. The manner in which they are accustomed to living, requires that they both take funds from that account to live the way they enjoy life. Both Hagen and Josef were thinking that the real estate boom in Florida needs to rekindle soon so that they continue their deceptions.

Things aren't great, but not that bad they thought. Little did they know what was coming?

****

Two weeks later Josef got two calls. The first was from Bram who was in Fort Myers.

"Joe agrees with us. He also wants to start the hotel." Stated Bram. "However, he is getting a lot of obstruction from Koop, Cutter and everyone else in Southwest Florida, including both the Cape Coral and the Fort Myers paper. Both have had editorials about the Hotel. One paper is calling Hyland, 'The bravest developer ever' by beginning the hotel project at this time. They are saying that without presales the project is doomed and so is Snook Point. The sales people at Snook Point are not even getting lookers. But Joe is adamant and he has Cathy putting in the first draw."

"Good, keep it going. Stay there as long as it takes to make sure the shovel hits the dirt on this project" Said Josef. "It is the lynch pin for the development. Cape Coral wants this and needs this. Real estate boom or no boom!"

"I will do that. I will keep you up to date." Said Bram. "Talk to you in a few days."

The second call was from Josef's wife Lena. She indicated that she just got back from the doctor and they had taken a chest x-ray as part of her problems that she had been having with coughing up some blood and irritation to her throat and chest. She was scheduled for an MRI the next day. Josef was surprised that they scheduled her so quickly for the MRI. But he and Lena had never been as close as Hagen and Sofie. Josef wasn't that concerned. Both Lena and Josef have been, or are seeing other people, from time to time, over the last several years of their marriage. Both are aware of this fact. Both have been all right with the open marriage concept for some time. Josef asked Lena to give Nicolaus Timmerman a call and have him look at the MRI, as a second opinion, after the radiologist has completed his review. Josef thought that Timmerman could make Lena feel better, no matter the outcome of the test, since the doctor and his wife have been very close. Lena agreed.

The next day, the radiologist and Timmerman were reviewing the MRI and some other tests Lena had taken and they both came to the same conclusion. Lena had stage IV non-small lung cancer. That type of cancer is the most advanced form of that disease. In stage IV, the cancer has metastasized, or spread, beyond the lungs into other areas of her body. The MRI confirmed that. The five year survival rate for this type of cancer was less than 10%. Lena was devastated. Over the next few months, Lena received chemotherapy and immunotherapies as a secondary approach. Nothing was working and Lena was not responding well to any of the treatments. Part of the problem was that Josef seemed somewhat concerned and fairly helpful during the treatments, but his mind was always somewhere else. His bigger concern was for his Florida projects. Therefore, Dr. Timmerman was the person Lena had to rely on most during this very difficult time.

Lena could tell the doctor anything and he was always there when she needed someone. Even Hagen would help out, from time to time, maybe because he remembered the grief Sofie went through, but Lena was always second to whatever was going on in Josef's life at the time. Josef even went to Florida for 10 days to check on the projects while Lena was in the midst of her treatments. Everyone in their circle of acquaintances, could tell how badly Lena felt about the lack of sympathy she got from her husband. Both of their sons were drug attics and had been through in-house treatment several times without any good results. So even Lena's own sons were not a great help during this period. Dr. Timmerman was furious with Josef and his sons. This was not the first time the doctor had been furious with Josef. Lena was an outpatient of the same cancer institute that Sofie attended several times. Sometimes she stayed for a week or more. She was failing quickly.

Just over three months after Lena was diagnosed, Josef and Bram went to Fort Myers to check on the Hotel. It had been started, but there were still no purchase agreements for any units. The price per unit for a three bedroom, three bathroom condo hotel room was still $1.5 million. Not even a bite on any unit. Joe and Josef discussed that maybe once the hotel was finished, they should form another management company and hire a brand named hotel Management Company to run the hotel, just as a hotel, and sell the units when the boom resumes. It was only a thought since there was still just under two years left before it would be completed. Josef told Bram to check on the "big named" hotel chains like Marriott, Hilton and Weston and see if any would be interested. Bram agreed to make the contacts.

But there was a bigger problem. The Chinese dry wall problem at Coconut Cove Park was becoming extremely expensive. 44 units had the problem and most of the owners were still living in them. The mold and odor made it almost impossible for people to live in. It was determined that to fix the problem the units would have to be completed gutted, and all new wiring and all new dry wall had to be installed in those units. The people who were living in the units would have to be housed somewhere for at least 4-6 months while the work was being completed. The costs was at least $150,000.00 per unit or more, depending on the size of the unit, plus housing costs! Josef was furious.

"This is not our fault." Said Josef. "There has to be someone responsible for this bad dry wall. How would we have known about it until it was installed?"

"I agree." Said Joe. "I have been talking to Koop and he believes that the general contractor should be responsible for all the costs."

"I am sure, that the general contractor has insurance that should take care of this." Said Joe. "We are not going to pay for this."

While Brian Koop and the general contractor and the provider of the dry wall were in the middle of trying to resolve the issues, all of the residents in the affected units hired an attorney to sue the developer for the costs to fix their units and for the cost associated with the time they had to live somewhere else while the disaster was being fixed. Attorney fees were mounting on this issue and no one wanted to purchase the remaining units in Phase 3. Interest was mounting on the loan! Also, others who had purchase agreements for units in Phase 3 were also afraid to close until the issue was resolved, and most of them demanded their deposits back or would sue the developer even though those units didn't have the Chinese dry wall problem. Phase 3 of Coconut Cove Park was really turning into a fiasco. One that AFC Bank had just become aware of.

Meanwhile, at the Bank, Hagen was meeting with the Board of Directors. The Board had several items that they wanted to discuss with Hagen. All were not good. First, the problems with the Chinese dry wall was delaying the closings of almost 125 units in Phase 3 at Coconut Cove Park. Interest was running much higher than forecasted and the costs to remedy the problem was not going to come from the

Bank. The Board wanted to know what solution Hagen and Josef had to resolve that problem. Hagen told the Board that Josef was at the project and trying to work something out. Hagen further explained that Josef's wife was going through treatments for stage IV lung cancer and Josef's mind and his efforts were focus there. The Board was not sympathetic. They reminded Hagen that the Bank had a 10% interest in the project and they were not even getting their pre-paid profits. They wanted to know where the money for the draws were going. Their profits were part of the draws. Hagen assured them that he would look into it and have a memo to them in a few days.

The next issue was the hotel at Snook Point. The Board had not seen any purchase agreements and the hotel was in the process of being constructed. What was their plan to pay back this very large loan? The board has committed a large amount of funds for that project and, as of that meeting, there was no realistic chance that the hotel would be sold out by the time it was completed. This was a very large and troublesome problem. Which brought up the last issue. This issue was to be kept confidential even from the Bank's partners in the Florida projects. ABN Amro, has contacted the Board, and the Board was putting Hagen, the President of the Bank, on notice of ABN's intent to make an offer to purchase AFC Bank. Again, this was to be very confidential. ABN wants to send some forensic accountants into the AFC Bank to review some of their larger loans and especially the ones that the Bank has set up as a subsidiary to own a portion of the project for which the loans were made. Those would include all of the loans on the Florida projects. This will take some time to complete since they are all complicated. However, the Board wanted to know if there was something they needed to know about those loans that they didn't already know. And they wanted to know right then and there. Hagen assured the Board that they have been kept up to date on everything dealing with those loans. Hagen was really nervous and knew that unless something drastic happen, or ABN decided not to continue their acquisition, there would be huge problems with him and Josef. Hagen had to tell Josef when he returned from the States. Hagen thought what a turn of events that never could have been anticipated. But one thing Hagen knew was that he was not going to jail no matter what Josef had to say.

Josef and Bram came back from Florida several days later. Hagen and Josef saw each other at the cancer institute when both were visiting Lena. Josef brought Hagen up to date on the Chinese dry wall situation and the Snook Point hotel situation. Josef wanted to discuss them as well as the larger cash flow problem happening at the mine. Hagen brought Josef up to date on the Board meeting including the confidential information about the possible acquisition of the Bank. This infuriated Josef! But Hagen had nothing to do with any of those issues. They both had to determine what they were going to do. Josef was so upset that he didn't even go in and see Lena. But Hagen did go visit her. Dr. Timmerman was with her. Nothing was said between Hagen and Timmerman. The bad blood was still there.

Four months later, in July, 2008, Lena passed away. Josef, Hagen and Dr. Timmerman were with Lena when she passed. Dr. Timmerman could tell that it was more of a relief than anything else for Josef. Even Hagen took it worse than Josef. Hagen knew that Josef probably couldn't wait to tell his current girlfriend, who happen to be Laura Wills daughter, that he was finally free. Laura Wills, Joe Hyland's broker for his real estate company, was not very happy about her daughter's relationship with Josef. But her daughter, Alyssa, loved the way Josef flaunted over her and especially how he spent money on her. Jewelry, trips, clothing. Life was good for Alyssa. She was 20 some years younger than Josef, and Josef loved it. Dr. Timmerman signed Lena's death certificate and funeral arrangements were being made. During Lena's last four months on this earth, the Chinese dry wall issue had been resolved. The general contractor's insurance company, after much discussion and a proposed law suit was presented to the insurance company, agreed to pay for their insured to completely gut the units affected and install new wiring and dry wall. In addition, the insurance company paid for up to 6 months of housing and food for the affected owners living in those units. The problem was solved. Other law suits were still going on by the purchasers for the Phase 3 units who didn't want to close due to the crash of the real estate boom that was getting worse each week. However all of the law suits were being settled by Koop, mostly by splitting the deposits with the purchasers. The remaining amounts of the deposits were being sent to the Bank. Some of the purchasers actually walked instead of suing and left their total deposit in the amount of a 20% deposit which was sent to the Bank.

The Bank was not very happy at receiving just the deposits. Interest was mounting and the units for which the deposits were taken, could not be resold. The prices were just too high. Joe would not reduce the price for the units. He was adamant that he did not cause this and he was not going to take the fall for it. The hotel construction was going faster than anticipated and they expected it to be complete so a grand opening could occur on New Year's Eve, 2009. ABN Amro was still going to go ahead with the acquisition of the AFC Bank, but no audits had been scheduled as of the date of Lena's funeral.

Joe came to Amsterdam for Lena's funeral. It was hard for him to travel. The stress of everything that was going on with his business was turning his life upside down. He really believed, in the depths of his heart, that he had done nothing wrong. How could this real estate market effect someone who did everything right for his employees, his purchasers and his partners? Joe just could not face reality. He drank more, ate less and got into drunken fights with Ivana, especially when she was also high on something.

The funeral was just a grave side service and didn't last long. Josef not only did not make any of the arrangements, he did not even speak at the service. A minister who Dr. Timmerman asked to speak, said some kind words about Lena. A chapter in Josef's life finally ended. What a relief.

At the funeral, Josef asked Hyland, Hagen and Bram to get together for dinner the next evening so they could discuss the Florida projects. After the funeral, Josef left and called Alyssa and told her he had purchased a ticket for her to come to Amsterdam for a few days. She could now stay at Josef's home. Josef was in need of some real comfort knowing that maybe the worse was coming. Alyssa packed and was on a plane several hours later. Josef picked Alyssa up at the airport and they went back to Josef's home. Josef said that he really needed some comfort. Having Alyssa there was just the cure. However, Josef did not want anyone to know that Alyssa was there so soon after Lena's passing. Alyssa understood and took the time she could get with Josef and not complain. Josef told Alyssa that things were starting to happen in Florida which may cause some drastic measures. Josef wanted to make sure that he retained not only his freedom, but the money he had been entitled to for the years of hard work, travel and sacrifices when it came to family. His two sons were both out there somewhere in Europe, probably high on some form of new drug. They probably didn't even know that their mother died, or worse, couldn't care. Josef apologized to Alyssa that he had to go to meet Hyland and Hagen for an important business meeting and would be back as soon as he could.

Joe, Josef, Bram and Hagen meet at an off the beaten trail restaurant, Blauw, where Josef was sure no one would see them together. The restaurant was an Indonesian restaurant, with some of the best choices of fish, meat and vegetarian rijstraffels, all fresh, well spiced and all full of exotic flavors. Josef liked good food and wine. The four had a lot to talk about. Both Joe and Hagen gave their condolences to Josef on the passing of his wife. Josef thanked them. Little did they know that Alyssa Wills was back at Josef's home? After they all ordered including Josef ordering his two bottle of expensive 2005 Fairsing Pinot Noer, business was at hand.

It was July 2008, and the real estate boom was close to becoming a full crash in Southwest Florida. Prices were decreasing but not as fast as other location in Florida. Joe looked like he had lost some weight and his skin had a light white tone. He ordered several drinks, instead of drinking the wine Josef ordered. Then he had to excuse himself to go to the rest room. Once there he vomited and his stomach hurt like he was just punched in the gut. After a few minutes, he cleaned himself up and he came back to the table. And even before he sat down, he called the waiter over and order a Crown Royal neat. Josef didn't think much of it. He had seen Joe drink hard many an evening. Joe liked to party. But Hagen was curious what was happening. Was Joe sick? The business meeting went on.

"I understand that the Chinese dry wall situation is being handled and the general contractor's insurance company is handling the remediation and all of the housing costs for the owners." Started Josef. "Are they also handing the units that the developer company still has in inventory with the dry wall problem?"

"Yes and they have been more than cooperative about this whole fiasco." Said Joe. "However, there is still one owner who refuses to let the general contractor fix his unit. Koop has drafted a full release for all of the 44 unit owners with the dry wall problems, including the developer. They and I have all signed the Agreement. The unit owners with the dry wall problem have all been moved out to a hotel on Fort Myers Beach during the remediation, except for one asshole."

"And what does that asshole want from us?" Asked Josef.

"He wants his money back and $200,000.00 in damages." Replied Joe. "Koop says he is stupid. We have provided a complete reasonable cure, at no cost to the affected owners. No judge, in their right mind, would find for this asshole!"

"Let him complain" said Josef. "He'll find out the cost of attorney's fees to fight this and he'll give in."

"The general contractor pleaded with him even when his attorney was with him, but he still refused." Said Joe "Our contractor said this was a onetime offer. All of the remediation will be done at one time. The contractor will not come back and fix his unit if he didn't agree at that time. Koop was there and confirmed that fact with the asshole's attorney. Even his own attorney told him to sign the release, but the asshole wouldn't. His attorney fired him on the spot and told him to get another attorney."

"End of case." Said Joe. "Let's move on. How many units in Phase 3 are left to sell?"

"64. 30 condo units and 34 duplex units." Said Joe. "Of those 64 units we have sent full deposits to the Bank on the units the purchasers walked, and some portion of the deposits, where law suits were filed and we settled the claim. The Bank has applied all those forfeited deposits to the construction loan. All of the law suits on all of those units have now been settled."

"We need to sell them quickly." Interrupted Hagen." "The Bank is nervous about the interest being paid for construction on the Phase 3 loan."

"What else is the Bank nervous about?" asked Josef.

"Everything" said Hagen. "I have been asked to give the Board of Directors a daily report on all the Florida projects. That is not good. It is more likely than not that ABN Amro will be putting in an offer for the Bank in the next few weeks. That means forensic audits on all of our loans."

"What is the problem with that?" Said Joe. "The Bank is aware of the prepaid profits and that the loans are for more than 100% which include all necessary professional fees. Hell they own 10% of all the projects and are getting their profits upfront."

"Are you really that naïve Joe?" said Josef. "You know Hagen and I are skimming some of those proceeds on every draw. Cathy Cutter puts them together every month. You sign off on them."

"I sign off, but I assume she has put them together as you requested every month without any skimming." Said Joe.

"Each draw consists of payroll, your salary, which, by the way, is much higher than usual for what a managing supervisor would normally get, your office overhead, etc, etc." Said Josef. "Don't tell me you are an innocent bystander here."

"I am not felling real well." Said Joe. 'Do you mind if I go back to my hotel and you all can bring me up to date tomorrow?"

"Hell no." barked Josef. "If you fell sick, go throw up in the toilet. Your here as long as I need you here." Said Josef.

"Where are we on the hotel at Snook Point" asked Josef.

"It is way ahead of schedule. We have lots of sub-contractors working on the job." Said Joe in a low and sickly manner. "Few developers are building now and there are lots of subs looking for work. Robb & Stucky decorators are working on the decorating of every room and the first floor entry way and restaurants. It is on schedule to be completed this December and the grand opening event is being worked on by Cathy for a New Year's Eve grand opening." As Joe could hardly finish the sentence since he felt so sick.

"Go back to your hotel Joe." Angularly said Josef. "You are no good in that condition. We'll talk in the morning. Now get out of here!"

Joe, left the restaurant and went back to the hotel where he continued to vomit and cough up blood. This had been slowly happening since Joe's percentage of ownership has been receding each time a new project started. He also had come to the realization that it is him, and only him, on all of the personal guarantees. It was only a few months ago Joe couldn't have cared about signing guarantees. How times change! He is extremely worried about some new Bank looking at the loans and not being as favorable on draws for the borrowers and guarantors as AFC Bank had been. Not only that. Joe has let Ivana be a really bad influence on him. She is spending money faster than Joe can make it and she drinks like a fish and encourages Joe to join in to "have some fun". Living with her at Largo Del Sol is making Joe think twice about having her around. She was fun for the good times, but she doesn't seem to care about the bad times. Let the truth be told, Joe has just been her sugar daddy.

Many people have been concerned with this turn around that Joe has been slowly making. He is drinking much more and earlier each day. Decisions that he needs to make are put on hold. Cathy Rutter has spoken with Brian Koop and Laura Wills about Ivana and Joe's problems. They all understand and believe something needs to be done, but until the hotel is completed, they needed Joe to keep going. The hotel had to be completed. The Bank, the Amsterdam investor and the City of Cape Coral expected the hotel to restart any problems the development companies were having. Cathy, in effect, started to make some of Joe's decisions and started to take over the developments. Koop called her for decisions, Bram spoke with Cathy direct on many issue. Things at Joe Hyland's companies were starting to unravel. But the hotel needed to be complete.

Josef and Hagen were still at the restaurant. They were discussing the other Florida projects. All of the remaining partners and Bram, at the restaurant, understood that nothing more needed to be done at Snook Point once the hotel was completed and up and running. Bram relayed to Josef and Hagen that there were no major hotel chains interested in managing the Hotel. It was the wrong time and the hotel was built as a condominium. The rooms were too big and too expensive. They all came to the conclusion that they would have to manage it themselves. They would need to hire a management company to take care of the hotel and all amenities. Bram was again charged with that task.

The mine was still not bringing in enough cash to handle all of the payroll and the payments to the Bank. They couldn't even get their skimming money from the loan. After some conversation, Josef and Hagen both agreed, it had to be put up for sale. Bram was again chosen for the task of finding a buyer. At least the sale proceeds, whatever amount it turned out to be, could be paid to the Bank to pay down the loan. Snook Point was the main development they wanted to continue with.

The Hidden Woods development in Orlando was going slow, but there were possible purchasers for building homes. But no one was still living at Hidden Woods. Preferred builders were showing lots and their homes, but no buyers. Plenty of lookers, so see what happens thought Josef and Hagan. They may continue with that development. Or, they may just sell that development also. The amount owed on the remaining loans were huge!

International Capital Park was not performing as they wanted. The zoning and density was taking much longer than anticipated and the attorney fees were mounting day by day. The State of Florida was reconsidering the second entrance to the airport. The University of Central Florida was moving so slow, they believed the University may have changed their mind about the hospital. Again, after some conversation, Hagen and Josef decided to sell the parcel. Bram was given the task to start that selling process.

The elephant in the room was the ABN Amro purchase of the Bank. All three of the men sitting and eating their dinner and drinking fine wine knew a big storm was on the way. No one wanted to mention it. Hagen was nervous, not only about his job, but about possible jail time. He could not handle that. Josef was thinking about how he could spin his way around the audits and blame it on someone else. And Alyssa was waiting for him back at his home. Bram was just disgusted with where his job has brought him. He has been Josef's mule. Could he be held responsible for some reason? Maybe he needed an attorney?

Bram had just been charged with doing tasks that may mitigate the Bank's problems. He was charged with selling failing projects at the worst time in real estate history. He was also charged with getting the Snook Point hotel cash flowing. Bram got up and said he wanted to go back to the hotel. In effect, Bram didn't want to hear any more that could further incriminate him. Bram had to do something for himself and not just Josef. Everything was beginning to cave and he was right in the middle.

After Bram left, Josef asked Hagen, how much money was in the Community Banks in the States. Hagen said just over $10 million. Josef thought it should be much more with over a billion dollars in loans. Josef actually started to believe that since Hagen was the only signature, that maybe Hagen was skimming money from Josef. As Josef has said many times, 'don't deceive a deceiver'. But Josef decided not to say anything at that time.

Josef then paid the check and the men left and went their own ways. The storm was beginning to build.

CHAPTER 13

I T WAS NOW just over 3 months since Joe Hyland's funeral. Denise Hudak had just picked up the Immunity agreement drafted by the County Attorney's office for Cathy Rutter. She emailed the document to Brian Koop's office so he could review it and asked him to get back with her as soon as possible. Arthur Winslow wanted to wait to go back to Amsterdam until after he sat in on the interview with Cathy Rutter. Her knowledge of how the draws and funds were disbursed would help Arthur's investigation when he goes back to Amsterdam. The Immunity Agreement included any criminal liability for any information she was privy to, any documents executed by her and any funds that were disbursed by Cathy Rutter, or any bank, including AFC Bank to any person or company for any development that Josef Hyland, Hagan Vinke, Josef Rynsburger, AFC Bank or any companies or persons or other banks, associated with them and all developments involved with such persons or companies, including but not limited to Largo Del Sol, Coconut Cove Park, Snook Point, Alico Grand Mine, Hidden Woods or International Capital Park. The Immunity Agreement was 6 pages and Brian Koop had one of his criminal attorney look at the documents to make sure Cathy Rutter was covered criminally under the Agreement. Once it was approved by Koop's firm, Cathy Rutter signed the Agreement. Brian emailed the fully executed immunity Agreement to Denise Hudak's office and waited for her to call him.

The next morning, Denise was on her way to work when she stopped into The Grind coffee shop. The Grind was just adjacent to the entrance to Coconut Cove Park. She frequented the establishment nearly twice a week. It was ironic to her that one of the developments involved with Joe Hyland was so close to where she gets her coffee every week. She never did see Joe Hyland at the coffee shop and the owner of the shop, Janet Nelson told Denise that she didn't know Joe Hyland, although she had heard of him. Joe Hyland and the last owner of the strip center where the coffee shop was located had a long ongoing dispute over one of the exits to the strip mall. All Janet knew was that they settled it and everything was fine. Denise ordered her usual medium coffee and an almond biscotti. When she was putting her cream in the coffee, a person walked into the shop and Janet said welcome fairly loudly to a customer that she had not seen for some time. She called him Roger Spector. Denise's ears pooped up.

Roger and Janet had a conversation and Denise was doing whatever she could to try to listen without being obvious. Roger told Janet that after his father passed about 11 or 12 years ago, he moved in with his mother for a few months while she was going through the grieving process of losing a husband. After staying with his mother for those months, Roger decided he needed to do something with his life. He thought he had found his calling by going into partnership with a coworker and friend of his. But within several months working together, his partner turned out to be quite a turncoat. He was thrown out of his own company. Luckily Roger's family had a great friend, George Harvey. Janet knew George and even let him use the back conference room on occasions. He was President Bush's ambassador to France for a couple of years. Roger told Janet that for the last 10 years he had been the casino manager for the Wyndham Hotel in Aruba. He told Janet he loved Aruba and the job, but the hours are crazy. He was ready to come back to Florida to look for something here.

George Harvey had retired after his time in France and moved to West Palm Beach to a mansion on the Ocean. Roger told Janet he felt so isolated on an island. Several years ago, he did meet someone from Minnesota who was with 3 of her girlfriends while on vacation at the hotel. They really hit it off. She came back several times, the last time by herself and eventually they got married. She is staying in Aruba with their two young sons right now. Aruba is not a place to raise his kids. Roger was just back in Florida since his mother was quite ill and he came back to check on her. Denise was shocked. What a coincidence. She deliberated if she should speak with him or leave it be. However, she would kick herself if she didn't approach him.

After Roger got his latte and muffin, he sat at one of the booths. Denise walked over to the booth and introduced herself to Roger. He was a little confused.

"What does a County Attorney investigator want with me?" said Roger.

"It's a long and probably boring story, but your name has come up in one of our cases." Said Denise.

"There has got to be some mistake." Inquired Roger.

"It's no mistake. You used to work with Joe Hyland at GHIC, didn't you?" asked Denise. "He passed away over 3 months ago and we are investigating his death."

"Someone killed Joe?" Asked Roger. "He may be a jerk, but kill him, I don't think so. I didn't even know he died."

"Hence the investigation." Said Denise.

"Well I have the best alibi possible." Said Roger. "I was in Aruba managing the Wyndham Hotel Casino for a partnership headed by George Harvey. I live there with my wife and two sons."

"Glad to hear that, but you were really not a suspect in Joe's death." Said Denise, which she knew to be lie. "We were looking for you to talk about the development company you were involved in with Joe Hyland and how that all related to Josef Rynsburger and Hagen Vinke."

"Names out of my past. I have tried to forget them." Said Roger.

Denise and Roger sat and chatted for about an hour. Denise did take a few minutes to call Alex to tell him she found Roger Spector and was chatting with him. He was amazed. Roger did tell Denise the plan that Hyland, Rynsburger and Vinke had for the development of residential projects in the Fort Myers area. Vinke was on the foreign loan committee for AFC Bank. He was also working his way up to President of the bank, although Roger didn't know if he actually did become President. Denise told Roger that Vinke did become President. Roger indicated that the plan was to have AFC Bank become a 10% owner in the development company, Rynsburger a 40% owner and Joe and Roger a 50% owner. Since the Bank was a partner and Vinke was on the loan committee, the Bank could loan the development companies more than 100% of the amount needed for acquisition loans or construction loans. This way, no one had to put up any money for anything! Vinke would convince the Bank that the additional funds were for professional fees and miscellaneous cost. Most important, since the bank was an owner, the extra funds could also be for pre-paid profits for the owners. So the Bank could loan out money, get it right back as pre-paid profits, and have the development company pay interest on those same funds. What a con job by Vinke to make the loans look really good. All the overhead by Joe and Roger's Development Company including payroll, rent, copy machines, you name it, and even the partner's salaries were packaged in the monthly draws. No one had to pay a cent. The Bank paid it all, including their monthly interest.

Denise discussed with Roger whether or not if he actually knew if those facts were accurate. If so, Denise thought, without saying anything to Roger, that maybe it could be considered fraud or theft. Roger could not definitely say that it was true since he was only there for a few months. Cathy Rutter was the only person who did all of the draws and no one was able to do the draws except Rutter. Then Denise took a leap out of the blue. Denise asked Roger if Rutter could had known that the pre-paid profits targeted to Roger and Joe were actually skimmed off the top of the draws by Vinke and Rynsburger? Specter could not confirm what Rutter knew. He couldn't even confirm what he knew himself, it was only speculation on the part of Roger. He was tossed out of the company before the first draw was even sent to the Bank. This all happen over 12 years ago. But Roger would believe anything when it came to Rynsburger. Roger considered him a low life.

One other matter Roger confided to Denise. Joe and Roger were each to get an unusually high salary for managing the developments which was also to come out of each draw. It was the plan that Joe and Rodger would wait for their profits until after the loans for each development was paid off. Roger didn't know if this really happen since he never got paid anything before he was tossed out.

Roger and Joe, at one time over dinner, discussed the possibility that the prepaid profits for which Roger and Joe were to be entitled to may be skimmed off the top of the draws by Vinke and Rynsburger. Roger really never trusted Rynsburger, but again it was just speculation.

But it would sure be a good way to screw their partners. If it did happen, Roger thought that the best way to do it would be to wire transfer those funds to some bank somewhere in the world. That would be a huge deception by Vinke and Rosenberger against the partners actually running the developments. However, at the formation of the development companies, Josef was so good to Roger and Joe, that both of them did not believe anything like that could be happening. Again, everything that Roger was telling Denise was all purely speculative. Roger really did not know anything for sure.

Denise told Roger that besides Largo Del Sol, their development company also started 5 other projects including purchasing a mine on Alico road and two developments in Orlando. Roger wasn't surprised. As Rynsburger always said, 'money doesn't matter'. Denise told Roger that they all got into big trouble when the real estate market crashed. Both Vinke and Rynsburger died. Joe was left holding the bag. Whatever was left in the development companies was foreclosed on by the Bank. So the bank got all their money upfront and then took the remaining properties through foreclosure. What a deal. Denise told Roger the deception was exposed when AFC Bank was purchased by a larger bank. Vinke committed suicide and we still are investigating Rynsburger's death.

"Couldn't happen to nicer people." Said Roger. "I wish I could help more, but I was out of it years ago."

"You did. Do you mind if I get your contact information in case we need to get hold of you in the future." Asked Denise. "But I think you answered all of my questions."

"No problem." Said Roger. "By the way, how did Joe die?"

"Not sure, But I believe it was stress and alcohol." Said Denise. "But that is what we are investigating. Thanks for your candor and help."

Denise then went on to work with a whole lot of speculative information when it came to interrogating Cathy Rutter. Roger then went to see his mother.

****

Roger went back to his boyhood home to visit his ailing mother. Several of Mable's close girlfriends and her sister Cathy were there, but Mabel was not in very good shape.

"Mother, have you seen the doctor? What has he said about why you look and feel this way? Asked Roger.

"Of Course, Honey." Replied Mabel. "He examined me and he basically said I was getting older and things happen to the body. I didn't want any more tests or any more needles jabbing me. I am here alone, Gene has been gone for a long time. My life has been good and I have many wonderful friends. You have set up Skype for me so I can see and talk to my grandkids. I am not complaining."

"I just feel terrible leaving you and going so far away from you when you are in this condition." Complained Roger.

"Don't you worry, I have a great circle of friends, although some of them are getting old also." Replied Mabel. "But Cathy is here. You have a wonderful, good paying job for a great man. I was so proud when the President appointed him ambassador to France."

"I love you Mother. I will Skype you when I get back to Aruba." Reluctantly said Roger.

Three months later, Roger's mother passed away of old age. She never got to see her grandkids in person. 'Old Age' is not truly a cause of death. To 'die of old age' means that someone has died naturally from an ailment associated with aging. Using those terms on a death certificate are rarely used and discourage by the medical associations. The same usually goes for 'dying of natural causes'. Since Mabel didn't want any more tests or procedures it would be difficult for professionals to identify an underlying cause of death when the deceased had multiple underlying ailments simultaneously. So her death certificate said that the cause of death was 'heart failure'.

One thing did stick with Roger as he boarded the plane to Aruba. He fully understood why his mother said she was 'proud' of George Harvey when he became an ambassador? She had not seen him for years. Very strange that George nor his mother ever told Roger who his real father was. But Roger was grateful. He really had two great fathers.

****

Denise got back to her the office about 45 minutes later. Alex Tarian was there waiting for Denise. He wanted to know how in the world Denise found Roger Spector. Denise told Alex that some coincidences do actually exist. She just happen to hear the owner of the coffee shop she frequents call out his name. Denise went over to him and introduced herself and indicated that her office had been looking for him for some time. Actually, Denise told him their office actually gave up on trying to find him. But after Denise explained the reason her office was looking for him, he open up completely and gave Denise some very interesting information about Hyland, Vinke, Rynsburger and even Cathy Rutter. The information Roger gave Denise, even though it was purely speculative, would help dictate the questions Denise will ask Rutter. It was Denise's belief that Roger had no reason to lie about the speculative information he gave Denise. Even though Denise didn't believe that Roger had any reason to lie to her, it was also Denise's belief that Rutter did know about the fraud and theft and deceptions that were occurring with AFC Bank. Alex told Denise to set up the meeting and go get the information so they can try to wrap up the investigation. Denise told Alex that she thought that having Arthur Winslow at the meeting would help his white collar crime investigation. Alex told Denise to go do it. My goodness, Denise thought. How long have they been trying to wrap this matter up?

Denise contacted Brian Koop and thanked him for getting the Immunity Agreement finalized and executed. They discussed a mutual date and time that would work for all of them. The meeting was to be at the County Attorney's office in the Lee County Court House in Fort Myers. Both had to confirm the date, with their boss or client, Brian with Cathy Rutter and Denise with Arthur Winslow. However, when Brian heard that Denise had to approve the date with Winslow, Brian said that the meeting would not go forward until The Feds signed off on the Immunity Agreement. The current Agreement was just with Lee County and not the Federal government. Denise apologized to Brian and said that it was her fault. She had just recently came up with some information that may make part of the case a Federal matter. Brian, of course wanted to know what that information was, however, Denise said she would speak with the FBI first and see if they would sign off on the Immunity Agreement and include all Federal crimes dealing with the same matters. Brian told her to email it to him once that was done and then a meeting could be arranged. They both hung up and Denise needed to continue to move on with the investigation.

"Shit." Said Denise out loud to herself. "I should have thought about that. I must be getting old."

Denise called Arthur's office and left a message for him to call her back about the Hyland investigation. She said on the voice message that some definitive facts have come to light. She had met Roger Spector, by accident, and he completely open up about many aspects of the possible deception Arthur was investigating.

Arthur called Denise back about two hours later. Denise had been preparing a list of questions she wanted to ask Cathy Rutter. Arthur asked about Denise's meeting with Roger Spector. Denise explained the situation of their meeting and the discussion that they had about the Hyland matter. Denise indicated that Roger was no longer a suspect in Joe Hyland's death since he had an air tight alibi. Arthur asked if she checked with his employer to make sure he was where he said he was at or around the time of Hyland's death. Denise had anticipated that stupid question. She confirmed that he was in Aruba at work for nearly 12 hours a day, almost every day for over 10 years before Hyland's death, even including the day Hyland died. He was not a suspect.

Arthur then said that he would have to check with the United States Attorney in the Tampa office to see if an Immunity agreement could be given to Rutter for her part in this theft, fraud, deception, or whatever crimes may have been committed. Arthur said that the U.S. Attorney would have to determine whether there would be jurisdiction in Florida to go after any of the people or companies involved in these crimes. Arthur reminded Denise that Hyland, Vinke, and Rynsburger were all dead. All of Hyland's development companies were dissolved and have no assets. Arthur was not sure if the U.S. attorney would: (1) have jurisdiction in Florida in order to impanel a Grand Jury for an indictment for fraud or theft against Cathy Rutter or any of the AFC Bank loan committee members that were still alive; and (2) if there is even a case, since, as far as Arthur knew, none of the loan committee members probably ever received any of the 'dirty money', if there actually was any 'dirty money'. Again, as far as Arthur knew, the loans were legal in Amsterdam, no matter how much the amounts of the loans were. Add to that the fact that Arthur didn't even know where the money went. It's possible no one anywhere even knows whether all of the skimmed money was already spent, or if it was sitting in some bank somewhere in the world. Denise asked Arthur to talk to the attorney in Tampa as soon as possible and get back to her. She would wait for his answer before she spoke with Alex. Denise was not happy. All of this work for what? She was getting the realization that Joe Hyland's death was not a homicide and there were just no other people or companies around to prove any wrong doing. It was coming down to Catty Rutter, and Denise wasn't even sure she was part of the conspiracy.

A little over an hour later, Denise received a call from Arthur. He had spoken with one of the attorneys in the Tampa office. The attorney said that any criminal matter under the fact situation of this development scheme, will be quite difficult, if impossible, to prove, especially due to the amount of time that has passed. Assuming that the Federal Government could prove Cathy Rutter had any part in this conspiracy, Cathy Rutter would be the only person that would be prosecuted. The U.S. Attorney does not believe any of the Board Members or Loan Committee members would have been involved in any theft or fraud. That's just too many people. The U.S. Attorney indicated it would be in the usual course of action to give immunity to Rutter, as leverage only. She would then tell the authorities the names of the perpetrators of the theft or fraud. Then the government would charge those people who Rutter would name up the 'food chain' to prove the fraud or theft. Rutter would then be the main witness in the case. However, since all of the possible perpetrators involved are dead, and all of the entities involved are dissolved, and no one has any idea if there is some huge bundle of cash sitting in some bank somewhere in the world, there is really no place for any prosecutor to go.

If Rutter was indicted through a grand jury bill, Rutter would, very likely, use the defense that she was just an employee doing what she was told to do and she had no input in the scheme or deception to skim money from foreign bank loans and actually may not have even known about it. Rutter had no ownership interest in any of the companies and there is no evidence Rutter received any consideration other than a normal employee paycheck. Rutter's financials have been investigated and all sources of her net worth have been verified as correct. Therefore, the United States Attorney is not inclined to give her any immunity, let alone pursue the case. However, if there was some evidence of a homicide somewhere in this scheme in Florida, and Rutter knew something about that or may have had something to do with the homicide, even in some minor fashion, the government would give the case another look.

Arthur continued with the conversation he had with the Tampa attorney. The authorities in Amsterdam may want to look at the situation in their jurisdiction to determine if there was someone or any entities or Banks involved in the fraud or theft, or maybe even possible homicides of Vinke or Rynsburger. Both of those deaths occurred in The Netherlands. Or maybe someone can find some funds form the developments in U.S. banks and Rutter or someone complicit with her had control of those funds, the U.S. Attorney's office would take another look at the case. Again, Denise was unhappy.

She sat for a long while and let everything she just heard sink in. The only other person alive involved in this scheme was Bram Meulenbelt. However, he probably was in the same position as Rutter. Or was he? Maybe he did receive a portion of the money that was skimmed off the top of the loans. Or, maybe not. But, he may know where the money may be, if there is money in a bank account. Or, maybe not. If there is a bank account somewhere holding the skimmed money and neither Hagen of Rynsburger lived long enough to withdraw the funds, maybe Denise can find it. Follow the money. But she would need Arthur's help for that. The estates of the two men who died would have been probated in The Netherlands. The money trail starts in Amsterdam. Denise thought that even if she found some, or all of the skimmed money, who would it belong to? The foreclosure of all property involved with this scheme was dismissed with prejudice and cannot be reopened. All of the real property deeded through the Settlement Agreement between ABN Amro and Hyland and his companies was transferred to ABN Amro when ABN purchased AFC. All of that property more than likely has been sold to good faith third parties in the last several years. All issues dealing with this scheme during negotiations for the sale of AFC and ABN Banks must have been resolved. Otherwise the sale would not have happen. Everyone, who could be a suspect is dead. Whose money is it? However, Denise remembers Luke and Arthur discussing Hyland's ex-wife yelling at Hyland's funeral about some hidden money. She thought Brian Koop or Cathy Rutter, or someone knew where it was. Leigh was a little flaky. That's probably why she believed it was really her money. But Denise knew that Leigh Mowery's rant was just conjecture, with no real proof.

Where does that leave Denise? She seems to be just going in circles. Is she over evaluating all of this? What does she tell Alex? Before calling

Alex, Denise thought that it wouldn't hurt if she gave Leigh Mowery a call to find out her basis for believing there was some hidden money around somewhere. Mowery never invoked her right to counsel. Denise could speak with her. She isn't even a suspect and wouldn't even need to be given her rights. What would she have to loose.

Denise knew she had her cell phone and home number somewhere in her office. But she couldn't remember where she put it. Denise was hoping that she would never have to speak with her again. At least that is what she wished for, but Denise was grasping at straws! It took a while, but she found her numbers. By this time it was getting late in the day and she thought that she needed a night off to think about what she would ask Mowery.

So she decided to go to the French connection for a drink. Too many lawyers would be at the Veranda for happy hour, which was the best place for lawyers to meet and talk to each other under a social atmosphere, and she wasn't in the mood for lawyer's talk and all the questions they would ask her about the County Attorney's cases. And the happy hour at the Veranda was always so crowded. She wasn't in that mood. The French Connection was a nice quite after work bar and grill. Mostly paralegal and administrative assistant types there. They tended to stay in their own crowd. So Denise walked the 5 blocks from the Court House to the French Connection. She was right, just a few groups of people in their own groups. A few lawyers, but all with their paralegals or administrative assistants. They wouldn't bother her. She asked for a gin and tonic with two limes. She sat there, for an hour and contemplated what had just transpired in the Hyland matter over the last months since the funeral. Probably all a waste of time. Just before she was paying her tab, Alex called her to find out where she was and what was happening on the meeting with Cathy Rutter. Denise said that some other issues came up after speaking with Koop and Arthur and that she would call him the next day. Alex said Ok, but let's wrap this thing up all ready! Denise thought maybe that will happen sooner than he thought. Denise went home, cleaned herself up and went to bed.

****

The next morning, Denise took a chance and called Leigh Mowery at her home in Louisville. Leigh answered the phone.

"Ms. Mowery, this is Denise Hudak. You may remember me, I interviewed you at the Ritz about 5 or 6 weeks ago." Started Denise. "I am an investigator with the Lee County Attorney's office."

"I remember." Said Leigh. 'What can I do for you? I thought I gave you all you needed at that time. Do you still think someone killed Joe?"

"We still don't know if he was murdered or not. We are still investigating." Replied Denise. "But that is not why I am calling you. No one believes you are a suspect. I am interested in some of the aspects of your life with Joe Hyland. I know you lived with Joe for a while, then at one of Joe's holiday parties, you and Joe surprised all the guests by the fact that you were getting married that evening. A surprise marriage party. Quite unique." As Denise went on.

"That's true. It was unique and fun. We surprised a lot of people, although there were quite a few that knew it was going to happen. Joe told some of his closest business friends. " Said Leigh very cordially as if she was anxious to tell her story.

Denise tried to gain her confidence so eventually she could ask Leigh about the skimmed money.

"Tell me about when you started to work for Joe and how you ended up going together." Asked Denise.

Leigh's life had change so drastically since Joe asked her for a divorce. Her life back in Louisville after her separation from Joe was not anything like her life was before she left Louisville for Fort Myers nearly14 years before. Many of her old friends had left town, had families or jobs and were not that interested in rekindling the same relationship they use to have with Leigh. Time changes people and mindsets. Leigh lost contact with all of her old friends due to the fact that Joe would demand all of her time. They were either at work in his office, or in evening meetings with business associates, politicians or his Amsterdam partners. Leigh had conflicting feelings about her time in Fort Myers. At one time she was the 'Bell of the Ball' during the height of the real estate boom and Joe's busiest time with his 6 projects going on. Joe always had time for her and their 'play time', as Leigh called it. Every night was taken with something that related to business one way or the other. Any potential client who may purchase a million dollar condominium unit was wine and dined to try to close the deal. Joe was a charmer when it came to selling. He really went into the wrong profession. As a salesman, he could have sold anything and made a fortune. But the life he chose was his passion.

"So tell me about moving in with Joe." Asked Denise tying harder to get her confidence.

"We stated going out about five or six weeks after Cathy Rutter hired me as her assistant and to help Joe out when Cathy was busy. Cathy and I became very close friends. We ate breakfast and lunch together almost every day." Said Leigh as she was flattered that finally someone wanted to know about her life. "Most of the time one of us would take a car run down to Juicy Lucy's fast food restaurant and get a breakfast sandwich. Lunch was Juicy Lucy burgers and the best fries ever invented. We did that at least 3 days a week." Continued Leigh. Joe asked me one day if I wanted to have dinner that evening. It was just the two of us and we really clicked. I believe I fell in love that night. We were at the Pawnbroker restaurant which was just a few blocks from the office. It was always known as the best bar to be seen at, except maybe the Red Lion Business Club, and everyone would come to our table to say hello to Joe. He was starting to become like a celebrity in town. A young developer who everyone believed had lots of money, or how else could he be building hundred million dollar developments." Leigh went on. "It was about a year later after the second tower at Largo Del Sol was almost finished, that Joe took me up to a double condominium on the eighth floor of tower one and asked whether I wanted to move in with him. Of course I did. But I couldn't understand why we were going to live in two separate condos." Leigh said questionably." He finally explained it to me and I'm sure you know the story, everyone else in Fort Myers does." Continued Leigh. Denise didn't even need to continue to ask questions.

"Joe was not heavily drinking when we lived together. He loved his Crown and water and his vodka on the rocks, but he was responsible about it. We worked hard every day and played each night at a different clubhouse or restaurant most every night. We had the use of Josef's limo when Josef was not in town. That was wonderful. Most every night we had one or two couples or clients with us. It was like a fairy tale. Florida Everblades games four or five times a month. We had season tickets with Brian Koop and Robert Coulson. The season had 40 plus home games. Too much hockey for me, but, they all loved hockey. They would have rather had a National Hockey League game, but the only game in the area was the Everblades. Always dinner in the Hockey Club before the game, and night caps after the games. If any celebrity or Broadway Show was in town, we had seats in the first four rows center for every event." On and on went Leigh. Denise needed to get to the money.

"After you got married around Christmas in 2003, what changed?" asked Denise to start to change the subject.

"Ivana came along." Leigh disgusting remarked. "She worked for Laura Wills, the broker for Joe's real estate company. She would call Joe whenever she had an excuse. A client was coming to town. There were problems with sales people's commission splits. Whatever to get him to go to lunch or meet for a drink after work." Leigh confessed. "She loved to drink and screw, and Joe was her target. I don't know if Joe was tired of me after we got married, but he ignored me more at work and home than at any time since we met." As Leigh started to cry. "She took over his life. He started to drink more and come home at all hours of the night. Sometimes he didn't come home. And I am certain they were using drugs." And then a pause by Leigh.

"I don't mean to bring back bad memories." Admitted Denise. "Let's move to a different topic."

"She is a Vamp!" said Leigh. "She ruined my marriage, my life, my job."

"I still can't believe Joe just one night said that we were getting divorced. He offered me all of this money and wanted me to leave town. He said he still loved me, but he just wanted to be friends." Confessed Leigh. "He was having Brian draw up the Divorce Agreement and he would always take care of me. He asked me to move out of the condo that week. Can you believe it?" said Leigh. "All of that money and move me out so that Vamp could move in with him. All they wanted to do was drugs and drink and screw." Again Leigh started to cry. "Everything he worked for started to change at the end of 2004. I wasn't even invited to the holiday party that year. And I still worked at Joe's office." As Leigh started to get her composure back. "Joe was making more money than he ever did. He spent it crazy on her! So I left. I took the money he offered me and left. No agreement, no divorce, just left." Said Leigh calmly. "I was still married to him, but he was screwing her! Finally, I just decided to feel good taking the $50,000.00 of his money every three months." Continued Leigh.

"When did the money stop? "Finally Denise got a word in.

"Some time in 2006." Angrily stated Leigh. "I don't know if he just wanted to stop giving me money, if the money he was getting from Amsterdam was reduced, or he was just too drunk to know he forgot to send me the check." Said Leigh.

Denise then started to discuss the fact that the real estate market was starting to change around 2006 and Joe was starting to have problems with sales. Denise brought up the fact that she had mentioned at Joe's funeral that he was hiding money. Denise wanted to know why Leigh made that statement, was she privy to some kind of skimming of funds by Joe or his partners as part of the loan draws each month. Leigh said to Denise that Cathy took care of all of that. Leigh didn't even get to look at the draw request, let alone touch them or even type any part of it. Draw requests were the 'Holy Grail' each month. Leigh admitted that when the draw money came in, only Cathy was allowed to distribute the funds. She would send a portion of the draw funds to a payroll company that took care of all of the office payroll, taxes and those issue. That was all out of the office. The rest was distributed by Cathy. Denise was curious if Cathy paid any funds to Joe or if he only got paid by the payroll company like all other employees. Leigh said that Joe only got paid by the payroll company and only his costs that he had receipts were paid by Cathy. However, every once and a while, like three or four times a year, Joe got a check at the condo through the mail. Leigh had no idea from who, how much or what it was for. It may have been from his investments, since he did invest some of his money with a broker. After another twenty minutes or so of meaningless talk, Leigh mentioned the fact that Joe had installed a large safe in his condo after they moved in. Denise tried every which way to try to find out what Joe kept in the safe, but Denise came to the conclusion that Leigh had no idea. However, as of the day they were talking, Leigh believes there were millions of dollars in that safe. But there was no evidence that it was true. Daniel and Southern Trust Bank are the personal representative for Joe's estate, but there are disputes between the two of them and it was Leigh's understanding, from speaking with Cathy Rutter, that no one had been in Joe's condo since he died. Joe had purchased some huge expensive home and moved into it before the foreclosure was filed by the Bank. The Vamp got to decorate it to the nines!

Denise thought a safe? What's in it? How can they get into it? With the evidence they have acquired to date Denise was not sure that Alex could even get a search warrant to get into Joe's condo. Denise would have to work with the personal representatives and see what she can do.

Denise had to actually say she had a meeting so she could get Leigh off the phone. Leigh really wanted to talk to someone, but Denise was now sure, after dozens of questions concerning the death of Joe, Vinke and Rynsburger, Leigh had no idea about any skimmed money from the Bank or anything about anyone's death. Except for a safe in the Largo Del Sol condo, Denise learned nothing from Leigh.

Now Denise had to face her boss and have a long talk with him about what they are really trying to accomplish with this investigation.

CHAPTER 14

HAGEN VINKE RECEIVED a call from one of the Board members of the Bank. He was asked to attend the meeting to be held on August 14, 2009 at 10:00 AM. That was in two days. Vinke asked the Board member if he needed to prepare anything for the meeting. Vinke was told just to be at the meeting, since he was the President of the Bank and some decisions had to be made by him. His input would be appreciated. Vinke had a feeling this meeting had to be about the purchase of the Bank as well as audits of certain loans. The Board was not going to give Hagen advance notice of any problems. If the Board knows about the skimming of some of the loan funds by Hagen and Josef, they are going to demand all those funds be returned to the Bank. They are going to want Vinke's resignation, and they may even think about turning Vinke and Josef into the authorities. The Board may even want to contact the Federal authorities in the States since the proceeds of those loans were transferred there and were spent there and even stashed in some U.S. banks.

Hagen's mind stopped for a minute and he said to himself that he was getting ahead of himself. He has no clue what the Board meeting is about. There could be dozens of reasons for him to attend. He attends Board meetings almost every time the Board meets. Hagen then calmed down. He did give Josef a call to give him notice of this Board meeting. Hagen would let him know if it had anything to do with them. Josef reminded Hagen that the Snook Point hotel was on schedule for the grand opening on New Year's Eve and he should invite the full Board to attend. Tell them, that they will be compted a room for 3 nights and they should bring their wives. After that day, cash flow will begin at the hotel. After all, they are an owner.

Josef went on, remind them Bram has several potential purchasers for the International Capital Park property. A sale will greatly reduce the outstanding balance on the loans. In addition, several of the builders at Hidden Woods are interested in purchasing all the lots and the amenities. That will take them out of that project and those funds would also reduce the loans. Things were looking up. Hagen still knew in the back of his mind that he and Josef had deceived the Bank on those loans and have stolen a lot of money, actually more money than Josef even knows. Selling the two projects would help, but it doesn't change what the two of them did.

"How about the mine property?" Asked Hagen. "Any bites?"

"Not yet, but I told Bram to price it right. It is losing money daily!" Said Josef.

"Ok. I'll talk to you after the Board meeting." Calmly said Hagen.

Hagen was still extremely nervous. The word on the street is that the Bank is going to be sold. Any forensic audit would reveal everything that has gone on with Hyland's developments for the last 10 years. The current Board and maybe even past Board members who were aware of the amounts of the loans and the 10% interest of the Bank in the projects may have to answer to the shareholders. What a scandal! Ever since the real estate market started to slide, Hagen's life has been in shambles. His wife died, his sons wouldn't come to the funeral, he has been lonely, his job is more stressful each day and working with Josef Rynsburger is getting harder and harder. The only bright spot during these time has been someone who Hagen has deceived, Nicolaus and Elisa Timmerman. Each day, Hagen becomes more and more depressed. He would really like to talk to Nicolaus about it, but he knows Timmerman has no intention of helping someone who literally robbed him. Hagen's mind was rushing. Everything that could go wrong was going through his mind. When Hagen got home that night after a very stressful day at work, he did a stupid thing.

Years ago, both of his sons were hunting enthusiasts. They joined a hunting club and both purchased several guns. Each purchased a Remington Model 870 rifle and a 9 millimeter Glock 26 semi-automatic hand gun. Both of those weapons were for goose and duck hunting as well as target practice. Years ago, his sons took several trips with their gun club to hunt ducks and goose. The best hunting areas for ducks and goose in The Netherlands is the Northern Wadden coast around Ijsselmeer and in Zeeland waterways. Hagen's sons went there several times with their club. Hagen remembers the dinners Sofie cooked roast duck for the family. He can almost smell the aromas. He misses those times. The semi-automatic Glocks were also used by his sons mostly for target practice, but were used on their hunting trips also. Hagen hated the fact that his son's purchased the firearms, but they were always locked and safely put away. All four weapons were locked in a gun safe, but none of them had been used in years. Also in the safe were 12 boxes of ammunition for the rifles and revolvers.

In The Netherlands, gun ownership is restricted to law enforcement, hunters, and target shooters. Self-defense is not a valid reason to own firearms. A hunting license requires passing a hunters safety course. To own a gun for target shooting, the applicant must have been a member of a shooting club for a year. Once obtained, firearms must be stored in a safe. The authorities would be required to annually inspect the weapons. Hagen's sons had complied with all of the statutory requirements. Hagen has had a visit annually, to his home, from the police to inspect the firearms and to ask when they were last used.

Hagen looked at the gun safe for almost thirty minutes. He knew the combination since the police came every year to inspect the firearms. He continued to think the worse about the Board meeting the next day. But, finally he did come to his senses. He poured himself a drink, went over the Banks financials and overdue loans and tried to anticipate what the Board meeting's agenda would be. After 3 drinks, Hagan finally fell asleep.

The next day, Hagen got up at his normal time and got ready for work. He always made sure he was at his desk before 8:00 AM. The meeting was at 10:00 AM. He had a hard time concentrating, but his assistant was constantly interrupting him for signatures on documents and other normal business matters. She reminded him twice about the Board meeting that morning, as if he really needed that. At 9:55, Hagen got up. Put on his jacket and walked to the Board room. All of the Board Members were already there. It seems that they had met a little earlier for some reason. Hagen was then invited into the room.

The Chairman of the Board, Lambert Van Leewen, came right to the point.

"Hagen, as you have been aware, ABN Amro has provide to the Board, about four weeks ago, a written offer in the form of a Letter of Intent to purchase our Bank." started Van Leewen. "Our lawyers and accounts, both in house and our private professionals have been reviewing the terms and conditions. The Board, several days ago executed the Letter of Intent, subject to shareholder approval, and requested that ABN provide a full Purchase Agreement and all other regulatory documents for the Dutch National Bank in order to merge the two Banks." Continued Van Leewen. "During that time, several audits were performed on random term loans and random loans where the Bank has an interest in the projects for which the loans were intended, as per Dutch law." Continued the Chairman.

"I was aware of a possible merger of the Bank, but really never thought this Bank would entertain a merger from such a large Bank" Replied Hagen to try to be nonchalant.

"We didn't either." Said Van Leewen. "But this offer is too good to be true. Our Bank has been very profitable. We have spoken to several of the largest Shareholders and since the offer is an all cash offer, it seems that the Shareholders will more than likely accept the offer." Continued the Chairman.

"What can I do to help?" replied Hagen. "I am a substantial Shareholder, yet I have not seen the offer. What are the term?" Asked Hagan.

"They are quite lucrative. Our Bank has been valued by several Certified Accounting firms at $145.00 per voting share and the offer is for $210.00 per voting share." Said Van Leewen. "Therefore we are preparing for this acquisition to happen. However, the terms and other matters associated with the acquisition shall remain confidential."

"No problem, Lambert, you can count on my discretion." Stated Hagen.

"We know that Hagen, but there are several issues that must be resolved prior to any public press release about the purchase." reluctantly replied the Chairman. "They deal with several of your loans. And I am a little embarrassed about those loans since the Bank is a participant in the equity of the projects involve in some of those loans."

Chairman Leewen went on to describe about two dozen clients of the Bank who have term loans with minor issues that had to be resolved. All of those loans, and any other non-audited loans with the same minor issues will be required by ABN to be remedied before finalizing the purchase. The Board is aware of these clients, some of whom are Shareholders and the Board does not believe that there will be any problems dealing with those issue. However, there were some issues dealing with the various remaining development loans that that the Bank has with the 5 developments Josef Rynsburger, Joseph Hyland and the Bank are involved. ABN does not like loans based on 100% of loan proceeds to the value of the security. So it can be imagined what the issue must be with ABN when ABN sees dozens of loans at over 100% loan to value. Of course the issue could be cleared if all of the owners of the development companies that are the borrowers on those loans pay down the outstanding principal to get to an 85% loan to value. AFC Bank may be able to come up with their 10% portion. The Bank's Shareholders may not be happy about it, since it is a lot of money, but it could be done. AFC has no idea if the other partners, who are also borrowers, could do the same. But even if the other partners could do the same, there is the issue of pre-paid profits. AFC Bank may be able to refund the pre-paid profits received to date on all current loans. However, that would really be a problem with the shareholders, since those funds come right out of the shareholders pockets, and that is also a lot of money. Again, would the other borrowers be able to do the same? Chairman Leewen was trying as gently as possible to explain to Vinke the difficult issues that must be fully discussed and resolved before the Bank could take the offer to purchase AFC Bank to its shareholders for approval.

"Hagen, do you understand these issues as I have explained them to you so far? Questioned Leewen.

"I do." Answered Vinke as he knew what was coming next.

"Good," Replied the Chairman. "None of us on the Board are happy with this situation since we were all participants in these loans. Whether someone on the Board desires to argue that you and Rynsburger promised us great wealth, or life in the Promised Land to approve those loans, it still does not make any difference. The Board approved the Loans, period." Reluctantly said Leewen.

"These dozen or so loans are huge, well over a billion American dollars." Continued the Chairman. "The Bank's liability is only 10% of the amount. The other borrower's liability is 90%! How are the requirements of ABN Amro going to be accomplished to finalize this purchase?"

Hagen Vinke just sat there and put his head down. After a short lull, without a peep in the room, Hagen looked up and said to the Board, "It's my responsibility to talk to our borrowers and see what can be done. Unfortunately, I really don't believe that the borrowers will be able, at this time, to come up with well over $150 Million."

Then the Chairman rose from his chair, walked over to Vinke, and sat on the board table right in Vinke's face and said, "Hagen, I only wish that was the only problem."

Vinke knew what he was talking about, and he just put his head down and almost started to cry.

"You do know what is coming next, don't you?" Said the Chairman. "Why in the hell would you allow your friends and some of the biggest customers of this Bank to steal from the Bank? How much of the stolen funds did you get?"

Hagen Vinke again just sat there, but this time he did cry.

"Stop that crying and be a man!" said Leewen.

Not one of the other Board Members even said anything.

"I want you, here and now, to tell everyone in this room what your plan is to get this Bank out of this unspeakable predicament?" declared Leewen. "This a multibillion Euro transaction that would make hundreds of shareholders a whole shit full of money, but there are over a dozen loans sitting on the Banks books that just may kill the deal."

Hagen, who could have told the Board that 3 of the 5 developments may be generating substantial funds to pay off as much as 50% of those loans in the next several months. As Josef told Hagen, International Capital Park is close to being sold; Hidden Woods is also close to being sold; The Alico Grand Mine is up for sale; the Snook Point hotel will be finished in a few months and start generating revenue, but Vinke knew that all of that really didn't matter. He stole money from the Bank.

"I didn't think you had any reasonable answer." Declared Leewen. "Tomorrow morning, I want you to report to the local police and turn yourself in." said Leewen. "And bring with you your brothers in crime. Now go back to your office, clean it out, and get out of this building." None of us at this table ever want to see you again except when we testify against you in Court. We will deal With ABN Amro and attempt to work something out."

The Chairman got up and walked back to his seat and sat down. "Gentleman, we have a lot to discuss and all of us are going to have to determine how we are going to convince ABN Amro that the funds that were stolen and the $150 million that are missing from the Bank will not be included in this transaction. We, as the responsible people to handle the matter, must do so in a fashion whereby the public will never know this fiasco ever happen." Sadly announced the Chairman. "Maybe, the bad loans can be assigned to all or some of the directors so a foreclosure could be initiated on the collateral, and then when the owners of the loans receive the properties and sell them, the owners of the loans can sue each and every one of the bastards for every cent they have to make up any difference lost! I hope ABN will entertain something like that. Or maybe after confidential discussions with ABN we can work something else out. We will just have to take our licks on this terrible issue." Again declared the Chairman. "But one thing I do know is that these bastards will not get away with what they have done to this great institution! Now Vinke, get out of here!"

Hagen Vinke got up out of his chair, a broken man, and went back to his office got the keys to his car and went home. He poured himself a drink. He then went to his son's gun cabinet, opened it and took out a 9 millimeter Glock. He put 6 rounds in a clip and put the clip into the gun. He cocked the gun and put one of the six rounds into the gun's chamber. He laid down the gun and went into his den. He thought about calling Rynsburger to tell him what happen. But he didn't. Instead, he went to his desk, sat down, took out a piece of his best stationary and picked up a ball point pen and stated to write:

My Dear Nicolaus:

I have been such a damn fool.

I have been greedy, a thief, unprincipled, an uncaring fiduciary for hundreds of shareholders of my Bank. I worked for most of my adult life as an untrustworthy friend to my wife, my sons and to many good people like you and Elise.

I have thought about this day for a long time, but I have also been a coward. I can blame certain people for what I have become, but the only person there is to blame is myself.

There are certain matters that I must get off my mind before this day ends.

First, I apologies to you and Elsie for the money Josef and I stole from you when you and Josef were partners. I can blame Josef for talking me into it, but I take full responsibility for everything that I did. I did it willingly. I should have been a real man and looked into Josef's eyes and told him no. But I didn't. Yet you never held my sins against Sofie. You were her rock until the day she died. Even with the way you must have felt about me, you never wavered from a friendship with my wife that was true and real. No matter what I write in this farewell note, it will never be enough to thank you from the bottom of my heart for what you did to comfort my Sofie. I am a thankless fool who does not deserve anything from anyone. I know I have a lot of nerve to ask favors of such a kind sole, but please make sure I am cremated as soon as the autopsy is completed. Spread my ashes over the filthiest dump you can find. Please, that is my wish.

I have a last and most difficult favor. I ask this of you because of your gentleness, your compassion, your willingness not to degrade me when I openly stole from you, and your kindness and compassion towards Lena Rynsburger. Only a man like that can I trust with my last wish.

I have attached three new signature cards I received several weeks ago for three bank accounts. I am the only signature. I have dated all 3 signature cards August 1, 2009, which is two weeks ago. I have had the financial institutions put your name as the second signature on those accounts.

Please sign all three cards. In those three accounts are some of the funds that Josef and I have stolen from you and Elise, from AFC Bank and various other people over the last 10 years. Much of the stolen funds were used by Josef and myself for pleasures we really didn't need. Josef only knows about one of the accounts. The one in Fort Lauderdale, Florida, at the Flagler Community Bank. It has about $6.5 million. You see, I even stole from my partner! Can anyone be thought of as any lower of a scoundrel than me? The other two accounts have a total of about $10.5 million. One is in Fort Myers, Florida in the McGregor Community Bank and the other in Naples, Florida in the Tamiami Community Bank. The tax ID on the accounts are my Dutch Social Security numbers. Having those numbers will cause no one any problems except my estate. Once they are closed, there is nothing more the Bank can do to me. The bank will attach everything else I own, but will be unaware of the U.S. Banks. Please take all of the money from the three accounts and close them. Pay back yourself all the money I stole from you, plus any amount of interest or inconvenience I may have caused you and your wife. Then double it for your kindness to Lena and Sofie. Find my two sons in Florida. They work for Ikea in Ikea's Florida office. Please give them $1 million each. Try not to tell them it's from ill-gotten gains. Tell them it's from my estate. They despise me enough. Then find Roger Spector. George Harvey, who you know, will know where to find him. He is the person that Josef and I rejected and threw away when we started our deceptions. I ruined his life. I made him quit his very good job with George Harvey, loose his livelihood as a real estate agent and become homeless and penniless for a long time. Give him, from what is left, whatever he thinks is reasonable for what Josef and I did to him. The rest, I leave to your discretions. I couldn't find a better person than you to decide where the money should go. However, for reasons you need not know, do not go to the financial institutions for at least 6 months. The addresses of the banks are on the cards, please mail them to the banks tomorrow.

As for Josef, please take all the evidence left tonight including this letter and do to him whatever you see fit. He also is a greedy scoundrel. Thank you for everything.
Hagen Vinke

Hagen folded the note, put it in an envelope and wrote on the front 'Nicolaus Timmerman'. He believed that by asking Nicolas, in the letter, to take all the evidence, Nicolaus would come to the conclusion, that Hagen wanted Nicolas to take the gun as well as the letter. Hagen needed this to be suspicious. Hagen, who really was not in his right mind that evening believed the authorities would think that Josef had killed him. What a fool! The gun was registered to his son and the police had inspected it yearly. How would Josef taken the gun? Hagen was still attempting to deceive people, however, this night the only person being deceived was Hagen.

It was about 6:00 PM when he finished his note. He poured himself another drink, picked up the telephone and called Nicolaus Timmerman.

"Hello." Said the doctor.

"Hello Nicolaus." Replied Hagen. "This is Hagen Vinke. I know how you feel about me, but I have something very important that I need you to do and you are the only person I know that can do this." Hagen went on. "Before you hang up, please just hear me out. I need for you to meet me on the Berenstr Wolvenste Bridge at 11:00 PM. There is a bench on that bridge. Bring your doctor bag. I have something for you personally and I have something I want you to put into your bag. I know this all sounds suspicious, but it is the most important meeting I will ever have in my life. If you do not want to do this for me, please do it for Lena and Sofie. I know what I have down to you, but this will go a long way to make up for it. I beg you. Please come. If you don't, so many bad things will happen to so many good people." Begged Vinke.

Nicolaus could tell from the tone in Hagen's voice that this was important and that something unknown to the doctor was needed to be done. With that, Nicolaus said. "I will be there."

"Please come by yourself and do not tell anyone about this." Again begged Hagan. "And park your car far away from the bridge and walk to meet me."

Then Hagen hung up before Nicolaus could say anything else.

Hagen went back into his den. Put the Glock next to him on the small table next to his chair, and poured himself another drink.

****

Denise awoke the next morning after meeting with Roger Spector, speaking with Arthur Winslow and having a boring conversation with Leigh Mowery. It was the end of October, 2013 and there were Halloween decorations everywhere. Denise only bought Halloween candy one time. She never did it again since if there where any kids in her neighborhood, no one ever showed up. Her first year at her current condo, Denise ended up eating most of the candy she bought. It finally dawned on her that she should bring the remaining candy to her office. If there is anything workers in an office enjoy, it's free food, especially candy, cake or cookies. Denise arrived at her office about 8:30 and went to the kitchen to get a cup of coffee. There must have been 4 bowls of every kind of candy made. She grabbed a Milky Way and went to her office. She called Alex and gave his assistant a message she would be in her office when he arrived.

Alex showed up at Denise's office about 9:30 AM. Denise filled in Alex on her long day the day before when she had a fully executed Immunity Agreement against Cathy Rutter for Florida matters. When she called Brian Koop to set up a meeting, Denise made the mistake to tell Koop that she needed to confirm the date with Arthur. Once Koop heard that, he wanted to know why the FBI was involved with a meeting without a Federal Immunity Agreement. Denise screwed up. She spoke with Arthur, who spoke with the U.S. Attorney in Tampa. They would not agree to sign off on any Immunity Agreement. Not because they thought that Rutter was not guilty of something, but that they believed there was really no crime that they could move forward on since everyone involved was dead. Without a full Immunity Agreement for both Florida crimes and Federal crimes, there would be no meeting with Rutter.

On the other hand, Denise told Alex that she spoke with Leigh Mowery again.

"Why in the world would you speak with that nut again?' said Alex.

"I had nothing after yesterday's interviews. So I was grabbing at straws." declared Denise.

"What about Roger Spector?" Said Alex. "Didn't you speak with him? He had to have some information." Said Alex.

"Not really." Declared Denise. "The only facts he had was that only Cathy Rutter did the draw requests for every loan. He knew that although he left the company before the first draw was even prepared. Everything he told me was an educated speculation. He further believed that no one else could touch the draws. Even Leigh Mowery confirmed that when I spoke with her. However Roger was there for only a few months and Mowery is nuts!"

Denise then confessed there was one other relevant fact she obtained the day before. The fact that Hyland had installed a safe in his condo after Leigh and Joe moved into Largo Del Sol. Alex inquired what Denise thought would be in the safe. I have no idea, and neither did Leigh. The personal representatives have not opened the safe yet since there are some disputes between the two parties. Denise agreed that the safe could be empty, but most safes have important things in them. Whether jewelry, money, important documents, etc., something had to be in it.

Alex and Denise talked for about another half an hour about everything they had determined so far. Alex then said to Denise to get Luke and Arthur to arrest Rutter for fraud, theft, conspiracy, and any other crimes that can reasonably be brought under Florida law and Federal law. Denise thought that, if anything, it was premature. All she'll do is invoke her right to keep silent and we will have the responsibility to prove those cases beyond a reasonable doubt. Don't you think we should just have another conversation with Rutter, with Koop there and let her answer whatever questions she wants? Remember, you have signed an Immunity Agreement in her favor. If she refuses certain questions, on the basis that the Immunity agreement is not valid since we did not obtain a Federal Immunity agreement, her refusal then may point us in some direction. Only Roger Spector and Bram Meulenbelt are living witnesses. And not good ones at all. What a mess!

Alex believed there would be no reason for Rutter to speak to anyone about anything, so why try. If she is arrested, her attorney is going to ask the government, that if the government believes, there are sufficient facts to prove a crime against her, the government should empanel a Grand Jury. Otherwise Rutter and Koop will tell us to leave her alone and just go away. In addition, maybe Arthur can get his connections in Amsterdam to find some or all of the Board Members of AFC Bank, who approved the sale of the AFC Bank to ABN Amro, to give an affidavit or even testify about skimming of funds each time the Bank received a loan draw written by Rutter. Rutter had to know. With Spector, Meulenbelt and some Board members, maybe we can, at least, get an indictment against Rutter. And from there it may be a small leap to the homicide of Vinke and Rosenberger. That could give the Netherlands authority some incentive to help us in this matter.

Denise asked Alex, what about Hyland's safe. Alex was reluctant to get involved in a civil probate matter at this point. Let's first find out what the personal representative's find when they open the safe. Probate is all public information. They are going to have to sell the condominium and Hyland is dead. We'll find out what is in it when the Court orders the personal representative to open the safe.

Alex told Denise to get Luke and Arthur and arrest Cutter.

****

It was 10:30 PM, August 14, 2009. Hagen Vinke was sitting on an empty bench on the Bernerstr Wolevenste Bridge, just next to the ledge of the bridge overlooking the canal. He had his suicide letter in his jacket inside pocket. He had the 9 millimeter Glock with a round in the chamber and 5 rounds in the clip in the revolver. The revolver was in the back of his belt under his jacket. He was scared, depressed and even a little reluctant. But he knew what was going to happen the next morning. He would be arrested, jailed, and go through hell on earth. The thought of jail was something he was not going to let happen.

About 15 minutes later, Nicolaus Timmerman had just parked his BMW about a half a block away from the bridge. Nicolaus was not sure what was going to happen. He got out of the car and started walking towards the bridge. He had his doctor's bag with him, as instructed. Nicolaus had a feeling, Hagen wanted him to put something in the bag. As Timmerman came on the bridge, he sat at the other end of the bench.

"Thank you for coming." Said Hagen. "I assume you are alone."

"Yes, Hagen." Replied Timmerman. "What is this all about?"

"I have a letter with me. I just wrote it tonight. I need you to read it." Begged Hagen. "Do not say anything to me about the content of the letter until you have read it fully. Please promise me."

"I agree." Said Timmerman.

Hagen took the envelope and letter out of his inside pocket of his sports jacket. Hagen took the envelope with the letter in it and handed both to the doctor. Timmerman took the letter out of the envelope, put his glasses on, and started to read the letter. Hagen looked around and made sure there was no one anywhere to be seen. As the doctor was reading the letter, the doctor honored his word and did not say anything, but from time to time, the doctor would look up at Vinke as if he wanted to say something, but he didn't say a word, and went back and continued to read the letter. To Hagen, it seemed as if the doctor took forever to read the letter. As Hagen could see that the doctor was just about finished reading the letter, Hagen reached behind him, pulled out the Glock, and pointed it at his right ear. The doctor did not see this since he was totally involved in reading and rereading the letter. As the doctor finished the reading of the letter, a very loud shot rang out. Timmerman looked up and saw blood coming from Hagen's head and then Hagen slumped over and fell off the bench onto the sidewalk. The Glock also fell on the sidewalk.

The doctor had to think quickly. A 9 millimeter bullet from a Glock is very loud. It must have been heard for blocks. Hagen had no idea how loud a Glock could be, he hated guns. The doctor, now starting to understand what it was that Hagen wanted him to take, took out his handkerchief, took the revolver and the handkerchief and put them at the bottom of his doctor bag with the envelope and letter. Timmerman, not knowing much about guns, had no idea a shell casing was lying on the bridge. That must have been the reason Hagen told the doctor to bring his bag. The doctor could hear sirens and knew that the police were on their way to the bridge. Thinking quickly, he moved as fast as he could and put his doctor bag in his trunk under the spare tire. He moved even faster back to the scene of the suicide and started to give Hagen CPR knowing, in his mind, that Hagen was dead.

People started to come out of their apartments and crowded around to see what had happen and watch the doctor giving CPR. The authorities arrived about 7 minutes after the shot was heard, with two police cars. The immediate police reaction was to grab the doctor and take him away from the body. The doctor said to the police that he was a doctor and he was trying to save the man. An ambulance then showed up with paramedics. They quickly checked out the pulse, examined the body of the bleeding man and quickly came to the conclusion that the man was dead. The police patted down the dead man to try to find some identification. They found a wallet in his inside sports coat jacket. He was Hagen Vinke. His address was on his identification and his electronic card to the AFC Bank was there indicating he was the President of the Bank. The man in charge of the police at the scene told one of the officers to go to Vinke's home and search for any clues that would answer questions as to what may have happen. That officer found only two things. An open gun safe, one revolver missing and an open bottle of Scotch with a glass next to it. The bottle was about half full.

The police immediately took the doctor away from the scene of the corpse and started to interrogate him. They asked him who he was, why he was there and what he was doing with the body when they arrived. The doctor explained who he was, showed his medical and personal identification and told the police he was trying to revive Mr. Vinke after he saw him take a gun to his head and shot himself. The doctor was well known by several of the police officers and one of the officers was actually Timmerman's patient. The police wanted to know why he was there. The doctor told the police that Mr. Vinke had phoned him late that afternoon to meet him at that location at 11:00 PM to discuss something very personal. The doctor knew that his phone records would be checked, but it was the truth. The doctor further told the police that Mr. Vinke was a good friend of the doctor's family, as well as a patient. Dr. Timmerman thought it was a little peculiar for such a meeting at such a place and time, however, he felt he needed to accommodate his good friend.

The police asked what form of transportation the doctor used to get to the location. Dr. Timmerman told him that he walked. He lived only a few miles away and thought the exercise would be good for him and that Hagen would probably have his car and would be able to drive him home after they talked. The doctor, for obvious reasons, did not want the police to examine his car. The doctor continued with his conversation with the authorities and told the doctor that Mr. Vinke had done something, very bad which Mr. Vinke believed was illegal and would be an embarrassment for him at his work. The Board of Directors at the Bank even demanded Mr. Vinke turn himself into the authority's the next morning. Mr. Vinke said he wanted to confess the truth to someone who he knew well before turning himself in. Mr. Vinke said it was important to get it all off his chest to a close friend before he spoke with the authorities. Dr. Timmerman didn't even ask him what he had done at work, but due to their friendship, he offered to go with Mr. Vinke to the authorities in the morning if he felt that it would help him. Mr. Vinke thanked him and said it would not be necessary and that it would be better if he went there himself. The doctor did not argue with him and wished him luck. The doctor had also told Mr. Vinke that whatever he needs, he would take care of it for him. At that time the doctor turned away and started walking away from the bridge and then he heard a loud shot. The doctor turned around and Hagen had shot himself. The doctor rushed back to try to revive Mr. Vinke, and then the police showed up.

The police could not understand why he would call the doctor to come to meet him for his confession. The doctor reiterated the same, except to say that he had been a doctor for many years and sometimes patients, who are also friends with him, and also, his wife would ask for strange favors. The doctor was close with Mr. Vinke's family and was his wife's doctor while she went through her procedures for colon cancer before she died. Mr. Vinke was not a religious man so he had no clergy to call for this confession. The doctor continued that Hagen was a lonely man and how the doctor understood, that for some unknown reason, Mr. Vinke believed he had committed a terrible crime at his place of employment, and wanted to confess to someone. It is unusual, but not unheard of before.

The police were wrapping police tape around the crime scene and were searching for any evidence of a homicide or a suicide. There was no note, but more important, no gun. They did find a shell casing on the bridge. They marked it as evidence and bagged it. The doctor had told him that he may have seen the gun fall into the canal as Mr. Vinke was shooting himself. The police thought that this was all very unusual. In fact it made little sense. The police asked the doctor if he would come to the police headquarters to give his statement. Timmerman agreed to come first thing the next morning. The doctor then asked the police if he could take care of the body after the autopsy. As Mr. Vinke's friend, the doctor knew that Mr. Vinke wanted to be cremated as soon as possible after his death. Also, the doctor would like to observe the autopsy, if possible. Hagen really has no family to speak of and the doctor would take care of all the arrangements. The police saw no problem with those requests. The doctor was a well-known person in his profession in the City. There was no reason to believe that the doctor had anything to do with Vinke's homicide. The doctor said, again, he would come in first thing in the morning to give his statement. The police took the doctor home in one of the police cars, not knowing the doctor's car was but a half a block away. The police called in a forensic unit to examine the crime scene, look for a note and a gun. Neither was ever found. Hagen Vinke was cremated ten days later and Dr. Timmerman, as a personal request to the coroner, who the doctor knew well, asked if he could sign the death certificate and deliver a copy to each of his sons next time he went to Florida, where they both worked. The sons and their father were estranged and it would be important to the doctor to tell them the circumstances of the death. The corner had no objection. Again, there was no reason to believe the doctor had any alternative motive. The final determination of death by the corner, with the help of the witness statement of the doctor, was a suicide. Now, Timmerman wondered, what to do with the Glock and the scoundrel Josef Rosenberger.

CHAPTER 15

HAGEN VINKE'S CELEBRATION of life was not like as he may have anticipated 20 years before. His wife was dead, his son's estranged and may not have even known of his death. All of his colleagues at work were not in the mood to celebrate the life of a thief. So Dr. Timmerman and Elise had a small gathering at their home several days after the cremation of the body. A few of Hagen's neighbors and a couple of Hagen's co-workers, who knew nothing about the theft at the Bank, attended along with Josef Rynsburger and his friend Alyssa. That was all. There was an article in the local newspaper about the suicide, but the reasons for the suicide were not revealed. AFC Bank made sure of that. However a very charming obituary written by Dr. Timmerman did appear in the local newspaper. Nicolaus did not know what to do with Hagen's ashes. He knew what the suicide note said, but even the doctor was not about to comply with that wish. The doctor thought about bringing the ashes to Florida to give to his sons, in several months, but he also thought that that may not be a good solution. Timmerman had signed all three of the signature cards for the three banks in Southwest Florida and mailed them. He was going to wait for a response from the banks just to make sure there were no other requirements necessary. The

248

U.S. banks were not aware of the death of Hagen and the doctor did not mention that fact in his correspondence with the banks.

Josef and Nicolaus were really never very friendly after the dissolution of their partnership. However, Josef still did not know that the doctor was aware of what Josef did while they were partners. Josef attempted to break the ice, so to speak, and introduced Alyssa to the doctor and Elise, as a good friend of his, from the States. Nicolaus was sure that Josef and Alyssa were more than friends for a long time and even before Josef's wife's illness. Just one more reason for Nicolaus to dislike Josef.

It was Josef who first approached Nicolaus to suggest that someday in the near future they should go out on Josef's boat and spread Hagen's ashes over the Baltic Sea. Nicolas thought about that for a while and said that he may be interested in doing that so long as Hagen had no will with instructions as to the disposition of his ashes. He lied to Josef when he told him that no one seemed to know what Hagen would have wanted to be done with his ashes. Nicolaus said that if there were no contrary instructions, he would be in touch with Josef about setting a time. The gathering only lasted a little over an hour. Not much time for a man's whole lifetime. No old pictures or old stories were even told.

After everyone left the Timmerman's home, Josef came back to speak with Nicolaus.

"Doctor, as I understand it Hagen did not have any will." Stated Josef. "Are you aware of any?" asked Josef.

"No I am not aware of any. Why the inquiry?" asked Nicolaus.

"Well, Hagen was President of the Bank. He had to have some benefits, life insurance, stock and maybe other benefits." Stated Josef with some authority. "Don't you think someone should make inquiry into that? And what about his house and the property in the home? Maybe he even had some money in bank accounts somewhere. Maybe you and I should make some inquiries?" asked Josef.

Nicolaus was thinking that Josef is up to his old deceptions again. Josef wants to finds out about the money that they stole from the Bank and where it may be located. Nicolaus knew that Hagen was the only signature on the U.S. bank accounts. This was to make sure, if anyone found out about it, Hagen could say it was the Bank's money. How was Josef going to get the money out of the U.S. bank? He knows about one of the banks, but he doesn't know about the fact that Nicolaus is now the sole signer.

"Josef, why don't you let me talk to one of the officers of the Bank and see what they can tell me? As you know, Hagen has two sons in Florida. They are his heirs if there is no will. The Bank will know if Hagen has a safe deposit box which may have a will in it." Answered Nicolaus.

"He was my best friend. I think I should be involved in this venture to try to see who gets what from Hagen's estate." Declared Josef again trying to find money that he thinks is his.

"Hagen and I had some talks in the days before he died." Said Nicolaus which he knew never really happen. "Hagen spoke about some of his loans that were in default, especially some very large ones, which he believed could not be brought into compliance due to the large sums due. Someone who is currently a good customer at the Bank, should go talk to the Bank." Answered Nicolaus. "I know you have some large loans, and I got the idea, from Hagen, as to the status of those loans. Therefore, I think the Bank may speak with me alone, however, I will keep you updated."

"OK, thanks. And let me know when you want to go out on the boat." Answered Josef very unwillingly.

Josef and Alyssa then left. Nicolaus thought that he should try to contact Hagen's sons and have them come to Amsterdam and give them an update on what has happen and what their father's last wishes were. The doctor knew that they worked in the Ikea Florida administrative office. He would call them around 2:00 PM Florida time. That would be 8:00 PM Amsterdam time. But talking to someone at the Bank, may also be a good idea.

That evening, Nicolaus called Ikea in Florida and reached Thomas Vinke, Hagen's youngest son. Nicolas told Thomas about the last several weeks including the sale of the Bank and the suicide. His son didn't have much emotion over his father's death. Nicolas did not tell him about the theft from the bank, only that his father felt responsible, as the loan officer on some large loans that were in default, that he may cause the purchase to not go through. His son could not understand taking one's life due to someone's bad loans. However, be that as it may, that is what happen. Nicolaus said further that Hagen had entrusted Nicolaus to take care of some of his affairs including giving both sons some money he has in an account. However, since Nicolaus was not a relative and there were no relatives in Amsterdam, Nicolaus thought that one or both he and his brother, Rasmus, should come to Amsterdam to see if there is a will either in the home or in a safe deposit box. Nicolaus told Thomas he had several certified death certificates that could allow the sons to find out information about their father's estate and decide on what should be done with Hagen's ashes. Thomas said he would speak with Rasmus and make arrangements to come to Amsterdam to take care of the estate, but as to the ashes, Thomas said he would rather have Nicolaus take care of that since Nicolas knew his father much better than them. Thomas thanked Nicolaus and said he would contact him when they got to Amsterdam. Nicolaus knew that Josef would be furious. Nicolaus could tell Josef was adamant about getting to the U.S. bank account before anyone finds out about it.

The next day, Nicolaus went to the bank and spoke with the acting President, Rudolf Spaans. After a full explanation, other than the night of the suicide, Rudolf did indicate that Hagen had substantial stock in the Bank, an insurance policy of 1 million euros, and an account in the Bank with about 3500 euros. The stock was going be to worth about 250,000 euros when the purchase of the Bank was finalized. Rudolf explained there were some minor details that had to be finalized before the final purchase agreement would be put up for a vote by the shareholders. Rudolf expected close to a unanimous vote in favor of the sale. Nicolaus was very candid about the fact that Hagen confessed to him before he died that he had stolen some funds from the bank. Nicolaus was there the night he shot himself. Nicolaus assured Rudolf that he had no intention of making that public since Hagen had stolen money from him also. Rudolf was very candid also, indicating that any assets that the Bank can find that Hagen owned, including his stock, insurance policy and bank accounts would be attached by the Bank for purposes of reimbursement of the stolen money. Also, the borrowers of some loans who were also part of Hagen's plan would also be dealt with. Nicolaus thanked Rudolf for his candor. Then Nicolaus told Rudolf that both of Hagen's son were coming to Amsterdam to finalize their father's estate. Nicolaus requested that he could be kept up to date by the Bank on these issues. Rudolf could not give Nicolaus that assurance, but the sons will have to find out sometime about this matter and Nicolaus could be kept up to date through them. Nicolaus understood and thanked Rudolf, again, for his candor thoughtfulness during this time, and his information about Hagen's assets at the bank.

Nicolaus was sure that the Bank would put a claim into any estate open for Vinke by his sons. They would find out the full truth. But Nicolaus knew that he felt responsible to fulfill Hagen's last requests.

****

Early September, 2009, Josef and Bram came to Fort Myers to talk with Joe. While Josef was in the U.S., he made a call to the Flagler Community Bank in Fort Lauderdale, Florida. Hagen had opened their bank account at that bank for the funds Josef and Hagan were skimming off of Rynsburger's profits from the Bank loans for each of the developments. Josef wanted to speak with the manager. Jackie White, the manager, answered the phone. Josef attempted to find out about an account opened by Hagen Vinke that may have about $6.5 million in it. Jackie would know about any account with that amount of money in it without really having to take much time to look it up. The manager, a nice and very cordial person, asked Josef how he was involved with the account. He said his friend, Hagen Vinke, opened it and that the money was actually both of theirs. Jackie did finally look up the account and found there were two signatures on the account.

"What is your name again?" asked Jackie

"Josef Rynsburger." Answered Josef. "Is there still more than $6.5 million in the account?"

"I'm sorry, that information is confidential and only signatures on the account are able to access that information." Said Jackie.

"There is only one signature and he is dead." Said Josef "So what is the procedure to get the funds out of the account?"

"I'm sorry Mr. Rynsburger. There are two signatures on the account." Admitted the manager. "And I have no paper work, or death certificate, that would indicate that either one of those people may be deceased."

"What do you mean two signatures?" Questioned Josef. "Am I one of them?"

"No sir, and I cannot reveal anything about the account over the phone even if you were a signature, I do not know you." Admitted Jackie.

"I may come over to see you tomorrow about the account. Will you be there?" Asked Josef.

"You can come over, but I will not be able to discuss the account with you since you are not a signature on the account. However, if you bring with you a notarized Power of Attorney signed by one of the signatures, we can discuss the account." Said the manager.

Josef just hung up and could not believe that he just had that conversation. Who could the other signature be? Someone at AFC Bank? But, it couldn't. We stole the money from the AFC Bank. It was perplexing to Josef and he just could not get it out of his mind. Maybe, Hagen felt bad about taking Hyland's money and told him about it and maybe he had become a signature? Maybe I will cautiously ask about it when I see him. But if he knew he was getting his money, he wouldn't be in the physical condition he is now. What a strange turn of events. Who is deceiving who?

At 8:00 PM, the next day in Fort Myers, Bram and Josef met with Hyland for dinner at the Red Lion Business Club. They first discussed Hagen's suicide and the fact that the Board of Directors must have found out about pre-paid profits for the loans through ABN's audits of loans for the sale of the Bank, and Hagen was probably exposed since, he was not only the loan officer for the development loans, he was also President of the Bank. No one will know the actual reason Hagen committed suicide since Hagen did not leave a suicide note. And with the purchase coming up, Hagen must have been asked to pay back to AFC Bank the pre-paid profits, in cash, and deposit them with the Bank against the outstanding principal of the loans. AFC Bank could relatively easily come up with their 10%. Josef did not want to mention that the skimming was actually, not only Rynsburger's pre-paid profits, but also the 50% of Hyland's profits. Joe was unaware of that scheme. Josef was walking a thin line, at this meeting, since neither Hyland nor Bram were aware of this skimming scheme.

"Wasn't the pre-paid profits your profits Josef?" Asked Hyland. "As far as I know, Vinke didn't have any ownership in the any of the development companies. Also, AFC Bank not only knew about the pre-paid profits since they were receiving there 10% portion, they approved the loan that way. The other 40% was yours Josef." Asked Hyland again. "Why didn't Hagen ask you to come up with the money? Why would Vinke commit suicide over money owed by you Josef and not by him?"

"Good question, Joe." Said Bram.

"I remember an Agreement Bram gave me to give to Brian Koop and put it in his safe. The Agreement was written in Dutch." Said Hyland. "Were you and Vinke splitting the 40% pre-paid profits?

"That Agreement had nothing to do with these loans." Said Josef. "That was a completely different matter between Hagen and me. It's private and I will not discuss it"

"I don't believe you." Said Hyland. "Something is going on here, and all I know is I have guaranteed all the loans, including the pre-paid profits and I am going to be the fall guy! Why is AFC Bank not on your back asking you to return the pre-paid profit funds? Also, I would like to do a little mathematics. The development companies have loans totaling over one billion dollars. The pre-paid profits were figured, conservatively at about 5% of the loans. If you multiply that out, 5% of 1 billion dollars is $50 million. $25 million of that is my money and I have not seen a penny of it and maybe never will. On the other hand, you have received $20 million upfront. There is something wrong here. Tell me this is not true."

Josef had to do some fast talking, and to get his point across, he started to speak very loudly to Hyland to intimidate him and have other patrons of the club who knew Hyland take notice. Josef continued, in a loud voice to Hyland that if it had not been for Josef, Hyland never would have been able to be involved in these developments. Hyland would still be selling real estate at GHIC and not have become a multi-millionaire with all his boy toys, his woman and his prestige in this town. Josef practically embarrassed Hyland by accusing him of turning on the best friend he had ever had, who would do practically anything for him. If Hyland was still selling real estate, Hyland would be practically broke since real estate is hardly even selling now. An historic hotel will be opening in several months and Hyland is in the center of that development. Everyone in this town believes Hyland is responsible for it. The town loves Hyland. Damn the Banks. The loans will be paid, or some arrangements will be made. Hyland will get his profits, it may just take a little more time and some maneuvering. There is no way any bank, no matter how big, wants to have defaults on loans over a billion dollars on their balance sheet. The bank is being purchased, so something had to be worked out. Josef told Hyland to be a man, stop getting drunk every night. Stop taking drugs with his Bitch, go to work every day and straighten up. The biggest night of Hyland's life is coming on New Year's Eve!

Hyland stopped his accusations. But somewhere in his drunken and drugged up mind, things did not add up. Someone is being deceived here!

Josef then said to both Hyland and Bram, if they could now speak civilly about what they were going to do with the developments and the loans?

Both Bram and Hyland knew Joe was really pissed off. They decided to sit quietly and listen and try to work things out.

Josef had heard from Hagen, prior to his death, that AFC Bank and ABN Amro where very close to finalizing the purchase. Several issues, both large and small were being worked out. The shareholders of both banks will be voting on the purchase and sale of AFC Bank in a week or two. So some arrangements had to have been made on bad loans, including ours. It will then take several months, or maybe up to a year, to coordinate the two banks into one bank. ABN Amro will then hold the loan documents on the Hyland Development's remaining development loans. All of which are substantially in default. Without Vinke as the buffer, while the developments were being finished and sold out, one thing was for sure, a new loan officer will be assigned to all the development loans. What the new Banks's position on those loans are unknown at the time. But all of them needed to work hard to help each other and make the situation better.

Josef was still just to pissed off to even continue. He told Bram and Hyland that they should meet in the morning at The Grind for breakfast and continue this discussion. Also, Josef asked Hyland to call Koop to be at the meeting. That would cool off Hyland. Cooler heads would then prevail. While in Fort Myers, Josef was staying at his condominium with Alyssa. He needed to be with her right at this time. His partners were closing in on him, which he was not used to. And, more importantly, some unknown person had access to his money in the bank in Fort Lauderdale. Laura Wills, Alyssa's mother, and Joe's broker was not happy about Alyssa's relationship with Josef. She just didn't trust him. But, her mother knew, Alyssa was old enough to make up her own mind. Josef also was not happy about a relationship that has been going on. He again told Hyland, before he got up and left, to sober up and get his act together. Get rid of that Bitch, Ivana, he is with. She is bleeding him to death and he looks terrible. Josef knew they were using drugs, drinking all day and Hyland was not only losing weight every week, but he is becoming careless on his decisions with both Snook Point and Coconut Cove Park. They needed to talk the next day about some arrangements that may help Snook Point and Coconut Cove Park. The hotel was almost done and the Grand Opening event is being put together by Cathy Rutter. This opening event is going to cost more than $250,000.00, but it will be the biggest event in Cape Coral since the Rosen Brothers threw those coins on the Rose Garden and built the City! However, money used to be no problem, but now Josef is starting to believe that money is the problem!

That night, after the conflict between the men, Bram made several calls to several brokers in Orlando. Josef had previously, without Hyland's knowledge, authorized realtors to find eager purchaser who were looking for deals, and to put together purchase agreements for International Capital Park and Hidden Woods. The amount of the sales for those two developments, at fire sale prices, would not cover the debt, but about 55-60% of the acquisition loan for International Capital Park could be paid down and 60-65% of the acquisition loan for Hidden Woods could be paid down. Those pay downs could help the partners renegotiate all of the development loans, since all of the loans are already cross collateralized.

The loan on the hotel at Snook Point was almost $300 million and another $250,000.00 was being spent just for the Grand Opening event. Hyland was still under the impression that the hotel will pay for itself. Hyland was also still under the impression that the real estate boom was still going to come back. They could then sell the hotel rooms for about a million dollars each. Hyland is still not ready to face the reality of the current situation. Even with the confrontation he had with Josef that evening, Hyland believed everything would, in the end, work out. He just felt terrible about Hagen and was still trying to understand why he would commit suicide?

Everyone around Hyland was trying to tell him that even if things go as Hyland thought they would, he still needed to seek bankruptcy advice. It couldn't help to be prepared for the worse. That is what good businessmen do. Hyland, however, was not in the best of mind. Ivana was influencing him too much. She continued to tell Joe how things will change again and prices will rise again. They drank and took drugs together and waited for more millions to come in. Brian Koop was the person with the leading voice on the bankruptcy advice. Koop and most everyone else in a supervisor positions in the Hyland Development Companies could see, and could read everywhere, what was happening. Foreclosures were starting to escalate. Buyers were abandoning their deposits. Owners were trying to make deals with their lenders to sell their units and get out of the deficiencies that were rising daily. Prices of their units were dropping weekly and their loans were rising with the interest mounting. Banks didn't want the properties back. They were trying to make deals, but owners were not going to get off for free. Owners were being required to come up with at least a portion of the deficiency, or their credit ratings would fall, as defaults continue to rise every week.

The next morning, Brian got to The Grind early and asked Janet Nelson if he could use the conference room for an hour. She agreed and said she would make sure someone took their breakfast and coffee order. Josef, Bram and Hyland showed up about 15 minutes later and they all went into the conference room. Josef reported to Hyland that the two developments in Orlando had sold. He told Hyland to execute the purchase agreements as soon as Bram received them in a couple of days. Josef asked Koop to start working on the closings. Josef told everyone in the room that the purchase prices for those properties were substantially less than the outstanding amount due on the loans. Koop said, the Bank won't like it, but all of the loans are cross collateralized so they will just add the deficiencies to the other loans and fully release the loans on the selling properties so the purchasers will get clear title. One bad loan off their books.

Everyone in that conference room knew it was time to start to liquidate and pay off as much of the loans as possible. Josef reminded Hyland that he has guaranteed all of the loans and the new bank will want a large payment on all loans in the next few months. Josef had received a call last night from the new loan officer from ABN Amro. Just one more thing to go wrong for Josef the day before. However, the new loan officer, Mies Groot and several other officers of ABN Amro will be at the Grand Opening event on New Year's Eve. They are requesting a meeting with Bram, Hyland and Koop within the first couple of days after New Year's. The new Bank will have their U.S. attorney at the meeting. This meeting will determine the future of the Snook Point development, Coconut Cove Park and the Alico Mine. Hyland couldn't understand why Josef was not going to be at the meeting. After all, he owned 40% of the developments. Josef told Mr. Groot that a substantial amount of funds will be sent to the Bank in a few weeks after the closing of International Capital Park and the Hidden Woods development. Mr. Groot was aware that the amounts the Bank will be receiving will be less than the full payoff, but the Bank will still agree to fully release all of the properties so the buyers will get clear title. The remaining amounts owed under those loans will be added to the current outstanding loans. Their attorney, whom ever he or she may be, will be sending documents to Brian for review for the purpose to advise the partners on the ramifications on the transfer of those outstanding amounts and any penalties or other matters dealing with the closings. Josef continued to instruct Hyland to sell as many of the remaining units at Coconut Cove Park as soon as possible. Even lower the prices, something Hyland did not want to do. What the new Bank wants are more pay downs. Only sales will do that.

Hyland wanted to bring up the pre-paid profits Josef had received over the years and ask him to contribute those to the required pay downs. After all, Hyland had to wait until all loans were paid off to receive his profits. That may never happen. But, after last night, Hyland decided to keep quite. Josef still was perplexed about the Ft. Lauderdale Bank. Who is this mystery person who is now the only signature on the account? Hagan is dead. How can he find out who it is before the money is gone? And why has Josef not heard from AFC Bank concerning the pre-paid profits? Did Hagen confess to the Bank that it was only him and Josef was not involved? Would Hagen do that? Was Josef's ego that large?

****

Cathy Cutter was sitting at the main bar, on the third floor overlooking the 18th green, at The Riverview Golf & Country Club having a glass of chardonnay about 1:30 in the afternoon on November 12, 2013. It was almost 3 months after Joe Hyland's funeral. Luke Bradly and Arthur Winslow walked into the bar and sat down next to her. Cathy looked at them both and said that her attorney had never heard from any of the authorities about any Immunity Agreement, so it was her impression that this was all finished.

"What's up guys?" Asked Cathy." Can I buy you all a drink?"

"We're on duty Ms. Cutter." Said Luke. "The Immunity Agreement is all gone. You and your attorney just got too greedy."

"And that means what?" questioned Cathy.

"That means that you, Cathy Cutter, are under arrest for conspiracy in the homicides of Hagan Vinke, Josef Rynsburger, and Joseph Hyland; for bank fraud, embezzlement, theft, and anything else the FBI or Sherriff can figure out after all the facts are in." Said Luke.

Luke Blakely then read Cathy Rutter her rights and made sure she understood them. She did. They handcuffed her, put her in their car and drove her to the County Jail for processing. Alex Tarian meet them at the jail.

"Good afternoon Ms. Rutter." Said Alex. "It's nice to finally meet you."

"What the hell is going on here?" yelled Cathy. "Are you all out of your mind? If you all think that I killed someone, or was involved in the death of someone, or stole money from some bank, you are going to get the largest lawsuit this County has ever seen!"

"What else can we think?" Calmly said Alex. "You were the only one at Joe Hyland's office that handled the draw requests for over a billion dollars of draws. You were the only one in that office that disbursed the money from the draws. Not even Joe Hyland did that"

"That was my job. Does that make me a criminal?" again yelling Cathy. "Take these damn handcuffs of my hands!"

Luke Blakely took the handcuffs off Cathy's hands and told her to sit down nest to the processing window.

"Here is the deal, Ms. Rutter." Started Arthur, the FBI agent who felt that he had the best chance to charge Cathy Rutter with a crime. "These officers are going to start processing you in 5 minutes. That means a full body search, finger printing, felony snap shots, a brand new red jumpsuit and then put you in a holding cell with a dozen prostitutes, several mentally ill criminals and some other real bad people until tomorrow morning when you will be put into a Sheriff's van and transported to the Federal Building Courthouse, where you will be arraigned for which of the crimes you are accuse. Do you understand that?"

"Why are you doing this to me? What is it that you really want?" questioned Cathy in a much lower voice.

"You have been very uncooperative about the procedures that were used and the line items of each and every draw for every loan related to Joe Hyland's development company projects." Explained Arthur Winslow. "You have not agreed to tell our investigative officers and investigator's anything about where all the money went, where the bank accounts are located and why Hagen Vinke allegedly killed himself. After all you typed out the checks and the wire transfers. You know where the money went and what every penny was for." Continued Arthur. "Hagen Vinke died because of where you sent money. I don't know if someone killed him for the money or whether he killed himself because of the money. But there has been some kind of deception going on and we want to know all about them."

"I don't understand." Replied Cathy.

"Yes you do." Said Luke. "Before we process you and you become a permanent part of the criminal process here in Lee County, including your mug shot on page 3 of tomorrows News Press edition with a two column story, several of us thought that you may just want to sit down and answer all of our questions and completely reveal everything you know about Hyland's development companies and where all the money came from and where it went."

"So if subpoenas don't work, Immunity Agreements cannot be obtained and my lawyer always has to be present when you speak with me, and I have not told you what you want to hear, you all decided to do it the hard way. Obviously the easy way didn't work for you." Smugly said Cathy.

"That's one way to put it Ms. Rutter." Replied Alex. "So what's you decision?"

****

Dr. Nicolaus Timmerman was at home in early September, 2009, waiting for Hagen Vinke's two son, Rasmus and Thomas, to arrive by cab at the doctor's home. That morning Nicolas received his daily mail. There were three envelopes from the three banks for which he forwarded the signature cards per Hagen's last instructions. The first one he opened was from the Flagler Community Bank in Fort Lauderdale. This is the only bank account Josef Rynsburger believed existed. The letter thanked the doctor for sending the new signature card along with a copy of his passport. His name was added as a signature on the account. The other two banks, Tamiami Community Bank in Naples and the McGregor Community Bank in Fort Myers indicated in the two letters to the doctor that there were never such accounts ever opened at those banks. The letters continued that if the doctor wanted to open account he must send them some money to activate the accounts.

The doctor just could not understand how that could be. A person who commits suicide would not lie in their suicide note, at least not under the circumstances of Hagen Vinke. $10.5 million is a lot of money. Where is it and who has it? Did it actually exist or was Hagen sending some kind of message? But what message? This whole theft ring with Josef and Hagen and maybe even Hyland was confusing the doctor. Did Vinke commit suicide for something other than what was in his suicide note? The Doctor will be going to the States in a few days or so and he would try to sort all of this out. He would need George Harvey's input to help him do just that. Another very strange turn of events.

However, the doctor still had two tasks to take care of. Hagen's two sons and Josef. First the two sons. He had heard that Josef was in Florida at the present time, so the doctor had time to finalize his plans for how to approach Josef. As the brother's cab arrived at the doctor's home, both Ramus and Thomas get out of the cab and came to the door of Dr. Timmerman's home. They all introduced themselves, including Elise, who had some refreshments ready for the brothers. All of them then got some small talk out of the way. After all, this was the first time Nicolaus and Elise had meet the two boys. They spoke for a while about the brother's mother, Sofie, and the doctor and Elise had many good things to tell them about her. They gave their condolences and said what a fine woman and friend she was. The brothers may have had some different thoughts on that subject, but they kept them to themselves. However, they did thank the doctor and his wife for their kindness during her illness.

Then the doctor gave a full account of the night of their father's death and how the doctor was involved. The doctor left out the part about the suicide note and the fact that he had taken the gun. He did indicate that there was some money in a U.S. Bank that their father left for them. The amount was not discussed. The doctor indicated that he was a signature for that account and would be going to the States in a few weeks and would retrieve the funds. The two brothers gave the doctor their contact information so once the funds were withdrawn, the U.S. bank could wire transfer the funds to each of the brother's accounts.

The fact that the brother's father was being accused of stealing money from his employer was a shock to them. The doctor also did not mention that their father also stole a tidy sum of money from him. Some things are just better left unsaid. The doctor did indicate that he was not sure what assets or liabilities their father had left behind, but in speaking to their father's employer there were some substantial assets and benefits that their father was entitled to. The doctor thought it was best for the brothers to discuss those items directly with the bank. The doctor also suggested that they employ an attorney, since it was the doctor's impression that the employer was going to try to keep the assets and benefits as an off set for the stolen funds. The doctor gave the brothers a key to their father's home so they could stay there. He warned them that the police had been in the home and searched the home for evidence of a crime. However, the doctor assured the brothers, that no crime had yet been proven, and that the brothers should act as soon as possible to clear the estate of their father and take what they wanted and sell the rest. He was sure a lawyer could let the brothers know what rights they had and it was important for them to retain the lawyer soon. The brothers again thanked the doctor for his kindness and help in this matter. The doctor said he would drive them to their father's home and they could either rent a car the next day or use a taxi. Taxis are a great way to navigate the city easily. The doctor gave the brothers the name of several attorneys he had used in the past and if they could not help them he was sure they could give the brothers a referral.

After the doctor dropped the brothers at Hagen's home, he went and made several copies of the suicide note and death certificates so he could take them with him to Florida. He called George Harvey's office and told his assistant that he would be in town in the next few days and would like to get together to speak with him. He asked his assistant to let him know some times and dates George would be available. The doctor then went home and arranged for a plane ticket and hotel in Fort Lauderdale, Florida.

CHAPTER 16

IT WAS THE morning of November 13, 2013. Cathy Rutter had spent a night in a Lee County holding cell with a dozen hard criminals, hookers and drug addicts. She was brought by van to the Federal Courthouse at 6:00 AM. She had no sleep. She was scared as hell the entire night. Now, she was waiting her turn to be brought before Federal Judge Lowell Stassen for her arraignment. Cathy was wearing a red jump suit with the initials LCCJ, Lee County Criminal Jail. She was wearing none of her jewelry and no makeup. A very different Cathy Rutter than anyone knew. Her mug shot from the Lee County holding cell was on the internet that morning. Whether the local News-Press would pick it up was questionable, although there was always a news reporter from the local paper at every Federal arraignment to determine if there was a good story for the next day's edition.

It was Cathy's turn. The bailiff brought her into the Court room and announced the charges against Cathy, which got the attention of the local reporter. Three counts of conspiracy for murder, embezzlement of Federal Banks and theft. Arthur couldn't find any more charges to bring against her at that time, but he was still investigating. Alex Tarian was sitting in the spectator's booths.

"Mr. Tarian, what are you doing in my Court today?" Asked Judge Stassen. "Are you just slumming?"

"No, your Honor." Answered Alex. "We are just waiting for a second bite at the apple for one of the accused coming before you today."

"This defendant must be an important one." Retorted the Judge. "So, Mr. Stein, does your client have a plea?"

Harold Stein is Brian Koop's partner that handles criminal matters and has now taken over the criminal representation of Cathy Rutter.

"Not guilty, Your Honor." Said Cathy Rutter."

"Bail, Mr. Fable?" Asked the Judge.

"Remand, Your Honor. Ms. Rutter either killed or conspired to kill 3 people and to steal millions of dollars from several Federal Banks. She has substantial assets, a ranch in Montana where she goes on many occasions." Replied Prosecutor Fable.

"Mr. Stein?" asked the Judge.

"This whole prosecution is a hoax on the part of the Federal authorities. There is no proof that anyone was killed in the U.S. and how could she have murdered two people in The Netherlands. Ms. Rutter has never even been to the Netherlands. As to the embezzlement, The Feds have searched all of her assets several times and have come up with nothing. Any transfers of funds in any Federal Banks went to her employer as part of construction draws, not for the defendant's personal use. All of the authorities know that. All of Ms. Rutter's money was acquired through legitimate means. All of the records examined by the Authorities has shown that." Replied Harold Stein. "This has been a witch hunt for some time and the only reason Ms. Rutter is standing here today, is because the Feds want someone to pay for events that occurred years ago, but the real perpetrators are all dead!"

"Quit an acquisition Mr. Stein." Replied the Judge. "Mr. Fable, any response?"

"Ms. Rutter was with Joseph Hyland the night he died just several months ago. In fact it happen in her house. Ms. Rutter had access to billions of dollars for multiple construction developments, a great deal of that money is missing and Ms. Rutter was the only signature on the bank accounts where funds are missing. Ms. Rutter is a smart, cunning person who wants this Court to believe she is just a scapegoat. Don' fall into that trap, Your Honor."

"I remember this case." Replied the Judge. "Wasn't this the largest foreclosure action in the history of Southwest Florida? Joe Hyland was the developer. He died several months ago. Are you saying that Mr. Hyland was murdered?"

"Yes Your Honor." Replied the prosecutor.

"Your Honor…" Said Mr. Stein.

"Enough." Said the Judge. "Bail is set at $100,000.00. Next case."

Frank Fable could not believe the Judge placed such a small bail for Rutter. Although, the prosecutor is still trying to wrap his head around how Cathy Rutter had anything to do with Hagen Vinke or Josef Rynsburger's death. In fact the Lee County coroner still has not ruled Hyland's death a homicide. That is why the prosecutor didn't mention it at the arraignment. He was sure the Judge wondered the same thing. Fable went over to Harold Stein and said he wanted to meet. Stein said, not until we post bail and get my client out of your garbage pit. Within 1 hour, William Rutter had bail set for his wife. They went back to the Lee County Jail and picked up all her clothes, jewelry and her purse. Cathy changed and her husband took her home. The News-Press reporter could not get to the News-Press building fast enough.

On the way home, William had some questions to ask his wife.

"Go ahead and ask all you want. I have become an expert on criminal law these days. Any discussions between husband and wife is privileged so you can't testify as what I have to say." Said Cathy.

"Why would you say that to me? Did you do something wrong? Or worse, criminal?" questioned William.

"I have changed my mind." Replied Cathy. "I don't want to talk now. Let me go home and rest. I need to speak with Brian, then I will tell you the whole story. It's really not as bad as you think. Trust me." Calmly replied Cathy.

Not a word was said between them on the rest of their ride to their home. William was very confused and a little scared, but said nothing. As soon as they arrived home, Cathy called Brian Koop's office. She left a message for him to call her to set up a meeting with him and Harold Stein as soon as possible. She had something she wanted to tell them before Josef and Bram went back to Amsterdam.

****

September, 2009, Josef wanted to speak with George Harvey and Cathy Rutter to see if they knew anything about the Flagler Bank account in Fort Lauderdale. George was now living in West Palm Beach after his stint as Ambassador to France for President Bush and he kept up to date through his connections into everything and everyone, including what Joe Hyland was up to. Cathy had worked with George and had a connection through Roger Spector. Plus she is the person who will still be drafting the draws for the convention center loan for the Snook Point hotel. That was the last piece of the puzzle for the commercial parcel at Snook Point. She will be supervised by Hyland since Vinke is no longer around to give her directions on wire transfers and payments. Cathy may be the one who is the second person who has access to the Flagler Bank account.

On the pretext of trying to maybe work out a joint venture with GHCI for a development outside of Southwest Florida, Bram set up a meeting at the Red Lion Business Club, in the bar for the four of them. Joe Hyland was not asked to attend. Josef thought that by the time they meet at the bar, Hyland would probably already be drunk and Josef would not be able to discuss the essential matters he wanted to find out, which is what is going on with the Flagler Bank account. Who is the new signor and why is there so little money in the account? This was a long shot and also taking a chance by meeting, but Josef was desperate.

At 5:30 PM, September 15, 2009, Josef and Bram were at a bar table at the Red Lion Business Club. Cathy Rutter was also already there. Perfect timing for Josef to speak with Cathy alone.

"Hello Cathy, I haven't seen you for some time." Started Josef. "How have you been?"

"Fine Josef, and you and Bram, everything going alright?" Replied Cathy.

"Not really. You should know all this. Vinke committed suicide a few months ago, The Bank is being purchased by the largest Bank in Europe and our development companies are in default under all our loans." Angrily said Josef.

"I know all that, Josef. But you don't have to take that attitude with me. I just work for Hyland." Countered Cathy.

"Bull shit!" You know everything that is going on. You do all the draws. You know how the angles work. What do you know about the night Vinke died?" asked Josef. "He had no note, no gun and no money. The optimum word is money." Said Josef.

"So what is it you want from me?" Replied Cathy.

"You know all about the money. You keep the books, both sets of them. You do the draws, including the money for pre-paid profits. You know the pre-paid profits for my interest goes into an account that Vinke wire transfers from the AFC Bank account in Aruba to another Bank here in Florida. If I know you well enough, you probably know the name of the Bank." with an angry look replied Josef.

"I know you and Vinke and probably Hyland have some scheme going to steal some money in case the whole development company went down the drain." Confessed Cathy. "I know there are two sets of books. However, I don't keep the second set, Vinke kept the second set. He is the guy that knows it all." Angrily stated Cathy. "I don't know what Hyland is going to do since you all put him on the hook and conveniently kept yourself off the hook, with no liabilities. He is now the one to review and accept the draw requests from the new Bank for the convention center at Snook Point. That is the only loan the new Bank will let you have monthly draws, since the new Bank wants just to have the hotel finished. All other developments are in default. People at the development company, including me and Hyland are not getting paid. Only the bare necessities are being paid. I am angry at Hyland also. You and he kicked out Roger Spector, my nephew, right at the beginning to get Roger's portion of his salary and profits. It was like a knife in Roger's back from you without any remorse. Roger quit his previse job, gave up his real estate brokers license and his dignity. You both are bastards!" as Cathy started to cry. "But the market crashed, and here you all are. Vinke, probably was found out by the new Bank through their loan audits. Remember, I worked for Wells Fargo for a long time. They purchased lots of banks. I know the procedure. You put Vinke in a bad position. You killed him as sure as you held the gun to his head. But here you are, probably looking for more money. Just a greedy son of a bitch!"

"OK, I have heard enough. You can deny all you want to, but you know more than you're telling me. I am willing to make a deal. I am not the bad guy you think I am. I am just a business man. So, where is the money?" exclaimed Josef. "Tell me and we can work something out. What is already done is done. Nothing we can do about that."

"You really are stupid." Exclaimed Cathy. "Do you really think Vinke would tell me where the Bank was or which Bank it was? I have no idea and have no idea how much money is in it. Or, in fact, whose money it really is."

Bram chimed in and said enough arguing. Bram was not really sure what the two of them were talking about, but it sounded like neither of them know anything about any money. Josef indicated that this was not the end of that conversation. And then Bram saw a glimpse of George Harvey walk in to the club. He mentioned it to Josef. Just like most politicians, it took George nearly 15 minutes to get to the bar. He stopped and shook a dozen people's hands and spoke with them about whatever they wanted to hear. Then George came into the bar and sat at the table. Everyone became cordial, but George could see that Cathy was upset.

"What's wrong Cathy? Did these bastards insult you in some fashion?" asked George calmly.

"What a way to start a friendly conversation." Said Josef. "I wanted to meet with you to see if you may be interested in financing and becoming an equity partner in a new development that Hyland and I are starting." Josef knew he had no new development in mind, but since his bank connection was now gone, maybe he could see if Harvey was interested in taking AFC Bank's place. Josef needs money to get the new Bank substantially paid down so Snook Point can begin additional construction and the remaining units at Coconut Cove Point can be sold.

"You got to be kidding." Replied George. "The real estate market is for shit! Why are you really here? I suppose you think Cathy has been stealing your money? I know what she does for you. She and I are very good friends. We speak a lot."

"What does that mean?" Said Josef.

"Have they mentioned Roger? Is that what got you upset?' asked George.

"Actually, I brought Roger up when they wanted to make a deal with me. Now, it seems they want to make a deal with you and probably steal some of your money." Said Cathy.

Josef was furious. He didn't want to hear any more. He told Bram to get up and they both stormed out of the club. Josef could not understand how George brought up Roger to Cathy. Where did that come from? Also, Josef was sure Cathy knew something about his money somewhere in some bank in Florida. He was now convinced she is the new signature. He needed to find that out soon. The next draw for November was coming up and he wanted to know how that was going to work. With Vinke gone, a new loan officer will be approving draws for the hotel development loan as well as the Snook Point acquisition loan. Cathy was the key. He would work on that and find out what he needed to do before the opening of the Snook Point Hotel on New Year's. That would be the next time Josef would be back in Florida. Maybe Hyland knew something. He had to check everything out, there was too much money at stake.

****

It was New Year's Eve, December 31, 2009. The Snook Point Hotel was mostly completed, all rooms furnished and ready for its first night of business. All that was left to finish was the construction of the convention center. All of the 250 rooms were occupied with all of them compted by the Developer of the hotel for anywhere from 1 night to 3 nights depending on the status of the guest. Brian and Linda Koop were compted for 1 night, but the four officers of the ABN Amro Bank and their companions were compted for 3 nights. Bram was still not able to make any type of arrangement with any of the big name hotel chains to put their Brand Name on the hotel and manage it for Hyland's development company. So The Snook Point hotel was still its name that evening.

Cathy Rutter had done another fine job in making all of the arrangements for the big party. The affair started at 8:00 PM at the main pool. The 475 guests that had compted rooms could check in as early as 5:00 PM that evening. That gave them time to look around the faculty and marvel at the most luxurious hotel Cape Coral had ever witnessed. Even the Ritz Carton in Naples and The Registry Hotel in Naples may not have been its equal in luxury. The remaining 250 gusts could arrive any time after 8:00 PM that evening. Cathy had booked one of the best 14 piece bands from Miami at $15,000 for the night plus room and board. No amount of money was spared for appetizers, a buffet dinner, desserts and an open bar. Dress for the night was mostly formal and the whole City of Cape Coral was excited for the opening of this facility. Joe

Hyland and Ivana Hollings had one of the suites for the evening. They were in their room getting ready about 3:30 that afternoon. Each with a drink in their hand and each already had several snorts of cocaine. Joe knew he had to make the first speech of the evening and introduce all the dignitaries, so he wanted to be as sober as he could. Ivana had no duties but to be a hostess, but being high on drugs and alcohol made her the kind of hostess she loved.

There were four of the highest ranking officers of the largest bank in Europe, ABN Amro attending the event. The sale with AFC Bank had been closed, but the two banks were still in the process of coordinating all of their systems and reassigning new loan officers to many of the large customers. Hyland's development company was one of the new Bank's largest customers. Even with the sale of the two Orlando projects closed, only about 55% of the amount owed on those loans had been paid back. The remaining amounts had been added to the Snook Point acquisition loan under the cross collateralizing of the loans. Still over a billion American dollars was still owed to the Bank by Hyland's Development Company, $350 million of it was just for the hotel. All four officers of the Bank were in Cape Coral and at the big party to see how all that money would be paid back.

At exactly 8:15, Joe Hyland was at the top of the spiral staircase in the lobby of the hotel with a waterfall running down beautiful colored glass right behind him.

"Welcome everyone. I am Joe Hyland the owner of this wonderful new addition to the City of Cape Coral. Each and every one of you were invited to this historic New Year's party because of your part in making this facility a reality. Let's all pick up our glass of Champaign and drink a toast to the opening of this wonderful hotel. Those of you who are staying with us will surely enjoy your rooms and the beautiful views of the mangroves areas, the Caloosahatchee River and Gulf of Mexico. The marina is specially lit up for everyone to tour that facility and see what a wonderful job the professionals involved in this project have done."

Everyone took a sip of their Champaign. Joe then went on to introduce about a dozen dignitaries from the Mayors of Cape Coral and Fort Myers, the new manager of the hotel, the food and beverage manager, and the four bankers who made the hotel possible with their generous loan and their foresight for this great City. Joe then told everyone to enjoy the food, drink and especially that wonderfully expensive band. They will be playing until 1:00 AM. Nobody in the neighborhood should complain about the noise since the Mayor of the City is in attendance. Everyone laughed and Joe went out and got himself another Crown Royal. The night was a success. Everyone had a great time. The weather cooperated until about 10:00 that night, when the temperature dropped a little. Those who were dancing and drinking didn't even notice, but all others either retreated to their rooms or sat by one of the several fire pits on the property.

About 10:30 PM that evening the four officers of the Bank approached Joe Hyland, Josef Rynsburger and Bram Meulenbelt. Hyland was not quit drunk yet, which made the bank officers feel more comfortable. Josef and Bram never looked drunk, even if they were. However, Ivana was completely plastered and could hardly stand. Joe told her to go up to the room so he could speak with the four gentleman. Ivana just waived her glass and told them she was off to be invisible again. Joe was somewhat embarrassed, but shrugged it off indicating that she was one of the salespersons for his real estate company having a little too good of a time. The bankers knew differently.

"Joe, you surely throw a great party." Said the speaker for the bankers. "Especially on our money!"

"Don't you all worry, this hotel will make a fortune for all of us." Joe said trying to calm their worries. "Remember, you all own 10% of this beautiful hotel."

"Joe our local lawyers who represent the bank are a law firm from Miami. Two of our real estate and litigation attorneys will be here at the hotel the morning of January 4 at about 10:30 AM. Please make yourself, your lawyers and anyone else you may want available for that meeting. The lawyers will not be staying the night. They just want to talk and see if we all can come to some type of arrangement for paying off your outstanding loans." Said the bank spokesman. The last thing the Bank wants is to own 100% of this beautiful facility." The spokesman continued. "Is the date and time all right? The four of us will not be there, but we will be anxious to see what arrangements can be made so all of us can enjoy the fruits of our long hard labors." Said the spokesman. "My condolences to all of you for your friend Hagan Vinke. I understand you all were very good friends. It's a shame our Bank doesn't have him working for us. He was a smart banker. We were so surprised when we heard of his death. We just can't imagine what would make someone do that. Again, our condolences. We are all going to retire to our rooms. We're just not big drinkers and usually don't stay out late, but I am sure we will see you over the next several days. Again thanks for the great welcome. By the way, the fruit and Champaign in our rooms were a great touch."

The bankers knew exactly why Vinke committed suicide. They just wanted to see the response, if any, from any of the others. There was no response. The party lasted until about 2:00 AM. The band agreed to play an extra hour, for an additional $1,000.00. Luckily most people who stayed that late were staying at the hotel. They're wouldn't have been enough jail cells in the City for the DUI's. Joe went to his room and Ivana had passed out. Joe poured a full glass of Crown Royal and drank himself to bed. He didn't have any food at all. Drinks were his only pleasure that night.

CHAPTER 17

GEORGE HARVEY AND Cathy Rutter were having their regular monthly meetings in George's office at The Riverview Golf & Country Club. It's always a closed meeting and it always happens around 6:00 AM when no one is around. This was a meeting which was important to the both of them, Roger Spector. George indicated that Roger wanted to talk to him about the Aruba job. George and Cathy were sure that Roger wanted out. He has a wife and a child and one on the way. Aruba is no place to bring up a family. Sending him to Aruba accomplished their goals, but now it was time to tell them what they really had in mind for him.

"I am Roger's biological father. I owe him a good life. I promised Martha that a long time ago and I am not going to give up now. I may be a son of a bitch when it comes to business and politics, I have made mistakes, and I am a stupid Queer that I believe no one knows about. But family comes first."

"I agree with you, George. Roger was treated terribly by Hyland, but mostly Rynsburger. My mother and Martha are sister which makes Roger my nephew. I now have a grandnephew and another on the way. I want to be able to see them and be part of their lives. I also want what's best for him. I also want to make sure Rynsburger and that good for nothing Bank get what's coming to them. Count me in on my pledge."

****

Roger had gone to Aruba as requested by George, but after two years into the training for the casino manager job, Roger contacted George, came back to Fort Myers, and told him, that he really didn't believe that being a casino manager in Aruba was the right business move for him. It was too far from his mother and he had met someone from the States and he was sure she would never agree to live permanently in Aruba. Roger was nervous about telling George this since George had spent a lot of money having Roger trained. However, that is when George told Roger, don't worry about it. I am sure the business training was worthwhile and that he thought that Roger would eventually change his mind about the Aruba job. George was just not sure how long Roger would take to make that decision. In George's mind, the longer the better.

But George wanted Roger to stay in Aruba a longer since he was not sure what Josef and Hyland's next move may be against Roger. They could black ball him from any real estate jobs in the area, or worse. George disliked Josef, and George's original deep believe in Joe Hyland's great prospects with GHIC had evaporated quickly after he left GHIC to go to work with Rynsburger. Especially when he convinced Roger to go with him. After Roger was literally tossed out of Hyland's development company, George thought it best that everyone thought that Roger had disappeared to places unknown. It worked. Roger made his decision, two years later, that Aruba was not the place for him, but George knew that was not the right decision at that time. George told Roger he that he had some other plans for Roger and that Cathy Rutter would also help to finalize those plans. He would explain all of this when George was ready to bring Roger back from Aruba in the future. Until then Roger reluctantly agreed to stay the course.

When Roger was on his respite from Aruba, he met with George in the back conference room of The Grind coffee shop, a place no one would see them together. He explained to Roger that it was his plan to keep Roger out of town for a while so Hyland and Rynsburger could not find him and do anything else to him, especially, if George were to give him a job at his and Bradly Whalen's new development close by the Fort Myers area. Who knows what Hyland and Rynsburger could have done while George and Bradly were developing their prestigious projects? George was so skeptical of Rynsburger that he was sure he had contaminated Hyland. If any illegal matters were to occur, Roger would be the first person they would point to. This theory was because of George's and Roger's feelings for the manner the original developers tossed him out of their development. This time out of the Country for Roger was all being done for his benefit.

Roger was surprised and asked George why he would go so far as to send him all the way to Aruba for a job George had no intention of letting Roger keep. He had been trained for the casino business and George had no intention of keeping him there. George said that the business training for a casino manager was a great learning process. The new hotel in Aruba was being built, and Roger would have a chance to observe it. The Aruba project would take almost 4 years to be finished. George knew Roger would not last the full 4 years and actually take the job. George and Cathy had plenty of time to wait. George could have stopped it at any time, but he wanted Roger to make that decision on his own after the 4 years were over.

Roger was curious what this new plan George and Cathy had for Roger. George told Roger that he was investing in a new project. With George's connection, George and the current owners of the Seminole Hard Rock Hotel & Casino in Hollywood, Florida, were bringing George in as a full limited partner into the Hotel Casino Partnership for the purpose of an infusion of funds to expand the hotel and reconfigure the casino to increase the number of slot machines and gaming tables and the hotel size. The casino size is currently 130,000 square feet. That will be increased by 20,000 square feet. There are currently 437 hotel rooms and 5 restaurants. That will be increased to 498 rooms, 20 of which will be suites and an additional expensive restaurant would be added. One of George's requirements was to put in the money and find a private lender who will loan the partnership up to 8 million dollars on very reasonable terms. Roger would become a full time manager in the project. Now that Roger has been fully trained in the casino business and the hotel business, he would be a perfect fit to help the management team at the project. George was putting up $2million for a limited partnership equity position and Cathy Rutter was loaning the Partnership several million dollars from sources she claims she will be having access to over various monthly amounts over the next few years. With George now living on the West Coast in West Palm Beach, he was just a few miles away from this new venture and could watch the growth on a weekly basis. Roger, down deep in his gut, knew why George and Cathy would be doing this for him. He said nothing, however. The problem that Roger had was this was not going to happen for several more years. He was not sure his new wife would continue to live in Aruba. George said, that if she loved him she would live wherever he was. The best part was that she would know that it would only be temporary for a few more years. You kids will be out of Aruba before they start school.

George told Roger, that in due time he would understand. But, for now, just let Cathy and George enjoy the eventual downfall of Josef Rynsburger. George has been around a long time and he has seen it all. What goes up, as fast as Hyland's development company is borrowing money, will eventually decline, especially since Cathy is privy to how the projects are being financed. That is the day George and Cathy will be there to pick up the pieces. George and Cathy had been waiting for this for a long time. George said that they will see who is deceiving who? Roger was still confused, but felt this may be an answer to a prayer. Sometime in the near future he and Holly could live close to her family and Roger would be only two hours from his mother.

Roger asked about salary, benefits, who would be the people he would have to report to, whether he would be required to live in a certain town due to gaming rules, and all of the normal questions a new employee would want to know before he agreed to a new job. George told him, not to worry, all of those matters have been negotiated by George and George knows Roger will be happy with them, especially since Roger could live in Fort Lauderdale, which is very close to Holly's home. Roger couldn't say anything bad, he just wanted to know when he could start. George said, the time will go fast. Arrangements will be made at the right time to move everything out of the Aruba condominium George provided for him to live and they would be put in storage until Roger found the perfect place in Fort Lauderdale. Roger was really confused. Why? Why would two people, even though he knew one was his Aunt and he knew one was just his biological father, do something like this for him?

****

It was January 4, 2010, Josef had returned to Amsterdam. Bram stayed to attend the meeting with the new Bank's attorneys. At about 10:30 AM that morning, Joe Hyland, Brian Koop, William Jones, Brian Koop's bankruptcy partner, Carl Finch, the attorney for ABN Amro Bank and the named partner in Harland & Finch, as well as Robert Adams, the bankruptcy partner for Carl Finch met at the Snook Point Hotel in a conference room. Harland & Finch was a 900 attorney law firm based in Washington D.C., with 22 office all over the world including an office in Amsterdam. Finch was from the Washington Office and Adams was from the Miami office. Coffee, juices, rolls, donuts and water were all set up in the middle of the conference table. Everyone introduced each other and made some small talk about how nice the hotel was. The Bank's attorney thanked Joe Hyland for his hospitality for this meeting. Joe said that they had the run of the hotel for the day and hoped they enjoyed the facilities and the restaurant and the bar. If any of them wanted to stay a night, Joe would make the arrangements.

Brian Koop stated the conversation. "You all called for this meeting, what can we do for you?"

"As you know we represent ABN Amro Bank. They currently hold all of the mortgages on the 3 development parcels your development company still owns. After the closing on the Orlando properties, that were just closed, all of those funds were paid to the Bank. Those funds were allocated as set forth in the Loan documents. First all costs incurred by the Bank were paid, which includes travel costs, all attorney fees were paid to date, all outstanding interest, at the default rate, were paid and then the remaining amount paid down the outstanding principal amounts on the two loans. That principal amount paid on the loan was $107,546,325.78 which was used towards reducing the Snook Point acquisition loan." All itemized by attorney Finch. "The total outstanding amount on the remaining loans for the three remaining project is currently, in round numbers, about $800,795,000.00 and default interest is still accruing each day."

"When you get back to your office could you have someone from your office, or the Bank, itemize all of this. My client would like to see the costs and interest calculations." Replied Brian Koop.

"No Problem." Said attorney Adams.

"As you know, my client wants to finish the hotel and will need to receive monthly draws to do so, even though your client's Bank is considering these loans in default." Said Koop. "It is to everyone's advantage to have the hotel completed. My client is also in the process of negotiating with several major brand hotel chains for an agreement to manage the hotel. My clients, real estate company is aggressively marketing the sale of the hotel rooms, both as a condominium and in the alternative, if sufficient amounts of sales are not obtained by the time the convention center is completed, we have time share documents ready to use and to market the hotel rooms as time share units. That will bring in substantially more funds for each of the hotel rooms."

"Mr. Koop, we are not naïve." Replied attorney Finch. "The real estate market will not support the prices you have placed on these hotel rooms at $1.5 million average per room. If you have to turn to time share than you have to sell 50 units per room for 250 rooms. That will take an eternity! So let's get back to the reality of the matter. We have a proposed plan."

Koop was interested how the Bank had any legitimate plan to have Hyland pay back that much money in such a short period of time. Finch stated that the Bank does not want to foreclose on this loan. The Bank wants to help Mr. Hyland pay back as much as possible under the terms the Bank is willing to agree to without any compromise or negotiations. Those terms include the following. First, so long as the following terms are followed, the default will be removed and interest will be due as if the loans were not in default. That will save Mr. Hyland a lot of money. Second, the bank will continue monthly draws for the construction of the hotel convention center until it is complete. The draws will be for construction costs only and nothing else. No salaries for the developer's employees or professionals. Third, all revenue from the hotel shall be submitted to the Bank on a monthly basis with an accounting, except for the payment of reasonable salaries, approved by the Bank, to all hotel employees, and reasonable expenses to keep the hotel operating during the construction period, at the discretion of the Bank. No salaries shall be paid to Joe Hyland or, his or the development company's attorneys or accountants. Forth, all rents on commercial units shall be submitted to the Bank on a monthly basis with an accounting. No commissions on those rents shall be paid to any real estate company. Fifth, all net proceeds of the restaurants and bars and other food vendors shall be submitted to the Bank on a monthly basis, with an accounting. The Bank shall determine if all salaries of food & beverage employees and all food and liquor costs are reasonable. Last, no new construction may be initiated at Snook Point without the Bank's approval.

As to Coconut Cove Park, it is the Bank's understanding, all construction is complete in the development. There are 48 units left to be sold. That development company will have 16 weeks to sell all of the remaining units to independent third party purchasers. The Bank does not care what price the developer needs to set per unit for those sales, so long as no final purchase prices are no less than 75% of the agreed sales prices set forth in the Loan Agreement for that loan. All net proceeds of the sales, as pre-approved by the Bank, shall be submitted to the Bank. No real estate commission shall be paid to Mr. Hyland's real estate company. Only outside realtors fees shall be approved. So long as this is accomplished the default on that loan will be waived.

As for the Alico Grand Mine, all defaults will be waived, so long as all of the proceeds of the mine are submitted to the Bank, on a monthly basis, with an accounting, less reasonable salaries paid to the employees, as approved by the Bank, and less all reasonable operating costs, as approved by the Bank. No salaries shall be paid to Joe Hyland or, his development company's attorneys or accountants. The developer shall continue to aggressively look for a purchaser for the mine to an independent third party, and if one is found, the Bank shall approve the purchase price and all reasonable closing costs. The Developer shall have 16 weeks to find that buyer.

You have asked for nearly the impossible, but assuming the developer accomplishes everything you have just outlined, and I assume you will send this in written form to me in the next few days, thereafter, what happens to any remaining amounts due under the loans?" Asked Koop.

"The Coconut Cove Park loan will be released and any remaining amounts shall be forgiven. The Alico Grove Mine loan will be released and all remaining amounts due will be forgiven. The Developer of Snook Point will deed the hotel and all other parcels in the Snook Point development to the Bank in lieu of foreclosure. All remaining amounts due under any loans associated with Snook Point will be forgiven." Replied attorney Finch.

"Bull shit" exclaimed Hyland. "The Snook Point property and especially the hotel will have to be renegotiated. I am not giving up the hotel."

"You heard what the Bank is requiring. No negotiations. Take it or leave it." Said Finch.

"Give us until we receive this proposal to give you my client's answer." Said Koop.

"It's not a proposal, it is the Agreement. My office will be drafting the Agreement for signatures and that is what you will be receiving. Not a word may be changed. We are talking about almost a billion dollars!" replied Finch. Now we are going to enjoy the faculties at our hotel. Thank you for your hospitality."

The two attorneys left the room and Hyland, Bram, Koop and Jones were all left in the room. They all felt they needed to discuss what to do. First thing Hyland did was go into one of the cabinets in the room, take out four glasses and a bottle of Crown Royal. Everyone, except Joe refused the drinks so early in the morning and before discussing the proposal. It didn't stop Joe. No ice. He just poured a full glass and started drinking.

"There is no way I can accomplish all of what the bank wants in 16 weeks." Said Joe. "It's Bull shit! Find a way to sue the Bank. Put the pressure on them. They have been taking pre-paid profits since day one. They have their profits and they took interest on those profits. I have received a reasonable salary, but no profits. I have even deferred my profits on the Largo Del Sol project, except for taking two units. Go get those shysters!"

"First, they're not shysters Joe. Let's be civil. I know the walls are caving in on you, but we need to see how we can get you out of this mess in the best possible manner." Said Koop. "Next, Bram, I hate to do this, since you have been such a reasonable voice through all of this, but you work for Rynsburger and we do not represent him. He has his own attorney. You need to leave. You have heard the proposal. Tell it to Josef and then you or he should let me know what your plan may be."

Bram left the room willing and understanding the situation. No one in the room had any idea that Rynsburger and Vinke were stealing funds from the draws as they took their pre-paid profits on each draw. They were also stealing Hyland's pre-paid profits each draw. The people in the room would be having a different discussion if they knew that Hyland was being deceived.

"I hate to be crude, Joe, but, how much money do you have these days. It matters for a few reasons. If you do not believe you can accomplish the Bank's proposal then we want to save you as much money as possible when the Bank files for foreclosure. That is their only remedy if you can't meet the 16 week deadline." Said Koop. "Second, we need to get paid. Unfortunately we have to eat also. We believe we're talking about $15,000.00 a month minimum in fees for the next 4 months."

"You are shysters! I have $3-4 million cash around to try to live during the time and work for nothing." Disgustingly remarked Hyland.

"You need to prepare for the worse, Joe." Said Bill Jones, the bankruptcy attorney. "Under Florida law there are some exemptions that cannot be taken away from you if you end up filing bankruptcy. And you may have to do that if they do start foreclosure or before if you're sure you will not make the 16 week deadline."

"Tell me more, Bill". Said Joe.

"Do you have any annuities, IRA's or 401(k)'s?" asked Bill. "Those are exempt under Florida law and the Bank cannot take them."

"No, I know I'm stupid, but no. However, I can put a couple of million dollars in those now." Said Joe.

"Won't work." Said Bill. "There is this law that if you transfer non-exempt funds, like the cash you have now, into exempt assets within a certain amount of years of owing creditors money, for the sole purpose of defrauding those creditors, the creditors can get to those funds. However, if the exempt asset is you homestead, more than likely a Court would let you keep the home, no matter how much it's worth"

"I have a home." Said Joe. "A condo at Largo Del Sol. I had two, but I had to transfer one to my ex-wife in the divorce."

"But that's only worth $600,000.00. Buy the largest home you can for several million dollars. It is more likely than not that the Bankruptcy Court will let you keep that Home."

"I hate it." Said Joe. "How am I going to pay the taxes and upkeep? I would need a job paying me lots of cash. If this crashes I am unemployed."

"Joe, you are the best salesman I know" Said Brian. "You can sell anything, cars, homes, snow to Eskimos!"

"I'll think about it." Said Joe, as he poured his second full glass of Crown Royal.

"Think hard, since that Agreement will be here in a few days and you will need to sign it. So start looking for a house and get some nice furnishings. You may want to put some cash away in your safe or safe deposit bank, but the court may ask you about that." Said Bill. "But do it anyway."

The two lawyers left the room, while Joe continued to drink and eat some of the refreshments on the conference table. Brian heard Joe call one of the suites and he heard Joe tell Ivana to come on down to the conference room since they have something serious to talk about.

Two days later the Agreement came by email from Finch's office to Koop's office with a request that the clients and the attorneys execute the document. Finch and the Bank had already signed it. Koop got Joe to sign it personally and as managing partner of all the development companies involved. Tick tock, 16 weeks to go!

****

It was the middle of January, 2010, and Dr. Timmerman was making arrangements to go to Fort Lauderdale to close the bank account at the Flagler Community Bank. He would then wire transfer $ 1 million to each of Vinke's sons and take the rest of the money and go speak with George Harvey. He would know where Roger Spector was and how much money he should get for what Rynsburger and Vinke did to him. Those were his instructions under the suicide note. However, Nicolaus was a little skeptical since Vinke had mentioned two other banks with double the amount in the Flagler Bank, but those accounts didn't exist. What did that mean? Maybe Rynsburger had an explanation. Nicolaus would find out soon.

Nicolaus called Josef and said he would like to take him up on getting together for a day or two of relaxation. The doctor said he had been working very hard and needed the time off. The doctor had a boat docked at the Waterstad on the Nieuwe Mass River. From there they could go out to the North Sea. He could confront Josef once they were on the North Sea. His plan was simple. He had Vinke's gun. He would use it to force anything he needed to know out of Josef. He could tell Josef what he thought of him and Vinke. The doctor would bring a syringe with an amount of insulin that would make a result of the injection look like a heart attack. He could then throw the gun and syringe into the North Sea and claim Josef had a heart attack while on the boat. After all, Nicolaus was Josef's doctor and the authorities would more than likely believe him. However, everything is a risk. Just like the Vinke suicide. One problem. An autopsy may be required and it may be very hard to get the authorities to avoid an autopsy. Getting away without any real investigation on the Vinke suicide was a magic fluke. Timmerman would not have enough influence to have that happen again. He would have to try a different tactic.

Nicolaus knew that Josef had a pleasure boat docked in the Venice port on the Dalmatian Coast. A couple of days on the Adriatic Sea, may be just what both of them needed. Nicolaus thought that was a great hoax to get Josef to Italy. Italy has no jurisdiction over a Dutch citizen who dies of a heart attack in international waters off of Italy. Nicolaus may be able to even have Josef cremated in Italy. There is really no family since he is estranged from his two sons, his wife is deceased and he has no other brothers or sisters and his parents are deceased. The perfect crime. The gun and the syringe would be thrown in the Adriatic Sea forever.

So Nicolaus contacted Josef to see if he would take a little time off together and they could go together to Italy, have some good food and long talks and a short cruise on the Adriatic Sea on Josef's boat. Nicolas would leave Elise to enjoy her few days of freedom from his nagging.

Josef was a little apprehensive at first, since Nicolas had been so cold to him since they broke off their partnership. Could there be some alternative motive? But what would that be. The only thing he could think of would be somehow Nicolaus found out about the deceptions on the loans with AFC Bank and Vinke. But Josef was a good talker. He could sell Nicolaus any necessary story about the loans to justify what happen. A couple of days may be just what Josef needed to take some time to think about the Flagler Bank, Roger Spector and Cathy Rutter. How does it all fit together? So Josef contacted Nicolaus and set January 22-24. They would drive to Venice and stay on the boat for a few days. They would have a couple of good meals and wine and take an afternoon cruise on the Adriatic. Josef would call the caretaker for the boat and tell him to prepare the boat for a long afternoon cruise, stock the wine cooler and the refrigerator with some good cheese and fruit. The two of them would only be out for about 4-5 hours. Josef asked the caretaker to be at the dock at 6:00 PM that evening to open the boat and have it cleaned. The stage was set.

****

It was Thanksgiving Day, 2013. William and Cathy Rutter were at their dining room table at 2:00 PM, just the two of them, trying to enjoy a traditional Thanksgiving dinner. A 12 pound roasted turkey, sweet potatoes, cranberry sauce, and fresh baked rolls and a pumpkin pie for dessert all made fresh at the Publix supermarket. Cathy has been indicted for the conspiracy of the death of three people. Brian Koop and Harold Stein have been trying to get Cathy to come to their office for several weeks to discuss the strategy as to how they will approach the charges. She keeps putting it off. Finally, Brian called Cathy. Again no answer. Brian left a message that the coroner has made a final determination on the death of Joe Hyland. It is no longer inconclusive, it is a homicide. The toxicology tests were tested 3 times over the last several months, at several different labs, and the coroner is now 100% certain that Joe Hyland was being slowly poisoned by someone. Very small amounts of ethylene glycol, the main ingredient for antifreeze has been slipped into something that he drinks or eats frequently. That message scared Cathy. She knows she didn't kill Joe. She still believes it was not a homicide. Brian's last message indicated that due to the new findings by the coroner, Cathy must be in Judge Stassen's court room at 2:00 PM on Monday afternoon after Thanksgiving for a motion by the prosecutor to increase bail due to the discovery of new facts. Cathy needs to be in Brian's office no later than 9:30 AM that Monday morning, or sooner. They need to discuss the increased bail motion and these new circumstances.

The authorities have upped the charge from conspiracy to murder in the first degree. Whether it is elevated to a death penalty case is up to the Lee County States Attorney. Cathy thought how can it be that someone even killed him and how could that have been accomplished? He was at her house for several hours and eating dinner when he passed. In no way was Cathy with Joe often enough to slowly poison him. Cathy was just overwhelmed at this whole situation.

In retrospect, Cathy never should have gone to work for Hyland Development Company, but what is done is done. However, due to the fact that once she started working for Joe, she could not give up the job. Even if she tried. It was fascinating. Life was going by so fast and things were always happening in a big way in the community. Cathy was in the middle of all of it. She knew what Joe had done to Roger, but she really didn't blame him. Maybe he could have changed Rynsburger's decision, but probably not.

Of the three people she has been accused of having some role with their deaths, Cathy wishes she did have something to do with the killing of Hagen Vinke and Josef Rynsburger. They were true scum. Of the three person's for which she is accused of their deaths, she would have never been involved in Joe Hyland's death. Cathy knows it was Rynsburger that really wanted Roger out of the companies. Joe had a terrible time coming to grips with just throwing a good friend out of the company, especially after Roger gave up so much, just like Joe did when he joined forces with Josef Rynsburger.

This Thanksgiving dinner was very quiet between Cathy and William. He was very aware that the charge of conspiracy to commit murder was just increased to murder one! The Rutter's were receiving phone calls from newspapers, magazines, tabloids and many calls from Brian Koop. They were ignoring the calls and even finally unplugged the phone. However, before they unplugged the phone, Cathy called Brian and left a message on his cell phone that she would be in his office at 9:30 AM Monday morning. William finally looked up at Cathy and said that he would like to go with her to see Brian and Harold Stein when she goes to meet the attorneys. Cathy was a little taken back on that request since William has never really been involved with her work or attended any attorney meetings with her before. William had had discussions with Cathy about how Joe was treating Cathy ever since the companies closed. William was concerned that Cathy just could not seem to stop helping Joe even though there was no more real estate business and Joe was, as far as they knew, going completely broke. William was not sure, but believed Cathy may even been giving him money. He probably used it to purchase liquor or drugs. Joe had no ambition to find another normal means of making a living. He could have attempted to be a salesman for anything and done well. There were dozens of people that would have wanted a sober Joe Hyland selling for them. However, Joe spent his time trying to connect with his old rich friends from over 4 to 8 years ago who were still around when the real estate boom was at its height. Joe was sure there was a way he could get some type of financing to repurchase Snook Point. He was delusional. The ABN Amro Bank settled with Joe several years ago and thereafter Joe had never accepted the settlement. Joe executed the Settlement Agreement, but never accepted it. He could not accept that the Bank had taken over ownership of all of his properties. He continued day after day to try to get Snook Point back. Everyone knew real estate was still in a deep recession, but Joe was oblivious. He drank and did drugs on his bad days and once a week or maybe even only once a month he tried to sober up enough to try to discuss partnering with new people or obtaining loans to repurchase some or all of the properties. Cathy never gave up on Joe. For whatever reason, William could not understand. This was hurting Cathy and also starting to affect William's marriage. William had to do something about it. That is why William wanted to get involved with Cathy on her defense. He knew that the only person that Joe was with almost every day was Ivana, and maybe even other woman. Ivana had been extremely upset when Joe lost the large home, which she decorated, and when Joe moved back to his Largo Del Sol Condo. He told Ivana she could not live with him there. He just threw her out. It took her days to find her own place. She had little money. But for a few friends at Joe's old real estate company, which was now owned by the ABN Amro Bank, she would have been sleeping on the street. The only thing Joe and Ivana had in common was drugs and booze. William wanted to make sure the attorneys knew that. Cathy was oblivious to that fact. She was sure it was just Joe who was drinking by himself.

Monday morning at 9:30 AM, William and Cathy Rutter were in Brian Koop's office with Harold Stein. Harold completely explained to Cathy the ramifications of the final coroner's report and the reason for the change of designation by the coroner. Harold did believe that this may be a death penalty case, and the State's Attorney has 120 days to make that determination. Harold told Cathy and William that bail could be increased substantially or maybe she may be remanded. She needed to be ready for this. However, Harold believed he had a good argument to try to stop this ambitious prosecutor from accomplishing any of that.

They discussed the facts that concerned the method in which Joe had been murdered which involved very minute amounts of ethylene glycol, on nearly a daily basis, over a long period of time. Cathy would see Joe, at work, almost daily after the settlement with the Bank. But that was years ago. She would only see him maybe once or twice a week over the last 18-20 months. She never drank with him and they usually meet in restaurants or bars. He would drink, but there was no way Cathy could stop that. Ivana was with him, sometimes, and Joe and Ivana saw each other almost on a daily basis. They did drugs and booze often. Starting most days very early in the morning. However, their relationship was never the same after he would not allow her to live with her in his condo. Joe ate very little and lost a lot of weight. There was no one there to cook for him. Ivana cared less about Joe eating. Cathy would invite him to her house every week so he would eat something. He saw doctor after doctor, who said to stop drinking, or be ready to die. His liver and heart were deteriorating on a daily basis, but he didn't care. He would doctor shop until he found a doctor that found other diagnosis for his conditions. Those were his doctor's until he died. They prescribed every pill available for every possible ailment from anxiety to depression to liver, heart and kidney problems. He took, Singuliar, Chantix, Xanax, amitriptyline, Oxazepan and Phenobarb. All of such medication just made his real condition worse. He was obsessed in getting back in the real estate business.

Brian then said to Cathy that the U.S. Attorney has indicated to him that a Judge had authorized a search warrant for the Rutter's home as they were sitting in Brian's office. Frank Fable, the prosecutor, was coming to Brian's office at 11:00 to try to work something out, to see if there was even a need for a trial. Brian was certain that the prosecutor would drop all of the other charges if she plead to Joe's murder. They may even drop the charge from murder 1 to murder 2. That would mean 15 years maximum. Cathy said she would refuse to plead to something she did not do. William wanted to know why they were not searching Ivana's home. Brian said, he just heard about this just that morning and he would speak with the prosecutor about it. At least it's an alternative theory of the case. Reasonable doubt.

Fable showed up at Brian's office at 11:00 AM and, as they thought, offered a plea bargain to a murder 2 plea. The prosecutor even agreed to lower the sentence recommendation to 3 to 7 years. Cathy refused. The attorneys met in private and Brian told Frank Fable about Ivana and her history with Joe. Especially over the last 20 months or so. Fable wanted to let the Judge decide. Brian wanted to know what the search warrant at the Cutter's home revealed. Again Fable said that he would discuss that in due time. Harold Stein felt that if something incriminating was actually found in the Rutter's home, the charge would not have been reduced to Murder 2. But, again that would have to be discussed at a later time.

That afternoon, the hearing before Judge Stassen went fairly fast. The prosecutor explained the updated findings of the coroner and that several of the pills that Hyland was taking, on a daily basis, were found, pursuant to a search warrant executed by Judge Rothman, in the Rutter's home. The prescriptions were in the name of William Rutter. No ethylene glycol was found in the home. The Judge asked Mr. Fable if he had anything else to offer at that time. When the prosecutor said no, the Judge asked what Mr. Fable was asking for in the terms of increasing Mrs. Rutter's bail. He indicated remand. Fable indicated that this may very well be a death penalty case. The manner and time Mr. Hyland suffered was unusually cruel.

Harold Stein then had his time to argue the issue of bail as well as the charges that were still pending. Harold Stein has tried many criminal matters before Judge Stassen and was highly thought of by the Criminal Bar in Lee County. Judge Stassen was aware of that fact. Stein first started with the bail issue. After retorting the possibility of a death penalty case, Stein indicated it's been over 3 weeks since the original bail had been determined and there has been no attempt by the defendant to flee the jurisdiction of the Court. In fact, she has made herself available for this hearing. Nothing incriminating was found at the Rutter's home and no other incriminating evidence has been even discussed by the prosecutor. Nothing has really changed in the last 3 weeks except for the coroner's report. Then Harold spoke about the alternate theory of the case. Ivana Hollings may not be the only person Hyland had been seeing over the last 20 months. ABN Amro Bank's foreclosure, and subsequent Settlement Agreement left Hyland with substantial assets. Mr. Hyland had been able to keep his Largo Del Sol condominium worth at least $600,000.00, several automobiles, the Winnebago Hyland had purchased for his father to live in before his death, his 30 foot Sea Ray boat and other various personal property, let alone over a million dollars in cash., This, more than likely, had made many of Hyland's dozens of former employees, who lost their jobs, very unhappy. Another alternate theory of the case.

The other charges of conspiracy for the death of two people who died in Amsterdam and Italy by suicide and heart attack should not have even been charged. Not a trivial amount of evidence has been produced to show some type of conspiracy, or deception, with anyone concerning those deaths. The authorities in those Countries have closed those matters. The theft and fraud charges were very hard for Stein to believe and even hard for Stein to believe that the Court could allow those charges, without some minute piece of evidence, to show where the funds are or where they went. The prosecution obtained, from a Lee County Judge, under some pretense, a search warrant for Mrs. Rutter's financials months ago. They examined every bank account, all her real and personal property, her revenue streams for the past 10 years, her acquisitions of residential homes and the sales of the same and where and how the money to acquire them came from and where the proceed went, or are located today. What else is left for the State to search for, financially, so that the State could possibly find evidence to show some unusual pattern that would go to the extent of fraud or theft? Where is the great deception? Frankly, Stein was surprised those charges were still pending. If this fraud or theft happen, it would have been 6 to 10 years ago.

The Judge asked Fable if there was some further evidence or argument that he wanted to say.

Fable, again went back to the fact that Mrs. Rutter was the person who drafted all of the draw request for over a billion and a half dollars while employed by the Hyland development companies. To this day there are several millions unaccounted for. Someone, dead, or alive had been attempting to deceive the Bank out of hundreds of millions of dollars. However, the prosecutor could not, or did not, say how such deception worked.

Stein retorted that Mr. Hyland and Mr. Vinke of the Bank signed off on every one of those draw requests. After that, Mrs. Rutter was instructed by the Bank and Mr. Hyland what to do with each penny of those draw request funds. Where is the evidence that she stole some of that money? Where is the evidence that there was some sort of deception on the part of anyone, let alone Mrs. Rutter? Even the Banks have not made any claim for any missing money. Let Mr. Fable show us the evidence, or at least, his theory that Mrs. Rutter stole some of those funds. The prosecutor, after a request by the Judge, said he had nothing further.

Judge Stassen then continued bail at the same amount and let Mrs. Rutter go home. He gave the attorneys 60 days to bring any relevant motions. The trial was set for March 10, 2014. The prosecution was astonished!

CHAPTER 18

ON JANUARY 20, 2010, Nicolaus called Josef Rynsburger concerning their short get together on Josef's boat near Venice. Josef had confirmed that he had spoken with his care taker and the boat would be in the slip, fueled and stocked and ready for a two day stay as of January 21. Nicolaus thanked Josef for the use of the boat and thought since the drive would take about 14 hours that they should plan on leaving early the next morning. Josef agreed. He said he had made arrangements with his driver who will be staying at a hotel in Venice. This way they would be able to take his limo. It would be more comfortable and they would be able to relax, have a drink, a snack, and even snooze a bit on the ride.

Josef said that he would pick up Nicolaus in the morning at 7:00 AM. That way they could get to Venice and stop at a restaurant for dinner before going to the boat. The driver will stock the refrigerator for a light lunch and a bottle of wine. Nicolaus was impressed. Why was Josef being so accommodating? Nicolaus would find out.

The next morning, Nicolaus finished packing and saying his goodbyes to Elsie. He had packed for a casual several days, but included some dressy shirts, since he knew Josef liked good restaurants and fine wine. Since Josef was providing the boat, the limo and the food, Nicolas knew he should be prepared to pay for the restaurants. He would like to see the reaction from Josef when he offers to pay. Nicolaus believes this is a 'fishing trip' for Josef to find out what Nicolaus really knows about what happen to the funds when they were partners. More importantly, if Nicolaus knew anything about the Flagler Bank money. As part of Nicolaus' packing, he included a copy of Vinke's suicide note and Vinke's 9 millimeter Glock 26 with 4 rounds still left in the clip, one already in the chamber and several vials of insulin and several syringes. Can Nicolaus really pull this off? He hated Josef for deceiving him and stealing his money as well as causing Vinke to commit suicide the way he did. Vinke was not one of Nicolaus' favorite persons, but Josef was the lynch pin that caused so many people to turn corrupt and deceptive.

At 7:00 AM the next morning, Josef was at Nicolaus' home. The driver was loading Nicolaus's luggage into the trunk and Nicolas was saying good bye to his wife. Josef said a few cordial words to Elsie and they were on their way. The 14 hour trip took them around Dusseldorf, Frankfort and when they reached Stuttgurt, which was about half way, Josef took out his bottle of Louis Latour Gevrey-Chambertin (2004), a very expensive Pinot Noir from Burgundy, France.

"Nicolaus, this wine reveals aromas of lightly-wooded blackcurrant. You will adore it with the cheeses and meats I have for our light lunch." Charmed Josef.

"I'll drink any type of red wine. The assortment of meats and cheese looks delicious." laughed Nicolaus.

An enjoyable way to travel. Both took a short nap so they would be prepared for a delicious dinner that evening. When they arrived near Venice, Josef said that the restaurant for which he had made a reservation was just a few miles away. 14 hours in the limo was a long time, but they made some small talk, spoke of each other's wives, spoke of the troubles of Josef's sons and and ate and drank like the millionaires they were. Actually, the time went much faster than Nicolaus thought it would. They arrived at the restaurant at about 8:30 PM a little earlier than they thought they would. It was quite crowded. The name was Ristorante Quadri. It was located just above the café of the same name and had an overstated Venetian ambience. Josef booked one of the beat tables with a view of Piazza San Marco, the best ambience in the restaurant. The price tag was quite high considering the wine ordered by Josef, but Nicolas expected that, and Josef did not say a word when Nicolaus paid the bill.

At 10:30 PM, the driver took both gentleman to Josef's boat. The bedrooms had the blankets pulled down and the heads were fully stocked. Nicolaus didn't even need to bring his shampoo. Each bedroom had a mini bar with juices, waters and, of course, some liquor and wine. Nicolaus just wanted to sleep. The next day would be a life defining day for him. Josef open a couple of after dinner liquors and read some business magazines before turning in.

The next morning, Nicolaus got up first. He heard some cracking and jingling noises in the galley. He looked out his door and there was Nicolaus's driver setting up croissants with jelly and butter and several espressos. Was this driver going to be around all the time? That may be a problem. Nicolaus threw some water on his face combed his hair and went into the galley. The galley was very small, so the food had to be served in the drawing room. Even that was small. Nicolaus was thinking of ways to get rid of the driver, without giving the driver any inclination of Nicolaus' plan. Oh! The best laid plans.

When Josef got up, he came out in his shorts and sat down on the leather davenport and had an espresso and croissant with lots of butter. Josef didn't wait at all and asked Nicolaus straight up why he suggested this little get together? Josef was not a patient man. Josef was under the impression Nicolaus was not too fond of him. When they had been together with their wives or friends, Nicolaus completely ignore Josef. Why? Then, Josef came right out and asked Nicolaus if Vinke had spoken to him about their partnership loans. Nicolaus and Josef both gave a look to the driver and then Josef told him to have some fun in Venice. Don't come back until after dinner. We would like to be alone today. When Josef tells someone to do something, they usually do it fast. The driver had learned that several times when Alyssa was around. The driver then left quickly. Nicolaus was not timid about asking Josef what he knew to be true. Nicolaus wondered what Josef would say about his and Vinke's little deception of at least a million of Nicolaus' Euros.

"So, Josef tell me did you and Vinke steal money form me during our partnership years?" calmly asked Nicolas. "Tell me if it is really true?"

"Nicolaus, I have no idea where you get your information. You and I and our families have been friends for years. I know your feelings about me and Lena. But that's different. At first I thought your cold shoulder was the way you perceived how I reacted to my wife's disease and her death." Replied Josef. "My relationship between my wife and I is personal, and really no one else should judge me. I am sorry I cannot live up to your standards when it comes to husband and wife relationships."

"Josef that is only one of your many faults. Marriage is something to be respected. If you want to play around, get a divorce." Wholesomely replied Nicolas. "Enough said."

"But, your arrogance when it comes to business is obnoxious! You can never be wrong. Your word is the only word." Sadly remarked Nicolas. "I saw that when we were partners. You never asked me about any properties, any opinions on which way the partnership should go. All decisions were made by you without any input by me. That is one of the reasons I wanted out." Said Nicolaus with his voice rising a little.

"To be honest, I did have some idea that you were cheating me out of some money. I wasn't sure, but it just seemed, with the market doing as well as it was, and rents so high, there was some money missing from my side of the ledger." Said Nicolaus a little more angrily. "But how do I prove it without a full audit. I didn't want to do that since our families were such good friends. I thought, before I did something I couldn't stop, I would do one more thing. I went to Vinke and asked him if he knew if anything unconventional was going on with the distributions of partnership fund between Josef and me. After all he was the banker for both of us." Nicolaus' voice started to taper off.

Then Nicolaus went into his room to compose himself for what was to come next. Josef started the engine and drove the boat out into the Adriatic Sea and then 20 minutes later stopped the motor and went out and dropped the anchor. Nicolaus came out of his room with a small athletic bag. It looked as if Nicolaus was going swimming.

"We're in the middle of trying to set the record straight on our partnership distributions and you want to go swimming?" said Josef. "So what did Vinke tell you?" asked Josef sincerely. "Vinke was a good guy, a good banker and loyal. I can't imagine he would lie to you."

"Josef, you don't know the half of it. You are the person who consistently said 'never deceive a deceiver', correct?" said Nicolaus with a smile.

"Of course." Said Josef. "Why?"

"Your good loyal friend was deceiving you." Said Nicolaus. "And, by the way, he told me that our partnership distributions were completely on the up and up. He said he reviewed them personally. So I never said anything. I just decided to end our business relationship. I still felt I was being cheated."

Then Nicolaus thought it was finally time. Nicolas told Josef that Vinke deceived Nicolaus when he was asked about their partnership distributions. Vinke was deceiving everyone. Vinke deceived his employer, deceived me, and best of all, Josef, he was deceiving you!

"What are you talking about?" asked Josef, this time in an aggressive manner. Vinke was my friend. He would do nothing to hurt or deceive me."

Then Nicolaus took out Vinke's Glock and pointed it directly at Josef.

"There is something I would like you to read." Directed Nicolas. "Read it twice if you have to. This day you will be educated."

"Nicolas what are you doing with that revolver? Put it away. Is it loaded?" nervously asked Josef.

"It's Vinke's Revolver. It was used by him to blow his brains out." Admitted Nicolaus. "I was there. Vinke called me that night and asked me to come and meet him since he wanted to tell me something." Arrogantly remarked Nicolaus.

"I know you saw him shoot himself? Nervously said Josef." But, I don't believe you.

"I did better than that. Vinke had written a long suicide note. I have a copy of it right here in my other hand." As he was still holding the revolver at Josef. "I want you to read it and then you tell me who the deceiver is?"

Nicolas handed the note to Josef. He started to read it. The expression on Josef's face was priceless to Nicolaus. Josef said that the note was a fake. While he was reading the note, Josef, on several occasions, asked Nicolaus to please put down the revolver. Nicolas has no intention of doing that. There was no way that Nicolaus was going to let Josef, a younger man try to get the revolver away from him. It was the key to Nicolaus' whole plan. Josef, as he continued to read the note, thought that Vinke would never say those things about Josef. Vinke would never ask Nicolaus to kill him. Josef and Vinke were partners, close partners! But Vinke was stealing from Josef? Could it be? Josef thought for a minute. It started to make sense. Vinke kept only himself as a signature on the Flagler Bank in Fort Lauderdale as security in case the Bank found out about the money. Josef then understood that Nicolaus was the second signature on the Flagler Account. Again, Josef was devastated.

"Did you send those signature cards to the 3 banks?" Asked Josef nervously. "I didn't know about the two other bank accounts. Was Vinke stealing all of Hyland's pre-paid profits? Had he made an arrangement with Cathy Rutter to help him with that deception? I thought he was my good friend. What happen to him?"

"What happen to him?" Questioned Nicolaus. "What happen to you? You really are a scoundrel. Even Vinke believed that."

"What are you going to do?" Very nervously asked Josef. "I can make it up to you."

"It's far too late for that." Claimed Nicolaus, as Nicolaus quickly jumped at Josef and shoved the syringe of a very large dose of insulin into Josef's thigh.

Josef immediately started to fell groggy.

"It won't be long now Josef. You are finally getting what you deserved years ago. Vinke may not have been an honest man, but he tried to repent on his terms. You could never repent." Nicolaus said nervously.

Josef fell to the floor holding his left side and arm moaning and attempting to scream at the same time. He would be dead in a few minutes. Nicolaus took the copy of the suicide note from Josef, went on the opposite side of the boat facing the shore, and took out a match and lit the note on fire. Nicolaus held it in his hand until it was almost burned completely and he dropped it in the water. Next, Nicolaus looked around and saw no one nearby, so he took Vinke's Glock, the rest of the syringes and the vials of insulin and threw them all in the Adriatic Sea where they would be lost forever.

Nicolaus checked Josef's pulse. He was gone. Nicolaus then sat on the floor for a few minutes, just to get his wits about him and prepare for the unknown. But he would continue with his plan. He went out on the bow of the boat, waited for a boat to come nearby, and started to yell, in Italian, "Help, help me, someone has just had a heart attack!" Several people some distance away yelled back to Nicolaus, "Do you need help?"

"Yes, please send an ambulance and get someone to help me get this boat to shore."

Within 5 minutes two boats had come to the rescue of Nicolaus's cry for help. They helped Nicolaus start the boat and helped him dock it and called the authorities. Nicolaus was just shaking! Nicolas had this story rehearsed for days. Josef was his patient and they were on this short holiday for Josef's mental health. Josef was a Dutch citizen. He had a massive heart attack right after breakfast. By then the Italian police were at the marina. The police covered Josef's body and questioned Nicolaus for about a half an hour. His story was creditable to the police. Nicolaus then told the Italian authorities about the driver. The authorities located the driver about an hour later. The driver confirmed the reason for Nicolaus and Josef's holiday. Nicolaus could speak enough Italian to understand most of what the police were asking. Nicolas asked the police to help Nicolaus get him to the closest mortuary where Nicolas could examine the body to see if there is anything more or something else unusual which may have caused the death. The Italian police, being their usual laziness, really didn't want to get involved with all the paper work and questions over a heart attack or natural death of a Dutch citizen. They confirmed Dr. Timmerman's credentials as a doctor, and his address and good standing with the Dutch Medical community. They had no jurisdiction over a natural accident like this that happen in International waters.

The police took them to a small mortuary and dropped off Josef's body and Nicolaus. The police just didn't want to know this happened and left once the body was dropped off. Nicolaus, spoke with the mortician and told him the story. He had been in a bad stage of health for a while and the last two days on the boat Josef was not breathing well. I told him to go to the hospital, but he said not in Italy. I did not have the medications that were needed in my bag with me. I thought Josef would have them. But he didn't. I gave mouth to mouth and CPR, but he was too far gone. I feel it's my fault. I suggested this holiday. Stupid me. He has no family. His wife is deceased. I am his only friend.

Do you have facilities for cremation? That is the only way I can get him back to Amsterdam. My wife and I can arrange a celebration of life for any friends he may have left. The mortician didn't even think twice. It would be down first thing the next morning. The mortician even invited Nicolaus to stay the night at his home. The plan was working very well. The dinner that the mortician's wife prepared was even better than the restaurant Josef choose the first night in Venice. The police just dropped them off and left, as if it never happened and were never to be heard of again. The mortician took care of the cremation, Nicolaus paid for the procedure, purchased an urn and asked the mortician to call a cab so he could get back to the boat so Josef's driver could drive him back to Amsterdam with Josef's ashes. What a tragedy! Nicolaus took care of the death certificate on the 14 hour drive back and filed the paper work and death certificate, the next day, with the proper authorities. What a wonderful world without one more scoundrel.

Josef's driver found the whole episode very unusual, but knew better than to ask too many questions. There was no blood or incriminating evidence anywhere on the boat that would disprove Nicolaus' statement of events. The driver drove Nicolaus back to Amsterdam. The driver asked what he should do now. Nicolas told him to drop the limo off in Josef's garage and go look for another job. It would probably be better off if you don't mention this to any of you future employers. If you need any letters of recommendations, just contact me. I know lots of people. Nicolaus enjoyed Josef's wine and cheese and meats on the 14 hour drive back to Amsterdam. Nicolas even smiled a little. Nicolas kept the window between him and the driver closed the whole way. The only communication between them was by internal phone. The first deed was complete.

****

It was the first week in April, 2010. The deadline on the Agreement with the new Bank and Hyland was coming soon. Joe had heard about Josef's heart attack. With Vinke gone, Rynsburger gone, AFC Bank gone, Joe was on his own. He had found a $2 million home in a beautiful development just north of the Riverview development on the Caloosahatchee River. Joe asked Ivana, when she was sober, to decorate it and gave her up to a $100,000.00 budget. She was in heaven, Joe was in the dumps.

The hotel convention center was complete and the Bank was no longer accepting draws from Hyland's development company. Revenues, including rents were coming in from receipts from the hotel, restaurants, bars and other commercial units. Companies were reserving the convention center for future gatherings for their companies. The City of Cape Coral was now on the map. However, unknown to the public, the revenues were barely enough to pay the employees. And those payments had to be approved by the Bank. The employees were not happy, they were getting paid but sometimes a week or so late. Some employees quit and moved on, but the Bank was sticking to the Agreement.

At Coconut Cove Point, of the 48 condominium units that were left to sell when the Agreement was executed, 28 were still not sold. All of the net proceeds of the sales of the 20 units sold were sent to the Bank per the Agreement.

As for the Alico Grand Mine, Joe had no prospects to purchase the mine. Revenues were coming in but nowhere needed to make the mine even break even. Some of the employees had quit there also since their wages were being paid late for the same reason as the hotel.

On April 16, Joe closed, in cash, on the large $2 million dollar home. He and Ivana were making arrangements to move into the home and Joe had Brian Koop draw up the necessary notices and documents to homestead the home to make it exempt from creditors. Joe also took $150,000.00 in cash and at least $100,000.00 of jewelry including 2 solid gold Rolex watches with full diamond faces, several diamond and emerald rings and other miscellaneous items and put them in his safe in the Largo Del Sol condo. The bank heard about the purchase of the large home and was furious. They did not know about his safe in the condominium. The Bank called their attorneys, Carl Finch and Robert Adams and demanded a meeting in Brian Koop's office to talk about this acquisition. The meeting had to happen within several days or the Bank was going to declare the Agreement void.

Brian Koop and Bill Jones, the bankruptcy attorney, knew that the Bank could not void the Agreement, but convinced Joe to meet with the Bank's lawyers. Brian instructed Joe not to say anything and let the attorneys do the talking.

The morning of April 18, Carl Finch, Robert Adams, Joe Hyland, Brian Koop and Bill Jones met in Koop's conference room as per the request of the Bank's attorney.

"You called this meeting." Said Koop. "Joe and this office have been keeping you and your client updated, every week since the Agreement was executed in January on all of the developments. My client still has a little less than a month to try to accomplish everything in the Agreement."

"This is Bullshit!" barked Finch. "I have never seen such a bad faith move on the part of any party to an Agreement in all of my 38 years of practicing law. Your client took $2 million and purchased a home and is homesteading it so the Bank cannot get to it if the Agreement is not satisfied. Either do not homestead that home and move into it, or our client has authorized this firm to file a bad faith law suit against Hyland personally and take everything he has."

"Where in the Agreement does it say that our client cannot spend his own money on anything he wants?" Said Jones. "The law is clear, an individual can use their own funds to purchase any priced home and homestead it even if it may be done to defraud creditors. However, our client is not saying he did this to defraud anyone. He has the absolute right to do what he has done."

"No sir!" Yelled Finch. "This is the lowest I have ever seen. I want each and everyone in this room to know that the Bank is aware of several millions of dollars that have been missing from the loans with AFC Bank. Our client has chosen to forget those funds so long as everyone works together in good faith under our Agreement. What Hyland has just done is worse than bad faith. It is downright deception!"

"Carl, we are unaware of any missing funds from the loans with AFC Bank. We have no idea what you are speaking about or what leverage you are trying to use to make Joe Hyland give up his Florida constitutional right of Homestead." Retorted Koop.

"I want to know here and now if this house purchase will be the Homestead for Joe Hyland?" exclaimed Finch.

"It is, and it is his right." Said Jones.

"Our firm is preparing a foreclosure action against Snook Point property, the Coconut Cove Point unit's unsold and the mine, and will be filing it in a week with the Lee County Clerk's office. This will be the largest foreclosure that this part of the world has ever seen. The papers throughout Florida will pick this story up. Hyland will be crucified! We will sue for all deficiencies under Hyland's personal guarantees and that includes the home he just purchased." Said Finch.

"That would be a big mistake, Carl." Said Koop." I would speak with your client and just make sure they are on board with this threat. Also, be careful what you may say to all those reporters for the newspapers that may bring up your foreclosure action. Remember, bad faith goes two ways. Slander and liable can be expensive!"

"We are out of here, see you in Court. And the several million dollars that are missing from the original loans, will also be part of the deficiencies. So I will give your client good warning that this may even turn into a criminal matter of fraud on a bank." Cried out Finch as he and his other attorney got up and left the building.

"Brian, I was afraid this was going to happen. I never should have bought that house." Said Joe. "I didn't even want it. I can hide my money someplace else where they will never find it. But it's too late now, you all advised me to buy this house."

"Joe, don't worry, they are just pissed they didn't see this coming and didn't put it in the Agreement." Said Koop." You know that you can't meet the terms of the Agreement that was signed a few months ago. You knew it when you signed it. It just gave you time to save some of you assets before the shit hit the fan, so we might as well start the fight now."

"I am absolutely sure that the Bank does not want to fight this in Court." Said Jones. "It's a looser, they were aware of how all of the development loans were structured. My God, the Bank owns 10% of all the developments! It's a battle this Bank does not want to take on. I am certain that when they see your answer to their foreclosure complaint, they will want to settle this whole thing, one way or another, but not in an open Court Room."

"I sure hope so." Said Joe.

"By the way, Joe, what's this about several million dollars that are missing from the original loan from AFC Bank?" asked Jones.

"No idea." Said Joe. "The only people that would know anything about something like that would be Hagan Vinke or Josef Rynsburger, and they are both dead! Otherwise you can speak with Cathy Rutter, but I am sure she knows nothing about it."

"Let me know when the Sheriff serves the foreclosure papers on you. We will not agree to accept service for you. They are being assholes about this whole matter. " Said Jones. "You can be sure that we will be drafting a counterclaim of bad faith against the Bank as soon as we receive the Complaint."

CHAPTER 19

Brian Koop and Harold Stein meet in Stein's office just after the Court hearing where Judge Stassen did not rule in favor of any of the prosecutor's motions concerning the turn of events where by Hyland's death was, in fact, determined a homicide.

"I believe the Judge seemed to be indicating to us that he was not really sure that there was sufficient evidence to prove that Rutter actually murdered Hyland. Maybe we should request for a preliminary hearing on the issues dealing with all of the charges to determine if the Judge determines that the prosecutor has sufficient evidence to move forward with a trial on any or all of the issue." Remarked Stein.

"Can that be down procedurally now that a trial date has been set?" Asked Brian.

"Well, I have never done it before, but the Rules don't really say anything about it, so why not try." Questioned Stein" "What's the worst that can happen, the Judge will rule against us and not allow the hearing."

Both attorneys discussed the strategy of this action. They looked at the evidence the prosecution has on Rutter for the murder of Hyland which is basically nothing. There are several other alternative theories of the case and the prosecutor hasn't even issued search warrants on

Ivana Hollings apartment or any of the other possible suspects who may be employees of the Hyland's development companies. They have just relied on the fact that Rutter drafted the draws for the acquisition and construction loans. What does that have to do with a murder? In fact, what does that have to do with fraud or theft? What evidence do they have that the State can prove, beyond a reasonable doubt, that Rutter is guilty of those crimes? The only people that can testify against her are dead. If the prosecution has someone who may have done audits of the AFC Bank loans when ABN Amro purchased the Bank, which may be able to show she is guilty of theft or fraud, let's find that out. Otherwise, maybe a motion to dismiss all charges may be timely.

"I'll start drafting the paperwork. I'll get my paralegal to set up a preliminary hearing date before the Court and we'll see what happens." Said Stein. 'Maybe the prosecutors will issue some more search warrants against other persons of interest or give us a list of their witnesses or at least something more to justify the charges once they get this motion."

"I'll contact Rutter and tell her what we are doing." Said Brian. "I'll tell her we have nothing to lose with this tactic."

****

Arthur Winslow, Alex Tarian, Denise Hudak, Luke Blakely and Frank Fable were all in Alex's office the Tuesday after Thanksgiving, 2013. The day before, Judge Stassen had just heard the motion by attorney Fable to increase the bail to remand or heavily increase the bail on Cathy Rutter due to the change in circumstances out of the Coroner's office that Joe Hyland had been murdered. The Judge changed nothing. Each of the persons in that office had some thoughts on this difficult case. Alex was running the meeting so he asked who wanted to start a discussion on the chances of convicting Cathy Rutter for Murder.

Frank started, and said that he would be the person who was going to be trying the case. His first thought was that the investigators in this matter have found not one iota of real evidence that Rutter is guilty of anything. There are a bunch of coincidences, but not even much in the form of circumstantial evidence for murder or, for that matter, any conspiracy of murder for two Dutch citizens that died in Europe! Then there are the charges of fraud and theft. Where in the world did anyone come up with those charges, Frank wanted to hear someone argue that those charges should stick. Everyone all heard Rutter's attorney argue, on the record, that all Rutter did was draft the draws for the loans. Someone else signed off on them and then a third person, Vinke, President of the Bank, told Rutter what checks to write or what wire transfers to initiate. She had no say in where any of that money went and most important, no one had convinced Frank that Rutter would receive one cent of any loan funds or how she was able to steal any of those funds. And, where would she have put the funds that you all say she stole? No one can find a cent of it. Frank wanted to hear someone tell him who his first witness should be at the trial who can show any proof of guilt.

There was a bit of a lull after Frank's opening remarks. Denise then took her turn, and indicated that she had never really believed that Hyland was even murdered. Denise had interviewed Rutter, Leigh Mowery, the ex-wife, and she was certain they were not involved in any foul play with Hyland. When she heard that the coroner changed the findings to murder by poisoning by ant-freeze, she was shocked. The police searched Rutter's home upside down and found nothing incriminating. He just happen to be at her home when he died. That does not make her a murderer. Denise still did not believe she was the murderer. Mowery was in Louisville, Kentucky while Hyland was being poisoned. That takes her off the hook. Josef Rynsburger died in 2010. He couldn't have done it. Hagen Vinke committed suicide in 2009, so he couldn't have done it. They're off the hook. An employee of Hyland's Development companies doesn't even make sense. Getting paid late or closing down a business because it went broke is not my idea of a motive for murder in this case. All the employees knew what was coming as early as 2009. Most, if not all of them got other jobs or left town to look for other jobs by 2010. Everyone in Hyland's real estate company who were racking in the dough during the real estate boom, were all kept on by the Bank when they settled the matter with Hyland. That leaves them out.

"Denise, your killing my case for murder here." Said Frank.

"Well, counselor, let's look who is left with a motive and an opportunity to poison Hyland." Retorted Denise.

"I'm listening." Said Frank.

The only ones that come to mind is Ivana Hollings or Willian Rutter. But William's motive would just be jealousy. Nothing to do with the developments. Maybe, Cathy and Joe were having an affair? However,

I highly doubt it. I did not find out anything that would put them alone anywhere during the time he was drinking and using. If anything she was the one person that tried to keep him alive. But an affair, no way. Also William was only in town about 12-14 weeks a year. Otherwise he was in Montana. That rules him out right there. And then there was one. So if you want my thoughts, if he was really murdered, and I am still not convinced of that fact, my money is on Ivana. He treated her like shit. All she was good for was a drinking and drug buddy. She lived with him at his condominium at Largo Del Sol until he purchased that monster house on the river. Hyland had her decorate it, and then he wouldn't let her live there. He kicked her out. In fact, she went to live with Cathy Rutter until she could find an apartment. Hyland stopped giving her gifts and money. He was going broke, his business was gone and he was getting sicker each day. He stopped eating and just drank. She had to be pissed. Maybe a search warrant on her apartment would be in order. That's my say.

"Anyone else?" said Frank.

"As to the fraud and theft charges, I had our accountants go through every piece of paper in William and Cathy Rutter's personal financial records for the last 10 years. We looked at tax returns, every checking and broker account in any of their names. Every penny balanced from income to expenses. It was somewhat complicated, but if she stole any money, we sure couldn't find it." Said Denise.

Luke and Arthur couldn't comment on the theft and fraud matter, but both agreed with Denise about the murder of Hyland. As to the deaths of Vinke and Rysenberger, there were some coincidences, but nothing that had to do with Rutter. Arthur was sure that Vinke's death was murder and not a suicide. They never found the gun. And a 9 millimeter Glock 26 was missing from his home. How can someone have a suicide without a gun and no suicide note? He was President of AFC Bank and had a lot of stock in that Bank. When ABN Amro purchased AFC, Vinke would have made a lot of money. It made no sense. Someone killed him. Vinke and Rynsburger were stealing money from the Bank and other people, probably customers of the Bank.

"My money is on Rynsburger, but he is dead." Said Arthur. "That is also a strange death. A man in good health having a heart attack in international waters off of the coast of Italy. Give me a break! However, there are two facts that are circumstantial. Dr. Nicolaus Timmerman was at both the suicide of Vinke, in fact he said he saw Vinke shoot himself, and he was with Rynsburger when he had his heart attack. No autopsies were performed on either man at the request of Timmerman and Timmerman signed the death certificates for both men. He's the man. Rutter had nothing to do with either death in any way that I can figure out. I plan to speak with Senior Officer Visse Jansen of the Amsterdam police and discuss the possibility of the Dutch authorities reopening both those cases. I would even enjoy going over there and helping, even on my dime."

Vinke was not only President of the AFC Bank who loaned all the money to Hyland, but he was also on the loan committee. There was some talk that he was getting kickbacks on the Hyland loans, but there was nothing the Dutch police could find to prove that. Even AFC Bank was an investor to the tune of 10% in each of Hyland's developments. ABN Amro would have not purchased AFC if there was some fraud or theft in those dozens of millions of dollars. Even Rynsburger was a 40% investor in Hyland's developments. What does that mean? He had no motive to kill Hyland, if anything he would want him alive. Even more, the Bank would have wanted Hyland alive since they were an investor. No one saw any fraud or theft anywhere.

"Again, you all are killing my case." Said Frank. "I am not getting involved in two potential Dutch murders in Europe. If you want to do it Arthur, go for it."

"So where does all this leave us?" said Alex. Do we need more time to get forensic accountants to audit $1.5 billion dollars in loans and construction? I don't think so."

"Denise has a good point. Let's get a search warrant for Ivana Hollings apartment and car." Said Luke. "It couldn't hurt. We're going no place here."

"I'll take care of getting it." Said Alex. "Luke and Arthur, you and a couple other officers should search her place as soon as the warrant is issued."

"Do it fast." Said Frank. "I have a funny feeling that Harold Stein is drafting a motion for preliminary hearing to see what evidence we have to try Cathy Rutter on these charges. I don't want to be laughed out of the Court Room."

****

A week after Josef Rynsburger had been murdered by Dr. Nicolaus Timmerman, no one had even contacted the doctor for a statement or anyone request any interrogation concerning the events in Venice. The police took a copy of his and Josef's passports and Dutch Identification cards. So they knew where he lived. The Venice police could have contacted the Amsterdam authorities, but, if they did, nothing happen. That surprised the doctor, so he thought, leave sleeping dogs lie. Elsie was shocked at what happen but didn't want to pry too much, since Josef was a patient of Nicolaus'. Nicolaus thought that it would be a perfect time to go to Fort Lauderdale and finish the second deed Vinke had requested in his suicide note.

It was February, 2010, and that month was a great month to be in Florida. The weather was perfect, however the traffic and the difficulty to drive on the crowded streets was a drawback, but now was as good a time as ever to complete his tasks and to recoup the money stolen from him. Nicolaus enjoyed having money. He told Elsie he had to finish a matter, in Florida, for a former patient who had passed away and he would be gone for less than a week. Nicolaus thought before he made arrangements for hotel and air flights, he would make sure that the people who he wanted to contact would be around.

The first person Nicolaus contacted was Holly Bedford, the bank officer who confirmed that he was a signature on the Flagler Community Bank account that Vinke opened. She told Nicolaus she would be around all month and he could come in any time during the work week to take care of any business he needed. However, she did request that he give her a days' notice, if possible. He had no problem with that. After Holly hug up with Nicolaus, she immediately called Arthur Winslow. During Denise's investigation, Denise found out about a bank account at the Flagler Community Bank that was opened in the name of AFC Bank. Hagan Vinke was the only signature. Holly told Arthur that she had recently received new signature cards adding Dr. Nicolaus Timmerman as a signor on the account. The signature cards were dated just over two weeks before Vinke committed suicide. Arthur said to call him as soon as she hears from the doctor. Holly agreed. She told Arthur that currently there was a little over $6 million in the account. Arthur then called Senior Officer Visse Jansen.

Next, the other person Nicolaus contacted was George Harvey who he had meet several times. Nicolaus was familiar with his reputation as a business man and as the ambassador for the United States for two years with France. Nicolaus also was the person who warned George about Rynsburger and his methods of deceiving people and stealing from banks. George said he would make sure he was around and he also requested a day's notice to make sure he would be available. As soon as George heard that Dr. Timmerman was coming to Fort Myers he called Catty Rutter. Both of them were aware that the doctor was present when Vinke either committed suicide or was murdered. They were also aware that he also was the only person present when Rynsburger had his heart attack. Both George and Cathy knew that Vinke and Rynsburger had stolen money from Nicolaus when the doctor and Rynsburger were in a real estate partnership. The money that was used to purchase the real estate for the partnership came from AFC Bank. The coincidences were just too many. Cathy and George were certain that Vinke and Rynsburger were, in some form or fashion, deceiving AFC Bank through draws drafted by Cathy. Cathy was too smart to let that opportunity pass. Vinke had requested Cathy, unbeknownst to Hyland, to open two other bank accounts in Fort Myers' banks under AFC Bank with Cathy as the signature and he would let her know when to disperse money and to whom. Vinke indicated the funds were mostly the pre-paid profits that Joe Hyland was entitled to receive when projects were completed. Cathy was smart and knew how to deceive a deceiver.

Dr. Timmerman had been contemplating about the more than $6 million in the Flagler Community Bank. He estimated that Josef Rynsburger and Hagen Vinke stole close to $2 million American from him while Nicolaus was Rynsburger's partner. Vinke only wanted to give each of his sons $1 million each. Nicolaus had, over the years, become fairly well off by practicing medicine and through some lucrative investments he had made. It seemed unfair for him to benefit from all that money and double his losses on the backs of two innocent and extremely nice boys who he and his wife had met after their father's death. Why should the sins of a father fall on the sons? So Nicolaus decided to take only what he estimated had been stolen from him in the Rynsburger partnership and send the rest equally to each of the two sons. Nicolaus felt good about that decision.

So Nicolaus made his arrangements for a flight to Fort Lauderdale for February 3, 2010, with a return flight from Fort Myers 6 days later. He booked a room for 3 nights at the Fort Lauderdale Marriot Harbor

Beach Resort & Spa. This hotel was only a few minutes from several great restaurants on Las Olas Boulevard. He decided he might as well enjoy his time in Fort Lauderdale. After all, it's been over 5 years since the partnership was dissolved and Nicolas had been deceived by those two crooks! With an additional several million dollars in his portfolio, why not enjoy! Nicolas then booked 3 nights at the Bonita Springs Coconut Point Hyatt Hotel just south of Fort Myers for 3 more nights. He would fly out of Fort Myers back to Amsterdam after he had finished his tasks, and had his chat with George Harvey.

Nicolaus was still a little confused about the other two banks that Vinke had mentioned in his suicide note. Those accounts had an approximate balance of $10.5 million. Nicolaus signed the signature cards, which had no bank account number on them, sent a copy of his passport and yet received two letters indicating that no such accounts had ever been opened. This was very strange to Nicolaus and for some reason he still could not get that out of his mind. It was a perplexing puzzle to Nicolaus, for which he desperately wanted to solve. That was the main reason Nicolaus really wanted to go to Fort Myers. Calling George Harvey was just a roués to come to Fort Myers and to go to both those banks and check and see if that money may actually be there, even with no bank account number on the signature cards. The people sending those letters may have been mistaken or looked up the wrong title to those accounts, or forgot to put the bank account number on the cards. However, Nicolaus enjoyed the company of George and would enjoy some time just chatting with him about his time in France and other interesting matters dealing with real estate developments and whether or not George had any further knowledge of any other deceptions that may have had occurred by the two crooks. If so, such deceptions may have to do with those other two mysterious bank accounts.

Nicolaus was sure to bring with him certified copies of Hagen Vinke's death certificates and all of the letters he received from the 3 banks, as well as every document he could get his hands on that would prove to those banks that he was actually Nicolaus Timmerman. Lastly, Nicolaus had the suicide note of Hagen Vinke, just in case he needed it for some unknown reason. But he had no intention of showing it to anyone unless absolutely necessary. He planned to burn the note before leaving Florida. On the flight over to Florida, Nicolaus was a little nervous about all this. It was a lot of money and who knows what the U.S. requirements would be for him, as a foreign citizen, to be able to withdraw all the money and close the accounts. He was sure there would be certain paper work. But after much thought, he really believed he was not doing anything illegal. However, the two mysterious accounts with approximately $10.5 million he really had no right to. However, in Vinke's note, Vinke never said who the money belonged to. It would have been very helpful if Vinke could have indicated, in his note, who Vinke and Rynsburger had deceived for those funds. Then, Nicolaus could actually go to the authorities to make sure those funds went to the right people. However, Nicolaus would have to disclose the fact that he did tamper with evidence by taking the suicide note and the Glock. That may be something he needed to have a second thought about. But by being honest about who those funds belonged too, would surely make the authorities understand and everything may, very well, come out all right. Nicolaus greed made him a little naïve. But, if the money does exist, he was grappling with how much of it should go to Roger Spector. That was another reason to talk with George Harvey. He trusted his opinion. The rest, Vinke said, was to be distributed in Nicolaus' discretion. Whether or not he should tell the appropriate authorities about the remaining amount, he would decide that matter after he sees if there are any problem with the Flagler Community Bank account. In fact, as to the Flagler Account, he was actually following the last request of a man who committed suicide. Nicolaus was certain, that no one in Florida, could know anything about his participation in either of the deaths of Vinke or Rynsburger. Nicolaus would just have to play this out as if it was just his right to distribute part of the money and recoup the remainder of the funds which he truly believed all of which was his. Again greedy and naïve.

After Nicolas landed at the Fort Lauderdale airport, he took a cab to the Marriot Hotel. That afternoon he called Holly Bedford and told her he would be at the Bank at 10:00 AM the next morning. He did ask her about any paperwork that had to be completed, but Holly just told him that as long as he had a certified death certificate for Hagen Vinke and proof of Nicolaus' identity and his Dutch Identification card, the rest could be handled there at that time. Nicolaus thanked Holly and said he would meet her the next morning. He then called a cab and went to Bottlest Winery, Bar and Grill on Las Olas Avenue for a nice quiet, expensive and relaxing meal. It would be his last.

****

When Arthur got the call from Holly Bedford, he spoke with Senior Officer Visse Jansen. Officer Jansen said that there was sufficient circumstantial evidence to charge Timmerman with both Vinke's and Rynsburger's deaths. Jansen requested that the FBI hold Timmerman on some charge, whatever Arthur could think of, until Officer Jansen could obtain the necessary extradition documents to have Timmerman transported to Amsterdam for those murders. Arthur agreed. Arthur was sure, after speaking with Jansen, that there was no conspiracy between Timmerman and Cathy Rutter for those two murders. They don't even know each other as far as Arthur and Denise had determined. The conspiracy charges against Rutter will probably be dismissed. Arthur also thought that maybe all of the other charges against Rutter should also be dismissed, but the prosecutor needs to do what is necessary, including the questioning of Ivana Hollings, to make that determination. Arthur then drove to Fort Lauderdale to be in the Flagler Community Bank at 10:00 AM the next day. Timmerman would be quite surprised. Arthur could almost anticipate the doctor's story. He knew it would be a whopper!

****

On April 29, 2010, at about 11:30 AM, a Sheriff's deputy rang the doorbell of Joe Hyland's new 4000 square foot home. Joe was lying on a lounge chair next to the beautiful kidney shaped pool with the hot tub bubbling and all three of the waterfalls activated. Joe had started to drink about two hours earlier. He still had not had anything to eat yet that day. The officer rang the doorbell at least 3 times. There was no answer. However, the officer heard someone, along with some music, around the back of the home by the pool. The officer walked around the home to the pool area and knocked on the pool door. Joe looked up and saw someone at the pool door.

"Come on in." Said Joe. "Do you want a drink? I have anything you want as long as its vodka or Crown Royal." Laughed Joe who didn't even recognize that this was a uniformed Sheriff's officer.

"No thank you sir, I am on duty." Firmly said the officer. "Are you Joseph D. Hyland? Are you the managing partner of the Traverse City Development Company, LLC?"

"I certainly am." Said Joe slurring his words. "Who wants to know?"

"Here you are Mr. Hyland." As the officer handed Joe a summons and foreclosure complaint. "Consider yourself served."

"What are you talking about?" asked Joe not quite sure what just happen.

The officer, turned around and left the pool area the way he came in and went back to his Sheriff's vehicle and drove off. Joe sat back down on the lounge chair and poured himself some more vodka. He put the papers down on a table and before the glass of vodka was fully consumed, Joe fell asleep.

****

The afternoon of April 29, 2010, the same day Hyland was served the foreclosure papers, Robert Adams, the bankruptcy attorney for ABN Amro called Bill Jones at Brian Koop's office. Adams informed Jones that Joe Hyland was served that morning both the summons and complaint for the foreclosure law suit that the two of them, with Brian Koop and Carl Finch, discussed several days ago. Adams told Jones that he had just sent Jones, by Federal Express, a copy of the same. Adams reminded Jones that Hyland had 20 days to Answer or otherwise file some other pleading or Jones' client will make a motion for a default judgment. Jones was well aware of that fact, however, Jones asked Adams if they would like to meet, with their clients, to possibly discuss a settlement instead of moving forward with this difficult, long drawn out and expensive foreclosure? Adams told Jones that he would speak with his client about such a meeting and get back with him some time the next day, due to the time difference in The Netherlands. Adams agreed.

Jones told Koop about the conversation with Adams and they both agreed that a meeting would be appropriate. First, Hyland did not, at least to the knowledge of the two attorneys, have the resources for a full drawn out legal battle that may take years to resolve. The attorney fees would run in the hundreds of thousands of dollars. After all, this was almost a billion dollar foreclosure and there were some wrong doings on the part of the Bank that may have caused the foreclosure. It would be in everyone's best interest to attempt to settle the matter, with a confidentiality provision, so the press could not find out everything that went on during the 10 to 11 years these loans were in effect. Koop new how Joe felt. Joe thought he never did anything wrong and he just followed what the Bank told him to do. Joe never received any pre-paid profits, other than two condos at Largo Del Sol, or any other illegal payments from anyone at the Bank. So Koop knew it would be difficult to convince Joe to settle, but both Jones and Koop needed to do their very best lawyering to convince Hyland that a settlement would allow Hyland to keep as much of his current assets as he could, as well as be in the best interests of all parties. Koop knew that the Bank was a partner in every development for which the Bank loaned money. The Bank knew what was going on in those developments and both Jones and Koop believed that the Bank would not want to have this dirty laundry plastered all over the front page of any newspaper.

After the summons and complaint was received by Jones, a meeting was agreed to in Koop's office on May 1, 2010. The bank temporarily gave Hyland a reprieve from filing any Answer or other documents with the Court unless a settlement could not be worked out. As soon as Joe very reluctantly agreed to this settlement conference, he started to liquidate as much of his assets as possible, except for one car, his condo and the big house. He stuffed some money he had in his bank account, and all the funds he received for the sale of any of his current remaining assets, into his safe in his condominium.

****

In February, 2009, a little over a year before ABN Amro would filed their foreclosure law suit against Hyland and his development company, Nicolaus Timmerman walked into the reception area of the Flagler Community Bank in Fort Lauderdale, Florida. Nicolas was sure that on that day, $2 million was going to be wire transferred to his Amsterdam Bank account and Hagen Vinke's two sons would each receive about $2 million each. Nicolaus was in a good mood. The dinner the night before was excellent and he had one of the best night's sleep he had in several months. Nicolaus asked to see Holly Bedford with whom he had an appointment. The receptionist told Nicolaus to have a seat, since Holly was not in her office and she would try to find her. Nicolaus had a seat and waited. Soon thereafter, Arthur Winslow and two FBI agents from the Fort Lauderdale office came to greet Nicolaus. Arthur introduced himself as a United States Senior FBI agent from the Tampa, Florida office. He introduced the other two officers as FBI agents from the Fort

Lauderdale office. Arthur then placed Nicolas under arrest for the two murders of Hagan Vinke and Josef Rynsburger. Nicolas looked at the three men and then he fainted.

Several minutes later, Nicolaus came to and Arthur offered Nicolaus some water. Nicolaus was in a daze and was not quite sure where he was. Arthur then also charged Nicolaus with attempting to commit fraud and theft of funds from a United States Federally Insured Bank. That charge would keep Nicolaus in the United States until Jansen could obtain extradition documents to send him back to The Netherlands to be tried on the two counts of murder.

'What are you talking about?" Exclaimed Arthur. "I did none of those things."

"Nicolaus you will have lots of time to explain your actions concerning those charges." Said Arthur. "But, you may be able to help yourself greatly, if you agree to cooperate with the United States Government on charges of fraud, theft, promoting illegal payments by a Dutch Bank and other numerous violations under the United States Treasury Department's Office of Foreign Assets Control and the Federal Deposit and Insurance Corporation Act." Arthur wasn't sure who those charges would really be against, since the only people Arthur knew who may have been involved in such matters were dead, other than Timmerman. But the charges would do for the time being.

Nicolaus started to compose himself again and finally came to the conclusion, that the suicide note that he brought with him to burn, was not the best idea. Arthur then called Alex Tarian and told him he would be in Alex's office first thing the next morning. He asked if Denise and Luke would also be there. Arthur said he would bring a prime witness with him concerning the charges against Cathy Rutter. Maybe a lot would be cleared up. The two FBI Agents took Nicolaus to his very luxurious hotel room and, with a search warrant in hand, packed everything in the room in Nicolaus' suit cases and took everything out of Nicolas' pockets including an envelope with a folded piece of stationary inside it. The FBI agents didn't read it at that time. They just put Nicolaus and his belongings in Arthur's car. Arthur and Nicolaus then drove back to Fort Myers. Nicolaus was handcuffed and his seat belt fastened in the back seat.

CHAPTER 20

I T WAS MAY 1, 2010. At 9:30 AM, Bill Jones, Brian Koop and Joe Hyland were sitting in Koop's law firm's main conference room. Both Koop and Jones were sure that this meeting with ABN Amro Bank and their attorneys would finally determine who was deceived by whom and for how much money. Hyland and all of his development companies dealing with Snook Point, Coconut Point Park and Alico Grand Mine were the defendants in the foreclosure law suit currently pending for just under $1 billion. The largest foreclosure suit that Southwest Florida has ever seen. About 9:45 AM, Carl Finch and Robert Adams, attorney for ABN Amro Bank showed up with Rudolf Spaans, the Executive Vice President of the foreign office of the Bank. Jones asked Finch if Mr. Spaans has authorization to settle the foreclosure law suit. Finch indicated that he had full authority. Before the discussion concerning the law suit began, Brian Koop's assistant brought in a menu from the restaurant across the street from the law firm so everyone could put in their order for lunch. Finch asked if they should also put in an order for dinner and breakfast for the next day. That comment did not go over well with either Koop or Jones and especially Hyland. Both attorneys indicated that either they settle the matter, at least in principal, by end of the day, or an Answer and Counterclaim would be filed by

Hyland in the next week. Everyone understood that Finch was just joking about the food, but the attorneys for Hyland wanted the Bank to know these negotiations where not going to go on for a long period of time. Everyone, including the clients, agreed.

"Gentleman, I know you all called this settlement conference, but I would like to open the discussion with a statement." Finch started. "My client, ABN Amro, was not the Bank that created the loans with the Hyland development companies for Snook Point, Coconut Cove Park or the Alico Grand Mine. Other attorneys representing AFC Bank were the ones that drafted the original loan documents and were the original lenders. We all understand that my client, ABN Amro purchased only the assets of AFC Bank, and they were no way involved in any of the loans in question except for a few million dollars to finish the convention center at the Snook Point Hotel." Continued Finch. "There may have been some problems with the draws for all of the rest of the funds over the 10 years before the acquisition of the loans outstanding, but ABN did not purchase any of AFC Bank's liabilities. So any counterclaim your client may have against a Bank would be the AFC Bank or their officers, directors or loan committee members. None of those people ever worked for my client. My client purchased the outstanding loans and your clients, Mr. Hyland and his development companies owe the money to my client. That is undisputed. So the questions here today is will the current owners of the three properties which are the subject of this foreclosure action, deed those properties to ABN, free and clear of all possible liens or title defects and will your client pay to ABN the amount of money that will become a deficiency, if any, after the Bank sells those properties to third parties?" Finch continued. "And three very important provisions of any settlement that may come out of these discussions are as follows. Number one, Joe Hyland and his development companies will give ABN, a current fully audited, financial statement; two, Hyland shall provide clear and marketable title, with title insurance, insuring marketable title for all the properties involved; and three, Hyland will transfer the home that he currently purchased on the Caloosahatchee River to ABN Amro."

Jones is writing all this down furiously while Koop is just listening. There is a short period of silence while Jones finishes his notes and Adams shuffles some more papers to Finch.

Koop then ended the silence and said, "Mr. Finch, we are all here to discuss a settlement of the issues presented in your client's foreclosure action. What you are asking for is everything in your law suit. If that is what you want today, you all took a long trip for nothing."

"I did nothing wrong!" Exclaimed Hyland. "Why are you all blaming me for the manner AFC Bank handled these loans. They were the ones that deceived all of us, and if anything, they owe me money for ...." Then Koop interrupted Hyland.

"Joe, please let the attorneys talk. Just listen and we can discuss all of that later. Please." Said Koop calmly. And then returned speaking to Finch. "Your client can take the position that they knew nothing of the deceptions that were going on inside AFC Bank by its President, Hagen Vinke, the Board of Directors, the foreign loan committee, and Josef Rynsburger. But everyone in this room, especially your client, knows about the wrong doing and illegal payments by AFC from those loans. Especially by the fact that AFC was a partner with my client. AFC took pre-paid profits out of draws and made my client pay interest on those funds that AFC stole." Continued Koop. "You know that my client can file third party complaints with the Court in this foreclosure action bringing into the law suit all of those people involved as employees of AFC Bank, who are still alive. You know that they will testify that, your client audited those loans, and where well aware of the wrong doings. It is more than just a guess on my part, and, more than likely, that your client adjusted the purchase price of those loans when ABN purchase them." Exclaimed Koop. "My client was just the worker bee who did all the improvements on all of the properties in which the Bank loaned money, while the Bank reaped all of their profits and other benefits. If it were not for the real estate crash, none of us would be here. Everyone has some dirt on their face in this matter." And Koop continued while Finch was becoming impatient. "Either your client is willing to discuss some type of reasonable settlement today, or we can all go home now. Your attitude with your opening statement is absurd. If that was what you thought you would get today you all are naïve!"

Again, a period of silence. Everyone except for Koop and Finch were taking continuous notes. Both sides continued their arguments on behalf of their clients for hours until 12:30 PM, when there was a knock on the conference room door. Koop's assistant came into the room with everyone's order for lunch.

Kopp, Jones and Hyland took their lunch into a smaller conference room to discuss where they were in the negotiations. The other side stayed in the main conference room. Koop told Hyland that he believed that an agreement in principal can be worked out that day, so long as, Hyland was willing to give up the big new home he purchased.

"God Damit!!" Said Hyland. "You all insisted I buy that home. I never wanted that home, now you're telling me to give it up. $1.6 million. That is a lot of fucking money and it sounds like a lot of bad advice."

"Joe, you buying that house is the reason we are here today. The Bank never would be here negotiating with you if you didn't take that money that they considered was theirs, and put it into an exempt asset, one that they cannot touch." Said Koop and Jones agreed. "Give them the house, so long as we can make sure you are able to keep everything else you currently have. And that's nearly several million dollars besides your condo, truck, boat, etc. Otherwise, had you not purchased that home, they would have wanted everything."

"This way, by giving them the home you are probably going to end up with more than if you didn't buy that home." Said Jones.

"I hate it, I hate it, I hate it!" said Hyland over and over. "I did nothing wrong, I did nothing wrong!"

"Joe, give us the authority and we will settle this matter today." Said Koop. "That will also save you thousands of dollars a month to fight this law suit, for which you will lose. You owe them the money. You know you signed personal guarantees. A judge will find some wrong doing on the part of the Bank, but that will not stop the foreclosure and transfer of the assets." Said Koop.

"Once the Bank gets the properties, they will fight you for your money. "Said Jones. "And no one will win that one since you will spend all your money on attorney fees and eventually just end up with a judgment against you. Listen to us, you pay us to give you advice. Now, take that advice."

"OK. But I am a very unhappy camper."

That afternoon, a settlement in lieu of a foreclosure was agreed upon, in principal, by the parties. The Bank took an unaudited list of assets owned by Hyland which included everything Hyland had less what he had hid in his safe. Even his attorneys were unaware of that. Everyone deceives someone sometime to get what they want. Hyland was furious about the big home. He still, after the agreement in principal was signed, didn't really understand why he was advised to buy that big home. Hyland believed he got screwed!

A Settlement Agreement was finally fully negotiated and executed by all parties and their attorneys. The one matter that was never determined, even though Koop tried on several occasions, was to determine who were the people at AFC and outsiders, if anyone, who actually deceived AFC Bank and Joe Hyland, and for how much money. ABN was not going to let Koop go in that direction. However, all of the properties involved, the Snook Point property that was not improved, all of the common areas and amenities, the hotel, convention center, commercial buildings and marina; the unsold 28 Coconut Cove Point condominium; the Alico Grand Mine and all the equipment associate with it; and the new big home on the Caloosahatchee River were deeded to ABN Amro. The Bank and Hyland and his companies all signed full, final and complete releases against each other and the foreclosure lawsuit was dismissed with prejudice so it could never be brought again. The Settlement Agreement included a confidentiality clause so no one would know the terms of a Settlement.

During the two months, thereafter, it took to finalize the Settlement Agreement language for signatures and releasing the foreclosure law suit, Joe Hyland drank more booze than ever before, took more drugs than ever before and hung around Ivana Hollings almost daily. Brian Koop was certain, Joe Hyland was not sober when he signed the final agreement, but nothing was said. Joe never even tried to get another job. He moved back into his condo, took money from his safe, from time to time, for booze and drugs mostly and was completely sober only several times before he died on August 10, 2013. He purchased a new car, expensive clothing and pissed away money. He went into three different inpatient drug rehabilitation programs during that time and never finished one of them. Joe did have dinner at the Rutter's every month or so and Ivana was never invited. Eating at the Rutter's was the most food Joe would usually eat in a week. He lost nearly 80 pounds before he died and looked nearly 75 years old. When Joe died his best friends were Crown Royal and any vodka he could get his hands on. When he was with Ivana, in his condo, it was Ivana that would always make the drinks and bring the drugs. Joe was virtually high for more than two years. The one thing Joe just couldn't recover from was the loss of the Snook Point hotel. That was the one development that, when anyone mentioned it, would put a smile on his thin wrinkled face. He was very proud of that development and what it meant to the City of Cape Coral. That hotel was his.

When he died, there was still over $60,000 in cash and over $300,000 in jewelry in his safe. No one knew the combination of the safe except for Joe and Cathy Rutter. Joe never knew about the bank accounts at Flagler Community Bank in Fort Lauderdale or the other two bank accounts, wherever they were located. Joe also, in the over 10 years of construction of his six large developments, never received one cent for any profits.

****

It was February 21, 2010, 10:00 AM, Alex Tarian, Denise Hudek, and Luke Blakely were all in Alex's office. Arthur Winslow brought Dr. Nicolaus Timmerman into the office about 20 minutes later. Arthur unlocked the handcuffs and told Nicolaus to sit down.

"Well, who do we have here?" Said Alex.

"This is the man that killed Hagen Vinke and Josef Rynsburger." Said Arthur.

"I didn't kill anyone!" Exclaimed Timmerman."

"Looks like we have a difference in opinion." Said Alex.

"Alex, didn't you get a search warrant for Timmerman's person and his hotel room in Fort Lauderdale? Asked Denise.

"I did." Said Alex. "And what did you find Arthur?"

"I found some letters from three banks in the United States, which is one of the reasons we're here today." Said Arthur. "Also, those letters seem to implicate our good doctor here, in bank fraud and theft from a United Stated Federally Insured Bank; numerous violations of the FDIC laws, and violations of the United State Treasury Department's Office of Foreign Assets Control Act. The doctor also had several certified copies of Hagen Vinke's death certificate, which was signed by our good doctor. Continued Arthur. "But the best of all is an original suicide note from Hagen Vinke. I have no idea if it's authentic, but, at best, it implicates our good doctor of aiding in a suicide, or, at worst, murder. It also implicates the doctor in the death of Josef Rynsburger."

"Have you contacted The Netherlands authorities, Arthur?" asked Alex.

"I have." Said Arthur. "Senior Officer Visse Jansen of the Amsterdam police department, is in the process of obtaining the necessary extradition documents to take Dr. Timmerman back to Amsterdam to be held on the charges of murder for the two Dutch citizens."

Everyone in the room was looking and reading the 3 bank letters and the alleged suicide note. Arthur called the FBI, Fort Lauderdale office and requested someone there get to a Judge as soon as possible to obtain a search warrant for an account at the Flagler Community Bank, to check and see if this account, in the name of AFC Bank, with the signatures of Hagen Vinke and the doctor, really exits. And, if it does exist, how much money is in it. The law enforcement individuals to whom Arthur spoke indicated that the search warrant would take some time, but they should know if they can obtain it sometime after lunch. While they were waiting for the search warrant, it was determined that Dr. Timmerman was to be put in a holding cell at the Lee County jail, while all the law enforcement authorities had a nice lunch at a place downtown where the best hamburgers and fries in the City are served. The FBI agents in the Fort Lauderdale office would call Arthur after the warrant was obtained. If they were to obtain the warrant that day, they would call and report the results of the search.

About one and a half hour later, just as everyone was finishing lunch, at Fords Garage, just across the street from the Court House, Arthur got his call. It was the Fort Lauderdale FBI. The agent on the phone told Arthur that a Judge signed the warrant which was carried out and the account mentioned in the alleged suicide note in the Flagler Community Bank letter, did exist. There was currently just over $6 million in the account. It was set up in the name of the AFC Bank A/K/A Rynsburger Investments, B.V. out of the Netherlands. The tax identification number used on the account was Hagen Vinke's Netherlands Tax Identification number with his home address. Hagen Vinke was the original signatory on the account. Dr. Nicolaus Timmerman was added as a signatory two weeks before Hagen Vinke died. Everyone thought that was very strange. That would leave the only signatory on the account today, as Dr. Timmerman. Looks like Vinke and Rynsburger and Timmerman deceived both AFC Bank and ABN Amro Bank.

The Fort Lauderdale FBI agent surmised that Vinke was embezzling the money, for his own use, and ABN Amro never knew about the account. The FBI agents determined that Vinke had wire transferred money, on a monthly basis, from funds that were to be sent to one of Hyland development company's account in Fort Myers, as part of draws requested by that company for several different developments in Florida. The diverted funds were first wired to an AFC Bank branch in Aruba, and then later wired by Vinke to the Flagler Community Bank. Arthur thanked the agent and asked him to fax the report on the search, as well as a copy of the Search Warrant for the bank account, to Alex Tarian's office in Fort Myers.

Everyone went back to Alex's office after lunch and after being briefed by Arthur on the results of the Search Warrant. Dr. Timmerman was brought back to Alex's office, again in handcuffs. The doctor sat down, his handcuffs were removed, and he was given the report that was found as a result of the search warrant, on the account at Flagger Community Bank. Nicolaus read it and then looked at Arthur.

"This proves I am innocent of assisting a suicide, or the murder of Vinke." Said Nicolaus. "The suicide note you have states that the money was in the bank. It was money that Vinke and my partner at the time, Josef Rynsburger stole from me, out of my partnership account at AFC Bank." Continued Timmerman. "Vinke, had been exposed as a thief by an audit performed by ABN Amro Bank accountants when ABN was in the process of purchasing the assets of AFC Bank. Some of that money in the Flagler Community Bank was legally mine. Vinke wanted me to have that money back. He also wanted to commit suicide instead of going to jail. He was very calm and in his right mind the night I met with him before he committed suicide. He knew what he wanted to do. I was overwhelmed and confused by all of those events. He also requested me to send some of that money to his two sons who were working in Florida for some corporation. Vinke and his sons had been estranged for some time. I don't know the reason for Vinke's change of heart on that subject. He just asked me to help him." Continued Nicolaus. "That is why I was in Fort Lauderdale."

"Still doesn't add up." Said Arthur. "Even if we take your word for it, which I don't, there was still over $2 million more in that account than what was stolen from you, and the amount Vinke says in the note to send to his sons. What were you going to do with the rest of the money? And what about the other two banks with lot's more money? What were you going to do with that money?" Arthur said accusing Nicolaus. "Just doesn't add up. You are guilty of the attempted fraud and theft of funds from a Federal Insured United State Bank."

Arthur then read Nicolas his rights, for the second time. He read him his rights in Fort Lauderdale when he was first arrested. Arthur then asked him if he was ready to make a statement concerning the money. Arthur said that if Nicolas would plead guilty, Arthur could speak with the Federal prosecutor in Fort Myers and try to work out something that would allow Timmerman to be extradited to the Netherlands on the charges of murder of the two Dutch citizens first. Then Nicolaus could argue his innocence to a Dutch Judge. After that matter is completed, and if Timmerman is found guilty and sentenced on any of the charges dealing with the two murders, the Federal prosecutor in Fort Myers may let the sentences for which Timmerman pleads guilty in the United States run consecutively with the Dutch sentencing. After all Dr. Timmerman was not a young man. However, if Timmerman was found innocent of all charges dealing with the two murders, Timmerman would then be required to return to Fort Myers to face a sentencing hearing on the bank charges and serve his sentence in the United States. Arthur wanted to know if Timmerman would agree to that deal.

Timmerman invoked his right to counsel, after all Timmerman never actually took any of the money from any United States Bank. Arthur then contacted the public defender's office in the Federal Building in Fort Myers and Timmerman and a public defender discussed the situation for several hours. Meantime, Arthur received a fax from Officer Jansen with the necessary extradition documents and said that two Netherlands police officers were on their way to Fort Myers to take Timmerman back to Amsterdam to be held over for trial on charges of the murders of Vinke and Rynsburger. Denise brought the extradition documents to the interrogation room so Timmerman and his attorney would both be aware of the status of the extradition.

After several hours, Timmerman's attorney told Alex Tarian that, if Timmerman can receive the deal offered by Arthur, in writing by the Federal prosecutor, Arthur would agree to plead guilty to the charges enumerated by Alex. However, as part of his allocution, Nicolaus would tell the Judge that he never took any money from any U.S. bank. He would, however, first return to Amsterdam to face the charges waiting for him there and fight those charges.

Everyone agreed. That was accomplished. Arthur was held in a Federal Holding cell for a night. The next day, Nicolaus appeared before a Federal Magistrate in Federal Court in Fort Myers, plead guilty to all of the bank charges, and allocated to those charges. Nicolaus said nothing about the death of Vinke or Rynsburger. The prosecutor and the Magistrate accepted Nicolaus' allocution and sentencing was deferred until after the Amsterdam Courts had adjudicated the fate of Dr. Timmerman on the two murder charges. Several days later, the Amsterdam police officers arrived in Fort Myers and took Nicolaus back to the Netherlands.

During this whole ordeal for Nicolaus and after many hours of integration, Nicolaus could not tell the Fort Myers authorities where the $10.5 million was located. He had no idea of the answers to those questions. The interrogators, after a total of 15 hours of interrogations, finally believed Nicolaus. Then the questions arose, where was the rest of the money? Was there any more money? Who did it belong to? Was ABN Amro entitled to it? This would be a puzzle that would not be solved, if at all, for some time. Who does the Flagler Community Bank money belong to? Should a Court decide that question? Does the government initiate the action to determine ownership of the funds, or is it ABN Amro's responsibility to bring the action? Or does someone else have that right? Does the Flagler Community Bank have to bring the action? Vinke was dead. Rynsburger was dead. Something for Alex to contemplate. Or does he even care to get involved? This whole case always had more questions than answers.

****

Alex obtained a search warrant for Ivana Hollings house, garage and automobile. Four Lee County Sheriff's officers and Luke Blakely went to Ivana's home. It was 10:30 AM, December 5, 2013. They knocked on Ivana's door several times and indicated that Lee County Sheriff's deputies were there to implement a search warrant. Ivana finally open the door after four attempts to get her to the door. She was in a night gown with an open robe and a drink in her hand. Luke identified himself and told her they were there to execute a search warrant in her home, garage and her automobile as he handed her the warrant.

"Come on in." slurred Ivana. "Does anyone want a drink?"

"Maybe you should put the drink down and just sit down while the deputies do their jobs." Said Luke "This shouldn't take too long."

"I don't need to sit, I am doing just fine. What the Hell you looking for?" Asked Ivana. "Maybe I can help."

"Just sit and relax and we'll be out of your way soon." Said Luke while Ivana ignored him and went and poured a little more vodka in the glass.

In one of Ivana's kitchen cabinet, one of the officers found something not labeled. Luke questioned Ivana about the substance and she told him she used it in coffee. Ivana would make coffee for Joe when he came over in the afternoons. He loved coffee in the afternoon, mostly with Crown Royal in it but also a little sweetener, but not too sweet. She used the substance with Splenda and this made the coffee much better and not overly sweet. Luke smelled the substance and couldn't tell what it was, but it could have been some type of sweetener or diluted anti-freeze.

"Did you put this in Joe Hyland's coffee at any time? "Asked Luke. "Did you put it in your coffee?"

"I hate coffee." Said Ivana. "I do, however, love vodka. What's this all about? Joe hated coffee too, unless there was Crown Royal in it and it had to be just right, sweet, but not too sweet."

"Did you ever put this in any of Joe's drinks? Asked Luke.

"I only use it for Coffee. It's like a sweetener." Again Ivana's words were slurring. "What are you trying to say?

"Whose coffee did you use it in?" asked Luke.

Ivana couldn't remember much, but she always offered it when anyone wanted some coffee. Luke was still not sure that Ivana was actually understanding what was going on. She was drunk.

The Sheriff's deputy bagged the substance as evidence. Luke recited Ivana her rights and put her under arrest for the murder of Joseph Hyland. The jar in Ivana's cabinet was the only possible evidence found anywhere in the house, garage or her car. Ivana was told to get dressed and Luke took her to the Lee County Jail and put her in a holding cell. He then sent the substance to the lab for analysis.

Frank Fable and Luke went into the holding cell to interrogate Ivana. She was still drunk and maybe even on some drugs. She said she wanted out of the cell. There were snakes and animals everywhere. She was hallucinating. The interrogation stopped.

"Is there anything you would like Ms. Hollings, coffee, soda?" asked Frank before he left the cell.

"Have you got any vodka, and get me out of here" Declared Ivana.

"This is not a joke Ms. Hollings, this is a serious charge that has been brought against you." Said Luke.

"OK. Then I want a lawyer." Said Ivana. Either some vodka or a lawyer, you guys decide."

"Are you invoking your right to have a lawyer or not?" said Frank. "Are you invoking your right to be silent?"

"Whatever." Said Ivana.

"Do you understand your rights Ms. Hollings?" asked Frank.

Ivana put her head down on the table on her folded arms and didn't say a word. Frank said to Luke that they would assume she has invoked all her rights. The two men wondered if she would ask for a phone call to call her lawyer. They waited quietly, for a few minute, to see what she would do. Ivana fell asleep.

The next morning, Ivana had retained Thomas Curtis, a well-known criminal defense attorney from Tampa. Curtis was with Ivana at her arraignment. He had not had any time to consult with Ivana before the arraignment. The Circuit Court Judge handling the criminal matter was Judge Manuel Gonzales.

"Alex, nice to see you in my courtroom again. It's been a while." Said Judge Gonzales.

"Thank you, Your Honor. Nice to see you." Answered Alex Tarian.

"Mr. Curtis, I have not had the pleasure, but your reputation precedes you." Said the Judge.

"Thank you, Your Honor." Answered Curtis.

"Does the defendant have a plea on the murder one count? Asked the Judge.

"Not Guilty." Said Ivana.

"Madam, you will address me as Your Honor. Do you understand that? Questioned the Judge.

"Yes, Your Honor, but I didn't kill anyone." Said a half sober Ivana.

"That's what not guilty means Ms. Hollings." Replied the Judge. "Alex, anything on bail?"

"Remand, Your Honor." Replied Alex. "This is a murder one charge. We contend the defendant poisoned a man intentionally over a long period of time with the intent to kill him."

"Mr. Curtis, any response?" Asked the Judge.

"Your Honor, I have not had time to consult with my client yet. I just arrived in Fort Myers this morning before this hearing." Said Curtis. "However, it is my understanding that the State does not have any physical evidence to show that the defendant has any poison at all, or what type of poison she may have used. They have searched my client's home, garage and automobile and found nothing. They have no motive or means for charging the defendant with anything at this time. I will make a motion that unless the State can show some means or motive for my client to kill anyone, the charges should be dismissed. And by the way, Your Honor, I believe there is also another person who has been charged with Mr. Hyland's murder, a Catty Rutter."

"Mr. Tarian?" Said the Judge.

"Your honor, all charges against Ms. Rutter have been dismissed, at this time, without prejudice. She is now just a person of interest and maybe even a witness in this case. We are still investigating the charges against her," Embarrassedly stated Alex. "However, the police have obtained what they believe to be a poison from the defendant's home in an unmarked bottle. It is in the lab for conformation of that fact. We should have the results late today or tomorrow. In addition, the police have returned to the defendant's home and are in the process of taking other liquids from her home for testing to see if there is poison in those containers." Replied Tarian. "The defendant lived with the deceased for over a year, but was evicted from his condominium with no explanation. The deceased supported her, and indicated to her that he would continue to support her, but he did not give her any funds for support for at least 12 months before he died."

"Your Honor." Replied Curtis. "What I just heard is that the State is on a fishing expedition to try to materialize some evidence to charge my client for this crime. The motive is ridicules. The deceased and my client are not married and never have been. They lived together for a time over two years ago. My client wanted to leave, on her own accord, due to the excessive drinking and drug use by the deceased. My client has a job as a realtor and can support herself and has been helped by her mother. All of her bills are paid to date. The State has no means or motive for this charge."

"Is that true Mr. Tarian?" Questioned the Judge.

"This is not a fishing expedition, Your Honor." Replied Tarian. "The State has good reason to believe there was much animosity between the deceased and defendant and that she was thrown out of the deceased home due to her alcohol and drug use and the deceased physically and mentally abused the defendant."

'Do you have any doctor's reports or hospital reports on this abuse Mr. Tarian?" Asked the Judge. "Has it been over two years since they have lived together?"

"Yes, Your Honor, it has been several years since they lived in the same home, but there are witnesses that will testify to the relationship between the deceased and the defendant." Replied Tarian.

"Not good enough counselor." Said Judge Gonzales. "I don't see any means or motive and you have not convinced me that a crime has even occurred. You have even dismissed the charges against your only other suspect. I have no idea if you even believe you know who may have murdered Mr. Hyland. Mr. Curtis, your motion is granted and all the charges are dismissed, without prejudice. Mr. Tarian, if you find some evidence or get an indictment from a grand jury, you are free to refile charges. Until then, Ms. Hollings, you are free to go. Next Case."

Ivana was not quite sure what just happen. She and Thomas Curtis went into a small conference room just off the courtroom to talk. Ivana's mother was also there. Thomas introduced himself to Ivana and indicated that her mother, Laura Wills, had retained him for her defense. As of that time Ivana was free to go home. However, before she left, Thomas wanted to discuss the case and Ivana's relationship with Joe Hyland. Thomas needed to know everything about Ivana and Joe Hyland for him to defend Ivana, if any further charges were to be filed. Tomas had called a lawyer friend in Fort Myers who said that Thomas could use one of their offices while he was in town. All three went across the street to the law office and discussed Ivana's relationship with Joe Hyland from the first time they met at the Red Lion Business Club through the day Hyland died. Ivan's mother was excused from that discussion to keep client confidentiality.

Thomas explained to Ivana that the police will be at her house if she goes back right away since they are still there under the original search warrant that was issued. He told her to wait a couple of hours with her mother somewhere and then go back to her house. He told her that her home will probably be all torn up from the search, since the police like to harass perceived criminals. Thomas never asked Ivana whether she had any poison or if she poisoned Hyland. He didn't want to know. However, Ivana continually denied poisoning him. Thomas also explained that if no poison is found under the current search warrant, he was sure the prosecutor would ask the Court for another search warrant for Hyland's condominium to see if they can find some there. He would object to that request since Ivana never actually lived with him at the condominium. She only lived with him in the home that the Dutch Bank got title to under the Settlement Agreement during the foreclosure. And, if they lose on that issue, they can argue that any poison in the condominium could have belonged to Hyland and not Ivana. However, more than likely, Alex Tarian will probably decide to convene a grand jury to indict Ivana for the murder. He told her not to be surprised if that were to happen. He assured Ivana that he would be available, night or day, by phone if anything came up. He also told her, in a kind manner, to try to get herself together and to stay off any drugs she may be using and to go easy on the liquor. It was obvious to him that she was very hungover. The cops will be watching her. Ivana felt much calmer after meeting and speaking with her new lawyer. She didn't even want to ask her mother how much it cost. It was a lot.

CHAPTER 21

I T WAS DECEMBER 4, 2013. Just under 4 months since Joseph Hyland died. The Lee County Coroner had finalized his autopsy report and had made a final determination that Hyland died by slow poisoning with a substance called 'ethanol glycol', or commonly referred to as anti-freeze. The police took at least 45 more bottles of labeled liquids from Ivana's home to have the County lab test for that substance. However, the lab determined that the unlabeled bottle of liquid was in fact SweatLeaf Sweet Drops, a commonly used sweetener. No anti-freeze was in the liquid sweetener or any of the other labeled liquid bottles the police took to the lab.

Alex asked Luke Blakely and Denise Hudak to join him in his office on that day. Alex was furious that he was assured by the Sheriff's office, and in particular, Luke Blakely, that Ivana should be charged and arraigned. No evidence of the poison had been found at Ivana's home and it's been two years since they lived together.

"Luke, what the hell did you do to me?" Exclaimed Alex. "I do not like being embarrassed and unprepared in front of any Judge, especially Judge Gonzales. So what's your next move to get me the evidence I need to go forward with this case?"

"I am certain she did it." Said Luke. "There are no other viable suspects and she must have gotten rid of the anti-freeze, or it's sitting somewhere else, probably in Hyland's condo. You can get a warrant to search his condo."

"Thomas Curtis is not going to let a Judge issue a search warrant for a condo that Hollings never lived in." Harshly criticizing Luke. "Even if we got the warrant, Curtis would argue it was Hyland's and not Hollings'."

"Alex, I know you may not want to convene a Grand Jury, but we all know there are plenty of witnesses out there that would be willing to testify to Hollings and Hyland's relationship." Squeamishly stated Luke. "There has to be a dozen people that saw them together over the last few years. They hated each other but loved to drink and do booze and have sex. The realtors in Hollings mother's real estate company will testify that she hasn't worked for almost a year and a half. She completely depended on Hyland for living expenses. Her mother hated giving her money. All of the realtors will testify to that."

"Doing drugs and drinking booze and having sex will not cut it. Hyland had no legal obligation to support Hollings." A frustrated prosecutor said. "Hyland may have had some moral obligation towards Hollings, that he ignored, and pissed her off enough to kill him, but there is no way I can get a Grand Jury to believe she killed him without some type of physical evidence. We need the anti-freeze or a witness that saw or knew Hollings was poisoning Hyland. Thomas Curtis is good. He will laugh us out of Court even with an indictment."

"Maybe she didn't kill him." Interrupted Denise. "I never even thought he was murdered. I still believe he killed himself, either by his lifestyle or he poisoned himself. He hated the world and he hated himself after the real estate crash."

"I can't even convince my own investigator that Hollings murdered Hyland." Stated Alex. "How am I going to convince 12 people that she murdered him? There is no statute of limitations on murder. Denise spend another couple of weeks investigating this matter and look at everyone who could have done this, including Hollings. Someone murdered Hyland. Someone is deceiving us. I don't believe Hollings is smart enough, but someone is. Find out in the next two weeks, so I can bring someone up on the murder charge, or we'll drop it until something surfaces that changes our direction."

The Sheriff's deputies followed Ivana for two weeks and found nothing. They checked her phone records every day. Denise investigated every realtor in Wills' real estate company. Denise looked at both William and Cathy Rutter again. Denise and Luke even tried long shots including George Harvey, Bradly Whalen and even Roger Spector who had miraculously surfaced. After two weeks, Alex was a very unhappy prosecutor. His attitude towards Luke and even Denise changed thereafter. Working together on other matters were never the same. This had never happen to Alex Tarian before. A very highly publicized murder occurred in his jurisdiction, with at least a half dozen suspects, but without one iota of any evidence as to who committed the murder. Local television news commentators, editorials in the Fort Myers News-Press and a half dozen letters to the editor, all of whom believed that the County Attorney's office completely botched the case. The next primary election was only 8 months away in August, 2014, when the current States Attorney will run against another Republican candidate or candidates, yet to be determined. Since Republicans nearly always win in general elections in Lee County, the primary will more than likely determine the eventual winner. If there is a new States Attorney next November after the general election, Alex Tarian's job may very well be in jeopardy. Alex was certain that the voters, candidates for the job and the media will still remember Joseph Hyland next August.

****

It was October, 1999. One of Joe Hyland's development companies had just purchased the Largo Del Sol parcel of land from GHCI and had closed on the acquisition loan with AFC Bank. Joe Hyland, against his wishes, had Roger Spector removed from the development company and any future developments where Josef Rynsburger would be involved. The funds from the acquisition loan had come into the bank account of Traverse City Development Company, Inc. The necessary funds, for acquiring the land, were then transferred, by wire transfer, to GHIC with Largo Del Sol Development Company, LLC, and a newly formed development company just for the Largo Del Sol Project. That newly formed company received the title to the land. Traverse City Development Company, LLC was always the managing partner for each future development company formed by Joe Hyland when a new project was acquired.

There were excess funds, after the loan transaction was completed, left in Traverse City Development Company, Inc.'s bank account in the amount of $1 million. Cathy Rutter was instructed by Hagen Vinke to wire transfer all of those excess funds to an account in the name of Rynsberger/Traverse City/SLS Investments, LLC. in a Fort Myers, Florida bank account. From there Cathy was instructed to wire transfer 10% of the excess, or $100,000.00, to SLS Investments, B.V., a Netherlands company in a bank account in the AFC Bank in Amsterdam. The monthly statements associated with that account would be forwarded to the AFC Bank c/o Hagen Vinke. Next Cathy was instructed to wire transfer 40% of the excess, or $400,000.00 to an account under the name of AFC Bank A/K/A Josef Rynsburger at the Flagler Community Bank in Fort Lauderdale, Florida. The monthly statements associated with that account would be forwarded to Hagen Vinke at his home address in Amsterdam. Hagen was the only signature on that account. The remaining $500,000.00 would be divided in half. One half of that amount would be wire transferred to an account under the name of Rynsberger/Traverse City/SLS Investments, LLC at the McGregor Community Bank in Fort Myers, Florida, and the other half to an account under the same name to the Tamiami Community Bank in Naples, Florida. The monthly statements associated with both those accounts would be sent directly to Cathy Rutter, who was to put them in a safe place where no one except Hagen Vinke would have access to those statements when he was in Fort Myers. Cathy Rutter was told that this procedure, for all excess funds of any loan, would be a bank requirement under every Loan Agreement every time there was a loan received by AFC Bank dealing with all future developments. Any excess funds for any future acquisition loans or construction loans were to be divided in the same manner and wire transferred to the same banks.

On that morning in November, 1999, Cathy Rutter and George Harvey met each other at GHCI's corporate office at 6:00 AM. This meeting would become a regular meeting each month, unless one of them were tied up somewhere else or out of town. Both of them had known each other for a long time. They had a common link, Roger Spector. Roger was George's biological son and Cathy was Roger's aunt. Roger knew that Cathy was his mother's sister, and know about

George's relationship, but never revealed that fact to anyone. Cathy had been hired as Joe Hyland's assistant and financial advisor for the Largo Del Sol development and hopefully for any future developments. Cathy was greatly underestimated by Joe Hyland, Hagen Vinke and Josef Rynsburger.

Both George and Cathy were very upset by Roger's removal from the development company, and in the manner and reasons it was done. They both knew that the decision to remove Roger was made by Josef Rynsburger and not Joe Hyland. Cathy was certain that the decision to remove Roger was made for several reasons.

First, it was Vinke and Rynsburger's intention to deceive AFC Bank and Joe Hyland each time a loan was closed for the acquisition of land or construction on that land. This was done by having each loan approved by AFC Bank, to be in an amount in excess of the amount of funds necessary for the intent of the loan. That excess would be documented, as pre-paid profits, and/or other miscellaneous costs, by the owners of the development companies. That excess funds, for each loan, would be divided, so that 10% would go to AFC Bank, 40% to Rynsburger and 50% to Joe Hyland. However, what was really happening to the excess funds of each loan was much different.

When a loan to a Hyland development was closed, AFC Bank would receive, though the Bank's subsidiary company the Bank set up in Amsterdam, 10% of the excess funds for their 10% interest in the development. In that way the Bank had a legal reason to approve a loan in excess of 100% of the necessary funds for each development. AFC Bank was very much on board with that procedure. Vinke was the President of the Bank, on the Board of Directors and on the foreign loan committee. All people involved were made aware of and approved all the loans and this procedure. The real estate boom was just starting and even the banks were starting to get greedy.

Then 40% of the excess would be transferred to a U.S. bank in an account under the name of AFC Bank A/K/A Josef Rynsburger. Those funds were designated as prepayment of Josef Rynsbuger's eventual profits for any particular loan. Most of those funds would remain in that Bank account and eventually, at some time in the future, be divided equally between Rynsburger and Vinke. From time to time, Rynsburger would ask Vinke to withdraw some of those funds from that account and equally divide them amongst the two of them for their private use.

That was one of the ways Vinke deceived AFC Bank and took money that was never supposed to be earned by Vinke.

The final 50% of the excess funds for every loan was to be equally divided and then transferred into two U.S. banks. That money should have been designated as pre-paid profits for Joe Hyland. But a different scenario occurred. Hyland agreed to a very high draw from the development companies in lieu of receiving his pre-paid profits upfront like Rynsburger and the Bank did. Hyland actually worked and managed all the developments while Rynsburger and the Bank were just investors. That is why Hyland agreed to wait until each project was complete and the loan for each project was paid off before Hyland would receive his 50% percent of the profits. Hyland didn't even know that the two U.S. bank accounts were even opened for the deposit of his 50% of the pre-paid profits. AFC knew about the accounts and thought Hyland was actually receiving his profits just as Rynsburger and the Bank were. Hyland never questioned this since his only communication with the Bank was through Rynsburger and Vinke. But what was really happening, unbeknownst to Hyland and AFC, is that Rynsburger and Vinke were depositing the 50% of the excess funds into the two separate U.S. banks for their own use, and stealing the money from AFC Bank and Hyland. A very large and highly fraudulent deception.

Second, Rynsburger was sure that Hyland could be deceived much easier than Roger Spector. Also, Hyland was a more competent real estate developer than Roger. Vinke and Rynsburger also believed it would be much easier to deceive one person than to deceive two people. Both were also certain that real estate values would rise quickly and for a long time. That meant there would be sufficient funds available, once each development was completed and the loan paid off, to pay Hyland all or at least a large portion of his promised profits.

Hence, Roger is gone.

George and Cathy discussed this situation for a long time. They needed to come up with a plan so Vinke and Rynsburger did not get away with this deception. Most of all, Roger must be vindicated. George knew that getting Roger a good paying job with GHCI would be no problem. But that was not enough. Both Roger and Joe Hyland should be compensated for these deception and Vinke and Rynsburger should be penalized. Both George and Cathy finally decided to think about it for some time and get together in several months to finalize some type of a plan. This was accomplished.

Several months later, George and Cathy meet at the same time and place and another deception was hatched. George was part owner of two local banks. He was on the Board for both of those banks. He had many connections in the banking world, the political world, the business world and the underworld. Making up false bank statements would be an easy task for George to have accomplish.

Therefore, each time there was a loan for a Hyland development, Cathy would follow all the instructions she was given by Vinke for the excess funds for each loan. However, there would be one important variation. Instead of the 50% being divided equally and sent to the Fort Myers bank and Naples bank, Cathy would wire transfer the 50% to two offshore banks as directed by George. George set up two offshore corporations and issued bearer stock to George, Cathy, Roger and Joe Hyland. George and Cathy then had a forged Power of Attorney form drafted, giving them Power of Attorney over Rogers and Hyland's funds. Neither George nor Cathy wanted Roger or Joe to know about what they were doing at that time. The holders of the bearer share certificates would be the owner of the shares of the offshore company. The offshore companies would each open an offshore bank account at a bank George had done business with on other occasions. One bank account would be at the Fidelity Bank in the Bahamas. The other would be at the Choice Bank in Belize. Only two of the bearers, George Harvey and Cathy Rutter knew that they owned stock in an offshore company. Shareholders of the offshore companies are not registered with any governmental agency. Therefore, the ownership of the offshore company would remain private. George and Cathy would tell Joe and Roger about the money sometime in the future when the real estate market starts to fall back, or other relevant events may occur for Roger and Joe to know about the money.

George would take care of having someone falsify bank statements for the Fort Myers and Naples Bank accounts each month so Cathy would have them available for Vinke to view, if requested. And if for any reason, Vinke asked Cathy for some of the money supposedly in the Fort Myers or Naples bank, George and Cathy would devise whatever plan necessary, under the circumstances, to satisfy Vinke with the requested funds so he would never be any the wiser of this deception.

So from 2000 until Hagen Vinke committed suicide, Cathy Rutter and George Harvey deceived Vinke and Rynsburger. Cathy continued to wire transfer 10% of excess funds for every loan to AFC Bank in Amsterdam. She continued to wire transfer 40% of the excess funds to the Flagler Community Bank. She also continued to wire transfer 50% of the excess funds to the two offshore banks under the names of the two offshore companies formed by George Harvey. George and Cathy had accumulated over $20 million, with a favorable high interest rate, in the offshore banks by the time Vinke and Rynsburger were dead. Neither George nor Cathy needed the money so they let it sit and accumulate. Funds were withdrawn only a couple of times when Vinke requested some of those funds. Rynsburger was never aware of any of those accounts. Another fraudulent deception by Vinke, or at least he thought it was.

When Joe Hyland was sued by ABN Amro Bank for foreclosure of the nearly $1 billion dollars, Cathy and George started sending Joe quarterly checks from "an unknown friend" for $20,000.00, for which Joe was told to cash at one of George Harvey's banks. That way Joe could pay his bills and attorney fees. The checks were from the offshore accounts but Joe didn't question who, what or where. He wanted and needed the money. Needless to say, Joe told no one, especially his attorneys, who would be obligated to tell the attorneys for the foreclosing Bank. Last thing Joe wanted was the Bank to find out about the cash he had accumulating in his Largo Del Sol safe. He had already accumulate some cash in the safe from his high draws and excessive expense reports out of the loan draws.

After Hyland and the Bank entered into the Settlement Agreement and everything concerning the legalities for all of the developments were completed, Cathy Rutter told Joe about Vinke's and Rynsburger's scheme to deceive him and the Bank. She didn't tell Joe how much money was in the accounts. Joe was too high on booze and drugs to really fully understand it all at that time. But, Joe took that news hard, however, he had surmised that something was going on since so much money was owed to the Bank at the time of the foreclosure. He always wondered how he would have ever made any profits. That news made Joe even more depressed. He now truly had someone to blame for his failure. But that didn't stop him from continuing his drinking, doing drugs and using Ivana when he wanted to. Cathy,

George and Laura Wills attempted to get both Joe and Ivana into inpatient rehab programs. Joe started three different programs at three different facilities, but never finished any. Ivana just refused. Joe's life as a developer or even a person who would contribute to society had ended the day the Settlement Agreement was signed. Snook Point and its City changing hotel/convention center was never going to be his. His death, and the manner in which he died, was cast on that day.

****

Several weeks after Joe Hyland died in 2013, Cathy Rutter went into Joe's condominium at Largo Del Sol and open his safe. She was looking for certain documents. Joe died single with no children. His only heirs were his brother, Daniel, and his wife and two daughters. Cathy was shocked at what she found in the safe. Besides the documents she was looking for, which were Joe's will and associated documents, she found a large pile of cash. She didn't count it. She found two gold and diamond Rolex watches and various other jewelry, all with diamond, emeralds and tanzanite. There were gold rings, bracelets, necklaces and broches. But Cathy was only interested in the will and associated documents.

Cathy closed and locked the safe and on her way out she saw lots of unopened mail on a table. At least 12 envelopes, addressed to Joe were from The Largo Del Sol Condominium Association, Inc. Several other envelopes were from a Fort Myers law firm that Cathy was familiar with. She knew that law firm had been hired by the Association to do their legal work. She took all of those unopened envelopes with her along with Joe's will.

When she got home, she opened the envelopes from the condominium association. All of the letters were demand letters for unpaid assessments totaling over $15,000.00. Interest and penalties increased that amount considerably. Why didn't Joe pay the association dues, thought Cathy? He had the money. For some unknown reason, he just ignored the association's demands. He never even opened the envelopes. Cathy found that very strange. Joe was a different person after the Settlement Agreement was signed. No one would be able to speculate what was in his mind during that period. Cathy, then opened the envelopes from the attorneys. He was being sued for foreclosure of that condominium unit for nonpayment of association dues. The most recent letter indicated an amount of over $27,000.00 due which would include all the additional quarterly dues, costs, interest, penalties and the association's attorney's fees. Joe must have been served by some process server since there was an itemized cost of $245.00 for process serving in the foreclosure complaint. He was probably drunk and just laid it down somewhere or just tossed it.

Cathy thought for a while and started to think that she should go back to the condo and get the money out of the safe and just pay the full amount so the condo would not be taken from Joe's estate. She decided, however, that before doing that she would call Brian Koop and ask his advice. Brian had not spoken with Cathy for a while, except for a few minutes at the funeral. He said that his firm had drafted Joe's will and he was aware of the foreclosure. The attorney handling the foreclosure called Brian as a curtesy before he filed the foreclosure. Under the terms of the will, there were two co-personal representatives appointed by Joe to handle the estate. One was Southern Trust Bank and the other was his brother, Daniel.

Brian told Cathy that he had spoken to one of the officers at Southern Trust Bank about the bank handling the estate, with Joe's brother, including the foreclosure of the Largo Del Sol condominium. Southern Trust Bank was not interested in getting involved with all of the legal matters involved in having the foreclosure comply with the Rules of probate and the time and effort to try to find hidden assets, if there were any, etc., etc. Brian could tell that the Bank just wanted out and to let Joe's brother handle everything. In fact, the Bank had filed a motion with the Probate court to be relieved as a co-personal representative. Brian told the Bank officer that after Joe Hyland had used Southern Trust as his escrow agent for years, and at one time had more than $80 million in escrow in the bank for the purchase of properties in his development as well as an account for the Alico mine, that Brian was astonished they would just reject him. But the Bank did just that and the Court approved their motion to have the Bank removed.

Brian then called Daniel. Brian asked why Daniel had not retained a lawyer to represent him as the personal representative for the estate. Daniel didn't want anything to do with Joe or his estate. This was a different person who spoke so highly of Joe at Joe's funeral. How Joe helped Daniel's family. Paid for tuition for his daughters to go to private schools. But Daniel said that the last three years with Joe had been Hell. Daniel and his wife were feed up with trying to encourage Joe to straighten out. Over two years of fighting with Joe was enough. Daniel was just not going to do anything else. Cathy told Brian about Joe's safe in the condo. Brian already knew about it. Joe told him after the Settlement Agreement was signed. Brian did know what was in it and he didn't have a key to the condo or know the combination for the safe. Cathy told Brian that she had a key and knew the combination. Cathy told Brian that there was enough money in the safe to pay off all the outstanding amounts to the association for the condo to be left in the estate. Daniel can sell the condo and get the proceeds of the sale as well as anything in the safe. Brian said great, but he requested Cathy call Daniel. Brian had tried too many times and was done with it.

Cathy thanked Brian for the update and his thoughts. Cathy did call Daniel and got the same response as Brian. Cathy even intimated what the safe may have in it. She did not want anyone to know she looked in the safe. It really was not her business. Cathy had to make a decision about the condominium and the contents of the safe. If Daniel refused to handle the estate and with Southern Trust out of the picture, how will Joe's estate be taken care of? No one cared about the condominium, or in her mind no one cared about Joe. How pathetic to her after all he did for the community and people for years. Yes, he had a bad last few years, but that should not take away from all the good he did in his life.

Cathy finally made a decision. She went back to Joe's condo, took out the cash and jewelry. There was $60,000.00 left in the safe. Cathy got 4 cashier's checks from George Harvey's banks for $10,000.00 each made payable to Daniel and his wife. She got two more $10,000.00 cashier's checks from two other banks one each made payable to Daniel's daughters. She boxed up all the jewelry and the checks and overnighted them to Daniel. She wrote a short note stating her sympathy for their loss and said she knew that Joe would have wanted his family to have the money and jewelry. She left all the furnishings in the condo, the safe door open with it empty and then forgot about it. It was time for her to move on. Cathy checked with the overnight provider, the next day, who confirmed the package was received by Daniel. Cathy never heard from Daniel or his family again.

****

Joe's casket was being transported to the burial site by limo. The mid-day rains were starting to come down a little harder. Only about 25 people went to the grave site for the final blessing by Minister Hilson. Daniel, his wife and his two daughters, Cathy and Ivana, Brian and Linda Koop, and several other old employees. All had their umbrella over them. The rest of the attendees had driven off to their homes, work or a bar. There were probably some people that day that lifted their glass to Joseph D. Hyland. Due to the heavy rains, the final blessing was short and to the point, after all, Minister Hilson didn't even know Joe. Nothing else was said at the grave site by anyone, but nearly everyone who attended the funeral that rainy day in Southwest Florida knew, in some personal way, that it was a sad day.

EPILOGUE

Joseph D Hyland:

He died in August, 2013 after nearly four and half years struggling with why his dreams of wealth and happiness were never fulfilled. Until the end of his life, he really did not understand the deceptions that were perpetrated on him. He died an alcoholic and drug addict. And he was murdered.

Cathy Rutter:

After she sent the contents of Joe Hyland's safe to Joe's immediate family, she and her husband William, decided to sell their expensive home in Fort Myers and all other real estate holdings they had in Florida, and Cathy moved to William's ranch to live full time. She thought about filing a law suit against Lee County for unlawful imprisonment and harassment, but she and her husband just wanted to leave Fort Myers. She, with George Harvey's approval took $5 million of the tax free offshore money for herself. She deposited it in chunks in several Montana banks with the proceeds of her real estate holdings. Neither the IRS, nor ABN Amro ever found out about the offshore funds. William and Cathy took long and expensive cruises every year thereafter, to different locations, for the next 10 years. Cathy, never came back to Florida again.

Daniel Hyland:

He and his wife lived a comfortable upper middle class life in Traverse City Michigan. He sold some of the jewelry that he received from Cathy Rutter and netted $35,000.00. He used that money and the $40,000.00 cash to buy a new car, updated his 25 year old home, and took week long trips to Washington DC and then the next year, to Hawaii. He gave each of his daughters some of the jewelry so they could use it for themselves. He had 5 grandchildren, two from the oldest daughter and three from his youngest. They enjoyed their grandchildren and set up a prepaid college funds for each. Both daughters contributed part of their money they received from Cathy Rutter for those college funds. They knew Uncle Joe would have liked that. Daniel retired from his job as regional manager for his local grocery chain at the age of 66 and received his full Social Security and a small pension. Daniel and his two daughters never went back to Florida again.

George Harvey:

He took no money from the offshore accounts. He set up two new offshore corporation, each with a different holder of a bearer share certificate. Then he set up two offshore bank accounts, one at Fidelity Bank in the Bahamas with $10 million with the bearer certificate owner as Roger Spector. The other account was for $5 million at Choice Bank in Belize with the bearer certificate holder in the name of Bradly Whalen, George's lifelong "closeted" companion for nearly 25 years. George and Bradly retired to George's West Palm Beach, Florida home, where they enjoyed life until George died in 2015. He left his entire estate to Bradly.

Ivana Hollings:

She purchased a gallon jug of ethanol glycol in a Sarasota hardware store in 2012. She keep the gallon jug in her mother's garage. She very slowly poisoned Joe Hyland over a period of seven months until he died. The doses were so small that even all of Hyland's quack doctors could not detect it. She despised the way Joe treated her the last several years of his life. She was never brought up on any charges again. She died of a heart attack in 2016, at the age of 55.

Leigh Mowery:

She lived in Louisville, Kentucky for the rest of her life. She sold her large home and expensive car and purchased a two bedroom condominium and a Chevrolet Malibu. She became a realtor and sold real estate until she retired at the age of 65. She lived off her real estate commissions and the investments she had made with some of the money her late husband had sent her when she left Fort Myers. She never remarried. She never returned to Florida again.

Dr. Nicolas Timmerman:

He was extradited to The Netherlands and stood trial for the murder of both Hagen Vinke and Josef Rynsburger. He was convicted on assisting a suicide and withholding evidence for the Vinke death. He was found guilty of murder, with special circumstances, for Josef Rynsburger's death due to his scheme of deceiving the doctor of over $2 million. He was sentenced to 5 years. He died in prison after 3 years at the age of 70. His wife Elsie died 6 months later. She never forgave her husband for those events and only visited him in prison several times.

Alex Tarian:

In August 2014, his boss, the then States Attorney lost the primary election to another Republican attorney who won the general election for State Attorney in November of that year. Alex was forced out of the States Attorney's office by resigning his position of Assistant Lee County Attorney for the criminal division on December 31, 2014. He went into private practice as a criminal defense lawyer and was very successful. He retired at the age of 66. His biggest regret was the fact that no one was ever prosecuted for the death of Joseph Hyland.

Denise Hudak:

She remained with the County Attorney's office as their chief investigator under the new States Attorney who was elected in November, 2014. She continued in the same job under several other States Attorneys for 10 more years until she retired at the age of 66.

Roger Spector:

After George Harvey's death, he returned to work as an Executive Vice President of GHIC. When Bradly Whalen retired to West Palm Beach, Roger took charge of the GHIC as its President and CEO of the publicly held company. He and the company did very well. During his tenure with the company, he increased the stock price of GHIC by 125% and initiated one stock split. He and his wife and two children lived in Fort Myers for the rest of their lives very comfortably. Roger was aware that George Harvey was his real father since he was 20 years old, but he said nothing to his mother or father before they died. Roger and his wife became very good friends with Bradly Whalen until Bradly died of aids in 2018.

Brian Koop:

He continued to practice real estate and banking law with his firm. He never communicated with any of the principals involved with the Joseph D. Hyland cases again. He earned more money between 2002 and 2012 than during all the other years he practiced law. Brian representing multiple real estate developers and builders including Joe Hyland during the real estate boom between 2002 and 2008 and again representing those same clients helping them keep as much of their assets as possible after the crash, between 2008 and 2012. He continued practicing law in Fort Myers until he retired at the age of 66.

Flagler Community Bank:

ABN Amro Bank filed a Declaratory Judgment lawsuit in the Circuit Court of Broward County in Fort Lauderdale, Florida, for the purpose of making a determination of the owner of the $6.5 million in the AFC Bank account. The defendants in that case were the estate of Vinke Hagen; the estate of Josef Rynsburger; the estate of Joseph Hyland; Dr. Nicolaus Timmerman and Cathy Rutter. None of those defendants answered the complaint. By default judgment, ABN Amro received title to the account and all $6.5 million plus accrued interest.

ABN Amro:

The Bank never was able to trace the whereabouts of the additional missing stolen funds from the assets of the AFC Bank. The Bank did not make any more foreign loans to anyone in the State of Florida for over 10 years after the Settlement Agreement was executed by the Bank and Joe Hyland. The 28 Coconut Cove Park condominium were sold within 12 months of the Bank receiving title under the Settlement Agreement. The purchase prices for those condominium were 20% to 30% less than the original asking prices by Joe Hyland. Snook Point hotel/convention center and all of the rest of the property in the Snook Point development was sold to a Developer out of Dallas, Texas. The new developer divided the 250 hotel rooms in half since they were built to be two and three bedroom, two bathroom condominium. That doubled the number of rooms in the hotel. The new owner contracted with Marriott Hotels to manage the hotel and the convention center and all commercial units. The new Marriott was a grand success in Cape Coral. ABN Amro Bank sold Snook Point development for $150 million. A loss of nearly $200 million for the Bank. The Alico Grand Mine could not be sold. The Bank operated it at a loss for 10 years. They then closed the mine and sold the property for development to a local developer for $35 million. A loss of nearly $200 million for the Bank not including the ten year negative cash flow. The Settlement Agreement with Joe Hyland was one of ABN Amro's largest losses ever.

Written Agreement between Hagen Vinke and Josef Rynsburger:

The Agreement written in Dutch between the President of AFC Bank, Hagen Vinke and Josef Rynsburger outlined how all the deceptions would occur with the loan funds from AFC Bank and Joseph Hyland. It further outlined how they would split the stolen funds and how the money would be hidden and when it would be distributed. After both of their deaths, Brian Koop asked Joe Hyland what Joe wanted Brian to do with the Agreement that was in Koop's firm safe. Joe told Brian to shred it. Neither Joe nor Brian ever knew what the Agreement said. However, ironically, the entire deception scheme was in Koop's law firm's safe just 100 feet away from his law office during the entire scheme.

Printed and bound by PG in the USA